Missing

Susan Lewis is the bestselling author of *A Class Apart*, *Dance While You Can*, *Stolen Beginnings*, *Darkest Longings*, *Obsession*, *Vengeance*, *Summer Madness*, *Last Resort*, *Wildfire*, *Chasing Dreams*, *Taking Chances*, *Cruel Venus*, *Strange Allure*, *Silent Truths*, *Wicked Beauty*, *Intimate Strangers*, *The Hornbeam Tree*, *The Mill House* and, most recently, *A French Affair*. She is also the author of *Just One More Day*, a moving memoir of her childhood in Bristol. She lives in France. Her website address is www.susanlewis.com

Also by Susan Lewis

A Class Apart
Dance While You Can
Stolen Beginnings
Darkest Longings
Obsession
Vengeance
Summer Madness
Last Resort
Wildfire
Chasing Dreams
Taking Chances
Cruel Venus
Strange Allure
Silent Truths
Wicked Beauty
Intimate Strangers
The Hornbeam Tree
The Mill House
A French Affair

Just One More Day, A Memoir

MISSING

Susan Lewis

arrow books

Published by Arrow 2007

6 8 10 9 7 5

This book is a work of fiction. Names and characters are the product of the author's imagination and any resemblance to actual persons, living or dead, is entirely coincidental

First published in Great Britain in 2007 by
William Heinemann
Random House, 20 Vauxhall Bridge Road
London SW1V 2SA

www.rbooks.co.uk

Addresses for companies within The Random House Group Limited can be found at: www.randomhouse.co.uk/offices.htm

The Random House Group Limited Reg. No. 954009

A CIP catalogue record for this book is available from the British Library

ISBN 9780434014590

The Random House Group Limited supports The Forest Stewardship Council (FSC), the leading international forest certification organisation. All our titles that are printed on Greenpeace approved FSC certified paper carry the FSC logo. Our paper procurement policy can be found at www.rbooks.co.uk/environment

Typeset by SX Composing DTP, Rayleigh, Essex
Printed and bound in Great Britain by
CPI Mackays, Chatham ME5 8TD

For James, with love

Acknowledgements

First and foremost I would like to express my thanks to Sir John and Lady Linda Jennings for making the Devonshire location of this book such a pleasure to research. In throwing open the doors to their beautiful estate I found myself afloat in inspiration, from the magnificent house and its picture book gardens, to the surrounding woods and the horse sanctuary where many deserving beasts are peacefully living out their days. I also thank John and Linda for the very touching story of Henrietta the goose, who is still skimming happily about their lake with her adopted family.

My sincere gratitude also goes to Jackie Bulley and her colleagues at the WI for their enthusiastic help with the book, and for the wicked game of skittles.

An enormous thank you to PC Robert Tansleigh at Teignmouth Police Station for talking me through official procedure at the time someone goes missing, and for showing me around the CID offices in Exeter.

My love and thanks to Ellie Gleave for so patiently exploring Chiswick, Richmond and Kew with me. Also to Jill Clarke for the quirky, but very valuable information about the clock at St Anne's Church.

A quick last note to Linda Jennings – the next time we don't know what something is perhaps we'll try asking instead of going looking!

Missing

Prologue

Everything seemed normal, so no reason to think something might change the course of the day, or of any days to come. The sky over Exeter was an infinite blanket of grey with no chinks to let through the sun, no planes to drop from their flights. The pavements were damp and puddled with reflections; the traffic was snarled, each driver guarding his space jealously, angry when forced to let someone in.

Jacqueline Avery was in the passenger seat of her husband's BMW. She was a slender, stylish woman with sleek blonde hair caught up in a velvet slide, pale brown eyes that saw much and spoke of little, and a mouth that might have been sensuous were it not for the lines left by tragedy, like debris after a storm. She was dressed with a sober smartness, her handbag and shoes the same black as her coat, and the two rings she wore were a slim gold wedding band, and a small amethyst that had once belonged to her mother. Miles, her husband, had bought her jewellery over the years, but she almost never wore it. She didn't like to be flashy, though Miles's taste was anything but. The truth was, she simply didn't want to be noticed, not even to be admired. There was a time when she'd enjoyed it, but that was during another existence – one that had no connection to now.

As usual Miles was listening to the news as he drove. She glanced at him, but only when she knew he'd turned to gaze absently out of the side window. He was a handsome man with dark, slightly greying hair, a Roman profile and an air of authority that had always been natural to him, even before he'd achieved his success. It was part of coming from an established family, where the men had always been in positions of power. The two homes they had now – one in Kensington, the other here in Devon – had both been inherited, as had the fortune that had been rapidly devoured by taxes.

Jacqueline preferred to be in London, which was where she was going now. Miles would drop her at the station, then return to Moorlands, the small estate that bordered the savage plains of Dartmoor. The relief she felt at leaving was like the slow release of a bad dream. Nothing about Devon seemed to work for her. While it soothed and nourished Miles, it made her edgy and fearful. It was too far from London. The people were different. Though no one was ever unfriendly, she knew she'd never share the sense of belonging that was so natural to Miles and their fourteen-year-old daughter, Kelsey. They were here most of the time now, since Miles had resigned from his position as editor of a national broadsheet, and then moved Kelsey to a school close to Okehampton. She still boarded during the week, and occasionally went to friends for weekends, but usually she came home to Moorlands.

Thinking of her daughter could easily make Jacqueline's head spin, while her heart ached with the guilt and horror of what she'd done. *Almost* done, she reminded herself. She'd never meant her any harm, she simply hadn't been in her right mind. Miles understood that, so did Kelsey, but they no longer trusted her and she didn't blame them. She should never have been a mother. Time had proved how incapable she was, and it just went on and on proving it.

Hearing her mobile phone bleep, she took it out of her bag and read the message.

`Still don't know who's picking me up. You or Dad.`

Jacqueline sent a text back.

`Dad.`

To Miles she said, 'I've just told Kelsey you'll collect her on Friday.'

He nodded, but was apparently too engrossed in some political story to enlarge on that.

She was neither surprised nor disappointed. Conversation wasn't something she wanted right now, so she wouldn't bother to tell him that Kelsey had called the night before. It wasn't particularly important, it had only been to ask the same thing. Jacqueline had told her she'd call back, because she and Miles had been in the middle of an argument at the time. They hadn't made up before going to bed, nor had either of them mentioned it this morning.

'That reminds me,' she said, as they pulled up at the lights outside Sainsbury's at Marsh Barton. 'Mrs Davies gave me a list of things she needs, so perhaps you can pop into the supermarket on your way home.'

'No problem,' he responded.

She put the list in the small well in front of the gearstick and rezipped her bag. She wondered if he was really as absorbed in the financial news as he seemed, or if it was an act to avoid speaking to her.

Dry-eyed, she turned to look out of the window. She used to love him, when she was able to love, but not any more. She wondered why he'd stayed married to her, but since she knew the answer she discarded the sophistry and asked herself instead what right she had to hurt him this way. The answer was none, of course.

He swore quietly under his breath as someone cut them up at the roundabout. She watched the other driver speed on towards the station, presumably late for his train. She wondered if Miles was already feeling the relief of her departure. After the tension of the past few days he must be, though she knew he'd rather have the issue resolved than let her go without getting what he wanted. But there was no point in discussing it further. It should be forgotten, swept away like dust. She was sorry that he loved another woman, but he'd been in love with her for three years or more, so it wasn't new. She and Miles had to stay together and he knew it, so why was he suddenly so insistent on having his freedom now? The timing was curious, she thought, though perhaps not altogether surprising.

As they drove alongside the River Exe she watched the

water gushing wildly over rocks and roots, always moving forward, stopping for nothing, a purposeful frantic rush to the sea. She looked up at the railway bridge and her hands tightened on her bag. In less than five minutes he would pull up outside Exeter St David's, wait for her to take her bag from the back seat, then after saying goodbye he'd drive away. Those were some of the things that might happen. She had no idea if he'd kiss her, or glance in the rear-view mirror before turning, or even wait for her to disappear inside the station. It all remained to be seen. All she knew for certain was that life could change in less time than it took a heart to beat, or a bird to take flight, or a person to go into a garage to pay a bill. And if Miles were being truthful, she suspected he would like to drive away and never see or speak to her again.

Maybe she wouldn't mind that so much either, never having to see or speak to herself again.

She frowned slightly as he turned off before they reached the station approach. Then, realising he was taking the short cut, she closed her eyes and rested her head against the seat back.

There really never was any way of telling what might happen next.

Chapter One

Since receiving the message, four days ago, Vivienne had been living on a knife edge. It had been so unexpected that it had taken her several moments to believe what she was hearing – not because of what was being said, but because of who was saying it. She knew the voice better than almost any other, but it was the first time she'd heard it for over two years and it was as though time had folded inwards, like a fan, bringing the past to the present, closing out both time and distance and even the heartache that had filled so many of the days between.

There had been no contact since, but the woman he'd told her would be in touch had rung a few hours later. Alice, her closest friend and business partner, had dealt with the call, while Vivienne struggled with the dilemma of whether or not to ring him back.

'I need to talk to you,' he'd said at the end of the message. 'Please get in touch as soon as you can.'

She still hadn't, but for the past four days she'd thought about nothing else. It was as though his voice had found its way to her memories, rousing them back to life, stealing through them like colour, warming them with feelings that were almost too powerful to bear. Her hopes were soaring out of control, while her heart tensed with remembered passion and her breath caught on the echoes of laughter. She wanted to capture it all again, go back to a time when they'd been so happy it didn't seem possible it could end. After hearing him, the images of all they'd shared had become so clear in her mind that it might only have been yesterday that they'd been forced to say goodbye. A lot had happened since that he knew nothing about, but she guessed he could probably say the same. What had been going on in his life during the past two years?

'Hello? Vivi, are you with us?'

Vivienne looked up from her computer screen to find her assistant waving at her, a cheery grin lighting up her impish little face.

'Alice for you, line one,' Kayla told her.

Vivienne reached for her extension and was about to say hello when Alice's voice came down the line in an avalanche of excitement. 'Brace yourself,' she commanded, 'because this is the news you've been waiting for. In fact, it's going to knock your knickers off.'

Considering where Alice had spent the past two days Vivienne's heart gave an anxious jolt, but she was laughing as she said, 'I never imagined the weekend was going to produce such results. In fact, I wasn't expecting any at all.'

'Weekend?' Alice said blankly. 'Oh, yes, that. We'll come back to it. Right now I need to congratulate you, actually *us*, because Irwin's project has just been given the green light. They're all systems go from next Monday and we, my sizzling little superstar, are on board to handle the publicity.'

Vivienne's eyes lit up. This was indeed the news they'd been waiting for, and it couldn't have come at a better time, for they were now so badly in debt to the bank that they'd lately been forced to discuss closing down the public relations agency they'd started together, a little over seven years ago. 'When did you hear?' she demanded eagerly.

'I just got the call – from Irwin himself, bless his frilly little socks. I've told Kayla to go and splash out on some champagne. We're celebrating when I get there.'

'Where are you now?'

'Still on the train. Just left Reading, so about half an hour from Paddington.' There was a shuffling of paperwork as she presumably rearranged her notes. 'OK, back to the weekend,' she declared. 'I should begin by telling you that they were seriously disappointed it was me who showed up and not you.'

Vivienne blinked. 'Are we talking about the Kenleigh Women's Institute?' she asked, needing to make sure they were on the same page.

'Of course. I did my best with the advice they wanted, but their confidence is entirely in you.'

'But I've never met them. Have I?'

'Not that they mentioned, but you do know – or at least *knew* – one of their husbands. Keith Goss.'

Vivienne was taken aback. 'You met Keith's wife, Sharon?'

'I did, and it seems her husband never stopped raving about how good you are at your job, getting him all that publicity and sponsorship when he was in training for the Olympics – which never earned us a bean, I might remind you, but I guess that's not really the point.'

Remembering those days only too vividly, and for many more reasons than the help she'd given Keith Goss, Vivienne forced her thoughts to remain with the gifted young swimmer who'd lost his life while trying to save one of his fire-fighting colleagues in a factory blaze. The tragedy hadn't only rocked the local community to its core, the rest of the nation had felt it too, for Keith's easy-going nature and cheeky grin had made him almost as popular with the sports-loving public as his athletic prowess. 'How is Sharon?' she asked. 'And the children?'

'Didn't see the kids, but Sharon was at the meeting. It's all about her, actually. I'll explain more when I get back to the office, but the bottom line is, you did Keith a favour once, now the local WI are hoping you'll do one again for his wife.'

Curious, Vivienne said, 'What kind of a favour?'

Alice's reply was drowned out by static, leaving Vivienne to recall the only occasion she'd ever met Sharon Goss, though it was doubtful Sharon had any memory of it herself, for it had been at Keith's funeral.

'Are you there?' Alice said, coming back on the line.

'Yes. Why didn't the woman who rang last week tell me it was about Sharon? I'd have gone down myself if I'd known.'

'Really? To Devon?'

'Of course.' Then, after a pause, 'Actually yes, I would have.'

'Well you might have to yet, but we'll discuss it when I get back. Are you OK? How was your weekend?'

'Fine.'

'Any more calls from you know who?'

'No, but there was an email waiting for me this morning saying he still needs to talk to me. I emailed back asking what about.'

'And?'

'No answer yet.' She looked up as Kayla came out of the kitchenette in her woolly hat and a parka jacket, saying, 'Can you ask Alice if she's got the Brennard file?'

'Tell her yes, I have,' Alice answered.

'Why do you need it?' Vivienne wanted to know.

Before Kayla could answer Alice said, 'We've had a similar enquiry, which Kayla and I have been drafting a proposal for.'

Vivienne's expression darkened as she looked at Kayla. 'What do you mean, similar?' she asked.

'Her name's Belinda Bellamy,' Alice replied, 'otherwise known as *La Belle Amie*. We didn't tell you, because we knew how you'd react, so before you go off on one . . .'

'I know what you're going to say, that we're in no position to be choosy, but cleaning up the image of porn stars isn't what we want to become known for.'

'If we want to survive it might have to be.'

Reluctantly conceding the point, Vivienne said, 'OK, we'll look at it when you get here. Now, tell me more about the WI and Sharon Goss.'

No reply.

'Alice? Are you there?'

Realising the connection had been lost, Vivienne hung up and returned to her computer. Alice would ring back when she emerged from whatever tunnel, or dip, or black hole of the English countryside she'd plunged into. Meanwhile it would be a good idea to start reacquainting herself with Irwin's movie, for six months had passed since their original pitch for the business.

Ten minutes later the phone rang again. Presuming it was Alice she picked up, saying, 'OK, where were we?'

There was a pause before the voice at the other end said, 'Now that isn't a question I was expecting, so I'm afraid I don't readily have an answer.'

The blood drained from Vivienne's face as her heartbeat slowed and her head started to spin. 'Miles,' she said, thrown by the intensity of her reaction, even though she'd known, since receiving his message last week, that it would affect her profoundly when they did finally speak. She just hadn't realised how powerfully the sound of his voice would move her.

'Am I interrupting?' he said. 'Is this a bad time?'

'No, it's not a bad time,' she assured him, and as though needing to confirm it she glanced at the clock. Five minutes to ten on a Monday morning. She took a breath to speak again, but suddenly too many thoughts were crowding her mind, while too many emotions filled the spaces inside her. She had never loved anyone the way she loved this man, and as the force of it came swirling out of the past, intensifying the hold on her heart, she had no way to resist it. 'Did you get my email?' she asked.

'I did, but I wanted to speak to you in person. Incidentally, I hope it was OK that I gave your number to the WI?'

'Yes, yes of course.'

'I was going to get in touch anyway, then they called and . . . Well . . . How are you?'

'Fine. I'm . . . Uh, it's good to hear you.' Was it? Yes, of course, but why was he calling? Had he found out what she'd been keeping from him? What would she do if he had? Suddenly it was hard to breathe. 'Is everything OK?' she asked, managing to push her voice through the tightness in her chest. 'It's been a long time.'

'Just over two years.'

She stood up, and carried the phone to the window. Outside an impervious world was going about its business, carrying on as though nothing extraordinary or momentous was happening anywhere, when it surely must be – not only here, in her small space, but in all the random vehicles crossing Kew Bridge, the planes flying overhead, the barges cruising the river. 'What are you doing these days?' she asked, wanting to delay the real reason for his call. It was safer this side of knowing, where hope still had a chance and dread could be ignored. 'I know you resigned.' There was an ironic lilt to her voice which echoed in his as he said, 'Faced with Hobson's choice I tried to remain as dignified as possible.'

She laughed, and felt the pleasure of it moving through her like warmth after an endless chill.

'As to what I'm doing now,' he said, 'I'm supposed to be writing a biography of our illustrious ex-prime minister, but I confess progress is slow and the subject is, shall we say, not always thrilled by the author's approach to his inimitable . . . achievements.'

Again she smiled. As the ex-editor of a national newspaper who'd made no secret of his contempt for recent government policy, or his loathing for the American mogul who'd acquired his paper by fouler means than fair, it was no surprise that a publisher was keen to get Miles into print. Not that his name had disappeared from the media since his very public resignation a year ago, for his opinion was regularly sought on any number of topics, from Middle East unrest to education reforms.

How exhilarating their time together had been, in so many ways, and inspiring and right – and doomed, though thank God she hadn't known it then.

'How are things in the world of public relations?' he asked.

She grimaced. 'They've been better, but it's starting to pick up again.' She only hoped she was speaking the truth, but Irwin's movie was a good sign.

She was gazing at her reflection in the window, a hazy figure merging with the slick, viscous strip of the river outside and the greyness of the sky. It could almost have been the ghost of her former self, staring back with haunted eyes and a pale, heart-shaped face. In reality, her eyes were a lustrous blue. Her cheekbones were high and naturally blushed, her mouth full and red, her hair long and heavy and almost black. 'We're still in Pier House, next to the river,' she said.

'. . . and close to home.'

'And close to home,' she confirmed, letting him know that she hadn't moved from the small town house she'd had when they were together, though the arrears on her mortgage meant this might soon become necessary. 'We have another partner now,' she continued. 'Pete Alexander. Actually, he's freelance, but Alice and I like to think of him as ours.'

'How is Alice?'

'She's OK. I'm sure she'd want me to say hi. Actually she's been in Kenleigh this weekend.'

'In response to the WI?'

'Yes. I'd have gone myself but I was . . . otherwise engaged.' What an absurd thing to say. She wished she could take it back.

'Does that mean what I think it does?'

Realising what he'd read into it, she said, 'That I've met someone else? No, I haven't.' Maybe she should have lied, but it was too late now. 'Where are you?' she asked, presuming he was at home in Kensington, since it was a weekday and he no longer had an office to go to.

'I'm in Devon.'

At that her heart gave a painful twist and her eyes closed, but it was impossible to shut out the image of him at the sprawling seventeenth-century farmhouse his grandfather had bought in the twenties and Miles had inherited six years ago. She'd loved the place almost as much as he had; it was where they'd spent every weekend and holiday while they were together, and they had even drawn up plans to modernise it in keeping with its heritage. They'd been so happy then, and in love, until fate had intervened to tear them apart.

'I guess I should come to the point of my call,' he said.

The earnestness of his tone caused her heart to trip.

'Actually, I should probably have said this at the start,' he went on, 'but I want you to know that I wouldn't be putting either of us through this if it weren't necessary.'

Experiencing a quick panic as the loss she'd felt when he'd told her it was over seemed to move out of the shadows to claim her again, she took a step back as though to escape it. 'This sounds ominous,' she commented with a shaky laugh.

'Maybe it is. I'm not sure.' Then, after a pause, 'I need to know . . . Have you seen or heard from Jacqueline recently?'

She became very still. It could hardly be a serious

question, yet he'd never have asked if it weren't. 'You mean your wife Jacqueline?' she said, as if there could be any other. 'Why would you think I've seen her?' A voice was crying out in her head, *you were separated when we were together, she has no reason to come looking for me.* She put a hand to her mouth, as though to prevent the words from tumbling out. *I'm not the cause of her problems,* she wanted to say.

Only when he answered did she realise how tense he'd sounded before. 'I guess that tells me what I need to know. She hasn't been in touch at all?'

'No, but why are you asking?'

He took a breath. 'The last time any of us saw her was over three weeks ago. She was supposed to be going up to London. As far as I know she got on the train at Exeter, but I haven't heard from her since.'

Vivienne's agitation was mounting. 'She always had a habit of taking herself off without warning,' she reminded him.

'But it's never been this long before.'

With a multitude of unworthy, as well as unnerving thoughts whirling around in her head, Vivienne said, 'What about Kelsey? Surely she must have . . .'

'She hasn't contacted Kelsey either. We've both tried calling and leaving messages, but I'm afraid things haven't changed with Jacqueline, she still disappears at random, and never answers until she's ready to.'

Feeling the craziness of his life mixing with the anger she felt at how resolutely it stood between them, she asked, 'Are you sure she came to London?'

'Only insofar as I dropped her at the station. I didn't wait around to make sure she got on the train.'

The image of Jacqueline Avery turning heads as she strode into the station at Exeter, all Chanel couture and chic blonde chignon, was an easy one to conjure, and perhaps even to admire. Yet it wasn't real, because very little about Miles's wife was what it seemed. She was like a book whose cover told the wrong story, a glittering window masking a room full of dark secrets. To look at her there was simply no way of telling that she often couldn't cope with her life, because there was nothing to see on the outside that set her apart from any other attractive woman of her age.

'You still haven't answered my question,' she reminded him. 'Why do you think she'd be in touch with me?'

There was a pause before he said, 'She thinks we're still—' He stopped and her heart turned over as she realised what he'd been about to say. 'She knows things can't go on the way they've been since she came back,' he continued, his tone betraying how hard he was finding this. 'We've tried talking about it, God knows we've tried, but the next day it's as though she hasn't taken anything in. I know she has, but she chooses to pretend—' He broke off again. 'I'm sorry, this isn't your problem. I just needed to know if you'd seen her.'

Though Vivienne's every instinct was warning her not to become involved again, she knew there was no way to avoid it, not only because of how she felt about Miles, but because of what Jacqueline's disappearance could mean for her. 'Did something happen before she left?' she asked carefully.

'Not really. She and Kelsey had a blazing row a few weeks ago. They were here in Devon at the time, and I was in London. I only knew about it when Kelsey called to tell me I had to get her mother certified or she wouldn't be held responsible for her actions.'

Feeling the tragedy of this being no normal teenage cry, she said, 'I take it you've asked Kelsey what it was about?'

'Of course. She says it was all the usual stuff, Jacqueline's coldness and refusal to listen or communicate. Her inability to let go of the past . . .'

Vivienne could feel her mouth turning dry, but the past didn't mean her – it meant a long time before she'd ever come into their lives. Then, remembering something he'd once told her, she said, 'What about the flat she used to have? Might she be there?'

'She sold it over a year ago.'

'Perhaps she's bought another without telling you.'

'I can't find anything to say she has, and I've been through her papers both here and in London.'

Vivienne swallowed hard. 'Have you contacted the police?' she asked.

'Not yet, but I think I'll have to.'

Her eyes moved to the door as Kayla returned with a bottle of champagne and a dripping umbrella.

'Sorry, I shouldn't be laying this on you,' Miles was saying. 'I'll ring off now. You have my numbers, in case you need to call.'

'If they haven't changed, yes.'

'They're the same.'

A silence followed that neither of them attempted to fill, but there was no need when they both knew what the other was thinking, and even feeling. It had always been that way with them, and finding it hadn't changed was perhaps more difficult to bear than all the other emotions that were burning inside her.

Finally, hearing the line go dead, she clicked off too and carried the phone back to her desk, suddenly realising she was shaking.

'Champagne's in the fridge,' Kayla shouted from the kitchen. 'Fancy a coffee for now?'

Vivienne barely looked up as she answered. A hundred more questions were starting to emerge through the longing Miles had left her with, but she wouldn't call back to ask them. She needed to think, to assimilate how Jacqueline's disappearance might affect her – and how she might handle it if she turned up here. The thought of it caused a shudder of unease in her heart, and putting her head in her hands she took a deep, steadying breath.

Had Jacqueline not decided to end her marriage three years ago and go to live with her sister in the States, Vivienne doubted she and Miles would ever have been more than a passing introduction at the launch of a new magazine. As it was, Miles was free to pursue an attraction that had been as instant and powerful for her as it had for him, and they'd dropped all the pretence and gone home together that night. Within a week he'd told her everything about his marriage and his life, and it was around the same time that they'd both admitted to something special happening between them.

Their relationship hadn't been easy, particularly at the beginning, when he'd regularly called Miami to find out how Jacqueline was, or to ask if there was anything she needed. She rarely wanted to speak to him, and when she did she merely told him to get on with his life and forget all about her. Kelsey should do the same, she'd say, and Vivienne could only imagine the hurt that must have caused the poor child.

It was mainly because of Kelsey that she and Miles had never flaunted their relationship in public, preferring to give his daughter some time to get used to her parents being apart before asking her to accept someone else in her father's life. Not that she and Vivienne didn't meet, because they did, but the troubled child's fear of someone stealing her beloved daddy's affections had made her hostile to Vivienne in a way that had caused several rows between her and her father. However, Vivienne had remained determined to work at it, and Miles wouldn't be dissuaded from envisaging a future with a new wife, and perhaps even a new family that would give Kelsey the siblings she'd always lacked.

Quite what Kelsey might have thought of her father's plans they'd never found out, because one Saturday evening, while they were in Devon and Kelsey was spending the weekend with a friend, Miles had received a call from his deputy editor warning him that *The News on Sunday*, clearly short of a story that weekend, was going to make a splash of his relationship with Vivienne.

Miles had been furious. Since he and Jacqueline were no longer together he could hardly be accused of cheating, so there was no doubt in his mind that the story was being run out of malice. The editor of *The News on Sunday* detested Miles with a Wagnerian fervour. Not that the animosity had shown in the article, far from it. Gareth Critchley was much too clever for that. He'd merely congratulated Miles on finding true love at last, because no one could have deserved it more after all he'd been through with his tragically disturbed wife. Then Critchley had sat back to watch the fallout that only he, Miles and a handful of others had known would follow.

It hadn't taken long, because within days Jacqueline was back from the States, by which time Vivienne and Miles were in London, and the scenes that followed would remain with Vivienne for ever. There had been no way she and Miles could have stayed together after that, for Jacqueline had shown them then, in the worst way imaginable, how far she was prepared to go to keep them apart.

Now, a little over two years later, just as Vivienne was starting to feel she might be able to get on with her life, Miles was calling to tell her Jacqueline had disappeared.

'OK, boss, if you don't want to answer the phone I will,' Kayla declared, plonking a steaming mug of coffee on the desk, and like the chirpily efficient assistant she was, she snatched up the nearest receiver, saying, 'Kane and Jackson, the one and only Kayla speaking. Oh hi, Alice. Yes, she's still here.'

Vivienne picked up the phone. 'Before we go any further,' she said to Alice, 'Miles has just called.'

At that Kayla's head came up and Alice fell silent.

'So what did he say?' Alice finally managed.

'Apparently Jacqueline's disappeared. No one's seen or heard from her for about three weeks.'

'Oh my God,' Alice groaned.

'Shit,' Kayla murmured.

'This goes to the top of the agenda when I get there,' Alice stated. 'Whatever else is going on in our world, nothing takes precedence over this.'

An hour later Alice was pacing up and down the office, a hand buried in her wavy, golden hair, a deep frown darkening her softly freckled features.

'So no one actually knows if she came to London?' she said, referring to Jacqueline. 'I mean, she could have waited for Miles to drive away from the station, then hopped into a taxi and gone anywhere? *If* what he's telling us is true.'

Vivienne started. 'Why on earth would he lie?' she challenged.

Alice looked at her incredulously, then slightly tempering her instinctive response to such naivety, she said, 'Try to remember, you're the one who's in love with him. The rest of us aren't clouded by rose-tinted specs, or delusions of romance that—'

'Don't be mean,' Kayla interrupted. 'She didn't ask to fall in love—'

'Kayla, when you've got a grip on reality that doesn't involve Hollywood, you can speak,' Alice snapped, 'until then, please leave it to me.' As she turned back to Vivienne Kayla poked out so much tongue that Vivienne couldn't help but laugh. 'Ignore her, she'll grow up one of these days,' Alice commanded, lending weight to Kayla's belief that she had eyes in the back of her head. 'Now, what I'm concerned about is this: when exactly did Jacqueline disappear? What prompted her to go ?'

'How can I possibly know that?' Vivienne protested.

'I don't suppose you can, but I think it's important, don't you, because the last thing you need is that woman turning up on your doorstep, or worse, dropping in on your mother for a nice cosy little chat, so we need to know—'

'You're making her sound like some kind of maniac,' Vivienne broke in. 'She has issues, we all know that.'

'And one of them is you.'

'Not really. Miles and I haven't even seen one another . . .'

Alice waved a dismissive hand. 'I'm aware of how long it's been, and I don't want him coming back into your life only to hurt you all over again. You went through enough the last time he broke up with you.'

'He didn't have much choice.'

'So he says.'

Vivienne looked at her in astonishment. 'What's that supposed to mean?' she demanded.

'All we know is what he told us.'

Vivienne's eyes flashed with temper. 'You know what Jacqueline did to herself and Kelsey,' she said angrily. 'They were in hospital for God's sake, and as far as I'm aware you never had these doubts about him before, so where are they coming from now?'

'Vivi, where marriages are concerned *no one* knows what's really going on, except those who are in it. And, I'm afraid, having a tragedy doesn't make someone a saint. Miles has his faults too, and no one knows them better than his wife. She's the one who's had to live with them all these years, and she's the one who's—'

Vivienne got up and began walking to the door. 'I'm not listening to any more of this,' she declared. 'It's bad enough that Jacqueline has taken it into her head to disappear. That you now think Miles is in some way responsible for her depressions and delusions . . .' She spun round angrily. 'Putting everything else aside, you met him often enough, so how can you stand there accusing him of . . . Well, I don't know what you're accusing him of, and I'm not sure I want to.'

'I was crazy about him, I admit it,' Alice said. 'It was hard not to be, but marriages break up all the time, Vivi. She'd have got over it, eventually, everyone does, so why didn't he—'

'You know very well that wouldn't be true in her case – and I had no idea you'd been harbouring all these horrible thoughts and suspicions. That you could think for a minute that Miles is some kind of . . . *monster* . . .'

'That's not what I'm saying, because I know he's not, but he isn't perfect either. No one is, and how do you know if you have the full story of what happened fifteen years ago? It's a long time, Vivi, they've been through a lot since then and you've only ever heard it from his side.'

Vivienne's hands went to her head. 'He's not a liar, Alice. I trust what he told me, and if you think I was gullible enough to be taken in . . .'

'Not gullible, just blinded, as we all are by love.'

Vivienne looked at Kayla, and to her dismay saw only solidarity with Alice, rather than sympathy with her.

'All we want is to stop you doing anything that's going to end in disaster,' Alice said gently. 'He's been in touch, next he might want to see you, then heaven knows where it might end, but whatever happens, you'll never be able to change his past . . . Oh God, Vivi, I'm sorry, I didn't mean to make you cry.'

'I'm not crying,' Vivienne declared, bringing her head out of her hands. 'I'm just horrified that we're even having this conversation. I always thought I had your wholehearted support . . .'

'That's exactly what this is. Me trying to protect you from yourself, because no one ever sees things rationally when they're in love.'

'For heaven's sake! Five minutes ago it was Jacqueline I was worrying about, now here you are telling me that I'm the one who's unhinged, because I fell for a sociopath.'

Looking suitably chastened, Alice replied, 'That's not what I'm saying at all, so why don't we try to start this again? Jacqueline does a disappearing act, Miles calls you and intimates she might have gone because he still has feelings for you.'

'He didn't say that!'

'But he did intimate it, and now we're extremely worried because we all know what she did to get him back last time.'

'Blimey, she might already be dead,' Kayla murmured. 'Three weeks is a long time.' Her eyes rounded with intrigue. 'Oh my God, what if he's offed her?'

'For God's sake!' Vivienne shouted angrily. 'I wish I'd never even mentioned it now.'

'But what if she *doesn't* turn up?' Alice said.

'Of course she will. She always does, so let's change the subject. I want to know what happened with the WI at the weekend? Better still, let's break out the champagne. We have a movie deal to celebrate, remember?'

'I'm up for that,' Kayla responded, heading for the kitchen. 'It's not the best, because they didn't have it, but it's dry and it sparkles.'

When Alice's eyes came back to Vivienne's they were softening with affection. 'I'm sorry if I gave you a hard time,' she said. 'I don't mean to be unkind, I just don't want to see you hurt the way you were before.'

'I know,' Vivienne responded. 'And I shouldn't have got so worked up.'

Coming to give her a hug, Alice said, 'You wouldn't be human if you hadn't. It's a very sensitive issue for you, I understand that, and I could see how shaken up you were the minute I walked in the door.'

'Please let's drop it now,' Vivienne said. 'We have work to do and champagne to drink . . . And phones to answer,' she added, picking up the nearest one as the main line started to ring. 'Vivienne Kane speaking,' she told the caller.

There was a moment's silence, which caused her a beat of

unease, until Alice's husband, Angus, suddenly said, 'Sorry. Are you there? Is that Alice?'

'No, Vivienne. How are you?'

'Snowed under, but not too busy to congratulate my girls on their movie deal. Alice left me a message. Dinner's on me tonight. Hope you can make it. Rose and Crown, Kew Green? Tell my wife I love her, and book us a table if you get a minute.'

'We'd starve without you,' Vivienne informed him, only half joking. And putting the phone down she said to Alice, 'Angus loves you, and is taking us to dinner tonight.'

Rescuing two fizzing mugs from the tray Kayla was carrying, Alice passed one to Vivienne, saying, 'Here's to my husband, our accountant; Irwin, our saviour, and the WI for their crazy schemes, though they're not going to earn us any money, and frankly I'm starting to feel a bit doubtful about helping them since you got the call from Miles. Kenleigh might be some distance from Moorlands, but it's still in the same county.'

'I thought they were only after advice,' Vivienne replied, aware of the churning feeling inside her. 'Are you saying we're getting involved?'

Alice grimaced. 'Actually, I don't think we have much choice, and I know you're going to agree, because the reason for their auction is to help Sharon Goss, who – I'm sorry to break it to you like this – has leukaemia.'

Vivienne's face drained. 'Oh my God,' she murmured, unable to comprehend life's cruelties as she pictured Sharon's slight, tragic figure beside her husband's grave, and how she'd tried to throw herself onto the coffin as it was lowered. It was Miles who'd caught her and wrapped her in his arms before taking her back to the car, while Vivienne had followed behind with the Goss's two frightened little children. 'Of course we have to help,' she said forcefully. 'Just tell me what they need the money for? Medical treatment? Transport? Living?'

Alice's smile showed her admiration for Vivienne's response, which though no surprise, was no less touching for that. 'Sharon's not able to earn any more,' she answered, 'so she's worried about how she's going to take care of her children while she has her treatment. Apparently the first bout has already left her up to her eyes in debt, and the stress of it isn't doing her any good at all.'

'Of course not,' Vivienne agreed, with feeling. 'Just thank goodness the local WI has stepped in to try and help out. I take it that is what's happened?'

Alice nodded. 'And they in turn are calling on you, because you're the one Sharon has all the faith in, because of what you did for Keith.' She took a breath. 'I think, however, that it's looking as though they'll have to put up with me, because after the call from Miles we can't let you go trundling off to Devon . . .'

'Don't be ridiculous. Of course I can do it. I have to.'

'Vivi, once the press get wind of the fact that Jacqueline's missing, they're going to be crawling all over the place.'

'But Moorlands is at least ten miles from Kenleigh, and anyway, whatever's going on in my life cannot take precedence over Sharon Goss's needs. Her husband's dead, Alice, and her children might be about to lose their mother. What can be more important than that?'

Alice looked at her, knowing that Vivienne was fully aware of the answer, so there was no need to spell it out.

'OK,' Vivienne said, 'of course you're right, but Jacqueline's likely to turn up at any minute, so we can't let her disappearance affect our decisions.'

Alice began to speak.

'No,' Vivienne interrupted, 'putting my previous association with Sharon aside, we agreed when we started this agency that we'd alternate on the high-budget projects, and it's your turn, so the movie's yours, while I'll do what I can to help Sharon and the WI.'

'While Pete takes on *La Belle Amie*,' Kayla piped up, 'to bring us in a bit more dosh.'

Vivienne looked at her.

'They're willing to pay top whack to get us,' Kayla cried. 'Her agent's already said so, and it's easy money. Everyone wants to interview someone like her, all tits, ass and a career full of shags. And she's willing to talk about it.'

'If she weren't, we couldn't help her,' Vivienne pointed out, 'but I'm still saying—'

'Let's get back to the WI and Sharon,' Alice interrupted. 'Without disputing who's going to handle it for the moment, the idea they've come up with is to hold a slave auction.'

'You're kidding!' Kayla exclaimed in shock. 'They'll never get away with that.'

'My reaction to a T,' Alice told her, 'at which point I was informed that Vivienne would understand right away what they meant, because slave auctions happen all the time in the country.'

Vivienne was laughing. 'They do,' she confirmed. 'It's when someone offers their skill – gardening, cleaning, plumbing, you name it – to the highest bidder. The money, of course, goes to the good cause, not the tradesman.'

'I understand that now,' Alice informed her, 'but it did give me a bit of a turn when they first said it. Anyway, they're fully aware that an ordinary slave auction isn't going to raise much cash, which is why they've come to us – or you – to see if we can turn their sow's ear into a silk purse, I quote.'

Vivienne was already looking thoughtful.

'Actually, I should add that a few of them have already cooked up a scheme that might just work, given the right spin. They're thinking that instead of putting local tradesmen under the hammer they could put toy boys up there, or gigolos, or I forget what they called them now, but essentially they reckon they'll get more interest if there's a bit of a sexy angle to it.'

Vivienne blinked several times. 'Well, they're right about that,' she replied, 'but what are these boys supposed to do for the highest bidder? Actually, don't answer that, I don't think I want to know. Are you sure it was the WI you saw?'

'So they said, and I've no reason to doubt it, but I have to admit they weren't the middle-class blue-rinsers I'd imagined. Much more colourful, in fact, especially Stella Coombes. Have you ever met her?'

Vivienne shook her head.

'Then if you do you're in for a treat.'

Vivienne took a sip of her champagne as she continued to think. 'So how have you left it with them?' she asked.

'A bit up in the air, really, but I don't think they're going to take much sorting out.'

'In which case there's no reason for it not to fall to me. In fact, I've already got a fair idea of how we can do this, but first tell me more about Sharon's condition.'

After exchanging glances with Kayla indicating that, as usual, they were impressed by Vivienne's quick thinking, Alice said, 'Like anyone suffering from leukaemia – at least I think it's anyone – she's in need of a bone-marrow transplant. The search is on for a donor, obviously, but it turns out that "our Sharon" as they call her, is a rare tissue type so they're having trouble finding a match. If, *when,* they do – actually, even before that – she needs help taking care of her children, meeting the bills, paying off her debts, finding a bit extra for the treats, all the usual stuff. It might be easier if she had some family backup, but it turns out she's something of a waif, because both her parents are dead, so are Keith's, and there are no sisters or brothers or even extended family capable of helping out in a way that's going to make a difference. Which is why Stella Coombes, in the shape of the local WI, has stepped in to lend support, but money's obviously really tight, and it's only going to get worse.'

Vivienne's expression showed how hard she was thinking. 'How much time does Sharon have?' she asked, bluntly.

'We're talking months, and not all that many,' Alice answered gravely.

'Oh God,' Vivienne murmured, finding herself being caught up in the poor girl's terror.

'Which is why,' Alice continued, 'they need to get the auction under way as soon as possible. Like I said, I'm willing to take it on myself while you do the movie . . .'

'You could always let Pete handle it,' Kayla suggested.

'No, we'll give him *La Belle Amie,*' Vivienne told her. 'It's more his thing. And Alice, *you're* doing the movie, while I sort out the auction. If we stage it right it could turn out to be big news for us, even if we don't get paid.'

'See,' Alice said to Kayla, 'she's a genius, because she's obviously already got some plan worked out that's going to benefit us too.'

'Maybe,' Vivienne said, 'but our main concern right now is to give Sharon some financial peace of mind.'

'And what about you and the press and Jacqueline?' Alice wanted to know. 'Because you don't need me to remind you that you've got a lot more at stake this time around.'

'You're right, I don't need reminding, but why don't we think about Sharon first, then deal with any other problems as they arise, because for all we know, they just might not.'

Chapter Two

Miles Avery's sunken dark eyes appeared solemn and slightly wary as he shook hands with Detective Inspector Sadler. The inspector's parka jacket was dripping rain on the grey flagstones of the entrance hall, where a cosy seating area was presided over by a wall of abstract watercolours, and a hand-carved wooden staircase began its ascent to the upper floor. At the far end of the hall, opposite the door, a floor-to-ceiling arched window framed an exquisite view of stone terraces and balustrades, and the wide, sloping sweep of the lawns down to a small lake, rippling now in the rain. All around the grounds thick clusters of trees were already changing colour with the season, while on the hillsides that protected the valley deep, dense woods grouped like a haze-shrouded audience across the horizon.

Though Miles stood at least a head taller than the balding police officer, it wasn't so much his height, at six feet one, that was unusual, as Sadler's lack of it. Having had experience of short men – at best defensive, at worst downright hostile – Miles was trying to keep an open mind as he closed the front door, while Mrs Davies, the housekeeper, took the detective's coat.

'DC Elaine Joy,' Sadler said, turning to introduce the ruddy-cheeked female officer who'd accompanied him.

Miles's expression was polite as he greeted the young DC, who was doing a poor job of concealing how thrilled she was to be in this important man's house.

'He's not that important,' Sadler had informed her snappily before they'd arrived. 'He only edited a newspaper, for heaven's sake.'

'And owns that lovely house and grounds right next to

the moor. And writes all those columns. And tells dumbass politicians where to get off when they need to. In my book, that makes him important, but if it's bugging you, sir, I won't say it again.'

Miles Avery was also a bit of all right, DC Joy was thinking to herself, as the housekeeper carried off their coats and Miles directed them towards a set of double doors. Not that that was any surprise, she'd seen him on the telly or in the papers often enough, so was perfectly aware of what he looked like, but it had to be said, in the flesh he was definitely not a let-down. Of course he was a bit old for her at forty-five, and probably a bit posh too, considering her own humble roots, but since she wasn't here to assess his looks or suitability, she quickly reasserted her professional neutrality and followed him and Sadler into the sitting room.

For quite a large room it was surprisingly cosy, with a wood fire crackling in a wide, open hearth, and all sorts of colourful paintings hanging on the walls that weren't of anything DC Joy could recognise, but she liked them anyway. The furniture wasn't what she might have expected, since it was kind of shabby and plush all at once, and covered in downy cushions and throws – in fact, it was just the sort of thing a person could sink into and spread out on to watch the TV. Not that there was any sign of a telly in here, though it could be hidden in one of the antique wood cabinets, or, for all she knew, one of the paintings might transform itself into a screen. Anything was possible these days, especially if you had the money, and there wasn't much doubt, looking at this place, that Miles Avery had plenty of that.

Noticing the young detective taking in her surroundings, Miles treated her to a friendly smile before his eyes were drawn back to Sadler as the detective said, 'I hope we're not interrupting anything. We probably should have called . . .'

'No, it's fine,' Miles assured him, waving them towards one of the sofas while he went to stand with his back to the fire. 'Can I get you anything? Tea? Coffee?'

'No, we're OK, thank you,' Sadler replied, before Joy made the mistake of accepting.

Miles's expression was benign as his eyes moved between the detectives. He wasn't particularly surprised that a senior officer was following up on yesterday's routine visit from the two PCs who'd come in response to his call, but he did wonder how much digging around Sadler might already have done into his family's affairs. It was that thought, amongst others, that was making it necessary for him to conceal his ingrained antipathy towards the police as best he could. 'I was told yesterday,' he said, 'that someone would be contacting the transport police.'

Sadler nodded. 'It's been done,' he said. 'They're still checking the CCTV tapes. Naturally, we'll let you know when they come back to us.' He cleared his throat. 'I've looked through the information you gave the response team yesterday, but I'm afraid it might be necessary to go over the same ground . . .'

'That's fine,' Miles assured him.

Sadler looked at him with cautious eyes. There was something about this man that was already getting under his skin, but for the moment he couldn't put his finger on what – apart from all the privilege and dosh, not to mention how well connected he was, a fact that rarely made Sadler's life easy. 'You say it's been three weeks since you last saw your wife?' he said matter-of-factly.

'That's right.'

Miles's expression, DC Joy was thinking, had become not so much defensive as guarded, though not in a hostile way, more sort of . . . well, like he didn't really want to be going through this, and who could blame him for that?

'And there's been no contact between you during that time?' Sadler prompted.

'None at all. As I told the officers yesterday, I dropped her at the station in the morning, just after ten, then after calling in at the supermarket I came straight home. As far as I knew, she was catching the train to London.'

'But we don't know whether she did or not?'

'At the time I assumed she did, but since I didn't go into the station with her, I'm afraid I can't confirm it.'

'You've been in touch with her friends and family . . .'

'Of course. She has a sister who lives in the States, though she's in Edinburgh with her husband at the moment. She hasn't heard from her.'

'Friends? Locally and in London?'

'She didn't have a wide circle – in fact it would probably be more accurate to say she had more acquaintances than friends. I've tried a few, but no one's heard from her recently.' His eyes went to DC Joy as she started to make notes.

'Was anyone at your house in London three weeks ago?' Sadler asked. 'Someone who could confirm whether or not she showed up?'

'I'm afraid not. My daughter was at school, and I was here.'

'But you've been to London since, to check for yourself whether or not she arrived?'

'Of course. There's no sign of her having done so, but the cleaner's been in since, so it's hard to be certain.'

Sadler chewed thoughtfully on his lip, and for a while they let the clock and fire fill the silence. 'We'll get in touch with the Kensington and Chelsea police,' he said finally. 'They'll need access to the house. Is there anyone close by with a key?'

'The cleaner. But I'm going myself the day after tomorrow, if it can wait that long.'

Appearing to note the lack of urgency Sadler nodded slowly.

Miles glanced at DC Joy and smiled again. Starting, she smiled back, and blushed as she returned to her notebook.

'You told the response team,' Sadler said, 'that it's not unusual for your wife to go off for a few days without saying where she's going.'

'She does, from time to time. She feels the need, occasionally, to get away from me, and the house . . .'

'From you?'

Miles appeared faintly amused. 'Does that make us unusual?' he asked.

Instead of answering Sadler said, 'Where does she go?'

'She used to have an apartment in London, but she sold it about a year ago, so I'm not sure where she goes now.

Probably to a hotel. She's never said and I don't ask, because she doesn't want me to know.'

Seeming to find this both odd and intriguing, Sadler said, 'Why wouldn't she want you to know?'

'I think it makes her feel powerful to make me worry.'

'And do you worry?'

'Of course.'

Sadler was watching him closely. 'Are you sure she was intending to go to London when you took her to the station?' he asked.

'It's what she said, and there was a train due about ten minutes after I dropped her so I had no reason to think anything else.'

Sadler's brow was creasing as he said, 'But no one knows if she actually got on it.'

'I'm hoping the CCTV cameras will help us with that,' Miles reminded him.

Sadler looked at Joy as she said, 'Can you tell us if you and your wife had a row or anything before you took her to the station?'

Miles's expression was unreadable as he turned to her, but as he was about to answer the door opened and a stunningly pretty young girl with long blonde hair and her father's deep-set dark eyes put her head round.

Miles beckoned her to come and join them. 'My daughter, Kelsey,' he announced as Sadler rose to his feet. 'Kelsey, this is DI Sadler and DC Joy.'

Very politely Kelsey shook the detectives' hands, then went to stand with her father.

'I collected Kelsey from school last night,' Miles said, feeling the need to explain. 'She wanted to be here now that the police are involved in looking for her mother.'

'Do you have any idea where she is yet?' Kelsey asked.

'I'm afraid not,' Sadler replied, sitting down again.

Kelsey glanced up at Miles, who gave her a reassuring smile. 'I'm sorry, Inspector,' he said, turning back to Sadler, 'where were we?'

'We were asking,' Joy responded, 'if you and your wife had had a falling out before you took her to the station.'

'No, we hadn't,' he replied. 'Nothing out of the ordinary had happened at all.'

'So no row, no accidents that we know of, no reason to suspect foul play – at this stage. I take it there's been no ransom demand?'

'If there had, I'd have told you,' Miles assured her. 'There's been no communication at all.'

Sadler said, 'Then is there anything else you can tell us that might help explain why your wife would *choose* to absent herself from home for so long?'

'She's often given to spells of depression,' Miles answered.

'It's all to get attention,' Kelsey piped up.

Miles allowed a moment to pass, then said, 'My wife can be very withdrawn at times, hardly speaking at all, while at others she'll be as communicative and responsive as the rest of us.'

Sadler glanced at Kelsey, waiting to see if she had anything to add, but it seemed she didn't. 'I'm sorry to ask this in front of your daughter,' he said, 'but is there a chance your wife might be involved with someone else?'

'You mean another man? I suppose we can't rule it out,' Miles replied, 'but I would strongly doubt it.'

'I can tell you now that she's not,' Kelsey confirmed. 'That's not what she's about at all.'

'Then what is she about?' Sadler enquired.

Kelsey's only answer was to move in closer to her father.

Tearing his eyes from her, Sadler said, 'And what about you, Mr Avery? Are you—'

'No, I'm not having an affair,' Miles cut in.

'Dad!' Kelsey hissed.

Miles sighed as he looked down at her. 'You know very well,' he began, but letting it drop he said to Sadler, 'I was involved with someone a couple of years ago, when my wife and I weren't together.'

Sadler glanced at Joy to make sure she was getting this down.

'I called her yesterday,' Miles continued, 'to ask if she'd seen or heard from my wife. She hadn't.'

'Why did you think she might have?'

'Because Jacqueline has never been able to accept that my relationship with Vivienne is completely over.'

'And could your wife be right?'

'I've just told you, Inspector, I am not having an affair.'

Sadler glanced at Kelsey, as though expecting her to contradict her father, but she seemed to have nothing more to say. 'Is your wife likely to be a nuisance to . . . I'm sorry, what was her name?'

'Vivienne. Vivienne Kane.' He waited for Joy to write it down, then said, 'My wife, by nature, is a very passive and private person, so no, I wouldn't say she was given to pestering people.'

'So not violent, or aggressive in any way?'

Miles shook his head.

'Except for what she did to me,' Kelsey muttered.

Sadler's eyebrows shot up. 'What did she do to you?' he asked quickly.

Kelsey waited for Miles to answer, but in the end she was the one who said, in typical teenage-speak, 'My mother gave me like an overdose when I was twelve years old that might only have killed me if Dad hadn't come back when he did. I mean, I know that's not violent, exactly, because she didn't hit me or anything, but you've got to admit, it is a bit random.'

'I'm afraid it was my wife's way of forcing me to end my relationship with Vivienne,' Miles explained.

DC Joy could hardly have looked more appalled. She found it hard to believe that a mother had used her own daughter in that way. 'Was your wife charged with anything at the time?' she asked.

'No, but she has been receiving psychiatric treatment—'

'What you should really be asking,' Kelsey broke in, 'is what made her all screwed up in the first place, because she wasn't always like it—'

'Kelsey—'

'. . . but no one's allowed to mention what turned her into a mental case,' she went on defiantly. The accusation in her eyes was unmistakable as she glared at her father, but as Joy watched her she could see through to the anxiety of a confused and angry child.

Looking at Sadler, Miles said, 'What my wife did to our daughter was an isolated incident brought on by intense stress. No one is more horrified than Jacqueline by what she attempted to do.'

'Have you spoken to her psychiatrist since she disappeared?' Sadler wanted to know.

'Yes, but apparently it's been several months since my wife's last visit.'

'And you weren't aware of that until now?'

'I had an inkling, but short of carrying her there, I can't force her to make her appointments.'

'We'll need to speak to the therapist.'

'Then I'll get you the name and number.' As Miles walked across the room to the dining area, Sadler said to Kelsey, 'Where do *you* think your mother might have gone?'

Kelsey shrugged and shook her head. 'She never tells me anything,' she said in a tone that was meant to indicate she couldn't care less, when there was little doubt that she did.

Thinking of how close his own teenage daughters were to his wife – apocalyptic rows notwithstanding – Sadler found himself feeling sorry for the girl, since it was clear that she'd lost out on the normal type of mothering.

Having found what he was looking for, Miles came back and handed a small business card to Joy so she could note the details.

Sadler said, 'I'm afraid, from what your daughter's told us, Mr Avery, that it seems we can't rule out the possibility of your wife being a possible danger to others.'

Miles's face paled. 'What happened with Kelsey wasn't a serious attempt on her life,' he stated shortly. 'She knew I'd be back any minute . . .'

'Nevertheless . . .'

'She tried to kill herself at the same time,' Kelsey said. 'Dad, you should tell them these things.'

Sadler looked from father to daughter. 'So she could also be a danger to herself?' he said.

Miles didn't deny it.

'How long ago was this attempt on her life?'

'I told you, when I was twelve,' Kelsey replied. 'Which means, just over two years.'

'Has she made any other attempts?'

'Nothing to be taken seriously,' Miles said gruffly.

Sadler's expression darkened. 'So there have been others?'

'It's mainly talk. Once or twice she's taken a few too many pills, not enough to do any real damage.'

'Is she on any medication now?'

'Antidepressants of some kind, I think. You'll have to ask her doctor exactly what they are.'

'I see. We'll be sure to do that.' Then, after pondering for a moment, 'The fact that you called Ms Kane to ask if she'd heard from your wife suggests to me that you're concerned for her.'

'I've called a lot of people to find out if my wife has been in touch.'

'But presumably they're not all ex-lovers.' Sadler's eyebrows went up.

Miles's hostility was starting to show, but he said nothing to that, and in the end the inspector allowed himself to be stared down.

'So, we're agreed,' Sadler began pedantically, 'that your wife could not only present a risk to others, but to herself?'

'If you must put it that way, but as—'

'I think I'd be failing in my duty if I didn't.'

'As I said,' Miles persisted, 'she's a very private woman.'

'Which precludes nothing.'

Miles didn't argue.

Getting to his feet, Sadler muttered something to Joy as she stood too. Then, referring to the report from the response team, she said, 'We're getting in touch with the phone companies, terrestrial and mobile . . . I see you've already been asked about credit cards and bank statements.' She looked up expectantly.

'My wife spends most of her time in London, so all her papers are there,' Miles told her. 'Obviously I've looked through them already, but I'll do so again when I go back in a couple of days.'

Joy nodded and returned to the report. 'OK, DNA samples were taken yesterday. Doctor and dentist also in

London. Can I just check that the personal details we have are correct? She is forty years old . . .'

'She will be in a few weeks.'

Checking the date the response team had taken, Joy nodded and continued. 'She has blonde, collar-length hair, brown eyes, pale complexion, no distinguishing moles or birthmarks. She's five foot seven, slim, and when you last saw her she was wearing a black knee-length coat over a skirt, not trousers, low-heeled black shoes, and she was carrying a dark-coloured bag with a beige design that could belong to a designer . . .'

'It's Fendi,' Kelsey informed her.

Joy smiled her thanks.

'Is anything missing from her wardrobe?' Sadler asked. 'Anything to suggest a prolonged stay away? Has she taken her passport?'

'I'll check again to see if anything's missing,' Miles replied. 'As for the passport, it's more likely to be in London.'

'The response officers asked for some photographs,' Joy reminded him.

'Of course,' and going to a small table between the two sash windows Miles took out an envelope and passed it over. 'They're reasonably recent,' he said, as Sadler shook them out and Joy came to look over his shoulder.

Sadler and Joy gazed down at the shots of a softer, slightly more engaging woman than either of them had expected to see. Yet there was something about her eyes, Joy was thinking, that seemed to set her at a distance, in spite of the pleasant smile on her lips. However, this was just one captured moment in amongst many, so one could tell nothing of what was really happening in her mind, much less her life, on that day.

After sliding them back into the envelope, Sadler said, 'I'm sure you'll let us know if she does get in touch, or if anything else comes to mind that you think might be helpful.'

'Of course,' Miles said, and standing aside he let Sadler lead the way to the door.

*

A few minutes later Sadler was circling his mud-spattered Ford Focus around the gravelled courtyard, while peering out at the rain-misted gardens to where a stream cut a gully alongside the drive before snaking off to join the lake. With such a profusion of game roaming freely around the place, pheasants, partridge, deer, rabbits, it almost wasn't necessary to ask if Miles Avery owned a gun, but Sadler would ask, if it became relevant. He wondered how much he'd like to live in a place like this. He guessed quite a lot, but since his grandfather had not been chairman of a big oil company, nor his father a canny investor, he was never going to inherit the fortune that had evidently come Miles Avery's way.

'So what did you make of all that, Detective Constable?' he asked, accelerating carefully over a humpback bridge to start heading down the tree-lined arc of the drive.

Pleased to be asked, Joy inhaled thoughtfully. 'Well, if we're to believe all we were told,' she began, 'I'd say Mrs Avery sounds like a pretty mixed-up sort of woman. Kind of sad though, I think, rather than mad. I can't make up my mind whether he cares about her or not. On the one hand he seems quite defensive where she's concerned, but three weeks is a long time for someone you love to be missing and not report it, even if she does have a history of taking off on her own.'

Sadler was nodding.

'Also,' Joy continued, 'did you notice how he spoke about her in the past tense when he said, "She didn't have a wide circle of friends"?'

Impressed, Sadler said, 'Yes, I did. A slip of the tongue? Or something more sinister?'

Joy glanced at him.

'The daughter's bothering me,' he said, hooting the horn to send a family of pheasants scuttling out of the way. 'I think she's probably even more mixed up than the mother. And lonely.'

Joy's eyes widened in surprise. Sadler didn't have much of a reputation for being the touchy-feely type, but on the other hand, he did have three girls of his own.

'I don't think being a part of that family has been easy,' he expanded, as they juddered over a cattle grid before turning out of the gates into the country lane.

In complete agreement with that, Joy remarked, 'It'll be interesting to hear what the psychiatrist has to say.'

'Mmm, won't it just.'

Joy turned to rub a circle in the steamy passenger window. 'I definitely got the impression he was holding something back,' she went on.

'I don't think there's any doubt of it. In fact the daughter told us as much.'

'You mean when she said about what made her mother all screwed up?'

He nodded. 'And the fact that no one's allowed to mention it. It's going to be interesting to find out what our trusty team has dug up on the Averys while we've been away.'

Joy took out her mobile to check if there were any messages from the officers they'd left trawling old records, but finding none she tucked it away again and stayed thoughtfully silent as she gazed out at the passing hedgerows and small glimpses of rolling fields beyond. They were travelling away from the moor now, but having been born and brought up in these parts she never failed to feel its presence whether it was visible or not. 'So what next, sir?' she finally asked.

'That depends on the CCTV. If it's not showing Jacqueline Avery getting onto a train I'll recommend contacting the local media. Maybe someone will remember seeing her at the station either getting into a taxi, or being picked up by someone else after her husband drove away.'

'And if it does show her getting on a train?'

'We'll liaise with the transport police, and the Met at Kensington and Chelsea.' He made a soft tutting sound as he thought. 'What time did the housekeeper tell the response team Mr and Mrs Avery left the house?' he asked.

'Twenty past nine, and he was back an hour and a half later. That could work, even with the stop-off at Sainsbury's she mentioned.'

'Mmm,' was all Sadler said.

'Are you going to recommend a search?'

'Not immediately. We can't just go blundering in without any solid reason to.'

'But three weeks, sir. No one lets their wife go missing for that long without reporting it.'

Sadler cast her a glance. 'And there was me thinking he had you all suckered in and eating out of his hand,' he teased.

Joy flushed. 'I'm not going to deny he's attractive,' she retorted, 'and powerful and charming and seriously rich . . . Which reminds me, do you think we should check out his finances?'

'I most certainly do.'

'And this Vivienne woman? It might be interesting to get an idea of what she knows about her ex-lover's wife.'

'If he is an ex.'

Joy turned to look at him.

'If the relationship was serious enough to cause Mrs Avery to stage a suicide and murder attempt,' he said, 'then we need to look into it. We also need to find out what reports were written up at the time of the incident with the daughter, because something must have been. Do we know how long the Averys have been married?'

Without consulting her notes, Joy said, 'Seventeen years.'

'So if he's forty-five now, that would make him twenty-eight when he got hitched and her . . . ?'

'Twenty-three.'

'And the delightful Kelsey came along three years later, give or take.' He slowed up behind a straw-bundled tractor and began tapping his fingers on the wheel. 'Give me your first hunch on this, Detective Constable,' he said after a while. 'Are we going to see Mrs Avery again, or aren't we?'

Knowing how Sadler liked hunches Joy sat with the question, trying to get a feel for what she was thinking. In the end all she said was, 'I don't know, sir. I really don't know.'

After showing the police out and going to check that Mrs Davies hadn't been unduly upset by their visit, Miles returned to the sitting room to find Kelsey slumped in one of the armchairs, staring into the fire.

'So what happens now?' she asked, as he flopped down on the sofa the detectives had vacated.

'I'm not sure,' he answered, looking and sounding extremely tired. 'I didn't ask.'

There was a paleness around her mouth as she said, 'I reckon you should have told them everything.'

With a short sigh he began to massage his brow. 'They'll find out on their own,' he said.

Her eyes were clouded with misgiving as she sat watching him, but with his head back he wasn't able to see her expression. 'What about the row you had with Mum the night before she left?' she asked.

His hand stopped. 'What row?'

'She told me about it.'

Lifting his head, he looked at her closely. 'So you have seen her – or at least spoken to her?' he said.

She shrugged. 'Not since that night. I called to find out who was picking me up from school and she told me she'd have to call back because you were in the middle of a row.'

His face was starting to darken. 'Why have you never mentioned this before?' he asked.

She coloured slightly. 'I don't really know. I mean . . . So how come you didn't tell the police?'

'Because there was no row,' he answered. 'We had a discussion which led to her starting again about Vivienne, so I went to bed. We even slept in separate rooms.'

'So nothing new there,' Kelsey said acidly.

Sighing, Miles let his head fall back again and stared up at the ceiling.

After a while Kelsey went to sit with him. 'I'm sorry,' she whispered, moving into the circle of his arm.

'It's OK,' he said, stroking her hair.

'It's going to get into the papers, about Mum, isn't it?'

'I expect so.' He sighed again, knowing how eager his enemies would be to make a circus out of this.

Reaching for his hand, she wound her fingers around his. 'You don't like the police, do you?' she said. 'I could tell. I think they could too.'

'It's not about liking. It's about what happened in the past.'

They sat quietly then, listening to the wind hurtling about the chimney, and feeling the presence of the police in the room as though their curiosity was lingering.

In the end Kelsey said, 'What are we going to do if she doesn't turn up?'

Without hesitation he said, 'She will.'

'But if she . . .'

'She'll be fine.'

She lifted her head and waited for his eyes to come to hers. 'Maybe we'd be better off without her,' she said bleakly.

'You know you don't mean that.'

She looked away, staring at nothing, until, in a voice he could barely hear, she said, 'No, but you do.'

Chapter Three

Gareth Critchley looked like a man whose relationship with personal hygiene was in need of therapy. His crumpled shirts were clearly unable to get past old issues, his jutting chin seemed to be bearing a grudge against his razor, and as for his gummy whorls of greying hair, word had it that the closest contact they made with shampoo was when he passed it by in Boots. Despite this, none of his reporters could claim ever to have caught a seriously malodorous whiff drifting from his revoltingly flabby frame, or from his loosely hinged lips when he was spraying about his instructions. What plenty of them had caught, however, was the sharp end of his caustic wit when they'd failed to deliver, or a playful thump in the gut when someone managed to pull off an exclusive.

Today, so far, things seemed to be going well for the Critch, as he was more generally known. Confirmation had just come down from upstairs that circulation was up again on last quarter, thus securing his contract for another twelve months, plus a handsome bonus. No sooner had those happy little nuggets been served up with an invitation to lunch in the boardroom, than one of his spry little army of stringers had called to really make his day . . .

'Ah, if it isn't my favourite fluffball,' he said, looking up as Justine James, a reporter who'd always considered herself a cut above the rest until he'd introduced her to the error of her judgement, appeared in his doorway. 'Come in, sit down. I've got something for you I think you're going to like.'

With her close-cropped silvery hair, doe-like brown eyes and sumptuously red mouth, Justine James created a winning cocktail of sternness and seduction that carried right through to the lacy push-up bra visible behind the open buttons of her maidenly white shirt. Her skirt was long and woollen, covering slightly plump thighs, which, to her dismay, had begun accumulating dimples at an alarming rate over recent years. However, they were hardly an issue where this poisonous little oik was concerned, for she'd rather cut her legs off at the hips than ever let him anywhere near them.

Fortunately, turning to close the door allowed her a moment to curl her lips with all the contempt she really felt, before she was forced to conjure a look of polite interest from the extensive repertoire of false expressions she'd acquired over a decade and a half of journalism. As she went to sit in front of his desk she could only hope that none of the nervousness she was really feeling, and knew he'd want her to feel, was showing, for she'd rather kiss his arse than give him the satisfaction. On second thoughts . . . Anyway, whatever he had to say, at least it didn't seem as though he was going to yell it across the newsroom this time, the way he had when he'd stripped her of her column.

'You're fucking losing it, Justine!' he'd yelled in his vulgar, loud-mouthed way. 'You're writing for the middle-aged hausfrau and we don't do middle-aged hausfrau here any more, that was in Avery's day. So I'm giving your page to Eleanora until you manage to get yourself a granny by-pass.' Eleanora, Justine's twenty-three-year-old, mini-skirted, plummy-mouthed assistant whose gift for gossip was equal to Beckham's for soccer. Justine should have seen it coming, and perhaps she had, but like a lot of women her age, she tried to ignore the freight train of youth that was coming up so fast from behind that sooner, rather than later, it was bound to derail her.

Nevertheless, the ignominy, and the hatred she'd felt for the Critch in those moments, as her colleagues had either turned away or watched her with pity – and relief it wasn't them in the firing line this time – had outclassed anything she'd ever felt before. This even included the indignity she'd suffered when her adored mentor, Miles Avery, had quit this smutty (though not in Miles's day) little Sunday tabloid to go and edit a daily broadsheet and hadn't taken her with him. Everyone had expected him to, and when he'd started poaching various other members of his team, she'd felt certain it was only a matter of time before he got round to her. But he never had, and the blame for that, Justine knew, lay wholly at Vivienne Kane's door. There had never been any love lost between the two women, and once Miles had become involved with the PR bitch Justine had known that whatever chance she stood of being rescued from the Critch had died.

'What's your relationship like with Miles Avery these days?' Critchley asked, not bothering to look up from whatever he was writing on one of his lawyerly foolscap pads.

Jolted by the question, Justine peered at him warily, then decided to take the safer option by not answering right away. First up, she'd like to know why he was asking before committing herself, and second, instinct was already warning her that he didn't want to hear that she and Miles had, at least on the surface, made up their differences some time ago, when Miles had explained his reason for not hiring her.

'I know you think Vivienne's behind my decision,' he'd said, 'but you're wrong. I have the greatest respect for you and your work – you know that, it's why I hired you and gave you the breaks that helped make your name. You've come a long way, and uncovered some great scandals in your time, but the truth is, your talents are better suited to *The News on Sunday* than to a daily broadsheet. You're great at all the pithy, gossipy stuff – one of the best, in fact – and you've got a natural outlet where you are, as well as a much wider readership.'

'That might be true,' she'd responded, 'but you can't tell me Vivienne hasn't influenced you . . . Be honest, Miles,' she said, as he made to protest. 'I know it anyway, so you might as well come clean.'

'Vivienne does not make the decisions about who I hire and fire,' he'd retorted sharply, 'and frankly, knowing me as well as you do, I'm surprised you even think it.'

There hadn't been much arguing with that, unless she'd

wanted to fall out with him completely, and she wasn't foolish enough to do that, so she'd let the matter drop. However, in spite of his denial, she remained convinced that Vivienne Kane was responsible for blocking her escape from *The News*.

'Well?' Critchley prompted, his freckle-flecked fist still sweeping back and forth over the page.

Justine's eyes went back to him. 'I haven't seen Miles for some time,' she said, still hedging.

'That wasn't what I asked.' With a flourish he drew a line under his sloping lines of scrawl and finally looked up. 'He dumped you royally a few years ago, and we both know it,' he said bluntly. 'And I'm not only talking about the way he never offered you a job when he took off out of here. You always had the hots for that man, and what really sticks in your craw isn't so much that he never rescued you from this hell you consider yourself to be in, but that he didn't even call you up when his wife bailed out and took off to the States.'

'You haven't got the first idea what he did or didn't do,' she sneered, aware that the sourness of her tone wasn't helping her.

He cocked a knowing eyebrow. 'You were waiting for the day Avery came free,' he told her brutally. 'You wanted him, and back then you were sure you'd get him. But it didn't work out that way, did it? No, it sure as hell didn't, because no sooner did the bleeding-heart wife take off than he goes and meets some PR totty and practically moves her in. That was a tough one for you, Justie. I remember cutting you a lot of slack at the time. Real torn up you were . . .'

'You're making this up,' she told him curtly.

'Am I? We'll see. When was the last time you had contact with him?'

'I can't remember,' she lied.

He shrugged, as though it didn't really matter. 'Does he know you wrote the piece that exposed his affair with the PR girl?' he asked.

Feeling herself flushing, she said, 'What do you think?'

His eyes turned to slits. 'What I *know*,' he said, 'is that you were banking on that piece bringing the wife back, and it worked, for which you should be congratulated. I guess it backfired a bit when she tried to off herself and the daughter, but it all turned out the way you intended in the end. He dumped the PR girl, went back to wifey and blamed me for the exposé. Trouble is, he still didn't give you a job.'

Aware of the loathing building inside her, she forced her way past it, and said, 'Since you're the master of spin I'm not going to argue with you.'

'Very wise, and I'm the first to admit there are many ways to tell a story, and you'll no doubt have a very different way of telling your own. Truth is though, things really haven't been going your way for some time now, have they? You've lost the page Avery gave you when he was running this paper, you're not doing so well in the general pool, and for all I know you're not getting laid.' He shrugged. 'Nothing I can do about your personal life, I'm afraid, but I can offer you the chance of reversing your professional misfortunes.'

Her expression turned to granite as she looked at him. What she wouldn't give to be able to tell him that whatever he was about to propose, which clearly had something to do with Miles, he could stick where no man nor beast would ever want to venture, because actually, she'd been offered a column on the *Mail*, or the *Express*, or any other paper come to that, just as long as it got her off this one. However, in spite of her many efforts to jump ship with a nice safe landing on smoother decks, she kept banging up against the same old problem: they wanted younger, fresher and more currently connected.

Meeting the coldness of her gaze with a smirk that made her itch to slap it, Critchley said, 'I've just heard that the wife's gone missing.'

Justine became very still. 'You mean Jacqueline?'

'She's been gone for three weeks, I'm told, and now the police have been called in to help find her.'

Somehow she only blinked.

He smirked again, and with a gaze that seemed to see straight through her, he said, 'Why don't you try to get us some scoop on this? There's something fishy about it, from what I've been hearing, and apparently your old friend Vivienne Kane's starting to hover about in the frame.'

Knowing it would give him more leverage than he already had to discover he was right about her feelings for Vivienne Kane, she forced her expression to remain neutral as she said, 'What exactly are you expecting me to do?'

He shrugged. 'Could be payback time?' His follow-up glance came at her like a dart.

'For me or you?' she challenged, without even flinching.

At that his eyes glinted as dangerously as a trapped rat's. No one ever dared mention, at least not to his face, the daily cartoon Miles had commissioned, and that still ran, called *The Grunt*, which charted the exploits of a crude, loud-mouthed and disgustingly salacious tabloid editor. The entire world knew it was based on the Critch, and it was no secret that the Critch was just biding his time, waiting for as cold a revenge as his sordid, but incisively clever little brain could come up with.

'I'll give you whatever you need,' he said, 'including your page back, if you give me something on that man.'

Justine eyed him frigidly. 'You seem to be assuming the wife's not going to turn up again,' she said, 'when history shows that she does.'

'I couldn't give a cat's ass what the wife's about,' he retorted. 'That man's got more skeletons in his closet than the underside of a churchyard, and you know it. It's time to start digging, Justie. Make a few calls, get this ball rolling.'

She merely watched as he scribbled a couple of numbers on a Post-it, hardly even thinking about whose they might be, for she was already considering how best to approach this.

A few minutes later she was back at her desk, the Post-it in one hand, while with the other she whirled her old-fashioned Rolodex searching for a contact she hadn't needed in a while. When she found it she pressed the number into her phone and after being diverted through to voicemail said, 'Roger. It's Justine. Call me back when you can. There could be a lot of beer money in it for you.'

Next she called one of the Critch's stringers – a sub on a local Devon paper – made a few notes as he brought her up to speed with what he knew about the police involvement in

Jacqueline Avery's disappearance, and then, pulling another old number from her Rolodex she pressed it into her phone and waited brazenly for the connection.

Vivienne and Alice were laughing at one of Kayla's outrageously silly jokes when Alice reached out to answer the phone. 'Kane and Jackson. Alice Jackson speaking,' she announced. Her smile began a rapid fade through to distaste as she listened to the voice at the other end. 'Justine,' she said, her eyes going straight to Vivienne.

Vivienne's smile died too.

'No, I'm afraid Vivienne's not here at the moment,' Alice lied. 'Can I help at all? I see. Well, if you can tell me what it's about I'll get her to call you back.'

She listened again, then said, 'I'll pass the message on,' and with an abrupt goodbye she rang off.

'She's got some nerve, calling here,' Kayla said sourly.

Alice's attention was on Vivienne. 'Apparently she's been hearing rumours,' she stated. 'Given the timing they have to be about Jacqueline.'

'Yeah, like, Vivi's going to discuss anything with her,' Kayla said hotly. 'She's got to be big-time delusional if she thinks that.'

Vivienne and Alice were looking at one another, each knowing what the other was thinking.

'The woman is best ignored,' Vivienne stated.

Alice didn't look so certain. 'Maybe you ought to find out exactly what she's been hearing.'

'I'm not giving her the satisfaction.'

'She's not someone to be on the wrong side of.'

'Nor am I.'

'She won't care about that.'

'She cares about Miles, though – and frankly, if she thinks I'm going to confirm or deny any rumours she might have heard about Jacqueline, or anything else, then Kayla's right, she's big-time delusional.'

'But what if—'

'No, Alice, I'm sorry, I'm not dancing to her tune,' and unwilling to sully her thoughts any further with the woman she despised above all others, she picked up the phone to call the much more fragrant, and delightfully quirky chair-woman of the Kenleigh WI.

'You're kidding me,' Pete Alexander cried, later that night, his electric-blue eyes boggling with astonishment. 'Justine James calls, and you haven't rung her back yet? Aren't you dying to know what the rumours are about? I mean, it's got to be *la pauvre* Jacq-u-line, obviously, but wouldn't it be good to find out what she knows?'

Aware of how keen Alice and Angus were to hear her answer, Vivienne only said, 'No,' and continued to sprinkle Parmesan onto her pasta.

'Vivi,' Alice said gravely, 'what if it's not about Jacqueline? You don't want—'

'Whatever she knows, there's nothing I can do about it,' Vivienne interrupted.

'But what if she makes it public about Rufus?'

'Then just like when she managed to bring Jacqueline back from the States, she'll have her own conscience to deal with,' Vivienne answered tartly.

'You don't know for certain she was behind that article,' Pete reminded her.

'For God's sake, of course she was,' Vivienne snapped.

'OK, I wouldn't put it past her,' he conceded, 'but she and Miles go back a long way . . .'

'Which is precisely why she was trying to get me out of his life. Everyone knew she'd set her sights on him.'

'I'm not denying that, but my money's still on the Critch. He's been after Miles's hide ever since Miles started running *The Grunt*.'

'Miles isn't a cartoonist.'

'But it was in his paper, which makes him as guilty as if he was writing it himself. Or that's the way the Critch sees it, and if you think about it, he's right, because Miles could have dropped that strip any time he liked, but he never did.'

'Which is why Miles holds the Critch responsible for the article that brought Jacqueline back,' Alice informed him. 'As the editor he carries the can. But I'm with Vivi. I think Justine wrote it – or at least gave the Critch the information he needed.'

Pete shrugged. 'You could be right, but imagine how you'd feel about the person who turned you into a laughing stock. You'd stop at nothing to get back at them, which is exactly how the Critch feels about Miles. As far as Justine's concerned, she's tough, I'll admit, and ruthless, but she's too shrewd to risk getting on the wrong side of Miles.'

Wanting to change the subject, Vivienne said to Angus, 'Would you mind opening some more wine?'

Giving her a wink, he reached behind him to take a bottle of red from the art deco drinks cabinet that occupied one wall of her softly lit dining room. The adjacent wall was almost entirely given over to French windows that in warmer days opened onto a small patio. This formed part of a secluded communal courtyard which sloped down to a locked gate opening onto the towpath and river. The opposite wall of the dining room was actually a counter top that divided off the bijou black granite kitchen, and the fourth wall was mostly doors, one opening into the hall that led upstairs to the sitting room and bedrooms, and the other into the garage where Vivienne kept her precious VW Beetle. It was a house she adored, and had had no problem affording during the agency's heyday. Now her mortgage was three months in arrears and a small pile of red bills was sitting next to the phone. Just please God some money came through soon, from Irwin's movie, or *La Belle Amie*, because it would break her heart to have to leave here.

As Angus refilled their glasses, Pete turned to Vivienne again, his sharp features and proud bald head aglow with intrigue. 'So how many times has Justine actually called?' he demanded, clearly determined not to let this go.

Vivienne looked to Alice for the answer.

'Three that I know of,' Alice provided.

Pete gave a shriek of laughter and rubbed his hands with glee. 'She must be incandescent by now,' he declared happily. 'No one ever blocks the Justine. Or they never used to, but we all know the days are darkening for poor Justie, so do be careful, darling, a panicky she-cat with a used-up ninth life is not an animal to mess around with.'

'That's what I keep telling her,' Alice agreed.

'Can we drop this please?' Vivienne said crisply. 'I thought we were meeting to discuss auctions and movies.'

'Oh we will, we will,' Pete assured her, 'but we need to get the important stuff dealt with first.'

Angus chuckled at the despair on Vivienne's face. 'Great dinner,' he told her. 'Nothing's burnt, underdone or even raw.'

Vivienne gave a gurgle of laughter. 'Something of an achievement for me,' she responded. 'I'm a latecomer to Jamie Oliver. If he weren't already married, I'd propose.'

'Oh, bollocks to Jamie Oliver – love him though we do,' Pete interjected. 'If you won't talk about Justine, then tell us more about Miles.'

'The police were in touch with Vivienne this afternoon,' Alice informed him, while staring at Vivienne. 'And you still haven't told me what they said yet,' she prompted.

Vivienne shrugged. 'They just wanted to know if I'd heard from Jacqueline, which I haven't. Or if I have any idea where she might be, which I don't. And if I'm still seeing Miles, which I'm not.'

'I bet they think he's bumped her off,' Pete said decisively. 'Boy are they going to have a shock when she turns up again. But hey, what if she doesn't? Oh God, what a scandal.'

Vivienne's eyes flashed. 'It's not a joke, Pete,' she snapped.

His hands shot up. 'Sorry, no offence,' he cried. 'Can see I was well out of order, so sorry again.'

'Actually,' Vivienne said, 'the police also wanted to know where I was on the day she disappeared, and if I have an alibi to confirm it.'

'Oh no!' Pete cried, clasping his hands to his cheeks. 'They surely don't think *you've* done away with her? Oh my God, this is too much. There's our dear little agency poodling along like an empty checkout, then suddenly we've got slave auctions in the countryside, biggish-budget movies, and our very own murder mystery. Agatha Christie must be turning in her grave.'

'Pete, will you at least try to be serious,' Alice chided, sensing Vivienne's humour failing again.

'Darling, I am,' he insisted. 'Tell us,' he said to Vivienne, 'have you spoken to Miles again since he called to let you know she'd gone up in a puff of smoke?'

'No. I've had no reason to.'

Pete couldn't have looked more pained. 'But Vivi, it's all you've ever wanted, to get back with him . . .'

'Time to leave it,' Alice warned.

'No! No,' he protested. 'Well, OK. But darling, you've got to find out what the Justine wants. *Please*.'

'Pete,' Angus said firmly.

'She can give you some great publicity for your auction,' Pete pointed out.

'I'd rather sink it than let her anywhere near it,' Vivienne retorted. 'Now are you happy about taking on *La Belle Amie*? I met with her and her agent first thing this morning. She's pretty forthcoming about her past career and how she got into it. Actually, probably too forthcoming, so you'll need to rein her in a bit.'

'Oh, listen to you,' Pete mocked, taking a mouthful of penne. 'Everyone wants to hear about sex, and the raunchier the better.'

'But she tends to go over the top, and we don't want to start building a reputation as a PR agency for sleaze . . .'

'Darling, you're such a *prude*,' he told her.

Vivienne was taken aback. 'I am not,' she declared.

'Yes you are.'

She looked from him to Alice and Angus. 'Is that how you see me?' she said.

'Not at all,' Alice assured her, a tad too quickly.

'No way,' Angus blustered.

Vivienne was clearly still bothered. 'Look, I just don't want us to become known for handling porn stars,' she explained. 'I know sex sells—'

'It does?' Pete interrupted, feigning shock.

Vivienne threw him a look. 'I'm simply saying, I'd rather we were the broadsheet version of PR than the tabloid. OK, maybe there's more money in the gutter stuff, and *La Belle Amie*—'

'Oh, you're just too image-conscious,' Pete protested, with a flick of his wrist. 'They're going to lap her up, pardon the pun if there is one there, which I'm sure there is. Anyway, what does she want us to morph her into? A soap star? Pop singer? Please don't tell me she wants to front BBC news, or some wildlife guff. Do you think she's up to writing a book? I reckon we could get her quite a good deal considering her background.'

'She'd need someone to ghost it,' Vivienne answered, 'and believe it or not, I think her ambitions lie in serious drama. To quote her, "Helen Mirren is my role model." '

'How delighted the Dame will be,' Pete chuckled. 'Mind you, at her age—'

'Are you going to answer that?' Alice interrupted, looking at Vivienne. 'That's the second time the phone's rung, and you seem oblivious.'

Vivienne looked at her in surprise. 'If it's important they'll leave a message,' she replied.

Alice glanced over as the bleep sounded, and once again there was a brief silence before the call cut out. She turned back to Vivienne.

Vivienne merely shrugged. 'Everyone who means anything to me is around this table,' she pointed out, 'except my sister who never calls me anyway, my gran who's forgotten who we all are, Kayla who's gone to the movies tonight, and my mother whom I've spoken to three times this evening, and who would definitely leave a message or call the mobile if she needed me urgently.'

'What about Miles?' Pete put in.

Vivienne's light-heartedness vanished. 'Does he strike you as the type who'd hang up without speaking?' she said shortly.

'It could be Jacqueline.'

'Pete! Just stop, will you.'

'Or Justine.'

As Vivienne sat back she threw down her napkin. 'All right, that's enough,' she declared. 'From now on those three names are banned in this house, and anyone who utters them has to leave.'

In a very theatrical way Pete pressed a finger to his rosy lips. 'Sealed,' he promised.

Alice glanced at Angus, who was helping himself to more

pasta. 'OK, getting back on track,' she said. 'We know Pete's going to handle *La Belle Amie* and, poppet of a porn star that she is, she's prepared to pay megabucks . . .'

'Most of which you're going to need upfront,' Angus interjected gravely.

'We also know that I'm going to take on Irwin's movie – working title, *A Deed Undone* – serious megabucks, at least for us, and Vivi's doing the auction which is going to earn us no bucks at all, but shedloads of goodwill, and there's never any knowing what it might lead to. That's me taking the positive view.'

'And why not?' Vivienne responded. 'The potential for publicity's pretty good considering who Sharon was married to. I've already contacted the local fire station, and at least six of Keith's old colleagues are willing to put themselves under the hammer. I have yet to talk to them about the skills they're offering, but it's definitely a promising start.'

'Absolutely,' Alice agreed, laughing at the way Pete was fanning himself down at the mere idea of a group of firemen strutting their stuff.

'Plus,' Vivienne continued, turning to Angus, 'I was wondering if your nephew might be willing to help out? It would be an amazing coup if we could get him.'

'You mean Theo?' Angus replied. 'I'm sure he would, if he's in the country.'

'Theo?' Pete enquired. Then, remembering, his eyes rounded with awe. 'Of course, Theo Kenwood-South is your sister's son. How could I have forgotten that?'

'More relevantly,' Alice said, 'he holds the Olympic gold for freestyle *and* he knew Keith Goss.' To Vivienne she added, 'We're having a family get-together this weekend, and Theo should be there, so we can put it to him then.'

'Fantastic,' Vivienne declared. 'And please send him my love. It's been ages since I saw him.'

'Oh please send him mine too,' Pete begged. 'I know he's never met me, but I simply adore him.'

Laughing, Alice turned back to Vivienne. 'When are you going to Devon?' she asked.

'Next Monday. There's a lot to sort out here first, which Kayla's helping me with. Has Irwin decided on locations for the movie yet?'

'Scotland for three weeks, London for two. Listen, if you're not going to answer that, will you at least let me?'

Vivienne shrugged. 'Be my guest.'

Turning in her chair, Alice tugged the phone across the counter top and picked it up. 'Hello?' she said into the receiver.

Everyone waited.

'Hello?' Alice said again.

Still no response.

'Is anyone there?'

Vivienne's appetite was starting to fade.

Alice looked at the receiver, then at Vivienne.

'Just hang up,' Vivienne told her.

Putting the phone down again, Alice said, 'Has this happened before tonight?'

All eyes were on Vivienne. 'I can read your minds,' she told them, 'so please don't ask if I think it's Jacqueline, because I really don't know.'

'But has it happened before?' Pete pressed, as Alice dialled 1471.

'Once or twice.'

'Number withheld,' Alice informed them.

Pete shivered. 'Sorry, but that sort of thing gives me the spooks.'

'It was probably a wrong number,' Alice retorted, with a quick glance at Vivienne.

'You're going to start spooking me too if you don't stop this,' Vivienne snapped, and snatching up the wine she refilled her glass.

Later, after everyone had gone, and she'd finished clearing up, she stood against the counter top staring down at the phone. She knew it was probably Justine making the calls, trying to catch her unawares, but at the same time she had to face the fact that it could be Jacqueline. Her heart gave a twist of unease to think of her out there somewhere, alone, unhappy and with a purpose only Jacqueline knew anything about.

However, she wasn't going to use these calls as an excuse to speak to Miles, even though she longed to hear him again. It would only end up worrying him, and that wasn't what she wanted at all. She wondered if he'd spent as much time thinking about her these past few days as she had about him. Since they'd spoken she'd hardly been able to get him out of her mind, not that he was ever far from it anyway, but now she couldn't help being concerned about the effect Jacqueline's disappearance must be having on him.

Finally turning out the light, she closed the kitchen door and started up the stairs to bed. To her surprise she found the TV on in the sitting room. She had no recollection of turning it on, and for one unsettling moment she thought someone else might be in the house. Then she remembered Pete and Angus had come up here just after arriving to catch some cricket result.

After switching it off she went to stand at the window looking out at the night, where only a single lamp post was visible at the open peak of the courtyard, turning the branches of a weeping willow to silver and reflecting like moonlight on the river below. Trying not to think any more about Miles was too hard, so she indulged herself for a while, recalling some of the times they'd spent here, at her house, when they'd been happy and so wrapped up in one another they'd needed no one else. There had been no reason to feel guilty about Jacqueline then, because she'd chosen to go and start a new life. Finally his wife had given Miles his freedom, and considering their past, no one could blame him for taking it.

Turning from the window she looked around the small sitting room where she and Miles had snuggled together on the squishy sofas, reading poetry to one another or watching TV. The shelves were full of books, many of which were his, and though none of the photographs around the room were of him, in their way they were a constant reminder too. She'd tried so hard to forget, but knew she never could.

She switched off the lamps and went back out onto the landing, glancing at the closed doors of the small guest bedroom which doubled as a study, and the neighbouring bathroom. It was too late to do any work tonight. She was tired and had probably had too much to drink, so leaving the doors closed, she climbed on up to the top level where the spacious master suite opened onto a small Juliet balcony with a view of the courtyard and river. Two large skylights allowed her, if she left the blinds open, to lie in bed and gaze up at the stars. Tonight she closed them by pushing a button next to the bed.

After taking a quick shower and shaking her glossy hair out of a clip she wrapped herself in a towel and went to sit in front of the mirror. As she picked up her hairbrush she was still thinking of Miles, remembering the way he used to lie on the bed watching her at night, seeming to love everything about her. He'd never seemed able to get enough of her, which was how she'd felt about him. She recalled how easy it had been to laugh and dream with him, how eagerly they'd talked about their future and the family they would have. They'd cherished every moment they'd spent together, and when they were apart not many hours would go by without them being in touch. The only cloud on their horizon was Kelsey's refusal to accept her. But time would sort that out, he'd assured her, and maybe it would have, if they'd been given a chance.

Putting down the brush she stood up and let the towel pool at her feet. Her limbs were slender and long, her hips boyishly slim while her breasts seemed too large for her delicate frame. She couldn't help remembering how he'd adored her breasts, and how she'd come to love them too for the pleasure he'd given her with his eyes, his fingers and his mouth. No one had touched her intimately since the last time they were together, and though she often craved the release she'd always recoiled from the mere thought of being that close to anyone but him.

Now Jacqueline had disappeared, and she knew she'd be asking too much of herself not to see it as a chance for them to be together again.

Chapter Four

Kelsey was standing at her bedroom window, watching her father loading up the car in the courtyard below. The rain had stopped an hour ago, leaving everything gleaming like silk in the sunlight, but more clouds were starting to roll over the treetops that separated their land from the moor. A big storm was forecast for later, and strong winds, the kind of tempest that could as easily set nerves on edge as it could exhilarate the senses.

Her eyes were drawn to a quad bike bumping down over a neighbouring field, scattering the sheep and leaving a dark trail in the grass behind it. It was the gamekeeper making his rounds, fattening up the birds ready for a shoot, and checking no poachers had ventured onto private land via the moor. She followed his progress in through one of their gates, which he diligently closed behind him before carrying on down past the lake, where he took a short cut through the woods to their neighbour's much larger estate.

Remembering that the ducks and geese needed feeding, she was about to turn from the window when her father spotted her and waved. She stared down at him, her eyes remaining bleak as he walked into the house, disappearing from view. For all she cared he could go away for as long as he liked – her friends were coming for the weekend, and it would be much better not to have him around.

Going into her bathroom, she poked about in a basket full of make-up and other stuff, looking for a scrunchie to tie back her hair. Finding a blue velvet one that she'd borrowed from her mother, she stretched it between her fingers, feeling it go tighter and tighter until it almost snapped.

Throwing it back, she rummaged around for another, feeling weird and restless and like she wanted to lash out with angry words, or her fists, or anything that might hurt.

Quickly twisting her hair into an old cloth band, she slipped a gilet over her sweater and jeans and ran downstairs to the utility room where they kept the large sacks of bird food. As she scooped the grain into small feeding pails she kicked off her shoes and was just digging her feet into her wellies when her eye was caught by an old Barbour hanging on the back of the door. She stopped and stared at it, feeling a bit sick, like there was something about it that was stirring up horrible things inside her. Then she felt annoyed and frustrated. There was loads of her mother's stuff around, so this coat was nothing special. In fact, her mother hardly ever wore it – it had only got all shabby like that because it used to belong to Grandma who loved to garden and go out hiking on the moor. She still really missed Grandma, and Grandpa, and felt mad that they'd had to die when she was only ten, but it was OK really, because actually she was fine.

Suddenly she wanted to cry and shout and throw up to get rid of the horrible feelings inside. It was like the time she'd put her arms round her mother, and her mother had stroked her hair, but when she'd asked her a question her mother didn't hear. Kelsey screamed and shouted, but her mother still didn't hear, and then her dad came and picked her up, telling her she'd had a bad dream, but everything was all right now.

Hearing footsteps she turned away quickly, tucking her jeans into the wellies and retying her hair.

'Ah, there you are,' Miles said, coming in with an armful of laundry. 'Is the machine empty?'

'I don't know,' she answered, keeping her head down.

Dumping the towels and sheets on a large wooden draining board, he opened the washing-machine door and began hauling out a tangle of tablecloths, napkins and tea towels.

'I'll sort it out,' she told him irritably. 'You can go now.'

There was a brief pause before, using the kind of tone that told her he'd picked up on her bad mood, he said, 'It won't take me a moment.' And sure enough, after pouring in the powder and whizzing round the dial, he turned to her, saying, 'You know you can come with me. In fact, I'd rather you did.'

'My friends are coming,' she reminded him stroppily.

'You can always put them off.'

'Yeah, like I'm really going to do that on the day they're supposed to arrive. What else are they going to do for the weekend? Anyway, even if I did come with you, I'd just be in the way.'

He seemed taken aback. 'In the way of what?' he demanded.

She shrugged angrily, her face turning red.

He waited.

In the end she said, 'So why are you going?'

'Because I have a lot of things to attend to,' he reminded her, 'such as looking through your mother's papers and checking the mail to see if anything's turned up that might help us to find her.'

Her eyes flicked back to the coat, and once again she felt weighed down by things that made her feel queasy and strange. 'Do you think she's all right?' she asked with a slight tremble in her voice.

His eyes softened. 'I've told you before, I'm sure of it,' he replied, wanting to hug her but sensing she wouldn't welcome it right now.

She turned away to pick up the feed pails.

'Kelsey, what is it?' he prompted.

'What's what?' she said tartly.

'I know you too well young lady, so come on, out with it.'

'There's nothing,' she cried.

Deciding he probably stood a far better chance of her opening up if he backed off and pretended to drop the matter, he said, 'OK, have it your way. Are you going to come and wave me off?'

Her jaw tightened.

'Is that a no?'

She slammed her eyes. 'If I have to,' she retorted. He didn't reply, so after a while she peered up from under her fringe and seeing the way his eyebrow was cocked, like he might laugh, she started to redden with rage. 'You are like, *sooo* annoying,' she told him, stamping her foot.

'Come on,' he said, and putting an arm around her he steered her outside to the courtyard.

'Where's Mrs Davies?' she asked, as they reached the car.

'The last time I saw her she was cleaning my study.'

'You remembered to arrange for Mr Davies to pick up my friends?'

'It's done. And Mrs Davies has agreed to stay over for the weekend.'

'Da-ad!'

'I know you don't want her to, but you're too young to be here alone.'

'Hardly alone when all my friends are going to be here.'

'All the more reason for Mrs Davies to be around. She won't get in the way, she's just going to prepare a few meals and clean up after you, which I don't imagine you'll be very happy about doing yourselves. How many have you got coming?'

'Three. Martha, Poppy and Sadie. You've met them all, and their parents, so you won't have to worry.'

After opening the car door he took her face between his hands and tilted it so he could look into her eyes. 'I'll be back on Monday,' he told her gently, 'Tuesday at the latest, but if anything happens about Mum, if the police get in touch, or she does . . .'

Her face darkened. 'She won't,' she snapped.

'She might.'

Her eyebrows made an imperious arch. 'Actually, I reckon she's got another family somewhere,' she said. 'One she cares about more than us.'

'You know that's not true.'

She turned to stare into the middle distance, struggling with the words that wanted to gush out in a terrible tirade. In the end, all she said was, 'If you ask me, we're better off on our own, but I know that's not what you want, and so what? Who cares?'

Understanding now what was bothering her, he said, 'Kelsey, I love you more than anything else in the world, and nothing's ever going to change that.'

Her mouth tightened.

'Nothing,' he repeated firmly.

'What about *her*?' she challenged.

'You'll always come first.'

'Oh yeah, like I believe that.'

'Good, because you should.'

Her attitude remained sulky, until finally she brought her eyes back to his. 'Yeah, well, I suppose you're first for me too,' she said grudgingly.

Smiling, he said, 'Tell you what, I promise not to hold you to that, because you're already growing up into a very beautiful young lady and before we know it you'll be out there in the world, going to university and making a life of your own. You won't want to be thinking too much about me then.'

At that her eyes widened. 'What makes you think I'm ever leaving home?' she demanded. 'You're going to need someone to take care of you in your dotage and don't forget, you'll be forty-six next birthday.'

Laughing, he gave her a hug and kiss, and got into the car. 'See the bottom woods over there,' he said, nodding towards the trees beyond the lake. 'Prince Charming's already on his way through, you just can't see him yet,' and with a playful wink he started off down the drive.

She stood watching the car right up until the moment it disappeared from view, then swallowing hard she pushed the tears off her cheeks. She always felt sorry after she'd been mean to him, because she loved him more than anyone else in the whole wide world, it was just that sometimes everything *really* got on her nerves.

Anyway, it was dumb to go on standing here like some kid who couldn't manage without her dad. She had the ducks to feed, and Henrietta the goose to cuddle. Henrietta was bonding well with the other geese Dad had bought to replace her lost family, which was good. They'd all be waiting for their food now, hungry and annoyed that it hadn't come sooner. She wasn't going to let them down, because she wasn't like that. She was like her dad who cared about things and people, and the horrible, frightening feeling she kept getting whenever she saw him go was just stupid. It didn't mean anything, because she knew he wouldn't let her down. It was only her mum who took off without telling anyone where she was going, and not bothering to let anyone know when, or even if, she was ever coming back.

'Hi, it's me,' Miles said into his mobile.

There was a moment's hesitation before Vivienne said, 'Hi. How are you?'

The sound of her voice brought the image of her more clearly into his mind, making the desire to see her stronger than ever. 'Fine,' he answered, glancing across the sprawling wilderness of Salisbury Plain as he drove past, grey and misty and infinitely arcane. 'How about you?'

'I'm fine too. Is there any news on Jacqueline?'

'No. Not yet.'

He could feel her concern, as if it were being spoken in words. It was one of the many things he loved about her, how she'd never failed to understand. More than anyone she'd know what Jacqueline's disappearance meant, and consequently what he was going through now.

'How's Kelsey taking it?' she asked.

'She's worried sick, but trying hard not to show it. Especially to me.'

'She always was very protective of you.'

His smile was weak. It was a truth he wished he could change, for Kelsey's sake much more than his own.

'The police have been in touch with me,' she told him. 'They wanted to know where I was the day Jacqueline disappeared.'

His insides sank. 'Subtle,' he commented, and flipping down the indicator he pulled out to pass a lorry.

'I guess they had to ask,' she said. 'They were also interested to know if we were still seeing one another.'

'They asked me that too.'

There was a beat before she said, 'You sound tired. Where are you?'

'In the car, on my way to London. I was wondering . . .' He took a breath. 'Would you be free tonight?'

She didn't answer.

'Just meet me for a drink,' he said. 'I feel like I'm going insane.'

'I know how hard this is for you, but she'll be all right. She'll come back and everything will be fine.'

'It'll never be that, and you know it.'

Because she did, he wasn't surprised by her silence. 'Vivi. I know it's been a long time, but nothing's changed for me.'

'Please don't say that.'

'Why? It's true. So I'm asking you again . . .'

'Miles, you have to know how much I want to be with you, but you've got enough to worry about. I'm not going to add to it.'

'How the hell would you do that?'

'You know very well. It'll be too hard for Kelsey, and other things have happened since we were together.'

'What things?'

'This isn't the time to go into them.'

He said no more, instead he let the silence stretch. She was going to change her mind. If he gave her the space to think about it . . .

'I'm sorry,' she whispered, and a few seconds later he realised the line had gone dead.

He drove on, thinking of her, imagining how she felt, the way they'd laughed and loved . . . It became so intense that he was almost grateful when his conscience rose up to push the memories aside. It wasn't that he felt a loyalty to Jacqueline any longer, the time for that had long passed, but his natural instinct to protect her always left him feeling wretched and scarred whenever he considered anything that might hurt her. And loving Vivienne as much as he did, finding happiness with another woman, would always do that.

As Vivienne let go of the receiver she took a deep breath and put her hands to her face. She'd known it would be hard to say no if he asked to see her, but until now she hadn't actually realised just how hard. The temptation to ring back to say she'd changed her mind was almost overwhelming, but she wouldn't. She couldn't . . .

'Are you OK?' Alice asked, finishing her call.

'Yeah, I'm fine,' Vivienne answered, removing her hands. 'That was Miles. He asked to see me.'

Alice's expression showed her concern.

'Don't worry, I said no,' Vivienne assured her, and getting to her feet she walked into the kitchen to make some coffee.

Alice came to stand in the door, her lively, freckled face as serious as Vivienne's.

'I don't want to talk about it,' Vivienne said, filling the kettle.

'Just tell me, has Jacqueline resurfaced?'

'Apparently not.'

Alice sighed, and was on the point of muttering something derogatory about the woman when she caught Vivienne's eye. 'Did you tell him Justine James has been trying to contact you?' she asked.

Vivienne shook her head.

Alice watched her spooning coffee into cups, then opening the fridge for the milk. 'Has he speculated at all on where Jacqueline might be?' she ventured. 'Or what might have happened to her?'

'No, and I didn't ask. I don't want to get into it.'

'What about you? Where do *you* think she could be?'

'I've absolutely no idea.'

Alice turned round as the main door to the office opened and Kayla and Pete came in.

'I'm going over to the deli,' Vivienne suddenly announced, and reached for her coat. 'Does anyone want anything?'

'I've brought some sandwiches back,' Kayla protested.

'Photographs,' Pete said, passing her a large brown envelope that he'd just collected from the post office. 'And I've got the list of choreographers you wanted. Remind me when you're going to Devon.'

'Monday, straight from my mother's,' Vivienne replied, belting her coat. 'I'll be back soon,' and picking up her mobile she left.

Minutes later she was walking along the towpath, inhaling the salty stench of seaweed that the tide had abandoned on the mudbanks, and feeling the greyness of the sky closing in around her as she dialled her mother's number.

'Hi, it's me,' she said, when her mother answered.

'Yes, I thought it might be. How are you?'

'Miles called again. He wanted to see me.'

Her mother's voice deepened slightly as she said, 'What are you going to do?'

'I want to see him, obviously, but . . .'

'Not yet?' her mother finished for her.

Attempting to swallow her frustration, Vivienne said, 'How's Rufus?'

'He's fine.'

'Has anyone been in touch with you? The police, or anyone from the press?'

'If they had, I'd have told you.'

Knowing that was true Vivienne felt some of the tension going out of her, and slowing her pace she turned to stare out across the river. On the opposite bank a fisherman was wading into the mud, while behind him joggers, cyclists and dog walkers were crossing one another on the leafy path. Spotting a woman with blonde hair she felt a jolt inside, and followed her progress to the small terrace where Alice lived. As the woman turned to descend the steps she waved to someone out of sight, and a moment later she was gone.

'Are you still there?' her mother asked.

'Yes. I'm hoping to be home around seven tomorrow night. Is that OK?'

'Of course.'

She took a breath. 'Mum?'

'Yes?'

'Don't think too badly of him. It's not his fault.'

'Not everything, no, but some of it is.'

Feeling a quickening of her temper, Vivienne bit it back and said, 'I have to go now. I'll call again later.'

After clicking off the line she was about to head back to the office when her mobile bleeped with a message. Expecting it to be from one of the journalists she'd already contacted about the slave auction, she opened it up and read the text. Seconds later her pace slowed to a halt as her heart started to freeze.

`U must b wondrng whr Mrs A is by now. Or do u alrdy knw?`

```
PS: I know about the little secret you're
hiding.
```

Snapping the phone shut, she ran back along the towpath.

'Read that,' she said, bursting in through the office door and thrusting her mobile at Alice. 'The last text. Read it.'

As she waited, Vivienne turned to an astonished Kayla and Pete. 'Someone seems to think I know what's happened to Jacqueline,' she told them angrily.

Pete's eyes boggled. 'No shit,' he murmured. 'Let me see that,' and taking the mobile he read the message too.

'We need to find out who it's from,' Kayla cut in, and whisking the phone away she started to check. 'Private number,' she pronounced.

'It's Justine James, obviously,' Vivienne fumed. 'She's trying to get to me and godammit, it's starting to work.'

'So what are you going to do?' Alice asked.

'What can I do?' Vivienne cried in anger. 'She's got my number, so I obviously can't stop her sending texts.'

'Maybe you should contact the police?'

Vivienne's eyes closed. 'No,' she murmured. 'No, I can't do that. Not yet, anyway.'

Alice glanced at the others.

'I don't think you're going to want to hear this much,' Kayla said, 'but while you were out the Justine rang here and left a message.'

'No, I really don't want to hear it,' Vivienne confirmed, going to hang up her coat. 'She's coming at me from all sides, so just keep her out of my hair and whatever you do, make sure she never gets through that door. Now, I need to speak to someone in Devon to get directions for next Monday.'

'I'll do that,' Kayla told her. 'You've still got a stack of calls to get through from this morning. I should just add though, that the Justine asked me to tell you that she's having dinner with Miles this evening.'

Vivienne stopped in her tracks, her heart somersaulting inside her. *PS: I know about the little secret you're hiding.*

'Remember,' Pete jumped in hastily, 'that woman knows how to press all the buttons, so don't dance to her tune –

unless, of course, you want to put the rest of us out of our misery and find out whether she really is having dinner with him.'

Vivienne looked at Alice, and knew right away that their minds were running along the same tracks. 'No,' she said angrily, 'this is just another trick to make me call her back. She's not seeing Miles at all.' She put a hand to her head, trying to make herself think. 'OK, I've got two options,' she said finally. 'I can ring Miles to find out if it's true, or I can do nothing and hope it ends up calling the damned woman's bluff.'

No one said anything, they didn't have to, because she knew from the way they were looking at her, that they were all thinking the same thing. There was a chance this might not be about Jacqueline, and if it wasn't, surely to God she shouldn't be running the risk of Miles finding out from Justine that he had a fifteen-month-old son.

'Miles,' Justine smiled, stepping in through the front door of his three-storey Kensington town house. 'How lovely to see you.'

'Hello Justine,' he responded, brushing her cheek with a friendly kiss. 'How are you?'

'Not bad,' she replied, as he closed the door. 'Still surprised by your call. It's been a while. You have to stop burying yourself away down there in Devon. We miss you in London.'

There was irony in his expression as he said, 'Come on through,' and after taking her coat he turned to lead the way across the hall into a large, brightly lit beechwood kitchen where the TV was on and the mouth-watering smell of spicy cooking was filling the warm air. 'Can I get you a drink?' he offered. 'There's red wine already open, or vodka—'

'Red wine sounds good,' she interrupted, looking around. It was a much more homely kitchen than she'd imagined, considering what she knew of Jacqueline, with all kinds of pots and herbs, and garlic ropes hanging from hooks around the range and overhead racks, and an impressive collection of gadgets snagged to the cream-tiled walls.

'I hope you don't mind coming here,' he said. 'I thought it

would be easier to talk than if we went out somewhere. One or other of us is bound to run into someone we know.'

'Here's fine by me,' she assured him. Then, noting a tajine on one of the burners, 'What are we eating?'

'Moroccan chicken.' He passed her a glass, then picked up his own. 'Cheers,' he said. 'And thanks for making it at such short notice.'

Her gaze remained on his as she sipped. She wouldn't tell him wild horses couldn't have kept her away, because he didn't need to know that. 'So,' she said, as he turned back to the range, 'I take it your dear wife is still in absentia.'

'She is,' he confirmed. 'May I ask how you know?'

She gave an incredulous laugh. 'You must be aware that your local TV station ran the story tonight.'

'But it's in Devon and you're here, and my guess is you knew before.'

'Ah, well, I'd be slipping if I didn't, but it was only the local stringer who tipped me the wink. Nothing sinister. No spies in the Avery camp.'

He gave her a quick glance and reached for the pepper mill. 'So what's the general opinion?' he enquired. 'Have I done away with her? Has she done away with herself? Or maybe she's found what she's always been looking for.'

'I'd say it's about sixty–forty in favour of you doing away with her,' she told him mischievously, while going to perch on one of the thickly padded bar stools.

'And which camp are you in?'

'Me, I'm torn. There's always the chance she's doing this to torment you, or to get some attention. After all, it wouldn't be the first time. However, it's equally possible that you finally flipped and decided to do away with her, for which not many would blame you, but if that is the case, I don't think you acted alone.'

Knowing that in spite of the tone, nothing had been said lightly, Miles denied her the satisfaction of appearing ruffled, and merely raised his eyebrows curiously as he said, 'And my accomplice would be?'

'Well, Kelsey might have had a hand in it,' she suggested. 'Revenge for all the years of rejection and bad parenting, as well as forcing that overdose down her throat a couple of years ago. Or, I'm wondering if Vivienne Kane might have had something—'

'Let's leave Vivienne out of this,' he said, cutting her off.

She smiled and took a sip of wine. She was starting to enjoy this now. 'Have you seen her lately?' she ventured.

'No.'

'Very wise. You wouldn't want to be calling attention to your relationship . . .'

'Justine,' he warned, 'there are limits to how much licence I'm going to allow you on this and you're pushing them very hard right now.'

'OK. This is me backing off,' she told him pleasantly, 'but you can't blame me for trying. It's my job, remember?'

Treating her to one of his famously sardonic looks, he turned back to his cooking.

She drank some more, and felt the pleasure of being with him steal through her with the same intoxicating warmth as the wine. It was remarkable, she thought, how being in his company could seem like the only really worthwhile place to be. He had that effect on others too, male as well as female: his charisma had often been discussed in offices and bars, and added to the list of qualities that made journalists so keen to work for him.

'So tell me what else is happening in your life,' she said, resting her elbows on the counter top. 'The last I heard you'd been approached by Channel Four news, so do I take it you turned them down?'

'We're still talking, but I have other irons in the fire.'

'So you *are* planning to go back to work? I mean apart from the weekly columns, guest editing and non-executive directorships. I thought maybe you were having too much fun as one of the idle rich.'

'Don't ever make the mistake of thinking I'm that,' he told her seriously. 'Practically everything I have – had – went into death duties and renovating the house, so believe me, I need to work.'

'Well, that's good news for some. I, for one, wouldn't mind having you as my boss again, but you already know that—'

'What's happening in your world?' he interrupted, clearly not wanting to discuss her ambitions.

With a dismissive wave of her hand she said, 'Oh, everything's pretty much the same. The Critch is his usual obnoxious self, the celebrities get younger and stupider by the day, and my colleagues get sassier and prettier by the minute.'

He cocked an eyebrow.

She mirrored his expression, but said no more, for she wasn't about to tell him how bad things really were. Knowing him he'd be fully aware of it anyway, for very little ever got past Miles. 'Can I do anything to help?' she offered.

'Actually, you could set the table,' he told her. 'I thought we'd eat in the conservatory. The heating's on. Everything's out there.'

After doing the honours, she wandered back into the kitchen and picked up her wine again. 'So how worried are you about Jacqueline?' she asked, bluntly. 'On a scale of one to ten.'

'I'd put it at eight.'

She nodded thoughtfully. 'High,' she commented. 'Where do you think she is?'

Taking a step back as a cloud of steam rose up from a boiling pan of couscous, he said, 'If I knew, she wouldn't be missing.'

'Very droll. So will you be making an appeal to the public, asking if anyone's seen her?'

'I believe that's what the police did this evening.'

'Not the same as the husband, or the daughter, doing it though, is it? How is Kelsey, by the way?'

'She's fine, considering.'

She watched him sample the chickpea sauce he had simmering around the chicken legs, then took some from the spoon he offered. 'Mm, heaven,' she declared, as the spicy flavours unfolded over her tongue. 'Will you marry me, if we find out you're free?'

'Tasteless.'

'No, I swear, it's delicious.'

His eyes narrowed, and returning to the stove he said, 'It's time I told you the reason I invited you here.'

Intrigued, she sipped some more wine.

'I want you to try and find out what Jacqueline was doing during the weeks before she left,' he stated.

Justine stared at his hands, not moving, not even sure she'd heard right.

'I'd rather not have you working against me,' he told her frankly, 'and we both know that's what the Critch will want. Not that I mind what's written about me, but it hurts children to see their parents lambasted, or incorrectly accused of crimes they haven't committed, and I think you'll agree my daughter's been through enough.'

'Of course,' she replied, 'but I have to confess to being surprised at your asking me, considering what happened in the past.'

He turned to look at her.

'Vivienne's convinced I'm responsible for the article that brought Jacqueline back from the States,' she reminded him. 'And as far as I'm aware, your daughter is too.'

'I know you better than they do,' he responded, 'so I'm in no doubt that the Critch forced your hand over that.'

Her eyebrows rose. 'So you do think I was involved?'

'As I said, I know your hand was forced – and I know your style, so I'm fully aware of which parts were written by you, and how much was added, or changed, by him. In my book I have you to thank for it not being even more damaging than it was.'

'The outcome was still pretty horrific.'

'Not even the Critch could have known Jacqueline would go that far, which doesn't let him off the hook. As far as I'm concerned, he's swinging high.'

She nodded her agreement. 'So what you're asking now,' she said, 'is that I try to keep the reins on him again?'

'Insofar as you can.'

'And what would be in it for me?'

'You'd have the inside scoop on what's happening with the search, if it comes to that. As you know, she could turn up again at any time.'

'At which point there wouldn't be a story?'

'No.'

'But if there is, you'd want me to run my copy past you

first, so you can have some control?'

He didn't deny it. 'The Critch is the only one I'm worried about,' he stated, 'and not without reason, as history has proved.'

She was regarding him closely, wondering whether now was the right time to ask if he'd be willing to give her a job at the end of it, or was he just going to use her to declaw the Critch, then drop her again? Deciding to let it wait for a while, she said, 'I can't tell you how relieved I am to discover I still have your trust. If nothing else, it proves loyalty has its rewards.'

'I'm glad you see it that way.'

She smiled, and felt a new warmth rising up inside her.

'I want you to come back to Devon with me after the weekend,' he went on, taking two warm plates from the oven. 'You can get some background on the place, and ask questions in a way I can't, as the husband.'

'What about Kelsey? I can't imagine she's going to be thrilled to see me.'

'She's going back to school on Monday, so she won't be there.'

'And if Jacqueline decides to show up? I'll be clotted and whipped before you can say pass the cream.'

He wasn't amused.

'That's not saying I won't come,' she assured him hastily, 'I just want to make sure we're both aware of the obstacles I'm facing.'

'I don't think there's any doubt about that, but you're not likely to run into either one of them.'

'Unless Jacqueline comes back. What about Vivienne?'

'What about her?'

Justine was trying to read his expression, but it wasn't possible. Judging it wiser not to go any further with that, at least for the time being, she merely shrugged and smiled and said, 'Sounds like we have ourselves a deal.'

'In that case, why don't you refill our glasses and take them through?'

Several minutes later they were seated either side of the table, with two candles burning between them, and several dishes of exotically scented food spread out around their plates. As they served themselves and ate he talked in some detail about the statements he'd given the police concerning the weeks leading up to Jacqueline's disappearance, and how very little had happened during that time that could be termed unusual, or out of the ordinary. Though Justine asked an occasional question, on the whole she listened intently to his words, while keeping a close watch on his eyes. He'd know she was assessing him, of course, so he was undoubtedly being careful not to reveal any more than he intended, but she felt reasonably certain that what she was hearing wasn't too far from the truth. What was intriguing her, however, was his consistent failure to mention Vivienne. She couldn't yet figure out whether this confirmed the startling information she'd learned only yesterday, that he and Vivienne had a child together, or proved the equally startling claim that he knew nothing about it.

The trouble with Miles was that it was almost impossible to tell what was going on in his head, particularly when he didn't want someone to know. However, if her source was to be believed, and she had little reason to doubt him, it was highly probable that Miles *didn't* know he had a son. Vivienne would have been afraid to tell him, because of the effect it might have on Jacqueline should she ever find out.

Heaving a gentle sigh, Justine sat back in her chair to drink the rest of her wine as he went into the kitchen to start making coffee. She could see him through the conservatory window, tall and stern, deeply thoughtful and as intractable as ever. Yet for all the armour that protected his emotions, she knew very well that after all he'd been through, finding out he had a son could as easily break him apart as it could push his poor wife right over the edge. It was why she wouldn't go to print with anything until she had incontrovertible proof that the boy existed. Knowing Miles as she did, if she managed to get one word, or even a single innuendo wrong about something so important to him, it would spell a very abrupt and permanent end to a once glittering career.

*

'Ah, sir, there you are,' DC Joy said, looking up as Detective Inspector Sadler came into CID with one of the sergeants. 'How did it go in court?'

'Don't ask,' he responded grumpily. 'Just tell me something to brighten my day.'

'Well, I don't think I can do that exactly, sir, but I do have something—'

'The Avery case,' he interrupted. 'Any sightings after the news broadcast?'

'Uniform are following up on a couple of possibles,' she answered, 'and we've been inundated with calls from the press . . .'

He waved a hand irritably. 'Has anyone seen her, that's what we want to know? There's nothing on those darned CCTV cameras, so we have to assume she never got on the train.'

Joy picked up a file and followed him into his office. 'I've spoken to the psychiatrist,' she told him, 'and this arrived from the Met a couple of hours ago. It's a bit surprising . . . I'm not sure why he never told us . . . Well, I think you'd better read it.'

Sadler eyed the file, took it, then sank down in his chair as he opened it. 'I could murder a cuppa,' he hinted. 'And a bacon sandwich with two thingamawhatsits of ketchup.'

'Would that be sachets, sir?'

'Don't get smart.'

By the time she'd gone dutifully off to the canteen and returned with his lunch it was clear to Joy that he'd finished reading the file. To her surprise, when she saw the look on his face she felt tears come to her eyes. Quickly blinking them back she set down his plate and cup and tried to assert a professional detachment, but after finding out what she had and now catching her boss's reaction, it was hard.

'Sad, isn't it, sir?' she said.

Still staring at the page in front of him, Sadler nodded slowly. 'Yes, Elaine, it's certainly that,' he responded, with a rare use of her Christian name.

Going to peer over his shoulder at the file, she said, 'I wonder why Mr Avery never told us.'

'He probably finds it hard to talk about,' Sadler replied. 'I know I would.'

'Even after all this time?'

He inhaled deeply. 'When a child is abducted and never found, time isn't much of a healer.'

Realising that was probably true, she continued to gaze down at the slightly faded photograph of a beautiful baby boy. 'So now we know why Mrs Avery's a bit unstable,' she said, swallowing another well of emotion.

With a protracted sigh, Sadler nodded. 'Do we know yet if Mr Avery's turned up anything in London that might help us to find her?' he asked.

'No word from him, sir.'

'OK, let's give him a call.'

As he reached for the phone, DC Joy said, 'I have a theory, sir.'

Sadler put the phone down again.

Surprised to find herself being taken seriously, she coloured slightly. 'I wondered . . . I mean . . . Mrs Avery's psychiatrist said she'd never been able to get over the loss of her child. Apparently she's had a couple of breakdowns and all the issues surrounding it are still a big problem for her, to the point that she finds it difficult to connect with other people, including her family. It sounds as though they've been through years of hell, actually . . . So I was wondering . . . I know this might sound mad, but do you reckon it's possible her husband might have helped her put an end to the suffering? I mean, she tried to commit suicide before . . .' She trailed off, knowing she wasn't presenting it well. 'I'm sorry,' she said. 'It's just that . . .'

'Don't apologise, DC Joy. I've been in this game long enough to know that anything's possible, and what you're suggesting had not occurred to me.' He stared hard at the file, not sure what to make of the idea. 'If the child's still alive he's about to be sixteen,' he pointed out. 'Do you think that's significant?'

Her face fell. 'I hadn't noticed that, sir,' she confessed. 'But I suppose it could be. Do you?'

'It coincides with Mrs Avery's fortieth,' he said, and flipping back through the file he began reading again. 'OK, let's get Miles Avery on the line,' he said a few minutes later.

After pressing in the number and hearing it ring, Joy passed the phone back.

'I'm sorry, Detective Inspector,' the housekeeper told him, 'Mr Avery's still in London.'

'I thought he might be. Could you give us the number there, please?' After jotting it down he was about to thank her and ring off when he decided to question her a little further. 'Has there been any sign of Mrs Avery?' he asked. 'Or any news?'

'If there had, I'm sure Mr Avery would have let you know,' she responded a little tartly.

'I'm sure you're right,' he said blandly. 'Tell me, Mrs Davies, did you know that the Averys have, or once had a son, who'd be coming up for sixteen now?'

'You mean Sam.'

'Do you know what happened to him?'

'He was snatched and never found.'

'And you didn't think it was important to mention that when we spoke to you?'

'You were only asking about her, not her son.'

'Indeed,' he said, letting his tone tell her how dimly he viewed her pedantry. 'Thank you,' he added, and rang off. His expression was dark as he said to Joy, 'OK, let's call the Averys' London number.' Then, treating her to a cautionary look, 'You might not like what's about to happen now, Detective Constable, so brace yourself.'

'What do you mean, sir?'

'I mean the benefit of the doubt stops here.'

'Gone, sir,' she responded, clearly not entirely sure what he meant.

Were the situation not so grave he might have smiled, but his expression was still sober when a few moments later Joy made the connection and passed him the receiver. 'Hello, Mr Avery?' he said, turning on the speaker so Joy could listen. 'It's Detective Inspector Sadler. I hope this is a convenient time.'

'Of course, Inspector,' Miles assured him. 'Do you have any news?'

'Not about your wife, no,' Sadler replied. 'But I am

wondering why you didn't tell us your *whole* family history when we came to see you.'

Silence fell at the other end.

Sadler was good at silences, so had no problem letting it stretch.

'Would it have made a difference?' Miles finally asked.

'You're an intelligent man, you must know the answer to that.'

Miles sighed. 'All I can say is it's not something I find easy to put into words.'

Though he understood, Sadler said, 'Perhaps I can do it for you?'

Joy flinched in anticipation as Miles said, 'You don't need to. I know the situation. He's going to be sixteen in a few weeks. Or he would be . . .'

Sadler waited, but this time Miles won. 'Do you think it's why your wife has gone?' Sadler asked.

'I have no idea what her reasons were.'

'Is there a possibility she could have found him?'

Joy's eyes widened.

'I doubt it,' Miles answered.

'Do you know where she is, Mr Avery?'

'I beg your pardon?'

'I'm asking if you're wasting police time.'

'I rather think it's the other way round,' Miles snapped and the line went dead.

Sadler handed the receiver to Joy. 'Get him back,' he said.

After pressing the redial she returned the phone, then poised a finger over the speaker, only pushing the button when Sadler nodded the go-ahead.

'Mr Avery, I'm sorry if I offended you.'

'I went through all this fifteen years ago,' Miles growled angrily. 'I was accused then of a crime I didn't commit.'

'Yes, we have the file here,' Sadler told him, knowing only too well how tough the police sometimes had to be on parents whose children went missing. He wouldn't have to point out the necessity of it to someone like Avery, since he'd be fully aware of how often parents were involved, and it would be naive to think that Avery's insight would have made his own experience any easier to bear. 'Did you happen to find anything interesting amongst your wife's papers?' he asked. 'Such as her passport?'

'Yes, it's here,' Miles replied. 'I should also tell you that she's virtually emptied one of our joint bank accounts.'

Sadler frowned. 'I see,' he said. 'May I ask what kind of sum we're talking about?'

'Somewhere in the region of forty thousand pounds.'

Sadler blew a silent whistle.

'Most of it was hers,' Miles continued, 'the profit from an apartment she sold about a year ago. It was in a long-term account, so she must have forfeited the interest.'

'When did the withdrawal take place?'

'According to the statement, about a month before she left.'

'Which suggests she was planning to go?'

'It seems that way.'

Sadler chewed his lip thoughtfully. 'Could she have used it to pay a ransom?' he asked bluntly.

Again Joy looked shocked.

Sounding less perturbed than he might, Miles said, 'Obviously the thought's crossed my mind, but I can't see her getting involved in something like that without telling me.'

'You're a big man in the media, so perhaps the kidnappers – if they exist – felt they could only trust your wife not to inform the police.'

'It's possible, but I don't think very likely.'

'Mm,' Sadler grunted, inclined to agree. 'It also doesn't seem a big enough sum,' he went on, almost to himself, 'particularly when you're known to be a wealthy man.'

'It's a general misconception,' Miles informed him. 'In fact, after two lots of inheritance tax, and some bad investments on my father's part, there was very little left when I took over the estate.'

'Well, I admit I'm intrigued,' Sadler said, sitting back in his chair, 'but as things stand, I'm not sure we can help you any further. If your wife has chosen to absent herself from the family home, which is what it's looking like . . . Well, there's no crime in that.'

Miles's tone was brisk as he said, 'So I take it you no longer consider her a danger to herself, or others.'

'Do you?' Sadler countered.

Miles didn't respond.

'You were at pains to tell us the other day,' Sadler reminded him, 'that your wife—'

'I'm aware of what I said,' Miles cut in. 'Now, I think I shouldn't take up any more of your time.'

'It's your decision,' Sadler told him.

The line went dead.

After putting the phone down Sadler steepled his fingers and began tapping them against his chin.

'Is that it, sir?' Joy protested. 'Are you really going to just drop it?'

His eyes went to hers. 'What do you suggest we do, Detective Constable?' he enquired.

She took a breath, all eagerness to reply until she realised she wasn't very sure. 'I'm still learning, sir,' she reminded him.

Sadler smiled. 'Then I'll tell you. First of all we're going to let Mr Avery think we've dropped it, then we're going to find out a little more about this missing forty grand. We only have his word to say Mrs Avery was the one who made the withdrawal.'

'You mean he might have taken the money himself to make it look as though she was paying a ransom?'

'Or absconding with a lover, or going off to start a new life.'

Joy could see the logic. Then her breath caught on another suspicion. 'Oh my God, forty grand might not be enough for a ransom, but it would for a contract – wouldn't it, sir?'

Sadler merely looked at her.

Joy shook her head. 'No, not someone in his position . . .'

'Position never precludes possibility.'

'But why would he want her dead?'

Sadler's expression was ironic. 'You've already floated assisted suicide,' he reminded her, 'and added to that, I can think of at least one more reason why he'd want her out of the way. Give me more information on Avery's personal life, and I'll probably come up with at least another two.'

'Oh my God,' Joy murmured, her eyes rounding like saucers. 'I think I know what you're thinking, sir.'

Sadler waited.

'I do believe that what you're thinking,' she went on clumsily, 'is *cherchez la femme.*'

'Well, that's one way of putting it, Detective Constable,' he replied, not entirely unamused. 'Or we could just call her Vivienne Kane.'

Chapter Five

Linda Kane's soft round face was alight with pleasure as her fifteen-month-old grandson wobbled about on his plump little legs in front of her, before making a sudden dash down the garden path towards his mother, shrieking and waving his fists in unabashed joy.

'Hello my darling,' Vivienne laughed, her voice catching with pride as she stooped to gather him up. 'Aren't you just the clever one, walking all on your own now?'

'Mum, mum, duh,' he gurgled happily as she buried her face in the wonderful baby scent of him and his paint-covered overalls.

'Have you been a good boy for Grandma this week?' she wanted to know.

'Muh, muh,' he shouted, and gave a squeal of delight for no other reason than he loved to make a noise.

Swinging him high to look up into his adorable little face, she laughed and shook him playfully. 'You are the biggest rascal in the world and Mummy's going to eat you all up,' she told him, loving the way his wispy dark curls glowed with an almost milky sheen in the light of the street lamps.

'Mm mum!' he gurgled, trying to grab her face.

'Come on, let's go in. It's cold out here,' and snuggling him against her as she picked up her bag, she went on up the path to embrace her mother, whose gentle brown eyes and faintly lined features were shining with love. 'Hi. Are you OK?' she asked, stepping in through the front door.

'Of course,' her mother answered. 'You look tired.'

'I am a bit, but not too tired for my boy,' she added, blowing a raspberry into his neck.

Rufus gave another yelp of pleasure, and taking two fistfuls of hair he started to bounce up and down.

'OK, young man,' his grandmother said, coming to the rescue, 'let's go and show Mummy your drawings. Prepare to be impressed,' she added quietly to Vivienne. 'They just about blew my mind.'

Vivienne let her take him, and after dumping her shawl and coat on the banister, she followed them into the cottage's cosy kitchen to inspect her son's latest achievements. 'Wow,' she exclaimed, when she saw the crayoned pages spread out on the table, 'did you do these?'

'He did,' Linda confirmed. 'I told you they were impressive.'

In fact, they were random sweeps and squiggles that depicted absolutely nothing at all, but Vivienne was well used to her mother's conviction that Rufus was going to be a great something when he grew up. This week it was clearly an abstract artist, while last week, after he'd staggered the entire length of the village hall to plunge into a pile of spongy balls, it was an Olympic athlete, and next week, after he'd hopefully mastered a few more words, he'd no doubt be a UN linguist.

'Are you hungry?' Linda asked. 'There's lamb casserole for dinner, but it's not ready yet.'

'I can wait,' Vivienne assured her, taking Rufus back. 'I just want to be with my boy for now,' she said, squeezing him, and noticing, as she always did, how like his daddy he was growing – at least, that was what she liked to tell herself, and who was going to contradict her? 'So what's on the agenda this weekend?' she asked, sitting him on the table in front of her to play pat-a-cake.

'Well, Rufus has a birthday party tomorrow afternoon,' Linda answered, checking the calendar magnetised to the fridge, 'and I have yoga in the morning. Other than that, we're free. How about you? Much work to do?'

'A little. I'm en route to Devon where I'll be for at least part of next week, then I'll come back here, hopefully for a long weekend, if not then for the night before I go on to London.' With a surge of happiness she said, 'Things are starting to look up, Mum. We've snagged two big paying clients this week, and another that's paying nothing, but could give us loads of prestige if we play it right, not to mention a young mother's peace of mind.'

Linda's tone was sober as she said, 'You told me on the phone, Vivi, but the question is, do you have any hard cash yet? Or at least a way of meeting your mortgage?'

Smiling past a pang of anxiety, Vivienne said, 'Not yet, but it's coming. Anyway, the important thing is that we keep up the payments on this place.'

'I've still got some savings left—'

'No!' Vivienne exclaimed firmly. 'I already owe you enough, and I'm not going to let you use up any more.'

'You're my family. What else am I going to do with it?'

'Mum, you're not even sixty yet, and look at you. You're gorgeous, a figure women half your age would die for . . .'

'Oh stop, I'm putting on weight like you wouldn't believe.'

'What I'm saying is, you've got plenty of years ahead of you, and already Rufus and I are taking up too many of them. You're entitled to your own life now, and you'll meet someone else – OK, maybe not as fantastic as Dad, but someone who'll appreciate you and understand how lucky he is.'

Colouring slightly, Linda said, 'What are you soft-soaping me for? There's no need, you know.'

'I'm just stating the truth, and telling you that whatever savings you have belong to you. It's bad enough that you won't let me pay you for taking care of Rufus . . .'

'What are you talking about? You settle all the bills in this house.'

'You mean I used to, but I will again, and this great heffalump is a full-time job. It would cost me a fortune for professional childcare—'

'It was never an option and you know it,' Linda interrupted. 'Maybe, if that poor wife of Miles's weren't—'

'Don't let's go there again.'

'But I think we should. The woman's disappeared, Vivi, and it's making me nervous. Miles told us himself how afraid she is of him having another son if he remarries. It's why she won't let him divorce her, and look what happened when she found out about you, what she did to her own daughter to make him give you up.'

'She was under enormous stress . . . No, I know what you're going to say. Sam went missing a long time ago, she should be over it by now, so maybe her problems go deeper than that, but think how you'd feel if you'd lost a child that way.'

'I'm not denying it's terrible. Horrible beyond bearing, but she's not the only one it's happened to, and people do manage to survive it and move on.'

'How do you know? Who have we ever met, besides Miles and Jacqueline, that it's happened to? They're in the news for a while, then we never hear about them again, so how do you know what it's like for them?'

'OK, I don't, but you can't tell me you're not worried about where Jacqueline might turn up, or what might be going on in that head of hers even as we speak. For all we know—'

'Let's not start speculating on things we know nothing about,' Vivienne interrupted, wanting to stop her mother's fear adding more fuel to her own. 'As far as I remember, Sam's sixteenth birthday is coming up, so think of how sad it must be making her.'

'It's not that I don't feel sorry for her,' Linda replied earnestly, 'but I have to tell you, Vivi, if she does anything to hurt you or Rufus—'

'It's not going to happen,' Vivienne cut in. 'You know very well that not even Miles knows about Rufus, or where you're living now, so let's end this . . . Rufus!' she laughed, catching him as he launched himself at her.

'Duh, duh, mum, mum, mum,' he cried, bouncing up and down in her arms.

Gazing at him with more love than words could express, she said, 'It must be time for your bath, young man. I'll just get my things in from the car, then we'll go up.'

'By the way,' her mother said as she settled Rufus in his high chair, 'I want to hear all about these firemen. Are you really going to teach them to dance?'

Vivienne started to grin. 'Not me personally,' she answered, 'but we're lining someone up to do that.

Actually, I've got some photos with me, so you can take a look at them if you like.'

'I wouldn't mind,' Linda twinkled. 'What skills are they offering?'

'So far we've got a gardener, a taxi driver, a painter and decorator, a car mechanic, a window cleaner, a DIY enthusiast and a Spanish teacher. I'm pretty sure there are going to be more, but it all depends on what their hobbies are and how useful they can be to others. Why don't you come down to Devon and make a bid on one of them yourself when the time comes?'

'I might just take you up on that,' Linda commented dryly, and stooped to pick up the bricks Rufus had just flung on the floor, while Vivienne went to bring her bags in from the car.

She was just struggling back through the front door when her mobile started to ring. 'Can you get it, Mum?' she called. 'I left it on the table. Tell them I'll ring back.'

'Hello?' she heard her mother saying, as she started up the stairs. 'No, it's— Yes, it is. Who's that, please? Oh, Annie. How are you? Yes, I'm fine, thank you. And you? I see. Yes, you'd better speak to her. I'll pass you over.'

Surprised to be hearing from her next-door neighbour, Vivienne let go of her bags as her mother came down the hall, and took the phone. 'Hi Annie,' she said. 'Is everything OK?'

'I think so,' Annie replied. 'I was just checking to see if you knew your garage door was open?'

Vivienne frowned. 'I'm sure I closed it when I left,' she said.

'Oh well, you know how they sometimes flip open again. Would you like me to go and close it? I'll get Geoff to come with me in case there's been a break-in, but the connecting door to the house looked closed as I went by, so hopefully there's no cause for alarm.'

'Thanks,' Vivienne said. 'Actually, can you let yourself into the house to make sure everything's all right?'

'Of course. I'll call back once we've checked it all over to put your mind at rest.'

'Thank you,' Vivienne said again, and clicking off she

continued up the stairs, reminding herself that Annie was right, the garage doors sometimes did flip back open after closing, so that was almost certainly all that had happened.

Finding the lamps already on in her bedroom, and the satin quilt turned back ready for her to get in later, she dropped everything on the bed and unzipped her bag. More than anything she wanted to believe that Jacqueline's disappearance was connected to Sam's sixteenth, but she couldn't help being afraid that she might have somehow found out about Rufus. She kept telling herself it wasn't possible, for she'd never even told Miles she was pregnant, never mind about the birth, and her mother had moved house before she'd even started to show, so the number of people who knew the identity of Rufus's father was limited to those she trusted implicitly. However, she couldn't stop thinking about what it would mean to Jacqueline to discover that Miles had a son. That kind of cruel twist of fate could prove the final straw for a woman whose suffering had never stopped over the years, and whose only reason for living had been in the hope she might one day find her child again.

Starting as her mobile rang, she quickly grabbed it and clicked on.

'Everything's fine,' Annie told her, and Vivienne practically unravelled with relief. 'No break-in, and nothing seems to be missing from the garage,' Annie continued, 'so it was obviously a random flip-up. The door's safely down now, so no need to worry.'

'Thank you,' Vivienne said warmly. 'Thanks for letting me know. I'll have to be more careful next time.'

'It happens to us all. Fortunately so far we've been lucky. Anyway, call if you need anything, we're here all weekend, then we're off to Canada for a month, don't forget.'

'I haven't forgotten, and I'll definitely keep an eye on the place. Have a wonderful time, if I don't speak to you before you leave.'

After ringing off Vivienne dropped the phone on the bed and went back downstairs to fetch Rufus for his bath.

As usual, as she played with him, squeezing spongefuls of warm soapy water all over his lovely slippery skin, and pretending to be shocked when he splashed her, she was thinking of how delighted father and son would be with one another. She found it easy to picture them together, Miles's hands so strong and tender on his son's chubby little limbs, and Rufus's delighted bubbles and squeals as he tried to grab his father's nose. She imagined them sleeping side by side, or playing in a park. She could see Miles feeding him, rolling him over on the floor in a mock fight, or trying to be stern and failing. She couldn't help it, but the longing for Miles to know his son made her forget how hard it might be for him to be reminded of the child he had lost – she thought only of how happy Rufus could make him. And more than anyone, she knew how much he deserved that happiness, for Sam's loss had always been seen as his mother's tragedy. No one had ever really considered how hard it had been for his father too.

Miles was in a taxi on his way to visit friends for the evening. Though he appeared relaxed, with his long legs stretched out in front of him, and one arm propped on the window edge, the deep line between his brows betrayed his inner tension. Right up to the last minute he'd been tempted to call and say he couldn't get to the dinner, but in the end he'd decided that a little relaxation with people he trusted not to gossip later, or push him to talk about Jacqueline, might do him some good. It might also help him to get a better perspective on whether or not he'd made the right decision to involve Justine James the way he had.

With a barely audible sigh, he turned to gaze out at the darkness. Everyone knew what a difficult time Justine was having at *The News*, so if she approached the investigation the way he wanted her to, she was bound to expect a ticket out of there as payment. Not that he was in a position to give her a job right now, but he could always open other doors for her, which he would, if she covered the story his way – or at least kept him informed of what the Critch was about. That kind of bold detail had yet to be spelled out between them, but she'd be fully aware of how he'd feel about the Critch dragging up the past and spilling it all over his Sunday rag. With Jacqueline missing there was every excuse to do just that, and whereas in other hands the story might be sensitively told, in the Critch's it certainly wouldn't. Of course Justine would be unable to influence her editor's approach, but few were better placed to warn Miles if the Critch was about to make a splash, or, far worse, if he managed to turn up anything new.

Looking down as his mobile started to ring, he saw it was Kelsey and immediately clicked on. 'Hi, how's it going down there?' he asked, hoping she was in a less tricky mood than when he'd spoken to her earlier.

'Everything's great,' she assured him chirpily. 'Mrs D is making some pasta for us this evening, then we're going to watch a couple of DVDs. I just wondered, Dad, would it be all right if we had some wine? Mrs D said I had to get your permission before she'll give me the key to the cellar.'

'How many are you?'

'Five, including Mrs D.'

'Then you can have a bottle of Pinot Grigio between you.'

'Oh Dad! That is like so mean. We'll hardly even get a glass each.'

'OK, two bottles, but make sure Mrs Davies has more than the rest of you.'

Sounding much happier with that, she said, 'So what's going on with you? Did you decide to go for dinner?'

'Yes, I'm in a taxi on my way there now.'

'Good, you need to get out, it'll do you good.'

Smiling at her parental tone, he said, 'I take it there's been no text or anything from Mum?'

'Duh! If there had I'd tell you. Anyway, if she can't care about us, why should we care about her?'

He toyed with the idea of telling her about the missing money, but decided it could wait for now. 'Has anyone tried to get in touch, from the police, or the press?' he asked.

'I don't know. I turned off the phones, like you said, but there was a bunch of reporters hanging about the gates earlier.'

Suppressing a groan, he said, 'Have they gone now?'

'Don't know.'

'Well, stay away from them if you can. I don't want them

hassling you. What time are you going back to school on Monday?'

'First thing. Mr Davies is going to drive us in the Land Cruiser, which is like really wicked because— Oh no, I better not tell you that, or you'll get mad, or worried . . . Anyway, we have to be there by nine, but he said he doesn't mind taking us that early.'

'And it's wicked because?' he prompted.

'Oh, Dad! I knew you wouldn't let it go.'

'So let's hear it.'

'Well, it's because we can see better into all the other cars, and sometimes if we spot fit guys we like give them a wave, or something. Now don't start going off on one, because it's nothing to worry about.'

'I'm chilled,' he assured her.

She laughed. Then in a slightly less cheerful tone she said, 'Have you seen *her* while you've been in London?'

'No, but I've spoken to her,' he answered carefully.

He almost felt the freeze. 'What for?' she demanded.

'I wanted to see her, but she turned me down. She's concerned about you—'

'Oh puh-leeze. I don't need her to be concerned about me—'

'Then forget I mentioned it. I just wanted you to know that I am in touch with her—'

'So where does that leave Mum?'

'It doesn't *leave* her anywhere, but this probably isn't a conversation we should be having now.'

Silence.

'Kelsey?'

Still no response.

'I know you're still there, I can hear your neural commotion.'

'Don't try to make me laugh, because it won't work.'

Able to tell she was close, he said, 'Would you like me to ring off now?'

'Whatever.'

'I'll leave my phone switched on in case you want to call. Have a good time all of you, and remember one bottle between you.'

'You said two!' she cried.

'See what a generous dad I am.'

'Oh yeah, like really.'

'Love you.'

'I suppose I love you too,' she retorted tartly, and the line went dead.

Clicking off his own phone he turned to stare out of the window again, absently registering the garish shops and randomly lit buildings they were passing, a blur of vivid colours sprawled across the black canvas of night. Though he was thinking about Kelsey, it didn't take long for Jacqueline to dominate his thoughts, and from there it was a short step to wondering about Sam and his approaching sixteenth birthday – and if that was why she'd gone. Did she really still believe he was out there somewhere, and that she could find him now, after all this time? Of course she did, because that was what it was like being the parent of a missing child, you never stopped wondering, or waiting, or asking yourself questions: Is he happy wherever he is, and loved? How is he doing at school? Does he have any idea who he really is? Is he still alive? Please God, don't let anyone be hurting him.

As usual the loss tightened like a fist in his chest, so he tried to turn his mind back to Jacqueline and their journey to the station the morning she was supposed to be getting on a train. He'd relived it so many times now that he soon let it go and began recalling instead his interview with the detectives. Of course he should have told them about Sam, but being helpful to the police didn't come easily to him, after his experiences fifteen years ago. He wondered if they'd realised yet that Jacqueline's fortieth birthday was going to coincide with their missing son's sixteenth. With a wrench inside that was like a dull scythe rending apart a scar to show a perfect picture beneath, he remembered how ecstatic they'd been when Jacqueline had given birth on her twenty-fourth birthday. It was a double celebration that had made them doubly happy to think of all the joint celebrations to come. Neither of them had ever dreamt, even for a second, that they wouldn't even reach the next one.

Shifting uncomfortably in his seat, he watched the Euston Road traffic lights turn from red to green, then let his eyes drift back to the darkness as the driver pulled forward. The woman Jacqueline had been then was a stranger to him now, someone he'd known a very long time ago, but had never forgotten, or stopped loving, if only for the memories that were buried somewhere beneath the mountain of pain. Many would say they were foolish to have stayed together once everything had started to break down, and he might agree, but Jacqueline had needed their marriage, and perhaps, in a way, he had too, at least for a while. The time had long passed, however, since he'd felt the nurturing strength of their connection; now he only knew its weight, as though it were dragging him to a place that might drown him.

Jacqueline felt a similar burden, he was sure of it, though he doubted she'd ever admit it. It was why she had to take herself off from time to time, to be free of him and the reason they were still together – or perhaps she just wanted to be alone with that reason. He had no clear idea of what she needed, because they'd never discussed it. All he knew was how he used to panic when she'd first started to go, not knowing where she was, or if she'd ever return. He'd often wondered if she realised how cruel it was to put him through such fear, considering their past, or if, in fact, it was why she did it. Whatever the reason, he'd eventually learned how to play the game, understanding that his role was simply to worry and wait until she was ready to turn up again. She always did, occasionally with an apology, but more often with no words at all.

He thought back to the night before she'd left, this last time, when he'd made it as clear as he could that no amount of blackmail, emotional or otherwise, was going to change his mind. Their marriage was over and had been for years, so it was time to go their separate ways. It had come as no surprise when she'd started accusing him of wanting to have another son with a woman who wouldn't be so careless as to let someone snatch him – it was a frequent refrain.

'You've always blamed me for what happened,' she'd

cried. 'And now you want to punish me by replacing him, as if he doesn't matter any more. Well, he does to me, and whether you like it or not, he's still your son and *no one can replace him.*'

He'd given up trying to reason with her, because he knew it was impossible. Nor did he deny it when she accused him of wanting to go back to Vivienne, because it was true. However, there was nothing to be gained from telling Jacqueline she was right, unless he'd wanted the scene to deteriorate even further, so he'd simply taken himself off to a guest room and closed the door. She hadn't tried to come after him, nor had she mentioned it again the next morning, which was typical, for she always backed away from the issues she was afraid to resolve.

Looking down at his mobile as it bleeped with a message, he saw it was from Jacqueline's sister, and immediately opened it.

`Any news?`

Texting back, `not yet`, he flipped the phone closed again and tucked it into his pocket. He didn't doubt Janice was concerned, but he knew very well that she considered Jacqueline his responsibility much more than hers, and he supposed she was right. For as long as Jacqueline continued to cling to their marriage and prop herself up with his conscience, she would be his concern, though he guessed it wouldn't change even if he did manage to divorce her. The pain of her loss, the guilt and despair of ever knowing what had happened to Sam, had devastated her life and time had proved she was never going to recover. It was as though a black hole had opened up in their world the day Sam was taken, and everything they had been before, or might ever be in the future, had simply vanished into it.

His eyes closed. Fifteen years on, and the horror of it could still affect him so deeply that he might have been back in that terrible time. Just a few short minutes was all it had taken. Time enough for Jacqueline to go into the garage to pay for her petrol. When she'd returned the car seat was empty. Their eleven-month-old son had been taken.

His eyes remained closed; his lungs were unable to draw in air as the sickening gulf of that empty space opened up in him again. It was a space that seemed to consume everything around it, as though nothing else had the right, or even the power to exist beyond it. It was a void that he had so often wanted to vanish into himself, as if somewhere inside its amorphous darkness and shadows he might find some kind of relief, or even, by some bizarre miracle, his son.

In all his life he would never forget the days and weeks that had followed that dreadful day; the search, the hope, the disbelief and indescribable fear as they'd waited for news, whilst living in mortal terror of a small body being found, or even one tiny scrap of recognisable clothing. The torment was like nothing anyone could ever understand unless they'd been through it too: the terrible imagining of what could be happening to their child, what vile or sadistic practices he might be being forced to endure, his lack of comprehension, bewilderment and pain – and the frantic crying for the parents who'd always kept him safe. Then there were the hours of pathetic, desperate hope that someone had taken him because they had no child of their own, so he was being loved and cared for and might even, one day, be returned to them. Such a merciless see-saw of emotions, such a pitiless streak in fate's plans.

There had been no witnesses to the abduction; no CCTV, no one to come forward and give as much as a clue as to what had happened, though traffic had been whirling around the roundabout in front of the garage at the time, and always there were passers-by. It turned out that Jacqueline was the only customer during those few fateful minutes, meaning that apart from the cashier, who'd been busy with her credit card, there was no way of being certain Jacqueline was telling the truth about her son even being in the car.

This was why, eventually, inevitably, the finger of suspicion had started to turn towards them.

He'd rather forget the nightmare the police put them through then. From supportive, caring human beings, they'd turned into predatory monsters of the law. Though he'd understood they were doing their duty – a child was missing with no convincing sign of abduction – the horror of being suspected of harming, or worse, killing, their own son was, he felt sure, what had ultimately persuaded Jacqueline that not only was she to blame, but that she needed to pay for what she had done. And, to one degree or another, she'd been paying ever since.

Had she not already been pregnant with Kelsey, he knew that they'd never have had any more children, because a part of Jacqueline's self-punishment was to deprive herself of love. She wasn't worthy of it, either as a woman, or a mother, so she cut herself off from him and Kelsey, both emotionally and physically, never seeming to realise that she was punishing them too.

That wasn't to say she didn't sometimes try with Kelsey, and even attempt to be a wife again, but he'd soon come to realise that the woman he had loved so deeply, and missed almost as much as his son, had gone for good. She could no longer function the same way, because she was incapable of trusting herself, or anyone around her. Life had dealt her one of its cruellest hands, and she lived in morbid dread of it happening again. For her there was no getting past it, or even trying to move on, until Sam came back. She even convinced herself that if she did attempt to let go she would lose what little chance they had of finding him. There was no reasoning with her, though many tried; she simply remained stuck in the belief that it was her fault, so she didn't deserve to be loved or have any kind of life until she found her son again.

He'd dealt with his own pain by immersing himself in work. It was his only escape. Without it he felt he'd have gone mad too – but then a story would come in about a missing child, or a paedophile, or some other horrendous abuse, and he would feel himself starting to fall apart inside as all the wounds were torn open again. If a child was found alive and well the relief he felt only seemed to intensify his loss, so that he'd have to take himself off to a private place where he'd weep and sob and plead with God to give him a sign that his son was safe. Or even tell him he was dead – anything except this never-ending hell of not knowing.

He felt certain now that in forcing Jacqueline to move from Richmond he'd sealed her inability to recover. She'd wanted to stay in that house for ever, waiting and watching, needing to be where Sam could find her, storing up Christmas and birthday presents so she could prove, when he did come back, that she'd never forgotten him. He'd tried to explain that the only way they were ever going to get on with their lives was to attempt to start a new one, but she was incapable of seeing it like that. Richmond was the only home Sam had known while he was with them, so it stood to reason it was where he'd try to find them. In the end she'd had to be tranquillised in order to get her out of the house. Since it had already been sold there was no alternative, and he could only feel thankful that Kelsey hadn't been around to see the doctors struggling with her, or the passers-by, and even the press who'd somehow got wind of it, all regretfully and salaciously lapping up the scene of this poor, tragic woman being drugged and carried from her home. By then Kelsey was away at school, only returning for half-terms and holidays which had been as difficult for her as they were for her mother. It was her father she turned to for love, and because he felt it more intensely than anything else in his life, he'd never held back from giving it.

As it turned out, the first couple of years in Kensington hadn't proved quite as difficult for Jacqueline as he'd feared. Though she'd started out bitterly resenting him for making her move, after a few months she began opening up to him in a way she hadn't since Sam had gone. There had still been rows, and spells of depression, but for the most part she was calm and actually seemed to enjoy redecorating the house to her taste. After a while they even started entertaining and accepting invitations, something she hadn't felt up to in years, and when he was promoted to the editor's chair and she threw a grand party to celebrate, she seemed so proud of him, and so like the woman he'd married, that he began to hope that a return to their physical closeness wasn't very far off.

How wrong he had been. How very wrong, for only days after the party a woman who'd contacted them at the time Sam had vanished suddenly got in touch again. It didn't matter that the police had interviewed her back then and established that she had mental problems, or that she was known to have pestered other couples in their position, her accusations of murder plunged Jacqueline back into a depression so black and severe that Miles had almost felt himself going down with her. At first he kept assuring himself, and Jacqueline, that it was only shock; this was simply the final, and probably most difficult hurdle they had to get over and if they just hung in there they'd make it. But as the weeks and months went by he began to realise he was losing her, particularly when she started behaving in ways she never had before, accusing him of sleeping with other women and even of hiding Sam from her. She'd beat him with her fists in an effort to make him tell her what he'd done with their son, or why she was the only one suffering like this. He had no answers to give her, but even if he had, when she was in such a state she was incapable of hearing them.

Then one day, about three years ago – twelve torturous years after Sam had gone – she'd suddenly announced that she was going to start a new life in America. No preamble, no forewarning, and certainly no discussion, at least not with him. It turned out she'd talked it over with her sister, and they'd both decided it was a good idea for her to go. To say he was dumbfounded would have been the understatement of his life, for until then he'd had no idea she'd even been considering it.

'We're no good for one another, Miles,' she'd told him bluntly. 'I know you still blame me for what happened, and I'm sorry, but I can't live with that any more.'

In fact, he didn't blame her, though he couldn't deny how often he'd wished she'd taken Sam with her when she'd gone into the garage to pay. 'When are you going?' he'd asked, ashamed of, and even shocked by, the relief he was already feeling at the prospect of her departure.

'Next week. I haven't told Kelsey yet. I thought you could do that, after I've gone.'

So he had, and until the day he'd seen the tears well in Kelsey's eyes, he knew he hadn't fully understood how dreadful her little life was. Just like any girl, she needed a mother, and though she rarely admitted it, he knew she loved the one she had and was desperate to be loved in return. Feeling his own emotions rise up as he watched her struggle, he'd tried to comfort her as he broke the news, but she'd pushed him away, not wanting him to think she cared. Only later did she allow the tears to flow as she clung to him with all the fear in her heart.

'You won't leave me, Daddy, will you?' she'd sobbed. 'You won't go too.'

'No, of course not,' he'd promised, holding her tight. 'I'll always be there for you. You're my precious girl and nothing's ever going to change that.'

Though his words had reassured her, he'd known how hard it was going to be to repair the damage Jacqueline had done. Nevertheless, he'd vowed there and then to try.

The last thing he'd expected during the weeks following Jacqueline's departure was to find himself becoming involved with another woman. All he'd wanted then was to feel himself breathing freely again as he devoted himself to Kelsey, doing everything he could to make her feel secure. She was so vulnerable and fragile and demanding of his attention that there shouldn't even have been room for anyone else in his life, but meeting Vivienne had soon shown him that his capacity for love was far greater than he knew. However, for Kelsey, Vivienne was a complication she couldn't cope with. It frightened and perplexed her to have her around, and she was too young to understand that her father had been starved of a normal relationship for so long that Vivienne's freshness felt as vital as air.

Though Kelsey hadn't realised it, it was Vivienne who'd enabled Miles to deal with the terrible tantrums his daughter had thrown during that time, when she'd blamed Vivienne for everything that was wrong in her life, rather than even mention her mother. And it was Vivienne's patience that had kept him together when he'd felt about ready to explode at how rude and impossible Kelsey was being at every turn. Now he shuddered to think of just how dysfunctional he and Kelsey must have been by the time Vivienne had come into their lives, but however bad it was, thank God it hadn't been bad enough to make her walk. But then the story of their relationship hit the press and Jacqueline had staged a panicked return to England to get her husband back.

'For Christ's sake why?' he'd roared, over her pleading and begging. 'You know it's no good between us. It hasn't been for years . . .'

'I can't cope without you,' she'd cried. 'Miles, please . . .'

'But you have, all this time, and you still can. Jacqueline, I'm in love with someone else now, please try to understand that. I need to get on with my life.'

'But we belong together, Miles. We always have. This past year has shown me that more clearly than ever. I can't let you go. You're—'

'You have to.'

'. . . Sam's father. You're all I have left of him, so without you there's no point to my life.'

'Jacqueline, please don't do this. You're stronger than you think. You don't need me any more.'

'I'll prove to you that I do. I'll show you how much I need you. I swear I will.'

And her way of doing that was to stage the most appallingly manipulative act of her life, when she'd drugged Kelsey, then cut her own wrists. That she could have taken such a risk with Kelsey's life had left him with no choice but to make sure it never happened again, and because he knew that in her heart Kelsey wanted to be with her mother, in order to keep her safe he'd ended his relationship with Vivienne and gone back to Jacqueline.

Now, as the taxi pulled up outside an address in Hampstead, he took out two twenties to pay, while reflecting grimly on how the tragedy of their lives had bound him and Jacqueline more tightly than any marriage vows ever could. In some ways he could almost detest her for the hold she had over him, but the pity he felt was too deeply enmeshed in the love they'd once shared for him to do that. He'd give anything to be able to take away her torment, to set her free from the past so she could finally live again, but because the torment was his too, he knew there was never any escaping it, only different ways of living with it. Sadly,

Jacqueline had never really found such a way, which was why, he guessed, she'd never really wanted to go on living at all.

'Oh my God, I have just had like the most brilliant idea. What don't we have a seance?'

Kelsey's lovely young features became instantly troubled as she looked at Sadie, who was lying flat on her back in front of the fire. With her huge brown eyes and round porcelain face Sadie was like an antique doll, precious, delicate and a little bit scary, Kelsey sometimes thought. She was only a couple of months older than Kelsey, but she'd already slept with six boys, or so she said, but no one ever really knew whether Sadie was telling the truth.

'No, what I think we should do,' Poppy giggled tipsily, 'is go and see if those reporters are still outside the gates. Some of them looked really fit.'

Kelsey's worried eyes went to Poppy's fluffy dark curls and heart-shaped mouth. She didn't really like Poppy much, or Sadie come to that, but she'd never let it show, she only smiled and tried her best to be friends.

'They're like way too old,' Sadie protested, trying to smother a hiccup. 'Anyway, it's chucking it down, so there's no way they'll still be hanging about.' She let her head roll round to look up at Kelsey, who was snuggled into an armchair with the last of her wine. 'What happened to Mrs D.?' she asked. 'Has she gone to bed at last? It's such a downer having her around.'

'Yes, she's gone to bed,' Kelsey answered, feeling stupid and angry that her father had insisted the housekeeper stay over.

'She's a fab cook,' Martha piped up from where she was sprawled out on one of the sofas. Martha's upturned nose and rosy cheeks made her extremely cute, in spite of the freckles that helped camouflage an angry rash of teenage spots. She was Kelsey's best friend, and had been since the day Kelsey started at the school, when she'd made her feel really welcome. She had even gone to the house mistress to ask her to arrange for them to share a room. Now they shared all their secrets, and Kelsey wished it was just the two of them this weekend, because she always got the feeling that the others didn't really like her very much. 'I could have eaten four more bowls of that pasta,' Martha declared.

'To wear on your arse,' Sadie murmured, taking another sip of the wine that had turned warm in her glass. 'Do you still have the key to the cellar, Kelse?' she asked, looking up again. 'Why don't we open another?'

'No, Mrs D. took it back,' Kelsey replied, torn between relief that she wasn't being forced to disobey her father, and embarrassment at the way Sadie always managed to make her feel like she needed to get over the adults in her life.

'Whatever,' Sadie said, yawning. 'Anyway, I still reckon we should have a seance.'

'No way,' Martha objected, yawning too. 'That is like so spooky and weird, and what if some crazy spirit gets out of control and tries to possess one of us? I heard that can happen. And they smash up houses and things.' She shuddered. 'No way am I doing it.'

'Don't be such a wuss,' Sadie snorted disdainfully. 'Everyone's doing it in twelfth year. It's really cool. You can ask it anything, like who— Oh my God,' she suddenly exclaimed, clapping a hand to her mouth, 'we could ask it where your mum is, Kelse. Wouldn't it be amazing if it told us?'

Kelsey's eyes widened in alarm.

'Yeah, and what are you going to do,' Poppy piped up, 'if her mother turns out to be, well, you know, like *one* of them, or something?'

Sadie wrinkled her nose. 'One of who?' she said. Then, getting it, 'Oh my God, what you mean she might be . . . Oh my God, what if she came through? That would be so—'

'Why don't you just shut up,' Martha snapped. 'This is Kelsey's mother we're talking about, not some random person none of us ever heard of.'

Sadie treated her to a seriously snotty look. 'Listen to you getting all stroppy,' she pouted. 'Just because you're scared.'

'You know what,' Poppy suddenly announced, 'I've just had the most brilliant idea. Why don't we find a boyfriend for Kelsey? Would you like that, Kelse? I mean, you've never had one, and it's about time. So who do you like? Tell us, and we'll fix it up.'

Kelsey looked from Sadie to Poppy, feeling her insides shrinking as she imagined all the local boys who regularly turned up in the school's back lane in the hope of meeting the girls. She didn't fancy any one of them.

'I know, why don't we choose someone for her?' Sadie suggested. 'We can draw up a list, and then pull one of the names out of a hat.'

'Why don't you just get off Kelsey's case.' Martha again came to the rescue. 'She's not the only one who's never had a boyfriend. In fact, if you ask me, I reckon you two are all talk, because I've never seen you with anyone.'

'Oh listen to her, like she's got all the boys running after her,' Sadie sneered.

'I didn't say that, but at least I don't go round making things up.'

Trying to avoid things turning nasty, Kelsey quickly said, 'Shall I make us some coffee? Or hot chocolate?'

'If you like,' Sadie replied, stiffly. Then, as Kelsey got up, 'You know, seriously, I reckon it would be a good thing for you to have a boyfriend, Kelse. Everyone's always saying about how close you are to your dad, and if you don't find someone soon, they're going to start thinking that it's like a bit weird or something.'

Kelsey frowned in confusion, until a bolt of horror hit her chest as she realised what Sadie was implying. 'That is such a gross thing to say,' she cried angrily. 'Just because I have a good relationship with my dad doesn't mean . . . Well, it doesn't mean what you're thinking.'

'Sadie, you are so way out of order,' Martha growled angrily. 'I've never heard anyone say anything like that.'

'I'm not saying they have. I'm just warning her that they will, if she doesn't get a boyfriend soon.'

Feeling as though she wanted to be sick, Kelsey grabbed up the empty glasses and stormed out of the room. By the time she reached the kitchen her head was spinning, as though all her thoughts and feelings were colliding and jarring and hating everything about one another. It was like she never wanted to speak to her dad again, but that would be horrible and then she'd have no one . . . Sweat was pouring from her skin. She was really afraid and dizzy and starting to cry . . .

Hearing footsteps, she quickly blinked back the tears and turned round as Sadie came into the kitchen.

'Kelse, I'm really, really sorry. I shouldn't have said that about your dad. It was dumb, and I didn't mean to upset you.'

'Tell her,' Martha said, pushing in behind her, 'that you're just jealous because you hardly ever see your dad.'

'Well thanks, just rub it in, why don't you?' Sadie retorted, her eyes filling with tears.

Kelsey immediately went to comfort her. 'It's OK,' she assured her, 'I didn't take any offence.'

'Like hell you didn't,' Martha muttered, 'and who could blame you. She's going through enough, what with her mother and everything,' Martha went on to Sadie, 'so she really doesn't need you making it worse.'

'I've already apologised, for God's sake,' Sadie cried, bringing her head up from Kelsey's shoulder. 'And anyway, maybe if she had a boyfriend she wouldn't care so much about her mum. She'd have other things to think about.'

'I don't care anyway,' Kelsey informed her. 'It makes no difference to me where she is, or what she's doing. She could even be dead for all I know, and it still wouldn't make a difference.'

It was half past one in the morning when Miles's mobile rang, not quite waking him because he hadn't fallen asleep yet, but certainly giving him a jolt. His first thought was of Jacqueline, but it was instantly obliterated by concern for Kelsey, and seeing it was her he clicked on quickly. 'Hello darling? Is everything OK?'

'Yeah, it's fine,' she answered. 'I just called to say goodnight.'

With relief, he said, 'Did you have a good time, you girls?'

'Oh, you know,' she said dismissively. 'Everyone's in bed now. Martha's sleeping in my room, and the others are in one of the guest rooms. Dad?'

'Yes?'

'Nothing.'
He waited.
'Do you think . . . ? I mean . . .'
Still he waited.
'Well, you don't think Mum's, you know, dead or anything, do you?'
Having guessed something like that was coming, he said, very softly, 'No, I don't.'
'So where is she? I mean, it's starting to get really embarrassing her not coming home and everything. I keep feeling as though people are thinking there's something wrong with us, for her not to want to come back.'
'Did one of your friends say that?'
'No, not really. Well, a bit I suppose. Anyway, it doesn't really matter. I only rang to say goodnight.'
'I can come back tomorrow if you want me to,' he told her.
'No. No, it's fine. My friends will still be here, and we've got like loads to do.'
'Such as?'
'Um, well, there's a shoot in the top woods in the morning, and they need some pheasant-beaters, so we're going to do that. Then in the afternoon we've got homework and stuff.'
'OK.'
Her voice was slightly strangled as she said, 'Sleep well, then.'
'Kelsey, what is it?'
'Nothing. Did you have a nice time tonight?'
'Not bad. You were right, it did me good to get out.'
'I expect it's quite nice being away from me.'
'Now that's a really daft thing to say.'
She took a breath and held it for a moment before saying, 'Do you miss Mum at all?'
'Yes, of course,' he answered, truthfully.
'So why aren't you looking for her?'
Smothering a sigh, he said, 'I've tried everywhere and everyone I can think of, darling. That's why I called the police. Remember?'
'Mm,' she said. Then, after a pause, 'Was *she* there tonight?'

'If you mean Vivienne, then no, she wasn't.'

'Have you called her again?'

'No.'

He heard her swallow and knew she was still close to tears. 'I'd better go now,' she said.

Wishing he could somehow transport himself back to Devon, he said, 'You don't have to. I'm happy to chat.'

'No, it's fine. I'm tired and Martha probably wants to turn out the light.'

'Where are you?'

'In your study. We all got a bit tipsy earlier. It was quite a lot of fun, actually. Anyway, I'm going now. You don't have to bother calling tomorrow. I'll be fine.'

He started to respond, but realising she'd already gone he disconnected too.

For the next few minutes he toyed with the idea of calling back, but reminding himself that she'd been mixing alcohol with far too many emotions, he decided to let it go till morning.

However, as he lay open-eyed in the darkness, he couldn't ignore the sinking sensation inside him. In the morning Kelsey would still feel anxious about her mother, and afraid of him restarting a relationship with Vivienne. So maybe it was time for him to reconsider the way he was handling this, because no matter what, Kelsey had to come first, even though the prospect of a future without Vivienne was one he immediately wanted to reject.

Chapter Six

As Vivienne sped past Exeter, leaving behind the sprawling mass of suburbia, she couldn't help wondering if being in Devon felt so exhilarating because of the times she'd spent here with Miles – or was there just something magical about the county that always filled her with gladness? As a child she'd often visited the coastal resorts, Dawlish, Salcombe, and Torquay, where she and her mother and sister had spent special, happy holidays romping about the beaches with her father, or sailing the estuary, or riding the fun fairs – or hanging onto their tent to stop it blowing away in the wind. They were precious memories, but the most treasured of all were those of walking or riding over Dartmoor with Miles, sitting snugly in front of roaring fires in old-fashioned inns, or working on his house and garden, transforming it into the home of their dreams.

Finding herself steeped in a pleasing nostalgia she eventually left the motorway to begin heading in the opposite direction to Moorlands, towards the remote village of Kenleigh. It felt strange to be going this way, as though she'd taken a wrong turn, but she was relieved not to be too close to the places she knew, for there was no doubt the memories would be much harder to deal with if she were.

In next to no time she was plunging deeply into the meandering forests of Haldon, where the trees soared skywards, and enticing nature trails snaked off into the sun-dappled beyond. She was now in territory she didn't know at all, for she'd never visited Keith Goss at his home, only at the fire station or swimming pool. Though she and Miles had done a lot of walking and riding during their time together, it had almost always been on Dartmoor, certainly never over this way.

Soon the dark density of the woodland began yielding to a landscape that rose and dipped in a gently billowing patchwork of ploughed earth and verdant meadows. She put down the window to inhale the scent of woodsmoke, mingled with farmyards and wild herbs and even a vaguely salty tang of the sea. Then, pulling into a lay-by to check she was still on the right road, she waited for a tractor to lumber by with a cargo of tightly packed bales before following it to where it turned into a field, allowing her to pick up speed again.

Two miles further on she finally came upon a small signpost directing her to Kenleigh. At the same instant her BlackBerry started to ring. Glancing down to see who it was, she immediately connected via the Bluetooth in her ear. 'Hi,' she said. 'How's everything?'

'Pretty good this end,' Alice told her. 'Where are you?'

'About three miles from the village, I think. I must have missed a turn somewhere, because I've obviously come the long way round.'

'Easily done. So what's first on your agenda?'

'I'm meeting Stella Coombes at the Smugglers. Is it easy to find?'

'Very. It's right in the middle of the village, so whichever way you approach, you can't miss it. Is Sharon going to be there?'

'Apparently she's hoping to make it, but one of her children has a football match he doesn't want her to miss.'

'What about the firemen?'

'No. Today's about organising, not performing, so I'll see them separately. Now tell me, did you have your family get-together this weekend?'

'We did, which is actually the reason I'm calling, because the delightful Theo not only wants to be one of your auction lots, he's offering to be involved in any way he can, whether it's publicity, organising, being some kind of gofer, you name it.'

Vivienne's heart swelled with triumph. 'That's fantastic!' she cried. 'We're going to have no problem promoting this now. The firemen were definitely doing it, but with Theo on board . . . Apart from being a national hero and drop-dead gorgeous, the boy was part of the same Olympic team as Keith Goss.'

'I think it might be more politic to refer to him as a man these days,' Alice advised. 'He's twenty-one now, and, as you say, an Olympic champion.'

'This is going to be so wonderful for Sharon to hear. I haven't mentioned a word of it to anyone yet, because I really didn't think he'd be able to find the time.'

'He assures me he's going to make it. He's talking to his coach today, as well as the powers that be at Bath University, which is where he does his training. He has to consult them, because he wants to offer their facilities as a part of the package everyone will be bidding for. So it'll be a day's coaching from Theo Kenwood-South at one of the nation's most prestigious facilities, plus five sessions of personal fitness training for the highest bidder, either in their own home, or at their nearest gym.'

Vivienne felt like swooning. 'The next time you speak to him, please tell him I love him,' she urged.

'I think he already knows that,' Alice informed her, dryly.

Laughing, Vivienne said, 'When, how, can I get in touch with him?'

'He'll contact us, as soon as he's sorted out his commitments for the next few weeks. Now, I'm assuming there was no word from Miles over the weekend or you'd have told me.'

'No,' Vivienne replied, aware of the twist in her heart. 'And before you ask, no more anonymous calls either.'

'That's good. How does it feel being down there?'

'Odd. I mean wonderful, because I love it so much, but this part is quite different to Dartmoor. Much less rugged and wild.'

'That's what I found. Oh, hang on, I've got another call.'

As she went off the line Vivienne slowed up at a Y-junction, and finally spotting a sign for Kenleigh lurking in a bush, she took the right fork to begin heading down another single-track country lane, where tufts of moist earth and moss wove a route down the centre, and leafy banks rose up into the hawthorns either side.

'I'm back,' Alice told her, 'and you'd better brace yourself, I'm afraid, because I'm about to tell you something you obviously don't know or you'd have rung me by now. There's a big piece in the *Mail* about Jacqueline today.'

At that Vivienne felt herself sinking inside. 'What does it say?' she asked, pulling into a passing point to allow a horsebox to go by.

'Needless to say they've dredged up the past, going over what happened when Sam disappeared. There're also a couple of mental-health experts talking about the long-term effects of that kind of trauma. No comment from Miles, but there is a picture of him, taken a few years ago by the look of it, and of Kelsey looking about twelve. Nothing about you, you'll be glad to hear.'

'Should I read it?'

'It won't tell you anything you don't already know, so maybe don't bother.'

'Is it in any of the other papers?'

'Most. The *Mail* has the biggest spread, though.'

'Well, with any luck it'll prompt someone to come forward and tell us where she is.'

'True, but it also means there'll be a lot of reporters hanging about Moorlands over the next few days. Are you OK with that?'

'I don't have much choice, but it's at least ten miles or more from where I'm going to be, so there's no reason for me to run into them. Besides, I'm hardly going to turn back now, when everyone's waiting for me. In fact, I'd better ring off, because I think I'm just about to hit the outskirts of Kenleigh. Very quickly, though, has Pete met with *La Belle Amie* yet?'

'He's with her as we speak, and I'm about to go off to a cast meeting, so we'll catch up again later. Will you be staying at the Smugglers?'

'No, apparently Stella Coombes has my accommodation in hand, so I wait to find out what treat I have in store.'

As she disconnected via her earpiece Vivienne tried pushing aside the feelings the call had left her with, not wanting Jacqueline's disappearance, or even Miles to become her focus now. She was here for entirely other reasons that mattered a great deal to the women she was about to meet, and to her relief, as she began passing between two rows of colourful cottages, each one painted in a different shade of blue, or yellow, or rose pink, she felt her tension starting to ebb. She really did love these Devonshire villages, and the gentle welcome they seemed to exude – and now Theo had committed to helping, she felt a pleasing rush of enthusiasm well up inside her.

Following the road round to the left she came to a high drystone wall that protected the churchyard, and just beyond that a central grassy area with toadstool pillars connected by looped black chains. What appeared to be the high street, and probably a more direct route in and out of the village, ran along the top of the small park, with a village store-cum-post office set back between a charity shop and a smattering of thatched cottages, next to which was a car park belonging to the pub.

As she turned onto the main street she caught a glimpse up ahead of red brick houses with grey tiled roofs and white-framed sash windows. These, she suspected, were some of the council properties that had been built during the early seventies to replace the prefabs that had gone up after the war. Apparently Sharon Goss and her children lived in one of them.

She'd just pulled into the pub car park and drawn up alongside a battered-looking Subaru, when someone startled her with a sharp rap on her driver's window. She turned quickly, and immediately started to smile, not only in response to the beaming, round face with its wind-mottled cheeks, pixie nose and crowning thatch of carroty hair, but at how accurate Alice's description had been.

'Stella Coombes is a cross between Benny Hill, Dennis the Menace and Wendy,' she'd claimed, and she clearly hadn't been joking.

'Hello, hello,' Stella gushed in her engaging West Country burr as she pulled open the door. 'Welcome to Kenleigh. I bin looking out for you. You did jolly well to get here so quick. Did you come M4, M5, or 303?'

'Motorway,' Vivienne answered, getting out of the car.

'Oh my,' Stella clucked, as she took Vivienne's hand in a rough, stumpy grasp, and to Vivienne's astonishment she went off into peals of laughter.

'I'm sorry,' Vivienne said, looking around uncertainly, 'did I miss something?'

'No, not at all,' Stella assured her. 'It's just me. Can't help laughing sometimes, specially when someone looks like you.'

Vivienne started to laugh too. 'What's wrong with me?' she asked, wondering what kind of paroxysms the woman might go into when she looked in the mirror. Not that she wished to be rude, but really, if anyone was strange around here, Stella Coombes had it in spades.

'Nothing's wrong with you,' Stella replied, dabbing her eyes. 'It's just that you and Alice . . . I've never come across a pair who look more like their namesakes. Her, with all her golden hair, and you . . . Go on, tell me, I bet your dad named you after Vivien Leigh.'

'Actually, you're right,' Vivienne admitted, 'but he spelt it differently.'

'With those twinkly blue eyes and all that black hair, you're the spit,' Stella informed her cheerfully. 'Anyway, come on in now, let's get you a drink, bet you're dying for one after the drive. It's a lovely day, innit? Bodes well that, the sun shining on your arrival. Some of the others is already here. Not everyone, because a lot of us has jobs. Meself, I'm a farmer's wife, well you knows that, so I'm a bit of an early bird, which gives me a couple of hours to meself in the afternoons.'

Vivienne followed her inside to find the pub's interior as dark and moody as any self-respecting smuggler's inn ought to be, with low, shadowy doorways and secret niches, a big stone fireplace, and crooked beams running through the peeling paint of a faded white ceiling. Chalked on a blackboard between two recessed windows was a delicious-sounding menu of fish, hiked out of the estuary that very day, it claimed, along with mussels, scallops, prawns and an abundant selection of local game.

'Aha, here she is,' the landlord cried, thumping a fist on

the bar as the door swung closed behind Stella and Vivienne. He was a tall, bullish man with kindly blue eyes, ruddy cheeks and a belly so big Vivienne had to wonder when he'd last seen his knees. 'Glad you came now,' he told her, 'because these ladies was starting to get out of hand.'

Vivienne smiled at his bawdy wink, and followed Stella over to the small group of mainly forty-plus women who were still laughing and clucking at the landlord's tease.

'What'll you have to drink?' Stella demanded, digging into a capacious pocket of her baggy jeans for a handful of coins. 'We're all on tea, herbal and normal, but if you wants wine or beer, we shan't think none the worse of you.'

'Tea's fine, thank you,' Vivienne responded.

'We'm meeting here,' Stella explained, while pulling out a chair for her to sit down, 'because the village hall's took up with something else today. Is someone pouring her a cuppa? Are you 'ungry? There's crisps and stuff behind the bar. Or I 'spect Jonty can make you a sandwich.'

'No, no, I'm fine,' Vivienne assured her, sinking into the chair and taking the cup and saucer someone was offering.

'Sharon just rang, she's on her way,' Stella told her, sitting down too. 'She's ever so grateful that you've come in person. It's going to make a big difference to her morale, having you around, I can tell you that. Not that she's doing badly, mind you. She's a brave girl. But after what you did for Keith and everything, well, it makes you a bit like one of the family, if you knows what I mean. It's not really a time for her to be dealing with strangers.'

'If I'd known it was for Sharon, I'd have come the first time,' Vivienne assured her. 'No one mentioned her on the phone.'

'No, well, she didn't want us to in case it seemed like emotional blackmail, or something, was what she said. I told her she was being daft, that anyone would want to help out in a situation like hers, but she got it in her head that you wasn't to know until you was actually here, and there was no talking her round.'

'Well, I'm here now, and I intend to do everything I can to help, but let's begin with some introductions. I know it might be a bit AA, but if you could tell me your names first, followed by whether or not you actually live in Kenleigh, how you know Sharon, and how much you think we need to raise to help her, it should give us a place to start.'

The woman next to her wasted no time. 'My name's Mary Allsop, and I lives at number three The Willows. I knows Sharon because she's my neighbour, and I think we need to raise a lot more than any of us here can on our own, which is why we've asked you to come and help. Oh, and by the way, we all reckons it's a brilliant idea to call in the fire brigade.'

Stella led a round of applause. 'Good on you, Mary,' she declared. 'Sharon's kiddies is going to need looking after while she has her treatment, and those chaps from the fire station is likely to get us a lot more bidders than the local lads would have managed.'

Wondering how they were going to react to the news of Theo, Vivienne kept it to herself for the moment, wanting the introductions to continue.

'I'm Eileen Rawlings,' said a platinum-blonde woman with a waxy complexion and ill-fitting false teeth, the sweep of her eyes telling Vivienne that she wasn't appreciating having her position as the glamorous one challenged. 'I lives at forty-eight Dodd Lane, which is behind the church, and I knows Sharon because we've lived here all our lives and my girl, Tina, who lives up in Bristol now, went to school with Sharon and Keith. Just like I went to school with Sharon's mam, Betty, God rest her soul. I don't know how much we needs to raise, but I'm happy to dip into my savings as far as I can . . .'

'Especially if she's going to get herself a nice bit of action out of it,' the woman beside her piped up.

Eileen chortled along with the rest of them. 'Can't wait to see my old man's face if he thinks I've won meself a fireman to come and sort out me chimney,' she told them, giving a nudge to the woman next to her.

'Might put his horse back in the stable,' someone else guffawed.

Vivienne laughed along with the others. Though their humour might lack subtlety their enjoyment of it was infectious, and as they continued to introduce themselves –

Lizzie, Cath, Gail, Janet and Fliss – she found herself warming to them more and more.

Then, as if on cue, the outside door opened and everyone looked up as a waif-like creature with a startling abundance of glossy black curls, starkly pale skin and a rich red mouth wafted in, like the heroine from the pages of an old-fashioned romance.

'Sharon,' Stella cried, 'you made it. Good girl. Everything all right?'

'Yeah, perfect,' Sharon said breathily as she straightened her ill-fitting wig and came towards them. 'He got sent off, silly bugger, so he didn't mind me leaving early. I'll box his ears when I get him home though, punching another player. I've told 'im about that before. 'Ello, you're Vivienne, aren't you?' she said, smiling shyly as she held out a hand to shake. 'I'm Sharon, the one what's causing all the fuss. Just shoot me and be done with it, is what I tell 'em. It's what they'd do with a 'orse, but they don't listen, none of 'em.'

'There's no fun in that,' Gail protested.

'Not when you've got risky ideas like you've got,' Sharon retorted dryly. Then to Vivienne, 'It's lovely of you to come all this way. Keith was always talking about you, so I felt like I already knew you. I hope that's not too much of a cheek, and you don't mind that we got in touch.'

'No, of course not,' Vivienne assured her, thinking how thin and frail she looked, in spite of the bagginess of her clothes that was presumably meant to disguise it. 'I'm glad you did, and I'm sure we're going to raise even more money than you think.'

'Bound to now we got the firemen involved,' Stella announced.

'I just hope you made it clear what we'm expecting of 'em,' Eileen piped up. 'Can't wait to get me hands on one of them helmets.'

'Listen to her,' Sharon said, 'there's been no controlling her since she started holding those Ann Summers parties back in the summer. I'm telling you, they're just using me as an excuse to get into all that kinky underwear.'

'Not true, we wants to make sure you're all right,' Lizzie chipped in hotly.

'Just teasing,' Sharon assured her, and sweeping a copy of the *West Country Times* off a window seat she sat down, hugging the paper to her meagre chest. 'So where are you up to?' she asked, eagerly.

Still trying to tear herself from the unholy images of their Ann Summers parties, Vivienne said, 'Actually, I have some news which I think is going to make a great difference to our auction. Theo Kenwood-South has agreed to take part.'

There was total silence as the enormity of the honour made several jaws drop.

'Bloody hell,' Stella finally pronounced.

Sharon's eyes were rounding with protest. 'But he's ever so busy,' she said. 'We can't ask him to give up his time for something—'

'She obviously already has,' Stella interrupted, 'and it's up to him to say whether or not he's too busy.'

'What a lovely lad,' Gail declared. 'I always liked him, even before he won his gold medal.'

'Course, he knew Keith,' Eileen added. 'I bet that's why he's doing it.'

'God bless him,' Mary murmured, shaking her head in wonderment.

Loving them for their appreciation, Vivienne was about to continue outlining her plans when Stella said, 'Reckon all the excitement's gone to me bladder, but before I takes meself off to the lav, do you have any more surprises like that up your sleeve?'

'It's the only one,' Vivienne assured her with a smile.

'They don't come any better,' Cath declared, as Stella got up to lumber across the bar. Then to Sharon, 'Have you ever met Theo Kenwood-South?'

'Only once,' Sharon answered, putting the paper back down to press her hands to her cheeks. 'He's really nice.'

'Here, in't that the woman what's gone missing?' Mary said, pointing at the front page. 'The one that lives over Haytor way?'

Sharon looked down. 'Oh, yeah, that's her,' she said, looking at a picture of Jacqueline. Then suddenly remembering Vivienne's connection, her eyes shot nervously to Vivienne's.

'They reckons she never went in the station,' Eileen stated knowledgeably. 'There's no CCTV footage showing it, they say, so they've only got her husband's word . . .'

'Eileen,' Sharon said awkwardly.

'He's the one who ran the *Telegraph*, in't he?' Mary asked.

'I think it was the *Independent*,' Cath told her.

'Whatever, it don't make him innocent, does it,' Eileen said tartly, 'just because he had a fancy job what paid him loads of money.'

Sharon's dismay was complete as she turned her eyes back to Vivienne.

'It's OK,' Vivienne whispered, putting a hand on hers.

'Do you reckon he's done away with her then?' Lizzie was saying. 'Thass what they'm implying.'

Eileen shrugged. 'Who knows? It's starting to look that way. Next thing you know they'll have the sniffer dogs and helicopters out going all over the place, but they'll have their work cut out, with him being nearly on the moor.'

'Right, shall we go back to—' Vivienne tried to interrupt.

'Must have been terrible having her kiddie stolen like that,' Cath came in tragically. 'They reckons you never gets over it. Well, how can you, when the poor mite could still be out there somewhere? You'd never be able to stop yourself hoping, would you? I know if it was one of mine I'd probably go off me head worrying and wondering and imagining all sorts of things.'

'Just goes to show it can happen to anyone, dunnit,' Mary said. 'They might be rich, but money and privilege didn't keep 'em safe from that, did it? Poor sods. She looks really nice, too. I can't imagine he'd want to get rid of her. I mean, why now, after all this time?'

'You never can tell what goes on behind closed doors,' Eileen said darkly. 'For all we know he might even have done away with the kid all those years ago and she somehow found out.'

Unable to take any more, either for herself or Sharon, Vivienne said in a voice that cut right across them, 'I think we should get back to the reason we're all here, and what our next moves are going to be.' It wasn't that she blamed them for gossiping, it was only to be expected, but she had no intention of listening to Miles's character being shredded by people who knew nothing about him, and even less of what had happened fifteen years ago. 'We'd just finished the introductions when you arrived,' she told Sharon, 'and now you know about Theo, we need to start discussing goals.'

'Our goal is to get her and those kids looked after while she's having her treatment,' Stella declared, as she rejoined the group.

'Of course,' Vivienne responded, 'but what we don't seem to have a clear idea of is how much we need to raise, and I realise we can't really know that until I've had time to talk to Sharon about how long the treatment is likely to take, and what sort of expenditure needs to be covered.'

All eyes were on Sharon, whose embarrassment was painful to see. 'I'll have to talk to the doctors and look at me bank statements and stuff,' she said. Then, in a strangled tone to Vivienne, 'Could I have a quick word with you a minute, in private?'

'Of course,' Vivienne replied, and putting her cup down she followed Sharon to a cosy niche at the far end of the bar.

'Look, I'm really sorry about all that,' Sharon said, her lashless eyes gazing directly into Vivienne's. 'They obviously forgot how we managed to get hold of you, you know, through Mr Avery, well, some of them might not even know . . .'

'You don't have to apologise,' Vivienne assured her. 'It's not your fault, and I promise I haven't taken offence.'

'Yeah, but I should've thought of this before, as soon as it got in the papers . . . I mean, if it's going to make things awkward for you, being here, if you feels you can't take it on now—'

'Don't say any more,' Vivienne interrupted. 'This isn't about the Averys, or your friends, or me, it's about you and your children, and that's the way we're going to keep it.'

Sharon's misery wasn't retreating. 'But it can't be very nice for you hearing people talk the way they did just now.'

'I'm a big girl, I can handle it. Anyway, I'm sure it won't happen again, once you've reminded them that I know Miles.'

'Probably not, and I will tell them, I just want you to know that if you decide you don't . . .'

'Enough,' Vivienne chided gently. 'Come on, let's go and sit down again.'

Sharon held back. 'You came to the funeral, didn't you?' she said, when Vivienne turned to her curiously. 'With Mr Avery?'

Vivienne nodded.

'I was a bit out of it at the time, so I don't remember much. They told me after that you was there, and how Mr Avery . . .' She swallowed and lowered her eyes in embarrassment. 'Made a bit of a fool of myself, didn't I? Frightened me poor kids as well.'

'You certainly didn't make a fool of yourself,' Vivienne told her warmly. 'You'd just lost your husband . . .'

'Yeah, but trying to chuck meself in a grave. Fat lot of good I'd have been to me kids if I'd managed it.'

Vivienne touched a hand to her papery soft cheek. 'I'm really sorry you're having to go through this,' she said gently, unable to imagine how worried and afraid the poor girl must be.

Sharon shrugged. 'Other people goes through much worse and manages to survive,' she said, and straightening her wig again she led the way back to the others.

'Right, where were we?' Vivienne said, as she sat down. 'Ah, I know, I was about to ask if you've come up with a venue for the auction yet?'

'Oh yeah, that's all taken care of,' Stella replied, tearing her maternal gaze from Sharon. 'Lady Blake's letting us use the big barn at her horse refuge. She's done auctions there before, so this won't be the first.'

Vivienne's heart turned over.

'My sister-in-law, Laura, is Lady Blake's housekeeper,' Stella was saying, 'that's who we got to ring Mr Avery for your number.'

At the mention of Miles Vivienne felt a current of embarrassment pass around the group. Obviously the connection was finally being made.

'Lady Blake's in Australia at the minute with Sir Richard,' Stella rattled on, 'but she told Laura she's got to open up the cider press for you to use while you're here. Or you can stay in the big house if you like, she said, but it's all closed up and under sheets at present, till they comes back.'

'That's very generous,' Vivienne murmured, wondering how she could refuse the offer, whilst already knowing she couldn't, because where else were they going to find such a perfect venue? And even if they could, did she really want to admit that she was turning down Susie and Richard's offer because their estate, and the horse refuge, were in the next valley to Moorlands?

'I think I'll just have to go with it for now,' she told Alice later on the phone, while attempting to keep up with Stella's Subaru which was careering through the country lanes like a souped-up pinball. 'It's only until Wednesday, provided all goes to plan.'

'But you have to go back.'

'By which time everything could have changed again. And if it hasn't, well, I guess I'll have to cross that bridge when I come to it.'

'OK. So how did you get on with Stella? Isn't she a scream?'

'Priceless. So are the others, actually. Sharon came. They're all completely blown away by Theo's offer to get involved.'

'We knew they would be. How is Sharon?'

'On the face of it she seems to be doing quite well. Her spirits are up, and by the time the meeting was over she had some colour in her cheeks, mainly thanks to a couple of firemen who dropped in to say hello. They're a raucous bunch of ladies, there's no doubt about that, and the men were lapping it up.'

'Sounds like you're going to have quite an event on your hands.'

'Tell me about it. Anyway, back to you, how did the cast meeting go today?'

'Before we get into that, I think I'd better tell you something I just heard on *PM*.'

Immediately Vivienne's insides started to tighten.

'The reporter who did the article in today's *Mail* was

being interviewed, and she said that since she wrote her piece the police have confirmed that they've . . .'

Vivienne frowned as she stopped. 'Alice?' she prompted.

There was only silence from the other end.

'Alice? Are you there?'

Still nothing.

'For God's sake,' Vivienne seethed. 'This is so not the time to lose a signal.'

As Justine James pulled up outside Miles's Kensington home she was no longer quite so focused on how appealing she might look in her loosely laced blue bustier beneath a shimmering black shirt, as she was on the interview she'd heard whilst driving over. Since it had been on Radio 4, she knew it was safe to assume that Miles had heard it too, so she might as well brace herself now for the explosion that was probably already under way.

Taking her small suitcase from the boot, she double-clicked the remote to lock the car and pushed open the black iron gate to his pocket-sized front garden. The front door was slightly ajar, so presuming he'd left it open for her she stepped inside and put her bag down on the marble-tiled floor. She was on the point of calling out to let him know she'd arrived when she heard him shouting, 'You don't understand. I have to speak to her . . . Yes, I heard what you said . . . I'm sorry, I know it's not your fault. Oh, for God's sake,' and she flinched as he banged the receiver down and came storming out of his study.

'Hi,' she said cheerfully. 'Bad time?'

Ignoring her, he turned down the hall towards the kitchen.

'Miles, for heaven's sake, what difference does it make?' she implored, going after him. 'It was bound to come out . . .'

He looked up, pale with anger. 'How did the *Mail* find out the police had spoken to Vivienne?' he demanded.

Shocked, Justine shrank from the accusation in his eyes. 'For God's sake Miles, so the police have questioned Vivienne Kane and Colleen Peterson found out. She's a journalist. It's her job . . .'

'Why are you defending her?'

'I'm not. I'm just pointing out what you already know, that the press is bound to be all over this because of who you are.'

'So this morning we have Colleen Peterson running a ludicrously ill-informed spread in the *Mail,* and now this evening we have the same damned woman being interviewed on the BBC like she's some goddamned expert on the case, telling the world that Vivienne's a part of the investigation . . .'

'Miles, try to be rational. Everyone knew about you and Vivienne when you were together, and why you broke up, so it stands to reason someone's going to call the police to ask if they've spoken to her.'

'Was it you?'

Her face flushed with anger. 'I don't give my stories away to other reporters, *or* other papers,' she retorted, 'and I sure as hell don't do their donkey work for them either.'

'But you have called the police to find out?'

'You asked me to work with you on this, so yes, of course I contacted the police. You must have known I would, so don't give me a hard time over it now.'

Seeming grudgingly to accept that, he turned and tugged open an overhead cupboard. 'I've been thinking,' he said, taking out a full bottle of Scotch, 'I'm not so sure it's a good idea for you to get involved in this.'

Her eyes rounded with alarm. He couldn't back out now, she'd staked virtually everything on it. 'Miles, the Critch is going to take you to the cleaners, given half a chance . . .'

'The *Mail*'s doing it for him.'

'Which is not what he wants. Christ, he hates them almost as much as he hates you, so no way does he want them walking off with your head on a platter.'

'Justine . . .'

'You did the right thing in asking for my help,' she persisted, 'and here's why. Between us we can feed the real story to the *Mail*, you know, everything that's happening with the search and what went on during the time leading up to it, whilst we give the Critch all the dirt he can deal with, and let him bury himself in it.'

He was shaking his head. 'This isn't a time to play games.'

'It's not games, it's a strategy,' she cried. Seeing he was about to protest again, she cut him off with, 'I thought you were trying to protect Kelsey, so please tell me how you're going to do that if you've got no one working with you.'

Though his face remained pale, as he glanced at her she could see she was starting to get through.

'Have you spoken to Kelsey?' she asked.

'She won't have heard about *PM*.'

'Yet. How did she take the spread in the *Mail*? Has she seen it?'

'I don't think so. She's back at school now, so I've only spoken to her briefly today. She didn't mention it.'

'Whatever, you have to try and gain control of this,' she pressed. 'Don't let scum like the Critch have a field day . . .'

'Colleen Peterson's on the *Mail*,' he reminded her.

'Yes, and she hasn't said anything that isn't true. OK, you might not like Vivienne's name being out there and attached to yours right now, but you knew very well it was going to happen. It had to.'

He nodded gravely, and seemed almost to withdraw into his thoughts as he said, 'Where the hell is she? She's not answering her mobile. Kayla says she's out of town, not due back until Thursday.'

'Maybe she doesn't want to speak to you.'

His eyes immediately sharpened. 'Do you want a drink?' he said sourly.

'Since you ask so nicely, I'll have one of those on the rocks.'

He began breaking ice into the glasses, then suddenly looked up. 'How did you get in?' he demanded.

Her freshly plucked eyebrows made a slow rise. 'The door was open,' she informed him, 'and it's Monday evening, which, I'm still hoping, means we're driving to Devon.'

After fixing her with a slightly less virulent look he thrust a glass at her, and picked up the phone to try Vivienne's mobile again. 'Damn!' he muttered, cutting the line as he was diverted through to voicemail. 'I need to speak to her.'

Justine watched him snatch up his glass and down the

Scotch in one go, before pouring another. 'I don't understand what you're getting so worked up about,' she said, perching on one of the bar stools. 'It's not as though anyone's accused her of anything, or that it's going to come as any great shock to the world to find out your friends and neighbours are being questioned. At the risk of sounding like a plod, it's routine.'

His eyes flashed again. 'We both know what's happening here,' he snapped. 'Colleen Peterson is setting up a story for the *Mail* that she's going to make run and run, based on nothing more than fragments of fact held together by salacious speculation and crass innuendo. Hell, you know how it works, you've done it often enough yourself. It sells papers, and that's what it's all about, isn't it? Fuck the truth, it's got no place on the bottom line.'

Her expression was sardonic, but she wasn't going to remind him of his own days on the redtops, or point out what a salutary experience it was being on the receiving end. Instead she said, 'I have a question for you. Try not to bite my head off, but why are you so concerned about Vivienne over this mild exposé, and not about the effect it might be having on Jacqueline?'

He stiffened, as his eyes came angrily to hers. 'In case it's slipped your memory,' he said tightly, 'I have no idea how to get hold of Jacqueline.'

'But you're worried about how this might be going down with her,' she insisted. 'I mean, if she's heard the news, which she might well have.'

'I'd have thought it went without saying that I'm concerned about her,' he snarled.

She smiled and shrugged. 'Sorry. It just wasn't looking that way.'

His eyes stayed on hers. 'What are you driving at, Justine?' His voice was dangerously low.

'Well, I'm just wondering,' she began tentatively. 'Are you sure you don't know where Jacqueline is?' she blurted courageously.

His glass hit the counter top so hard it was a miracle it didn't break. 'You know the way out,' he told her furiously.

She didn't move. 'What are you so afraid of, Miles?' she

challenged. 'OK, I know this is a tough time, and you're obviously at your wits' end, but the way you're behaving—' She stopped suddenly.

'Go on,' he prompted. 'The way I'm behaving . . .'

'Well, I'm sorry, but I can't help thinking you're hiding something. So I'm asking – are you?'

There was such a horrible silence then that she started to remember, for the first time in years, what it was to feel real fear in front of this man. Then, quite suddenly, it was as though she'd just been cut free from a noose. His temper deflated and he picked up his empty glass. 'As it happens, I'm not,' he said, swirling the melting ice, 'unless you think wanting to keep my private life just that, is hiding something.'

Her eyes went to the phone as it rang.

Miles picked it up, and hearing the voice at the other end he immediately turned away. 'Thank God,' he said quietly. 'I've been trying to get hold of you. Have you heard the news?'

Justine couldn't hear the reply, but she didn't need to to know who was calling. It was evident not only from his words, but from the softness of his tone as he spoke them.

She watched him walk into the conservatory and close the door behind him. Just these past few minutes had shown her that getting her old friend Colleen Peterson to run a story in the *Mail*, then drop Vivienne's name into the five o'clock bulletin, had been the right call. She couldn't put anything in her own name right now, but if everything went to plan this story was going to earn her a first-class ticket out of Critch hell and onto the *Mail*, because that was the deal she and Colleen had struck with the *Mail's* editor this past weekend.

She didn't like to think of it as a betrayal of Miles; after all, she'd more or less told him five minutes ago that it was what she was intending to do, and no way would she file anything to anyone that wasn't true. No, this was more a saving of her own skin, because if she'd learned anything during her years as a journalist, it was to take care of herself first, and never to trust an editor. Not even Miles. And if he thought he was going to pull out of their agreement now, then he needed to think again, because she was going nowhere until she'd found out for certain if that child really did exist – and if it did, what part was it playing in Jacqueline Avery's disappearance?

Chapter Seven

'No, I didn't hear the news myself,' Vivienne was saying into the phone. 'I just called Alice at the office and she told me. She said you were trying to reach me.'

'I was,' Miles confirmed. 'Where are you?'

She looked around the converted cider press that Susie Blake's housekeeper had unlocked for her a few minutes ago. Quaint and cosy, it consisted of no more than a small kitchen-cum-sitting room, and a staircase leading to a vaulted mezzanine bedroom with en suite bath. 'I'm out of town seeing new clients,' she answered briefly.

There was a pause before he said, 'I'm sorry this is happening. Your name shouldn't have been dragged into it.'

As aware as he was of what had happened the last time their names had been linked in the press, she tried to downplay it by saying, 'It was bound to happen, and after today there shouldn't be any reason to mention me again.'

With no little irony he said, 'They don't need reasons, the past is enough. Has anyone tried to contact you?'

'From the press? Apparently Kayla's fielded a few calls, and my email's looking pretty full, but don't worry, I'll go the no-comment route. I take it there's been no word from Jacqueline?'

'No.' He paused. 'It's looking as though she didn't get on the train.'

Vivienne's heart gave an unsteady beat, even though she'd already heard the rumour. 'So she could still be in Devon?'

'Possibly.' Again he paused. 'A lot of money's gone from one of our joint accounts.'

She frowned. 'What are you reading into that?'

'It was withdrawn about a moment before she left, so it doesn't seem as though her decision to go was impulsive, and if she's using cash, I can only presume it's because she doesn't want to be traced.'

Able to picture the strain on his face, she said, 'Are the police actively looking for her now, or just making enquiries?'

'I'm not sure. The missing money won't encourage them to set up a search. She's an adult. She has the right to disappear, if that's what she wants.'

But not to do this to you, she wanted to say. 'How's Kelsey?' she asked.

'Getting more worried by the day. I don't know if talking to her headmistress will help, or just make things worse.' He sighed wearily. 'I dread to think of the long-term effects this is going to have on her, as if she hasn't suffered enough already. She needs some kind of stability in her life.'

'She has it with you,' Vivienne reminded him gently. 'You're there for her, and that's all that matters.'

'I wish it was, but seeing the way . . . This is nothing short of a nightmare for her. How can it be anything else? Her mother's walked out on her again, and she doesn't know whether to feel afraid of her coming back after what happened the last time, or if she should want it as much as she seems to. She's all over the damned place. And what's going to happen if Jacqueline does decide to show up, which she presumably will, at some point? Do we carry on with the same farce we've been living for the past fifteen years? Pretending Sam's going to turn up at any moment. Maintaining a united front so both Mummy and Daddy will be there when he knocks on the door? Shopping for all the latest gadgetry and fashions a boy could want, so she can show him *when he comes back* that she's never forgotten him? It's got to end. Somehow, someone has to find a way of making her understand that she deserves a life too. For Christ's sake, we all do.'

'Especially Kelsey,' Vivienne murmured – and Rufus, she added in her mind, her heart stirring with the need to unite him with his father. 'It'll be all right,' she told him, wishing she felt as confident as she sounded. 'Somehow, we'll work this out.'

There was a long silence before he said, 'You don't know how much it means to hear you say "we", but I can't involve you in this.'

'The press have already done that.'

'You don't need to speak to them, and as long as we don't see one another there'll be no reason for the police to be in touch with you again, either. I just hope to God she's not . . .' He stopped, and she knew why. Words were almost impossible when there was such a cruel mix of emotions in his heart.

'I should go now,' she said softly. 'Please don't worry about me, I'll be fine. So will Jacqueline. Just focus on Kelsey.'

As she put the phone down her eyes drifted to the small terrace outside the kitchenette, where a regal-looking peacock was gazing quizzically in through the open door. It seemed to be asking what right she had to be there, and if she had to give an answer, it might be to ask the same thing. She was too close to Moorlands, too far into Jacqueline's world to feel either secure or right about being there, particularly if Jacqueline was still in Devon.

Getting up from the table where she'd dropped her laptop and BlackBerry on arriving, she went outside and watched the peacock. It strutted off past the pond that was scooped like an oyster shell into the lawn beyond the small terrace before soaring, honking and fluttering, into the branches of a nearby oak. She looked around, feeling the cool dampness of the air, and cocooned by nature in a way that was vaguely unnerving. It was as though she was being watched by a hundred hidden eyes. The country sounds were sibilant and persistent, scratching, rustling, croaking, and blending with the gush of the stream that bubbled and raced alongside the press. A sharp cracking noise made her turn quickly, but there was nothing to be seen amongst the mossy barks and golden branches of the surrounding trees.

With a growing anxiety she started across the stone bridge that linked the terrace to a gravelled clearing where her car was parked, and currently a family of pheasants was pecking about in the dirt. She was intending to fetch her overnight bag, but instead she found herself walking on through the small wood that cloistered the press, taking long, firm strides as though there were some purpose to where she was going.

The big old manor house, with its pale grey stone walls and elegantly turreted towers, was nestling grandly, emptily, in the weakening sunlight as she passed, while down at the gates the Lodge, home to Laura the housekeeper and her gamekeeper husband, would only become visible once the foliage had fallen.

Taking a path she'd occasionally followed with Susie, or Miles, she walked on to the stables, digging her hands into the pockets of her jeans and hunching her shoulders. She was heading towards an open field that sloped steeply down from the woods where local landowners often held their shoots, though she knew Miles had given up his gun some time ago after watching too many birds being shot for sport and then buried because they were never going to be eaten.

As she strode up over the field a mix of defiance and fear was powering her legs, and making her strangely lightheaded. It wasn't that she really believed Jacqueline was somewhere close by, in fact it was absurd even to think it, yet she was aware that this gesture was somehow challenging, as though she needed to prove to herself, or anyone watching, that she wasn't intimidated, or at all afraid.

When finally she reached the gate that connected the Blakes' land to the game-infested territory beyond, she stopped and leaned against it, taking a moment to catch her breath before going through. When she did she turned away from the woods that climbed on up to the moor, and went to stand on the crest that marked the boundary between Moorlands and the Blakes' much more sizeable estate. As she gazed down into the spectacular valley she felt her heart filling with its beauty. The evening sun was burnishing the fields in shades of amber and gold, glinting and sparkling, and spreading like honey down to the house itself. A blood-red creeper clung to the walls and framed the windows, while the grey tiled roof and rising chimneys shone like molten alloy. She remembered the times she and Miles had stood on this very spot gazing down at the home they were making their own – how close they had become during that one short year. Being in touch with him now she was aware of that closeness reasserting itself, as though no time had passed at all.

She looked on to the woods that dipped away from the far side of Moorlands' lake, spreading out like an enormous hand to the distant road beyond. They were quite separate from the woods behind her, where the shoots took place and the gamekeepers kept an avid lookout for intruders, though these woods too straggled over to the hill behind Moorlands to form its boundary with the moor.

As she gazed down at the house again she was trying to imagine Jacqueline inside, or crossing the courtyard to stroll down to the lake. Though it had been her home for the past two years, and for a while before she'd gone to the States, Vivienne knew she'd never had any fondness for it, so perhaps that was why her presence, at least in Vivienne's mind, seemed strangely ephemeral, almost ghostlike. Yet at the same time it was as though her disappearance had created an energy that was stealing through the trees like a wind, and drifting down from the moor like a mist. Even the scent of grass and earth seemed to be hers, while the sough of the air was the plaintive cry of a woman searching for her lost child; the anguished beat of a broken heart.

With a shiver of pity she turned around and began wandering back the way she'd come. As tormented and unpredictable as Jacqueline was, she surely had to know how much distress her actions were causing her husband and daughter. How could she not care? More to the point, how could she allow a child who'd vanished fifteen years ago to take precedence over one who was still there?

By the time Vivienne had collected her bag from the car and returned to the press the light had almost gone, and the feeling of being alone, and yet not, was creeping in on her again. Closing and locking the door behind her, she walked around the room pulling the curtains, then put a match to the fire the housekeeper had set. For a while she stood watching the flames lick up through the tangle of twigs and logs, then after opening a bottle of wine she'd found in the fridge she went to check her BlackBerry.

Amongst the emails asking for interviews or comments about Jacqueline she found half a dozen or so expressing interest in the auction, which she dealt with right away. Next she listened to a voice message from Kayla letting her know that a Devon-based choreographer was making contact with the firemen to start work on their auction routine, then she opened a text saying:

`I know you know where she is.`

As her insides jarred, the phone rang, making her start.

'Mum,' she said, clicking on quickly. 'Is everything OK?'

'Of course. I heard the news while I was driving back from town, so I'm wondering how you are. I take it you heard it too.'

'Actually I didn't, but I know what was said. How's Rufus?'

'Being made a fuss of by his aunt and uncle. Do you—'

Vivienne broke in sharply. 'Are they listening to this call?' she demanded, knowing how her sister would gloat if she was.

'No, they're in the sitting room. So what are you going to do about having your name dragged into it?'

Feeling more annoyed than she should, she said, 'There's not much I can do, is there?' Then, without thinking, 'I received another text just now, from the person who seems to think I know where Jacqueline is.'

Linda's tone was clipped as she said, 'But that's absurd. I think you should tell the police.'

'I'm considering it.'

'Do you think Jacqueline herself could be sending them?'

'It has crossed my mind, but why would she? What does it achieve?'

'That's asking me to think the way she does, and I'm not sure any of us can do that. Anyway, if it's not her, who the heck else could it be, apart from that dreadful Justine James?'

'Actually, I'm pretty certain that's who it is. She's trying to conjure up her own exclusive, meaning that if I contact the police she'll be able to go to print with the messages, as though they've been leaked by an insider.'

'She can't get away with that,' Linda declared hotly.

'You'd be amazed what the press gets away with when someone's fighting shy of publicity. Look at the things some of them are saying about Miles, slanting their coverage to cast him in the worst possible light, as if he didn't get enough of that when Sam went missing.'

'Well, maybe he should speak up for himself and tell them that if anyone's done away with her, she'll have done it to herself.'

Vivienne's eyes closed. 'Mum, don't say things like that.'

'You might not want to hear it, but you can't deny that a part of you wishes she'd put herself—'

'For God's sake,' Vivienne broke in angrily, 'don't you realise how it could sound to someone else if they heard you talking like that?'

'All right, be as sympathetic as you like towards the woman, just please excuse me if I put my grandson first and worry about him instead.'

'Don't even try to suggest he doesn't come first for me,' Vivienne shot back, 'because you know it's not true.'

'Of course I do, I'm just saying that it's as though all our lives are in limbo while Jacqueline goes about the world in her tragic, wounded-heart way. Something's got to be done to put an end to it, because Rufus has as much right to his father as little Sam did, and the only person stopping that from happening is Jacqueline.'

'Is *me*,' Vivienne corrected. 'I'm the one who took the decision not to tell Miles, and now we've got to make sure that no one from the press gets wind of Rufus's existence, because I don't want him finding out that way.' She shuddered. 'And I sure as heck don't want Jacqueline or Kelsey finding out like that either.'

'Sir, there's something here I think you're going to find extremely interesting,' DC Joy announced as she walked in through the open door of Sadler's office.

'And what would that be, Detective Constable?' he responded, continuing to read the computer screen in front of him. 'Shit, how many unsolved crimes can we be expected to declare when the investigations are ongoing—'

Cutting across the rant, she said, 'I've been doing a bit more digging around on the Avery case, sir, and, wait for this, it turns out that Vivienne Kane has a little boy of fifteen months who lives in Berkshire with her mother. No idea who the father is yet, but given the timescale I reckon it has to be Miles Avery.'

Sadler's head came slowly round to look at her.

'Since neither he nor Vivienne Kane mentioned the child when we interviewed them,' she went on, 'they're obviously deliberately keeping his existence a secret. Which would make sense when you consider how devastating it might be for Mrs Avery to find out her husband has another son.'

Sadler put out a hand for the file she'd brought with her, and started to read.

Joy waited quietly.

'I take it you realise what this gives us, if Avery is the father?' Sadler said darkly when he'd finished.

She nodded. 'A very good motive for murder, sir.'

His small eyes bored into hers. 'Pull the child's birth certificate,' he said. 'It should give us the confirmation of parentage we need.'

Taking the file back, she said, 'There's also the chance, sir, that Mrs Avery found out about the boy, and if that is the case, he could be at risk.'

Sadler inhaled deeply as he contemplated her words. 'How much contact have Avery and Kane had in the last two years?' he asked.

'None, according to them, until Mrs Avery disappeared, when he called to give Vivienne the news. Or, so he claims, to find out if his wife had been in touch.'

Sadler was still looking pensive. 'If we're to take him at his word, then he waited three weeks before alerting Vivienne Kane to the fact his wife was missing. That doesn't sound to me like someone who's worried about the safety of his son.'

'No, sir.'

'Which could mean he *knows* his wife doesn't pose a threat.'

'Or that he doesn't know he has a son.'

Sadler's eyes rose to Joy's. 'Get the birth certificate,' he said. 'If the boy does turn out to be Miles Avery's, we'll have sufficient grounds to order an official search for our missing person.'

After she'd gone Sadler closed the door behind her, wanting some peace for the next few minutes while he reviewed what they had so far. All they knew for certain was that a woman had disappeared, apparently without trace, either because someone had committed a serious crime, or she'd lost her memory, or she'd been abducted, or because she'd chosen to go. The memory option was, for the moment, a non-starter, since there was no history of her blanking out as far as he knew, and even if she had, someone would have found her by now. The possibility of abduction wasn't swinging it for him either, simply because it bore none of the hallmarks. So why would she choose to go? The fact that she and her missing son shared a birthday soon wasn't floating his boat in any big way. What was she going to do? Light fifty-six candles and blow them out all by herself? Of course she could be planning to celebrate with another suicide attempt, but if she was, why disappear so long beforehand, and why withdraw all that money?

No, much more likely, as far as he was concerned, was that Miles Avery, either with or without Vivienne Kane, had removed the obstacle that was preventing him from being a father to his fifteen-month-old son. Which, in its way, brought him back to the money. Someone should have found out by now who'd actually made that withdrawal, because banks didn't hand over that amount of cash without asking for ID, especially not these days.

'All we've got so far, sir,' Joy told him when he went through to CID to enquire, 'is that the money was transferred from Jersey to a branch in Knightsbridge, and that it was a woman who picked it up. She signed herself Jacqueline Avery.'

'Was Jacqueline Avery actually in London that day?'

'I'll check, sir, but even if she was, we still won't know for certain if it was her, because it's not her regular branch, so chances are no one there would have recognised her.'

Sadler's eyes were piercing.

'She'd have had to produce some form of identity, of course,' Joy went on, 'but I think our best bet is to talk to whoever handed the money over and ask for a description.'

Sadler nodded agreement. 'Get hold of Vivienne Kane,' he said. 'I think we need to have another chat with her.'

A few minutes later Joy came to find Sadler in his office. 'Apparently, Vivienne Kane's here in Devon,' she informed him. 'I've got a number for her.'

Sadler glanced up in surprise.

'Her receptionist said she's involved in something with the Kenleigh WI.'

Sadler's eyebrows rose further up his forehead. 'Well, I guess that saves us a trip to London,' he muttered. 'But before we go any further I want confirmation on whether or not the boy is Avery's.'

Justine was sitting beside Miles in his BMW, quietly watching the countryside go by as they drove past Stonehenge, where a hardy clutch of tourists was gawping at the monument from the periphery fence. Since he'd had a little too much Scotch the night before, he'd sent her home, saying he didn't want to drive while over the limit, so he was delaying his departure for Devon until lunchtime the next day.

However, instead of returning to her apartment, she'd passed an uncomfortable night in her car, determined not to let him take off without her, though he'd made no attempt to do so. And when he'd come out of the house, just after midday, to her relief he hadn't raised an objection to her joining him.

Now, as one of her three mobiles bleeped with a message, he said, 'I doubt there's much food in and it's the housekeeper's day off, so we can either stop at a supermarket, or go to a pub.'

'The pub option sounds good to me,' she responded, looking down at the text that had just come in. Her eyes were widening in amazement, and no small satisfaction, for it would appear that her little cat-and-mouse game with Vivienne Kane was paying off.

```
I know it's you sending the texts, Justine, so
let's meet. VK
```

Well, that was unexpected, she was thinking as she began composing a message back. She'd felt certain Vivienne would show the texts to the police at some point, which would then allow her, Justine, to report them, verbatim, in a sensational exclusive. After all, new angles were often hard to find in an ongoing investigation, so sometimes it was necessary to help them along. However, in this instance it seemed she might have hit on more than she'd bargained for, because if Vivienne was finally willing to meet it was quite possible, even probable, that she had something to tell.

Chapter Eight

Vivienne was sitting with her legs dangling over the edge of the stage of Kenleigh parish hall. In front of her, in haphazard rows spread out over a well-trodden pineboard floor, was a sea of foaming white hair, with the occasional bronze dash or shiny black cap bobbing up like seaweed amongst it. The turnout was impressive, considering it was a working day. There were at least thirty women present, some, she'd learned, from the neighbouring villages of Kenn and Kenton, but most were from Kenleigh.

For the moment she was listening to Stella – the branch chairperson – who was seated at her formal table reading out a list of upcoming events: various coffee mornings, a Christmas floral art class, a shopping trip to Bath, skittles, a quiz night on Friday. In fact, everything she might have expected from a meeting of the WI, whose gathered members were making notes in their diaries and asking the odd jovial question.

'All right, that's our normal business about done with,' Stella finally declared, closing up her file, 'so I'll hand over to Vivienne now. You've all got a copy of her plans for the auction, have you? They were on the table where you came in.'

Several hands rose in the air, waving their copies, and as no one claimed not to have one Vivienne opened up the laptop on the stage next to her, ready to begin. 'OK,' she said, tucking her hands in under her knees, 'I guess I should start by telling you that Sharon and I had a long chat this morning,' she threw a smile in Sharon's direction, 'and the sum we're now aiming to raise is much larger than you were probably expecting.'

A few eyebrows went up, and some of the older women exchanged eloquent glances. 'So how much are we talking about?' Eileen wanted to know.

'We're going to set a target of thirty thousand pounds.'

There was a moment's stunned silence before they all began muttering in amazement, and no little excitement.

'How on earth are we ever going to raise that much?' someone near the back called out. 'It's more than my old man earns in a year.'

'The answer's in the notes I've given you,' Vivienne told her, 'but for those of you who haven't had a chance to read them yet, we're going to make the auction a national event. It's the obvious way to go, and thanks to Theo Kenwood-South and the Devonshire firemen, plus Sharon's own profile as Keith Goss's wife, we shouldn't have any trouble getting the necessary publicity. In fact, I've already received quite a lot of interest, but what we're really after is one of the networks to televise it.'

'Telly? What do you reckon about that then?' someone near the front clucked delightedly. 'We'm all going to end up being famous.'

Vivienne laughed. 'I should also make it clear,' she went on, 'that the money's not all for Sharon. She isn't comfortable with being the sole focus, so if we do reach our target, fifty per cent of it will go to someone with a similar need.'

'That's a bloody good idea,' Mary stated approvingly. 'Yeah, I likes the sound of that.'

'Me too,' the woman next to her agreed.

'So how's the auction going to work then?' Eileen demanded.

'Much the same way as the slave auctions you're familiar with,' Vivienne answered. 'So far we have ten firemen offering their amateur skills, such as gardening, weight-lifting, DIY – it's all listed in your notes. However, instead of just standing next to the podium, or sitting in the audience, they're going to perform a dance routine, which a choreographer's devising for them.'

'Blimey, what a scream,' Mary chuckled gleefully. 'I can see 'em now in their helmets and boots.'

'I hope they'm going to be strip routines,' Eileen cackled. 'That'll get the bids up all right.'

'What about Theo Kenwood-South?' Gail demanded. 'What's he going to be doing?'

'Basically the same as the firemen,' Vivienne replied. 'He'll be the star turn, obviously.'

'When's he coming down here?'

'I'm hoping to hear later today.'

'It says here that one of the firemen's a bit handy at plumbing,' Mary read out.

'That'll suit you,' Eileen crowed, 'being a bit of an old boiler.'

Everyone burst out laughing, including Mary.

'The weight-lifter's offering some personal training,' Gail informed them.

'Oh blimey, somersaults in the bedroom, I'm coming over all hot now,' someone nearby claimed, fanning herself down with the proposal.

'You'm never going to be able to afford any of 'em,' Stella told her. 'Not if we'm going to be bidding against women all over the country.'

'Still can't see how we'm going to raise as much as thirty grand for a bit of plumbing and personal training,' Eileen said doubtfully.

'Don't forget the swimming,' Lizzie shouted. 'Imagine that, being close to Theo K-S in his dear little trunks and goggles. I can feel meself drowning already.'

As they all laughed Vivienne said, 'Provided we can get the right TV interest, and link up with a registered charity, it'll be easier to raise the money than you think.'

'You haven't told 'em yet what we're all going to be doing,' Stella reminded her.

As all eyes came to her, Vivienne wanted to hug the lot of them for how eager they seemed to help. 'If we can pull it off nationally,' she said, 'and I really think we can, then most of the bids are probably going to come in by phone, so we'll be needing you to man the lines. I have to talk to BT about that yet, but I'm hoping they'll donate their services and equipment for free. As it's in a good cause, and there's the chance of a lot of publicity, there's a strong chance they will.'

'Oh Sharon,' Mary said excitedly. 'You're going to end up with everything you need, my old love. Wouldn't even be surprised if we ended up with a donor.'

Sharon's face was pale as she rose to her feet. 'Sorry, but I have to go,' she said shakily. 'I've got to pick the kids up from school.'

Realising something had upset her, Vivienne quickly slid down from the stage and walked out to the lobby with her.

'Sorry, I know I'm being really daft,' Sharon said, dabbing her eyes, 'but it's bringing it all home a bit.'

'Of course it is,' Vivienne said, hugging her.

'And all that money. I know we talked about it this morning, but I've been thinking about it since . . . I don't know if I can go on telly asking for all that much.'

'You'll be going on to help promote the auction,' Vivienne reminded her. 'And Theo's going to be right there with you. And Stella. In fact, knowing her she'll do all the talking, and remember, we're aiming that high so that we can pass the extra funds on to someone else in your position.'

'Maybe they should get it first. It wouldn't seem quite so selfish then, would it?'

'You're not being selfish,' Vivienne assured her. 'You're simply allowing your friends to help you, and in return, you're going to help someone else.'

Sharon nodded uncertainly, then glanced at her watch. 'I ought to be going,' she said, 'but before I do . . . I know it's none of my business, but I heard the news last night . . .'

'You mean about the police questioning me?'

She nodded. 'It's just that with the Blakes' place being over by Moorlands, and all the press being there . . . Well, if you want to come and stay with me. The kids could always sleep . . .'

'Honestly, I'm fine where I am,' Vivienne assured her. 'Remember, dealing with the press is part of my job.'

Sharon nodded uncertainly.

'I really appreciate the offer,' Vivienne said earnestly. 'Thank you. Now you'd better go, or you'll be late. And if there's anything you need, just give me a call.'

An hour or so later, after an extremely rowdy but nonetheless satisfactory brainstorming session with the WI ladies, who'd readily offered the services of spouses, sons and brothers should they be required, Vivienne left them to it and carried her laptop and briefcase out to the car. Once in the driver's seat she switched on her BlackBerry and her heart sank to see so many emails, texts and voice messages. Much as she wished that they were all about the auction, she knew very well they weren't.

Ignoring them all for the moment, she got back on the road to Haytor before giving a voice command to connect to Kayla.

'Hey, boss,' Kayla cried on hearing her, 'did you get my message? I'm being inundated here by journos wanting to talk to you about Jacqueline. Don't worry, I haven't told anyone where you are, except I'm afraid I had to tell the police.'

Vivienne stiffened.

'They called here earlier, asking to speak to you, so not wanting to end up on the wrong side of the law or anything, I thought I'd better tell them how to get hold of you.'

'Did they say what it was about?' Vivienne asked, as she joined a dual carriageway to start heading south.

'Not really, but I suppose it has to be Jacqueline.'

'Do they want me to call back?'

'If they do, they didn't leave a number, which means it's probably not urgent, so if I were you I'd wait for them to get in touch again.'

'Thank you for your advice. Is Alice there?'

'Yep. She's just come in, but she's on the other line already, do you want to wait?'

'No, get her to call me when she's free.'

As she rang off Vivienne's expression quickly changed to one of concern, not only about why the police wanted to talk to her again, but because of the ludicrous problem she was now facing. Somehow she had to keep herself out of the public eye, while trying to push Sharon and the auction into it.

'Obviously it'll be easier once Theo's around,' she said to Alice when they finally connected, 'any word from him yet?'

'Absolutely. He can be on board from next Wednesday, apparently.'

'As soon as that? Excellent, but for how long?'

'Until the auction's over.'

'He knows we haven't fixed a date yet?'

'He says he'll fit everything around it.'

Vivienne laughed. 'Well, we can't ask for more than that,' she declared happily. 'However, I'm still going to need some extra help organising photographers and press calls etc., so I'll give Pete a call to find out what kind of time frame he's working to with *Belle Amie*. How are things going your end?'

For the next ten minutes they were engrossed in discussing Alice's various strategies for the movie, until eventually the subject returned to the auction.

'We need to move ahead fairly quickly now,' Vivienne said, indicating to take a left fork that led into a tangled network of country lanes. 'Sharon's seeing the specialist next week, and you only have to look at her to see the strain she's under. Putting some money in her account will help alleviate at least one burden of stress.'

'So what sort of time frame are you looking at?'

'I'm meeting with a local auctioneer before I leave here tomorrow, so he'll be able to give me an idea of how long it'll take to set up, but I'm hoping we'll be ready to go under the hammer by the middle of November.'

'So about three weeks from now? You'll have your work cut out.'

'Which is why I need the extra help. Thankfully the choreographer's taking care of the firemen, and as soon as Theo's around he can help prepare Stella and Sharon for the cameras.'

'He'll enjoy that,' Alice commented cheerfully. 'So how was it staying in the cider press last night?'

'Cosy. A bit lonely without Susie and Richard around, but it's going to work well as my HQ. The barn – or auction room, I should call it – is about five minutes away, at Susie's sanctuary, and I've got everything I need, landline, fax, printer, copier, video and DVD player, either right there in the press, or in Richard's office.'

'Sounds perfect. Any more calls from Miles?'

Vivienne's heart caught a beat. 'No, not today. No more anonymous texts either, before you ask, but I sent a return message to Justine James telling her I knew it was her texting me so maybe we should meet. And what do you know, ten minutes later I get a text back asking me to name the time and place and she'll be there. Signed JJ.'

'So you were right, it was her. What a bitch. Are you going to meet her?'

'No, of course not. But I might well mention the texts to the police as a form of harassment. Oh no, what's this, something's happening up ahead here.' Peering along the narrow road where the hedgerows and trees were beginning to merge into a greying dusk, she watched the tail lights of a car in front as the driver swung into an open gate, reversed, then came back to edge past Vivienne's Beetle. Right behind him was a plump woman in a tight-fitting wax jacket and muddy green boots.

'Is everything OK?' Vivienne asked, rolling down her window as the woman approached.

'Yeah, fine,' the woman answered in a broad country accent. 'It's just that me husband's running the heifers down from the top field any minute, so we've roped off all the driveways as far as the major's to make sure none of 'em takes a wrong turn. Where are you going?'

'Moor—' Vivienne cut the word off, stunned that it had almost come out. 'Uh South Dinley,' she said.

'Oh yeah, Richard and Susie's place. We've got 'em roped up at the moment, I'm afraid. Shouldn't be long though, but if you wants to go back and come down onto their land from the moor you can turn around where the other bloke just did.'

'Don't you just love that accent?' Alice's voice said in her ear.

'OK, thanks,' Vivienne said to the woman. 'I'll do that,' and winding up the window again she pulled forward to start making the turn.

'You're never driving up onto Dartmoor at night, alone,' Alice teased.

'No. I'm going to take the opportunity to go to the

Nobody Inn at Doddiscombsleigh, or Doddy as the locals call it. They do B & B, so I'll see if I can work out some kind of deal for the invited press. Anyway, where were we?'

'Can't remember, but I'm afraid I have to love you and leave you now. Angus has just turned up wanting a lift to the airport.'

'Where's he going?'

'Only over to Dublin for tonight and tomorrow. We'll talk again later.'

After ringing off Vivienne drove on through the rapidly darkening night, passing entrances to large estates where sprawling farmhouses and elegant homes were tucked away like secrets behind locked gates and dense prickly hedgerows. Eventually she connected with the road that led to the centuries-old inn which, if she remembered correctly, could boast over 200 brands of whisky, 700 of wine, and fifty different types of local cheeses. It was a pub she and Miles had often visited, usually for lunch on a Sunday when the roast was so scrumptious that people would come from miles around for the treat.

By the time she pulled up outside it was a little after five thirty. There weren't many other cars around, just an old Land Rover tucked away in a far corner, and an Audi estate which she parked alongside.

She found the lounge deserted, but a welcoming fire was crackling in the hearth, creating a warm, cosy glow that was reflected in the many pieces of brass and glossy black beams. A man in tweeds was in the adjacent bar, leaning against the counter chatting to the landlord, while either side of the electric fire in there two young couples were talking and laughing quietly amongst themselves, and barely even looked up as she came in.

After ordering herself a lager shandy she carried it to a corner table in the empty lounge, and took out her BlackBerry to start roughing out a workable agenda, so that she could approach the landlord with possible dates.

When the door opened a few minutes later she was so absorbed in what she was doing that she barely heard it. It was only when someone said her name that her head came up, and when she saw who it was her heartbeat almost slowed to a stop.

'Miles,' she whispered, getting to her feet. 'Miles, I . . .'

His dark eyes were reflecting her shock.

She started to speak, but the words dried in her throat. She'd dreamt so often of how it might be if she saw him again, what they might say, how overwhelming it might seem, and now it was happening, and it still felt like a dream.

His eyes were sweeping her face as though she were an apparition.

Realising she was shaking, she clenched her hands tightly as she said, 'I wasn't expecting . . . I mean . . .'

Neither of them was aware of the door opening, they only knew the emotions passing between them as he said, 'What are you doing here?'

'I'm seeing the WI.'

'Of course.' His smile was crooked, and amazed, and so wonderfully familiar that she could feel her heart swelling. 'This has been so hard,' he murmured.

'For me too.' She laughed as the words caught in her throat.

'Uh, excuse me,' a voice behind him said. 'Sorry to interrupt, but can I get anyone a drink?'

Miles turned round, and as Vivienne looked past him to see who'd spoken she blinked in confusion. Her eyes went back to Miles as her blood started to run cold. 'Is she with you?' she demanded. Then, without waiting for an answer, 'Yes, of course she is.'

'Vivienne, listen,' he said, making to grab her as she snatched up her BlackBerry.

'Don't!' she raged, pulling her arm away. 'I don't know what's going on here, but that you could have anything to do with that woman . . .'

'Charming,' Justine murmured.

'Vivienne,' Miles barked, 'will you just—'

'You might be willing to trust her, but I never will,' Vivienne seethed, and before he could stop her she was sweeping past him, only pausing at the door to say, 'Get her to tell you about the texts she's been sending me. Ask her what that's all about, and while you're at it, you might like to ask her if *she* knows where Jacqueline is.'

She was already in her car and starting the engine by the time he came out after her, but she was too angry to speak to him now, and backing dangerously across the car park she accelerated furiously off into the night, throwing up a hail of gravel behind her.

Justine was standing at the bar ordering drinks when Miles came back into the pub, looking both angry and worried as he tried to get Vivienne on her mobile. In the end, since she was evidently refusing to pick up, he called her office and started trying to bully information out of someone there.

To Justine's surprise the person at the other end must have caved in, because suddenly Miles was jotting down a number, and the next minute he was pressing it into his phone.

'Alice, it's Miles,' he said shortly. 'You have to tell me where Vivienne's staying . . . I know she's in Devon, I've just seen her . . . Alice, please listen. Something's happened. I need to know where she is . . . No, she's fine, I swear. I just have to . . . OK, if you must, call her first and tell her . . . Just tell her I have to see her.'

As he snapped his phone closed frustration was etched in every line of his face.

'You might as well have a drink while you're waiting,' Justine told him lightly.

His focus sharpened, and picking up one of the glasses the barman had just put down, he said, 'What did she mean about the texts you've been sending her, and knowing where Jacqueline is?'

Justine pulled a face.

'Don't play innocent, Justine. What the hell's going on?'

She shrugged. 'Come on, Miles, you know how it works.'

'How what works?'

'You try to provoke someone into saying or doing something . . .'

His eyes closed in despair. 'I knew I was a fool to get you involved in this.'

'Miles, I'd be covering it anyway!' she cried. 'And I'm on

your side, remember? You don't seriously think I'm going to do anything to jeopardise our friendship?'

'Sending texts to Vivienne goes a lot further than that,' he told her angrily.

She gave a sigh of frustration. 'Like it or not, you're big news,' she said crisply, 'and she's your ex, though judging by what I saw when I walked in . . .'

'You didn't see anything,' he growled. 'She's here working with the WI. It has nothing to do with me.'

'OK, I believe you, but she's still here, in Devon, and you're missing a wife, so tell me how I'm suddenly the guilty party here.'

Before he could answer his phone rang, and flipping it open he put it to his ear. 'Alice,' he said.

Justine watched him as he listened, his expression registering first confusion, then surprise. 'OK, thanks,' he said, and abruptly ended the call. 'I'm going after Vivienne,' he announced, throwing a ten-pound note on the bar.

'You can't just abandon me,' she protested. 'If you—' She stopped as his eyes suddenly glinted in a way she didn't much like.

'You still haven't told me what she meant about asking *you* where Jacqueline is,' he reminded her.

'I've no idea.'

His expression was darkening. 'If you know anything . . .'

'For God's sake, Miles, if I had that kind of information do you seriously think I'd keep it to myself?'

Since it hardly seemed likely, he let it go. After checking for his keys he was about to tell her to book herself into the pub for the night, when the arguments that would inevitably follow flashed before him. Having neither the time nor the inclination to get into it now, he told her to take a taxi to the house, and left.

Justine's eyes remained on the door long after it had closed behind him. She took another sip of her drink, and continued to reflect on the intriguing exchange she'd overheard as she'd come into the bar.

This has been so hard, he'd said to Vivienne. *For me too*, she'd replied.

Of course, they could simply have been expressing how

difficult they'd found the past two years, being apart from one another. On the other hand, they could just as easily have been referring to some kind of forced separation that they'd been enduring since his wife's mysterious disappearance.

Taking out one of her mobiles she put in a quick call to Colleen Peterson, the reporter she'd been working with on the *Mail*. 'The Berkshire address I texted you yesterday?' she said when Colleen answered. 'Have you sent a photographer over there yet?'

'Dan Figgis went earlier,' Colleen informed her. 'Apparently there's definitely a child inside, but so far he hasn't been able to get anything usable.'

'Is he still there?'

'Be serious, it's dark out in case you hadn't noticed. He's going back tomorrow. So, what's happening about the meet with Vivienne Kane?'

'I don't think it's going to happen,' Justine replied, 'but don't worry, you've got something much better coming your way.' Snapping closed the phone, she carried her drink to a table, knowing that even if Dan Figgis didn't manage to get a shot of the child she wasn't far off being ready to go to press with rumours of one, anyway.

'OK, Elaine,' DI Sadler was saying as he started out of CID, where momentum had stepped up since they'd received confirmation that Miles Avery was the father of Vivienne Kane's child, 'let's go pay Ms Kane a visit.'

Quickly grabbing her coat and mobile, DC Joy hurried after him. 'You're not going to call first?' she asked, catching him up in the corridor.

'I think a little surprise might serve us well,' he responded, digging into his pocket to make sure he had his keys.

Stepping aside for two uniformed officers to run past in answer to an emergency, Joy said, 'Will you let Avery know in advance about the official search for his wife?'

Sadler nodded as they continued out through custody. 'I'll speak to him before we brief Tactical Aid in the morning,' he said. 'They know we need divers and pilots?'

'DS Johns is arranging it.'

A few moments later they were getting into Sadler's Ford Focus.

'Do you know where the Blakes' place is exactly?' he asked, reversing out of the parking space and driving round to join the rush hour on Heavitree Road.

'More or less. It's kind of between Chudleigh and Haytor. Whatever, it's going to take us a while in all this.'

Sadler didn't disagree. Nor did he feel inclined to speak again until they were on the main road heading south from Exeter, when he said, 'Have you sorted out family liaison? There's a teenage daughter, remember?'

'I'll get right onto it, sir,' she replied, and opened up her mobile.

Chapter Nine

The rain was coming down in torrents, lashing the vaulted roof of the cider press and flooding the roiling stream outside. Vivienne was pacing the small room, waiting for the sound of Miles's car and wondering if she'd done the right thing in allowing Alice to tell him where she was.

Now that the initial shock of seeing Justine had worn off her anger had abated, though she still couldn't accept with any kind of equanimity the fact that he was even on speaking terms with the woman. Surely to God he'd accepted by now that she was behind the article that had brought Jacqueline back two years ago, and if he had she could only conclude that he either had some kind of blind spot where his venomous little protégée was concerned, or the wretched woman had something over him. And if that was the case, Vivienne damned well wanted to know what it was.

When at last the sound of tyres crunching gravel mingled with the storm she flung open the door, then turned back into the lamplit room to wait. A smoky yellow fire was gaining life in the wood burner, and the shadows on the walls were flickering and large. Deep inside she wanted to scream, for this was nothing like the kind of reunion she'd long envisaged. However, for Rufus's sake, she must put her own needs aside as she attempted to persuade Miles to cut all contact with Justine James. How she was going to do that without telling him about Rufus, she wasn't yet sure, she simply had to trust to the right words coming when she needed them.

As he appeared in the doorway, tall and filling the frame, her heart expanded with so much emotion that she had to force herself to look away. Now wasn't the time to give in to how much she still loved him.

She heard him close the door, and brought her eyes back to his face. As though it had a will of its own her body seemed to yearn towards him, but she didn't move, and nor did he.

'You're irrational where Justine's concerned, you know that don't you?' he said angrily.

Her eyes flashed with shock. 'I think you've just stolen my line,' she shot back. 'After what she did . . .'

'She's a journalist, for God's sake. You might not like some of the things she does to get a story, and frankly I don't either, but it's a cut-throat world out there.'

'Don't defend her to me. I know you've never believed she was behind the story that brought Jacqueline back from the States.'

'You're wrong, I know she was, but it was only a matter of time before our relationship was made public, so she took it upon herself to try and run it in a way that would do the least damage. She has no editorial control. That belongs to the Critch. She gave him the facts, and he spun them into a tale all his own.'

'For an intelligent man, Miles, you can be staggeringly naive at times. Don't you realise how resentful she is about being left behind on *The News*?'

'This is old ground. Let it go . . .'

'Don't patronise me. I lost you because of her and that story, and you came very close to losing your daughter, so I'd like to know what the hell she's doing here now, when your wife is missing?'

'She's here because she can keep me informed on what the Critch is up to, and because I considered it wiser to have her working with us than against us.'

Vivienne stared at him, dumbfounded. 'Miles, for God's sake—'

'I was thinking of Kelsey,' he broke in. 'I'm trying to minimise what they're going to say about me, and you know where the Critch stands as far as I'm concerned. Kelsey doesn't need that kind of shit. She's already going through hell because of her mother, I don't want her suffering even more because of the grudge that man's got against me.'

'But Justine's not the only journalist you know on *The News*.'

'She's the most dangerous, because right now she's fighting for survival.'

'And you're letting her anywhere near you? I don't believe this. Have you lost your mind?'

'If she's where I can see her, then I know what she's doing.'

As she started to answer they heard the sound of someone arriving outside.

Going to the window she pulled aside a curtain, and her heart sank as the car headlights went off. 'It's Laura, the housekeeper,' she said. 'I'll go and see what she wants,' and putting a coat over her head she went out into the rain.

'Sorry to interrupt if you got visitors,' Laura said, getting out of her mud-spattered Peugeot. 'I was just coming to tell 'e that there's a nice 'ot casserole on the stove, if you'm hungry. Can bring some over, if you like, or you can come and eat with us.'

Vivienne smiled past the frustration inside her. 'Sounds wonderful,' she told her, 'but I picked something up from the supermarket on the way back.'

Laura nodded, and looked pointedly at Miles's car. 'There's plenty enough for two if you changes your mind. Partial to a bit of game, are you?'

'Quite,' Vivienne admitted.

Laura tore her eyes from the car. 'I almost forgot,' she said, digging into a pocket. 'The key to Sir Richard's office. There's a code too – 1415. Nice and easy to remember. If you needs to go in you just goes round the back of the house. It has its own door.'

'Thank you,' Vivienne replied, taking the key. 'I probably won't need it this visit, but I will when I come back, so shall I hang onto it?'

Laura nodded. She continued to stand where she was, soft, silvery spikes of rain slanting through the halo of light shining around her from an outdoor lamp.

Vivienne waited beneath the tent of her coat, wondering if the old woman was hoping to be invited in.

'Well, I s'pose that's it then,' Laura said finally. 'You knows where we be if you d'change your mind.'

'Thank you,' Vivienne said.

After glancing at Miles's car again, Laura returned to her own and Vivienne stood watching as she turned it around.

'Meant to tell you,' Laura said, lowering the window before driving off, 'there's a shoot going on in the top woods in the morning, just in case you was thinking of going for a walk up there.'

Vivienne was still smiling. 'I've got an early start, so it wasn't my intention,' she said, 'but thanks for the warning.'

Laura blinked once or twice, then putting her foot down gently she started off down the drive.

Once the red tail lights had disappeared, Vivienne turned back across the bridge to the cider press. 'She came to invite me to supper,' she told Miles, closing the door. 'And to let me know there's a shoot tomorrow.' As she rehung her coat she added, 'I think she recognised your car, so I guess the gossip mill's about to start grinding.' Her head went back as she gave a growl of despair. 'Why can't people just leave us alone?' she said through her teeth.

Realising he'd said nothing, she turned to find him standing the other side of the table she'd arranged as a desk, staring down at something he was holding in his hand. When she realised what it was she felt a slow paralysis coming over her. She'd completely forgotten about the photograph she always carried of her and Rufus, the one she set up next to her computer, or bed, when she was staying away. In it Rufus had one fat, rosy cheek pressed up against hers, while his two little bottom teeth were proudly displayed in an exuberant smile.

She watched silently, painfully, as Miles continued to stare down at his son. Her mind was reeling as she tried to think what to say. Had he guessed? He must have, or he'd surely have put the photo back by now. In the end, when he turned to look at her the very paleness of his face told her all she needed to know.

'I want to see him,' he said gruffly.

Her heart leapt. 'Miles . . . I . . .' Was she really going to deny him?

He put the photo down and pushed his hands over his face and through his hair. 'Why didn't you tell me?' he demanded. His eyes were harsh and accusing as they came to hers.

'I wanted to, believe me . . .'

'How old is he?'

'Fifteen months.'

He almost flinched. 'And his name?'

'Rufus.'

His eyes closed as the emotions tore through him like knives. 'How could you?' he murmured. 'Knowing what you do . . .'

'Miles, try to . . .'

'Don't you think it was bad enough losing one son?'

'You haven't lost him,' she cried. 'He's with my mother. He's safe and that's how I want him to stay. Oh God, Miles, please try to understand. Not telling you has been the hardest thing I've ever done, but for his sake, and for yours . . .'

'If I'm his father, Vivienne . . .'

'There's no if about it. Of course you are, and I swear I want you to be together. You must know that. I love you, for Christ's sake. I'd never want to do anything to hurt you, but I was afraid . . . I still am . . . Jacqueline . . .'

'Damn Jacqueline,' he shouted. 'You had no right to keep this from me. You of all people must know what it means for me to be deprived of a son.'

'Of course I do, but please try— Miles, don't!' she exclaimed, as he slammed a fist against the wall. 'I was trying to protect him, you have to understand that.'

'From me? His own father?' he said savagely.

'No! From Jacqueline. She's so fragile, and unpredictable. I don't know if she could cope with—'

'But it wasn't your decision to make. Not alone. You've kept him from me, prevented me seeing him. Don't you think it's enough that someone did that fifteen years ago? Couldn't you at least have tried to put yourself in my place?'

His voice tore with emotion and his eyes closed as he tried to swallow the pain.

'Darling, I'm sorry,' she cried, going to him. 'It wasn't done to hurt you, you—'

Pushing her aside, he said, 'Do you have any idea what it's been like all these years, trying to stop myself imagining what happened to Sam, trying not to think about someone hurting or abusing him, feeling like the biggest fucking failure on God's earth because I wasn't there for him? And now you're depriving me of a second chance . . .'

'I'm not!' she shouted. 'You're not seeing this rationally, Miles. No one's taking Rufus away from you, because no one wants you to be with him more than I do. But we have to think of Jacqueline, especially now. What's going to happen if she reads it in the press and no one's there to help her come to terms with it?'

'You think she'd harm him?' he said incredulously. 'An innocent child?'

It was on the tip of her tongue to remind him of what she'd done to her own daughter, but it was too cruel. He knew it, and didn't need to hear it. 'I'm just afraid it might prove the end for her, what finally tips her over the edge,' she replied helplessly. She stopped and glanced over her shoulder at the sound of a car pulling up outside. 'Oh no, Laura what do you want now?' she muttered angrily.

Hoping to prevent the housekeeper from coming in, she reached for her coat to go and forestall her. As she opened the door she was aware of Miles picking up the photograph again, and turning to look at him she felt such a wrenching in her heart that she longed only to go to him and try once more to make him believe how much she wanted him to be with his son.

But footsteps were already crunching over the gravel. 'I'll get rid of her,' she said, but he barely seemed to hear as his eyes drank in the tender joy of his son's face, the radiant innocence and the unmistakable bond that mother and son shared. She could only guess at the torment going on inside him, the flashes of memory and resurgence of fear as he tried to see Rufus and not Sam, and to deal with finding out that, after all these years, he actually had a son again.

Stepping outside, she made to put the coat over her head, but stopped as she almost collided with someone coming across the bridge. A beat later she registered another person, then realising from their authoritative manner that they must be the detectives who'd interviewed her on the phone, and were wanting to be in touch again, her heart tightened with fury and alarm. *Why did they have to come now, when Miles was here? Why did they have to come at all?*

It was on the tip of her tongue to say it wasn't a convenient time when she realised there was a chance they'd recognised Miles's car, so to try putting them off would only make matters worse.

'Ms Kane,' DI Sadler said, gesturing for her to go back inside. 'I hope we're not interrupting anything.'

'No, of course not,' she retorted, acidly. 'Please come in.'

As she pushed the door open Miles put the photograph down and turned around. His face was still pale, his mouth tight with suppressed emotion.

Fixing him with her eyes in an effort to transmit a warning, she stood aside for the detectives to come in after her.

'Ah,' Sadler commented, wiping his feet on the doormat and looking at Miles, 'the proud parents.'

Vivienne winced, not only at the sarcasm, but at how close Miles had come to learning about Rufus that way. She looked at him and her heart gave an uneasy thud; his expression was as forbidding as she'd ever seen it, his whole demeanour one of simmering resentment.

'I suppose one of you was intending to tell us about Rufus Avery at some point,' Sadler said amicably, moving aside for DC Joy to close the door behind her.

Vivienne's eyes shot back to Miles, but his only reaction to learning she'd given their son his name was to flick a glance at her before returning his attention to Sadler.

'Well, were you?' Sadler prompted. The cider press seemed ludicrously overcrowded now, unable to support so much intrusion.

Sadler turned to Vivienne. 'Withholding information in a missing-person case isn't clever, Ms Kane. In fact, it could be considered a crime.'

'She did it for a good reason,' Miles said darkly.

Vivienne's eyes went to him.

'And since you know my family history,' he continued, still focused on Sadler, 'I don't imagine you've had any trouble working out that reason.'

'No, I haven't,' Sadler agreed, 'but I'm sure you understand, Mr Avery, what an awkward position that now puts you in.'

'But he's only just—' Vivienne began.

Cutting across her, Miles said, 'I understand perfectly, but it still doesn't mean I know what's happened to my wife.'

Sadler's eyebrows rose. 'You will admit, though, that the existence of your son provides you with a strong motive for wanting to . . . put an end to your marriage?'

'Of course I admit it. I'd be a fool not to, but even if he didn't exist I'd want to end it.'

'And of course you, Ms Kane,' Sadler said, turning to her, 'would also welcome an end to that marriage.'

Vivienne's eyes widened with astonishment. 'If you're insinuating what I think you are . . .' she began fiercely.

'Go on,' Sadler prompted.

'Well, of course I want my son to be with his father, but if you think I – or Miles – had anything to do with Jacqueline's disappearance, you need to think again. Neither of us has any idea where she is.'

Sadler allowed his scepticism to linger for a while, then returned his scrutiny to Miles. 'I'm sure Mr Avery can speak for himself,' he said mildly.

'Inspector, I can assure you, if I knew where my wife was I wouldn't be wasting your time.'

Sadler's lower lip jutted outwards as he digested the words. 'Well, that's good to hear,' he commented. Then, after a pause, he raised his head. Unexpectedly, he asked, 'Do you happen to own a gun, sir?'

Vivienne gaped at him incredulously as Miles frowned with annoyance. 'I do,' he replied.

'For which you have a licence?'

'Of course.'

'And would we find that gun at Moorlands, if we were to go there now?'

'It's in a locked cabinet in my study. The key is in the safe.'

Appearing impressed by the security, Sadler enquired, 'Has it been fired recently, by any chance? It's the shooting season.'

'No, it hasn't,' Miles said shortly.

'You wouldn't mind if we checked that?'

'Of course not.'

'This is outrageous!' Vivienne cried. 'You can't seriously think he's harmed her. For God's sake, you know who he is—'

'Status doesn't exempt him,' Sadler cut in. 'Now, Ms Kane, would you like to tell us what you were doing on the morning of August 29th this year?'

Vivienne's jaw dropped in amazement. She looked at Miles, who appeared equally as confused, until, registering the significance of the date, he said, 'It's when Jacqueline withdrew the money from the bank.'

Vivienne blinked as she turned back to Sadler. 'Please tell me I'm not reading this correctly,' she challenged incredulously.

He waited.

'You're actually asking me . . .' She stopped, still too stunned to continue.

'Where you were on the morning of August 29th,' Sadler repeated affably.

Vivienne looked at Miles as she dashed a hand through her hair. Then, sensing DC Joy's piercing scrutiny, she said, 'I'll have to check my diary, but I imagine I was at my office.'

'It would help if you could be certain,' Sadler told her. 'Better still would be if someone could confirm it.'

Vivienne was starting to feel dizzy. 'You can't seriously think I withdrew that money,' she protested. 'I have no access to Jacqueline's accounts.'

'No, but Mr Avery does, and someone, a woman, collected the money. We're trying to establish whether or not it was Mrs Avery herself, or someone passing themselves off as her.'

Vivienne's eyes went back to Miles.

'I understand you have a job to do, Inspector,' Miles said, sounding oddly much calmer now, 'but you could save yourself a lot of time if you removed Ms Kane from your inquiries. She has no idea where my wife is, nor did she collect the money from the bank. Nor, I should add, has she colluded with me on any level to effect my wife's disappearance.'

Sadler's eyebrows were rising high. 'And I'm to take your word for that, am I?' he said.

'You could, but I'm sure you won't. I'm simply trying to tell you that until the day my wife vanished Vivienne and I had had no contact for over two years.'

'Not even about your son?'

'No.'

Sadler couldn't have looked more cynical if he'd tried. 'Yes, well, I'd still appreciate knowing where you were on the morning of the 29th, Ms Kane. You too, Mr Avery.'

'I was here, in Devon,' Miles told him. 'I'm sure my housekeeper will bear me out.' At that moment his mobile started to ring. Glancing down to see who it was, he said, 'My daughter. If you'll excuse me,' and he clicked on.

'Dad! Where are you?' Kelsey cried at the other end. 'That horrible woman's in the house. She said you invited her, but—'

'Just a minute,' Miles cut in, 'what are you doing there? You're supposed to be at school.'

'I know, but I didn't want to go back and have everyone keep asking me where Mum is . . .'

'But you can't just stay away . . .'

'Well I have, and I don't want that woman in our house. You have to make her go.'

Glancing at Sadler, he said, 'Darling, I'm in the middle of something right—'

'I don't care,' Kelsey shrieked. 'If you don't come home now I'm going to tell her to fuck off. Or I'll call the police . . .'

'Kelsey, just go to your room if you don't want to speak to her.'

'Why should I? This is my house, not hers. I didn't ask her to come, so tell her to go away. Or to get lost back to London. We don't want her here.'

Miles took a breath and looked at the inspector. 'All right,

I'm on my way,' he said, and ringing off he glanced at Vivienne before saying to Sadler, 'I'm sorry, I need to go home.'

Sadler nodded affably. The yelling at the other end hadn't been lost on him. This was a man under a lot of strain, a teenage daughter, a missing wife, a police inquiry, and now Sadler was about to add to the load. 'We can talk again tomorrow,' he said, nodding to Joy to open the door. 'We'll be bringing a TAG team with us. You're aware, I'm sure, of what that means?'

Miles's eyes came harshly to his.

Sadler met the hostility.

'What does it mean?' Vivienne asked, watching the stand-off.

DC Joy spoke for the first time. 'A tactical aid team will be searching the grounds as well as the house,' she said, 'including the surrounding woodlands – and police divers will be dragging the lake.'

A cold fist closed around Vivienne's heart as she looked at Miles. He'd been here before, suspected of a crime he hadn't committed.

Miles's eyes remained on Sadler until, with a brief nod, he walked to the door.

Vivienne's insides were clenched in fear as they moved from Sadler to Joy and back again. 'He hasn't done anything wrong,' she told them after Miles had gone. 'I know him. He just wouldn't.'

DC Joy only looked at her.

'Please keep us in touch with your movements,' Sadler said, starting to leave. 'And don't forget about August 29th.'

She watched them go to the door, still trying to resist the enormity of what was happening, until with a sudden panic shaking her voice she said, 'Inspector, about my son.'

Sadler turned round.

'I swear to you, Miles didn't know anything about him until tonight,' she said. 'I couldn't tell him. I was always afraid of what his wife might do. I still am, if she finds out.'

Sadler's eyes narrowed. 'That's starting to look increasingly less likely,' he told her bluntly, 'but if you're asking that we don't go public about him, the only assurance I can give you is that no one from the media will learn of his existence from us.'

'Where the hell are you?'

Recognising the Critch's dulcet growl, Justine said, 'Actually, I'm in the sitting room of Miles Avery's country home,' and she gleaned a moment's satisfaction from picturing his piggy eyes widening with surprise.

'Mm,' he grunted, which was about as much as she was likely to get by way of approval. 'Is he there?'

'Not right at this instant.'

'So you can talk?'

'I would if I had something to say.'

'Very clever. I've just heard the police are going to start an official search of the place tomorrow.'

It was her turn for surprise. 'You mean Moorlands? Why? What's happened?'

'You're the one on the ground, and *you're* asking *me*?'

'This is the first I've heard of it, and I don't think Miles would have brought me here if he knew, so my guess is something's broken.'

'I'm not interested in your guesses. I want facts – on my front page. You've already lost out once to the *Mail*, when the police questioned Vivienne Kane. How the hell could you not have found that out? I got to tell you, Justine, you're not using your second chance well, so make damned sure you stick close to Avery from now on. I want to know everything that's happening down there, and I want some exclusives. Remember what they are?'

It was on the tip of her tongue to tell him to drop dead, or worse, but stringing him along, letting him think she was still helping to shape his revenge was going to make her own all the sweeter when it came. 'Got to go now,' she said abruptly. 'Someone's coming.'

As she clicked off the line she walked over to the fire, continuing to smart at the way he'd spoken to her, and still not yet over the outrageous reception she'd received from Miles's lippy offspring.

'What are you doing here?' the kid had demanded rudely.

'I'm your father's guest,' Justine had told her.

'So where is he?'

For two pins she might have told her that he was somewhere with Vivienne Kane, since that was almost guaranteed to upset the hormonal cluster. On the other hand, it would upset Miles too, so in the end she'd said, 'He's on his way. He had someone to see, so I came on ahead in a taxi.'

At that the girl had turned around and walked away, leaving Justine to find her own way to the sitting room. God only knew where she was now, probably squeezing her teenage spots in a bathroom somewhere, or practising vampire kisses on a nasty collection of dolls.

Realising she should be making notes on what she'd seen and heard at the pub this evening, she took out her PDA to start jotting down the salient points. A few minutes later she closed it up, and began mulling the idea of making a few calls about this search. She didn't doubt the Critch's word that it was due to happen, he never got anything like that wrong, but apparently he had no more idea than she did about what had happened to make the police call in the TAG boys now. Actually, at this stage of the game, that information could probably only have come from the police themselves, or Miles, so how lucky was she that she happened to be right here in the thick of it, while her esteemed colleagues were camped out around the gates. Or she guessed they would be by tomorrow morning. Right now it was raining hard, so they'd obviously cleared off for the night, believing Miles still to be in London.

Ten minutes later her pale eyes were sparking with anger. 'Are you serious?' she shouted at Miles, who was busying himself with turning on more lamps. 'I've just got here, and now you're telling me to leave? Apart from anything else, have you seen what the weather's like out there?'

'I'm sorry,' he said. 'Things have changed in the last couple of hours.'

She waited, smouldering with fury at finding herself about to be ejected just as events were really hotting up. 'Is that it?' she exploded. 'Surely I deserve a better explanation than that?'

'Probably,' he responded, 'but I'm afraid I can't give you

one. I just need you to leave. I'll take you to the station and pay for your ticket back to London, naturally.'

She glared at him, speechless with frustration, but absolutely no way was she allowing herself to be turfed out now.

'Justine, I know what's going through your mind,' he told her, stooping to put another log on the fire, 'so please don't waste your time trying to change my mind. I apologise for bringing you all this way. I tried to tell you in London that I was having second thoughts—'

'But the Critch *isn't*,' she cut in forcefully. 'He's going to crucify you, given half a chance, so nothing's changed there. You still need me on your side, so for God's sake tell me what's going on?'

Standing up, he brushed the dust from his hands and turned around. 'You'll find out soon enough,' he informed her.

At that she almost screamed with outrage. 'What? I'm going to read about it in the papers?' she spat. 'Well, thank you very much. I came here as a favour to you and now, because it apparently doesn't suit you any more, I've got to just up and go. Well, I'm sorry, Miles, it doesn't work that way. I already know they're going to start searching the place tomorrow, so I'm not leaving here until you tell me *why*, and what they're expecting to find?'

Though his voice was perfectly calm, there was no mistaking the edge to it as he said, 'You'll have to ask the police those questions, Justine, or the person who's leaking the information. For my part, I'm not prepared to discuss it any further. Again I apologise for allowing you to think—'

'To hell with your apology. You walk back in here like a thundercloud about to explode after being with Vivienne Kane and suddenly I have to go. Now why would that be, Miles? Let me see. They're searching your house tomorrow, definitely not something to put you in the best of moods, but then I have to ask myself why would that upset you so much if you've got nothing to hide? And then I say, it couldn't possibly have anything to do with the child your girlfriend's been hiding at her mother's place, could it? The little boy that's obviously yours, who you clearly don't want the rest of the world to know about?'

His face had turned deathly white. 'How the hell do you know about that?' he demanded, in a tone that chilled the heat of her fury.

'What does it matter how I—' She stepped back as he came towards her.

'This isn't a game, Justine,' he said, his voice dangerously low. 'I want to know how you found out, and who you've told.'

Her eyes flashed. 'So you're not in such a hurry to get rid of me now,' she sneered.

Grabbing her arm, he wrenched it up between them and twisted it hard. 'How do you know?' he growled into her face.

Unnerved enough not to push him any further, she said, 'I had her followed.'

'When? Why? What prompted you?'

'I've always kept tabs on her, ever since you two broke up. I knew it wouldn't be the end between you, that something—'

'If you've known about Rufus all this time, why have you never said anything before? It's a headline-grabbing story, especially now, so why haven't you run with it?'

Trapped by her own lie she had to think fast, then suddenly realising how she could win back his favour, she said, 'Believe it or not, I kept it to myself out of loyalty to you. I'm not going to be the one to slap that child's existence all over the front page. You want to protect him, and I understand that.'

His expression was loaded with cynicism, but he said no more, only pushed her away and turned back towards the fire.

Rubbing her wrist she watched him, quietly thrilled by the confirmation she'd just received that he really was the father.

'OK, so where do we go from here?' she asked finally.

He glanced up. 'I thought I'd made myself plain. You have to leave.'

Her eyes rounded with amazement. 'Even knowing what I do, you're still—'

His scowl was suddenly terrible again. 'If you're about to embark on an attempt at blackmail your career really will be over,' he warned.

'Nothing so crude,' she retorted, though of course he'd read her correctly.

He flicked her a glance, then checked his watch. 'There's a train leaving in just under an hour.'

'Forget it. I'm not going anywhere.'

'I'm afraid you are. I'll just—'

'But it's pouring down, and you've got this great big house . . .'

'I didn't realise Kelsey was going to be here, and she still holds you partly responsible for what happened the last time her mother came back.'

Justine flushed with guilt, but her mettle held firm. 'Does this mean I'm to believe Jacqueline's going to stage another return?' she dared to challenge. Then, quickly realising that she'd gone too far, she added, 'How was I supposed to know she'd pull a stunt like that?'

'None of us did, but it happened,' he growled, 'so perhaps you can understand why you need to leave now.'

With a certain amount of bravado she said, 'If you can find me a number for the Nobody Inn, I'll try to book in there for the night.' Then, when it looked as though he was about to object, 'For God's sake Miles, I'm hardly going back to London now, when so much is happening here. I've got a job to do, and like it or not, I'm going to do it, even if it means camping out on your doorstep along with everyone else.'

Looking daggers, he crossed to the dining-room dresser and took out a well-thumbed contact book. After giving her the number, he dropped the book back in the drawer, and waited for her to make the call.

'Please tell me,' he said when finally he took her out to the car, 'that I can rely on you to keep Rufus's existence to yourself, at least until we know what's happened to Jacqueline.'

She gave him a smile as he pulled open the passenger door for her to get in. 'Of course you can rely on me,' she assured him, 'but only because it's you. Were it anyone else, it might be a different story,' and with a playful wink she sank gratefully into the car.

Upstairs in her bedroom Kelsey was sitting in the window seat watching her father's car disappearing down the drive, red tail lights glowing through the trees in the darkness, like the eyes of a deer. It was raining again, slanting like tiny pins through the lights around the lake. The surface rippled and plumed, while the giant gunneras surrounding it rose and swooped as though peering down into the murky depths.

She'd been crying so hard that her chest hurt and her ribs ached. She wanted it to be over; she didn't want all this horribleness any more. Her mother should come back now. It was just stupid and spiteful staying away like this, making everyone worried and afraid. Not that she cared where she was, but Kelsey had sent more than a hundred text messages since Jacqueline had disappeared, and still she hadn't had a reply and that was just mean.

She pushed a fist to her mouth to force back another swell of emotion. It was all wrong. Everything was spiralling out of control and she didn't know how to stop it. Her friends wanted her to meet boys she didn't like, or they kept asking about her mum, and she was feeling such a freak because she was so different to everyone else. She hated them, and herself, and she wanted her dad to make them go away. Or he should go out and find her mum, not bring people like Justine James into the house when what had happened before was her fault.

Taking a breath, she dragged her hands over her face, stretching the skin and pressing in the bones. Then, wiping her fingers on her jeans, she hugged her knees to her chest and stared down at the lake. Her dad should have come up to see her before he left, but he hadn't, and anyway what did she care? He was going to be mad about her not going back to school, and they'd end up rowing and he'd wish he'd never had her, and she'd wish she'd never been born . . .

Catching a movement on the lake she watched one of the Muscovys come gliding out of the reeds, then climb up onto the platform of the duckhouse that her dad and the gardener had built especially for nesting. It was more than two years now since a flock of Canada geese had come along and turfed out all the other birds to make a nest for themselves. The eggs already laid had been destroyed, except one, as it turned out, which no one knew about until eventually it hatched along with all the snowy-white young of the Canada geese. Kelsey had named the little rogue gosling Henrietta. Though she was brown and dull and nothing like the others she was taken into the family anyway, a small bundle of dingy feathers, skimming happily about the lake with her parents and siblings until one day her world had turned into a frightening and lonely place.

More tears rolled onto Kelsey's cheeks as she remembered Henrietta's distress as her mother had swooped around and around the lake, trying to coax her small ugly goose to fly. But Henrietta couldn't. She was only able to paddle or waddle along helplessly, frantically, squawking and flapping her wings, desperate not to be left behind. In the end, Henrietta's father had come to put his neck gently over hers, stroking her softly, until turning to the rest of his family he'd led the long run down the lawn and they'd soared off into the blue beyond. Watching from the bank, Kelsey had been inconsolable. She'd sobbed and sobbed, unable to bear poor Henrietta's confusion and heartbreak. Nothing in her life had ever felt so terrible as watching the plain little goose being left alone on a lake that had always been such a happy and safe place to be. Vivienne had been with Kelsey that day, and had put her arms around her, holding her tight. Henrietta's tragedy was the only moment of closeness she and Vivienne had ever shared, but Kelsey had broken away quickly, before Vivienne could let go first.

If it weren't for Vivienne her mum and dad would work things out and they'd be a family again. It was all Vivienne's fault. Her throat seemed to close over then, because there was such a horrible mix of weird things going on in her head. Like she remembered when her mum had come back, and how much relief and happiness she'd felt because she hadn't left her after all. Then her mother had tried to kill them both, which was OK, actually, because it had meant she'd intended to take Kelsey with her. It had felt nice for her mother to want her, for once. The anger and bitterness had only come later, when Kelsey had finally realised that her mother was still looking through her, instead of at her. All she really wanted was Sam, and somehow Kelsey was in the way.

Suddenly, out of nowhere, she couldn't stand any more. So much anger and fear and confusion surged up inside her that her whole body was racked with despair. 'I don't want to be here,' she sobbed, pressing her hands to her head. 'I want to go away where no one can find me.' Her father would be sorry then. Everyone would. They might even stop thinking about Sam and her mother all the time, because she'd be missing too and it would serve them all right if they couldn't find her.

Chapter Ten

Vivienne was at the horse sanctuary, standing with Reg Thomas, the local auctioneer, whose broad face was tilted upwards as they watched two police helicopters swoop by overhead.

'You knows what all thass about, don't you?' Reg said gravely as the helicopters began to hover a few hundred yards away. 'They'm looking for the woman what's gone missing. Mrs Avery. I expect you've read about it, or heard it on the news.'

Realising he hadn't made the connection, Vivienne continued to watch without replying. She could hardly bear to contemplate the horror of what Miles must be going through now. It was too much, she was thinking. Finding out he had a son who'd been kept from him, the indignity of having his home turned upside down in search of his wife, knowing the police suspected him of playing some part in her disappearance, just as they had when Sam had been taken. She wished she could be with him to give him some support, and a sense that at least one part of his life wasn't falling apart. Though considering the conclusions the police were already jumping to over Rufus, she was hardly a safe haven for him now.

Remembering his anger last night at what he'd seen as a betrayal, she felt the remorse building up in her again. She couldn't imagine he'd feel any differently this morning, though she had no way of knowing, since he hadn't returned any of her calls.

'They'm going to have a heck of a job on their hands if they'm about searching the moor,' the auctioneer commented, scratching his head. 'Probably won't never find her if they has to do that.'

'You're assuming,' Vivienne said, trying to keep her tone light, 'that she's there to be found, and as far as I'm aware there's no evidence to say she is.'

He shrugged. 'True enough,' he conceded, 'but you got to admit, it's starting to look a bit suspicious now, with no sign of her going into the station and him not even contacting the police till three weeks or more after she'd gone.' He jammed his hands in his pockets and puffed out his chest. 'Met her once or twice,' he said, his owlish eyes moving out across the field where half a dozen or more rescued horses were tearing up tufts of grass and munching pleasurably. 'Nice woman. Quiet. Kept herself to herself mostly, but she was always polite. Brought some pieces in for auction a couple of months ago: an old Byzantine clock, and some paintings she said was done by her great aunt. All right they was, fetched a bit too. My missus bought one of 'em.' He shook his head and sighed. 'Bad business about her kiddie,' he said. 'Bad business all round. We don't know the half of it, do we, what goes on in other people's lives. Must be terrible never knowing what happened, if he's still out there somewhere, or if someone did away with him all those years ago.'

Vivienne smiled weakly. 'I can't imagine going through anything worse,' she said truthfully, and starting back towards the vast, newly built barn they were to use for the auction she took out her phone to check for messages. Still nothing from Miles.

'So,' the auctioneer was saying as he followed her in through the giant doors, 'all you've got to do is come up with a date, and I'll make sure the chairs and the podium and everything's all set up.'

'I'm contacting BT about putting in some phone lines,' she said, looking around to see if anything existed already. The walls were mostly bare, however, as was the cement floor where several footprints were scuffed into the chippings and sawdust, and large bundles of hay were waiting to be stacked onto a nearby forklift. 'We'll have to arrange for some kind of heating, too,' she added, with a shiver.

He was about to respond when the sound of a car pulling up outside made them both turn around. Stella was chuckling, even before she turned off the engine.

'Blimey, what a palaver I've had getting here,' she grumbled amicably, as she came to join them. 'Road's all blocked up by the press and police cars. Right bloody circus it is. Nearly ran one of them satellite things over when I was reversing to go round t'other way. Not sure the police has 'em under control. They looks a pretty rowdy bunch to me, all trying to get into the Averys' place. Bloody good job they don't know you're up here,' she said to Vivienne, 'or we'd probably have 'em swarming all over us too.'

Reg Thomas turned to Vivienne in surprise. 'Well, I never,' he said, shaking his head as he stared at her. 'Fancy me not . . . You'm the Vivienne Kane they bin talking about on the news, aren't you? And there was me going on about Mrs Avery . . .'

With as pleasant a smile as she could muster, Vivienne said, 'If you don't mind, I'm not here about that.'

'No, no, course not,' he said, clearly embarrassed. 'Hope I didn't say nothing . . .'

'You didn't,' Vivienne assured him quickly. 'Now, if we can just run through the arrangements we've made so far, and bring Stella up to speed.'

'No problem, you can leave that to me,' he told her as her mobile started to ring.

Thanking him, she hurriedly checked who it was, then went outside to take the call.

'How's it going?' Alice asked as soon as she'd clicked on. 'Have you heard back from Miles yet?'

'No. There's a lot of activity over at Moorlands, though. Helicopters, police, press . . . It's a nightmare. I can hardly bear to think what it must be like for him.'

'He'll handle it, I'm sure. I'm more concerned about you and what you're going to do.'

'I'm leaving fairly soon, and so far no one seems to know I'm here. Apart from Justine, of course, but she doesn't know my movements, and the sanctuary's pretty well tucked away in the next valley.'

'Someone's bound to phone in a tip-off.'

'By which time I should be long gone. Anyway, it's not my biggest concern right now. Miles is.'

'What'll you do if he insists on seeing Rufus?'

'I'll have to let him, of course. How can I not?'

'You should make him wait until all this is over.'

'Actually, I think he might anyway. He won't be any keener than I am to expose Rufus to the kind of media attention any contact between them is likely to create.' Her eyes closed at the mere thought of it. 'Oh God, Alice,' she groaned, 'to think that having a son could backfire on him like this, making it look as though . . .' She shook her head. 'I can't go there. It's too horrible, the way they're thinking.'

'But you told them he'd only just found out.'

'Of course, but they've only got my word for it, and clearly that wasn't enough to call off the search. I can only hope that Jacqueline sees what's going on and comes forward to stop it. Have you been watching the news? Is it getting much coverage?'

'Quite a bit, but there's not a lot to see. Just some shots of the gates, and the police coming and going. Divers are dragging the lake, apparently, but they haven't shown that yet.'

'They can drag all they like, they won't find anything,' Vivienne said heatedly.

Alice's response was too slow in coming.

'Oh for God's sake, not you too!' Vivienne cried. 'He hasn't done anything to hurt her. If anything it's the other way round, she's doing this to hurt him.' She looked up as another car pulled into the stable yard, and waved when she saw it was Sharon. 'This is such terrible timing,' she said angrily into the phone. 'It's not supposed to be about anything other than this poor girl and her family, but what chance do we stand of that now?'

'Not much, but Pete's happy to help run it with you, which means you can keep a low profile. The really important thing is to make sure the press stays away from Rufus, because it would be too much for your mother to handle if they start descending on her. Do you think the police will stick to their word and not leak it?'

'Who knows? I guess it depends on what happens in the

next couple of days. And on how cooperative Miles is being. They turned on him once before over Sam, now it's happening again . . . Oh God, I can hardly bear it. If they knew him, if they had any idea what he's really like, what he's been through all these years . . .' She stopped as a terrible thought suddenly clawed at her heart. 'Alice, you don't think they'll open up the case about Sam again, do you? *Please* don't say yes.'

'I guess it's a possibility,' Alice said tentatively. 'I don't really know how these things work.'

'I have to go over there. He needs me.'

'Don't be crazy. You can't with everyone camped out at his gates. Think of Rufus.'

Vivienne sighed. 'It's just . . . Oh, I don't know. If you could have seen his face when he found that picture last night. What have I done to him, Alice? I've made him miss all those months of Rufus's life.'

'He'll understand, eventually. He probably already does, but with everything else that's going on . . .'

'I hope you're right. Anyway, I suppose I'd better go now. I'm meeting the firemen and choreographer at twelve, so I'll call you later, when I get to my mother's.'

As she rang off she put on a big smile for Sharon, who was coming towards her. 'How are you today?' she asked, looking into the young woman's anxious eyes.

'I think it's me who should be asking you that,' Sharon answered. 'I just heard one of them on the radio saying about how you was with Mr Avery last night.'

Vivienne tensed. Clearly Justine hadn't wasted any time over that. 'Well, just as long as no one knows I'm here,' she said, linking Sharon's arm as they started towards the barn.

'Trouble is,' Sharon said, 'someone's bound to tell 'em. Eileen, or Lizzie or someone. What I'm saying is, well, if there's anything I can do. I mean, I don't want to give meself airs and graces, or nothing, but I knows my way around here. I used to work in Chudleigh.'

'Then maybe you can give me a route to the dual carriageway that won't take me in the direction of Moorlands.'

Sharon screwed up her eyes in thought. 'Shouldn't be a

problem,' she said, and looked up to see what all the increased noise was about. 'Blimey, there's at least six of 'em now,' she muttered, as a small fleet of helicopters passed overhead.

Vivienne was looking up too, her heart churning with the fear that something sinister had spurred an increase in police activity. However, she soon realised that what she was watching was the arrival of the airborne press.

Miles heard the knock on his study door, but didn't turn round as it opened and Mrs Davies came in carrying a tray of coffee. She was a neat, dumpy little woman with spiky grey hair and gentle eyes that regarded him uncertainly as he continued to stand staring out of the window at all that was happening in his garden and the woods beyond. It was a nightmare; like watching a plague of locusts at work, or a gang of rapacious vandals.

'I thought you might be in need,' she said, going to put the tray on his desk.

'Thank you,' he replied. His skin seemed sallow, and there was a pale line around his mouth showing the strain he was under, while a sleepless night showed in his eyes. 'Has Kelsey come out of her room yet?' he asked, still watching the activity outside.

'I'm afraid not.'

Knowing she'd be watching from her window he was tempted to go and force her door, since she was refusing to let him in. Feeling certain, however, that it would make matters worse, he decided to give her a while longer to come down.

'Is Tom still with the detectives?' he asked, referring to the gardener.

'Yes. I took some coffee in there too. Will you eat something now? I've brought biscuits, but I can . . .'

'I'm fine, thank you.' Turning, he said, 'This can't be very pleasant for you, so I want you to know I'll understand if you feel you want to leave.'

Her eyes widened with astonishment. 'Why would I want to do that?' she retorted. 'You and Kelsey need someone to take care of you, especially now.'

With a smile of gratitude he said, 'I hope your own interview with the police wasn't too arduous.'

'There wasn't anything I could tell them that I hadn't told them before,' she replied, sounding defensive and peeved that anyone might think she was going to change her story just because some new information had come to light. Though she had to admit it had come as a bit of a shock when the police had asked if she'd known Miles had a fifteen-month-old son, because she definitely hadn't.

'I didn't know Miss Kane,' she said hesitantly, but feeling she had to mention it. 'She was here before I joined you, but I . . .' She stopped as he turned back to the window. 'I'm just saying,' she went on valiantly, 'that if you'd rather I didn't mention anything about the little boy, you know, to the press—'

'Thank you,' he interrupted. 'For the child's sake it would be better if you kept it to yourself.'

She began winding her fingers around one another, while looking awkwardly about the book-lined room. 'Well, you knows where I am if you need anything,' she said.

He nodded, and only when he heard the door close behind her did he leave the window and go to fill a cup from the cafetière she'd brought in.

The anger and frustration inside him was deeply buried, held back by an iron control, along with the other terrible emotions that continued to torment him, as they had through the night. Finding out he had a son and that Vivienne had never told him was almost as hard to bear as all the other insanity that was consuming his world. Never would he have dreamt she'd do that to him. She should have trusted him, for God's sake. She should have told him the moment she knew she was pregnant. More than anyone he'd have understood her concerns, and she surely couldn't think he'd ever have allowed anyone to harm their son.

His eyes closed as the image of Kelsey, aged twelve, drugged and slumped awkwardly on the bed, slipped into his mind. It was one he would never forget; nor would he ever stop tormenting himself with what might have happened if something had delayed him that day and he hadn't come home in time. That Jacqueline could have done that to her own daughter . . . No matter that it was an isolated act to try and manipulate him when she wasn't in her right mind, it was enough to make anyone afraid of how far she might go when confronted by the prospect of him leaving, particularly if she ever found out he had a child – a son – by someone else. It had long been her greatest fear.

But Vivienne should have trusted him, goddamit!

Stifling another surge of anger, he drained his cup, replaced it on the tray and went back to the window. The divers were up again now, either standing on the bank, or sitting in the small boat they'd brought with them. Considering the lack of urgency he guessed nothing of much consequence was happening, nor did the combing of the lawns and garden beds seem to be sparking much excitement. What was going on in the bottom woods or overhead was impossible to tell, though the helicopters had moved some way off now, hovering closer to the moor. This morning's shoot in the top woods had been cancelled due to the search, which had no doubt infuriated the gamekeepers, who depended on the sport for their livelihood. He was sorry, but there was nothing he could do about it, though he guessed he'd be blamed and even, possibly, approached for compensation.

Thankfully the gates weren't visible from here, but it wasn't difficult to imagine the media bandwagon that had undoubtedly set up camp down there. His movements were going to be severely restricted over the coming days, he realised, unless he wanted to confront the unruly army of reporters with their microphones, tape recorders and cameras.

Hearing the door open again, he looked round and to his relief saw it was Kelsey. 'Are you OK?' he asked gently, seeing how pinched her face was.

She nodded and went to the small leather sofa, where she sat down cross-legged and bunched her hands in front of her, her eyes fixed on them sightlessly.

'Have you had any breakfast?' he said.

She shook her head.

He knew he should raise the subject of her returning to school, but now wasn't the time when there were other, more urgent matters they needed to discuss.

An uneasy silence lingered as he considered how to broach the subject of Rufus. God knew he was finding it hard enough to come to terms with himself, so how was it going to be for her, on top of all this other madness in her life? However, if he didn't break it to her now, it was inevitable that the police or someone else would, by the end of the day.

'They think you did it, don't they?' she said, her voice tight with a resentment that seemed to border on accusation.

Forcing himself past the anger he felt towards the police and press who'd put the suspicion in her head, he said, 'Yes, it seems like it, but they're wrong, of course, and we have to remember, we don't even know if she's . . .' Unable to utter the word, he left the sentence unfinished.

She looked up, and seeing the anguish behind the antagonism in her eyes he felt an overpowering need to hold her, as though his embrace might keep her safe from all the terrible blows life could inflict. Yet here he was on the verge of delivering yet one more.

'What is it?' she challenged, suddenly seeming angry and afraid. 'Why are you looking at me like that?'

'I'm sorry,' he said, drawing a hand over his unshaven jaw, 'I didn't realise . . .' Picking up a chair, he carried it over to the sofa and sat down in front of her.

'Why are you sitting there?' she cried, drawing back.

'Darling, there's something I have to tell you,' he said gently. 'I tried last night when I came home . . .'

Her face reddened as she turned quickly away. Clearly she didn't want to be reminded of how she'd told him to fuck off and die when he'd knocked on her door.

'It seems,' he began. 'Well, the fact is . . .'

Her head came round, and seeing her panicky tears he struggled to prevent his own. 'Oh Dad, please don't tell me anything horrible,' she begged. 'I didn't mean what I said last night. I was just mad and . . .'

'It's all right,' he soothed, taking her hand.

'No it's not,' she choked, grabbing it back. 'Oh God, I don't want this to be happening. I want it all to go away.'

'I know, sweetheart,' he said, and moving to sit beside her he pulled her head onto his shoulder, 'and it will soon, I promise.'

'Are you going to tell me something about Mum?' she asked, and he could feel the tension in her body as she braced herself.

He started to answer, but she looked up at him and her face crumpled. 'Oh no, please don't say . . . You didn't . . . Oh my God, you'll have to go to prison and . . .'

'Sssh,' he said, pressing a kiss to her forehead. 'No, of course I didn't do it, and I'm sure Mum's fine. What I have to say isn't about her.'

'Then what?'

'Well, I'm afraid it's probably not going to be easy for you to hear, but before I tell you, I want you to know how much you mean to me.'

'What is it?' she cried. 'Just tell me. Oh Dad, I'm really scared now.'

Cursing himself for how badly he was handling this, he said, 'I'm sorry. There's no need to be afraid, I promise. It's just that . . . Well, apparently after Vivienne and I broke up . . .'

She drew back sharply, her eyes smouldering with protest.

Hiding his dismay at the hostility Vivienne's name had provoked, he said, 'Darling, I . . . Well, it . . .' Realising there was no other way than to come right out with it, he said, 'Vivienne and I have a son.'

Her face started to freeze with shock.

'I only found out myself last night,' he went on. 'If I'd known sooner, believe me, it's not something I'd have kept from you, but it's important that I tell you now, before it gets into the papers, or you find out some other way.'

She was still too stunned to speak, though he was afraid of what might be building up inside her.

'Darling, I want you to know,' he persevered, 'that no one means more to me than you, and nothing's ever going to change that.'

'But you've got a son now,' she said, her voice seeming too thin and stiff. 'It's what you've always wanted.'

'*You* are what . . .'

She was shaking her head. 'It's all right, it doesn't matter,' she told him. 'I always knew I wasn't enough.'

'Kelsey, that isn't true.'

'Yes it is. You and Mum only ever really wanted Sam, I just got in the way.'

'Darling, you know how much I love you . . .'

'I know you say it, but only because you have to. The truth is, I'm not a boy so I don't really count. Well, you've got one now, with Vivienne, so I suppose . . . Oh my God, that's why Mum went, isn't it? Because you told her about . . . whatever his name is?'

'It's Rufus, and no, it's not why she went because, as I said just now, I didn't know about him myself until last night.'

She appeared confused by that, until she said through tight lips, 'So you were with *her*, last night?'

'For a while.'

'So she's here, in Devon?' Her expression filled with contempt. 'That is so disgusting, she just can't wait to step into Mum's shoes.'

'She's working here, and as far as I know she's not staying long.'

Her eyes went down, but her jaw remained tight and her fists clenched. 'Rufus is such a dumb name,' she sneered nastily.

'I'm sorry you think so.'

Her head came up. 'Well, I do, as it happens, but why should you care?'

Sidestepping the childishness, he said, 'I'd like you to think of him as your brother, if you can, because that's what he is.'

Dissent blazed from her eyes. 'No he's not. He doesn't belong to Mum, so how can he be?'

'OK, he's your half-brother. The point is, what's happening now is no more his fault than yours.'

'What if I said I don't ever want to see him?'

'Well, I'd be very upset if you took that stand, but it still wouldn't change how important you are to me.'

'That is such crap,' she cried furiously. 'You've never given a damn about me, or Mum, because you don't care about anyone except yourself. All that's ever mattered to you is your work, and how much time you could spend away from us – until *Vivienne* came along. Everything changed for you then, didn't it?'

'Kelsey . . .'

'Don't touch me,' she cried, punching his hands away. 'God, it's no wonder Mum went out of her mind being married to you. She was even lonelier than me, and that's saying something. But don't think I'm defending her, because she was as bad as you. Never thinking about anyone but herself or Sam. It was like I never even existed half the time. Well, don't worry, I won't be sticking around much longer. You can get rid of me, just like . . . you got rid of . . . her.' She broke off and dropped her head so he couldn't see her tears.

As devastated by her words as she'd clearly intended him to be, Miles said, 'I understand that you're angry and upset now, and you're right, I probably should have tried harder to understand . . .'

'Don't start making excuses,' she yelled. 'You sent me away to school because you didn't want me.'

'No, because I thought it would be best for you, but I was wrong, which was why I brought you to Devon as a weekly boarder—'

'Don't worry, you can dump me back there,' she broke in, 'then if you like, you won't ever have to see me again.'

'Kelsey, if you think that's what I want then I really have failed, because nothing would hurt me more.'

'Don't lie!' she raged. 'You've got your son now, so why would you be interested in me? Oh just fuck off,' she snarled, as he started to reply. 'You talk so much crap, and I'm sick of it, because the truth is nothing would make you happier than to get me and Mum out of your life so you can bring Vivienne back here. Well, you've obviously succeeded with Mum, and I bet the police are right, you have done away with her.'

His face was bloodless, his eyes glittering darkly as he said, 'If you seriously think—'

'Shut up,' she seethed, leaping to her feet. 'I don't want to hear any more. It doesn't interest me. You've got what you want – she's gone, and now I can't wait to go too.'

He flinched as the door slammed closed behind her. Though his instinct was to go after her, he knew it wouldn't do any good right now. She was too angry and afraid of what was happening. She needed time to calm down, then he'd try talking to her again, because he had to reach her somehow. God knew how he was going to manage it when her insecurities and fears were so deeply ingrained, and the police were out there even now expecting to find her mother's body.

Pushing his hands through his hair, he got to his feet and returned to the window. From the look of it nothing had changed outside, still a bunch of dark uniforms milling over the grounds, a few dogs panting and sniffing, and the ducks huddled up with the geese on the far bank, keeping clear of the divers. There appeared to be more helicopters now, which undoubtedly meant that news cameras were beaming progress back to the studios. He could almost feel pleased about that if it managed to reach Jacqueline and prompted her to put an end to this nonsense, but God knew if it would.

Hearing his mobile start to ring he turned back to his desk to check who it was, and seeing Vivienne's name he let the call go through to messages. There was nothing he could say to her now that was going to make this any easier for either of them. If anything, feeling as he did, it would only make matters worse.

Kelsey was sitting on her bed, hugging herself tightly, terrified that the feeling she'd had when her dad had told her about *Rufus* might come over her again. It had been like something inside her was sucking her down and down, making her smaller and smaller while the world grew bigger and bigger. She was shrinking into a horrible, ugly thing that no one wanted to see, or speak to, or have anything to do with at all, so she had to get plucked out like a weed, or crushed like a disgusting, mouldy crumb.

She felt sick and afraid and desperate to hold onto someone, but she wasn't going to let her dad in, even though he kept knocking. He didn't care really. He was just saying he did because he had to.

Suddenly huge waves of despair began tearing through her savagely, convulsing and pounding her chest, stealing her breath and making her want to scream out loud. *Mummy. Daddy.* The voice was shrill and terrified, but she couldn't let it out. She had to keep quiet, because she didn't matter the way Sam did. No one wanted to listen to her, so she rolled onto her side and clutched her knees even harder and almost didn't hear when her mobile bleeped with a text. She ignored it anyway. It wouldn't be from her mum, because it just wouldn't, and even if it was she didn't care. She didn't want to hear from her ever again. She only wanted to be dead, or to run away and never come back. If she had any money, or knew where to go, she'd start packing now.

In the end, just in case it might be her mum, she got up from the bed, breathless and trembling, her face ravaged by tears, and went to her dressing table to check. It was a message from Martha.

`Hey, wen u cmng bk 2 skul? Need my m8. XxM`

More tears welled in Kelsey's eyes and rolled down her cheeks to drip from her chin. Martha, her best friend. Immediately she started texting back, so relieved to have someone to talk to that her fingers were shaking and small, eager laughs were breaking through her sobs.

`Loads to tel u. bk soon. Cant w8 2 get out of here.`

The only trouble now was she had to ask her dad to take her back to school, and she really didn't want to see him in case he started talking about *Rufus* again.

She went to the window, trying to work out what to do, but seeing the helicopters she stepped back again. She didn't want to think about why they were there. It just made her angry and frustrated, like she wanted to lash out and hit someone, tear their face, their eyes, their hair. She had to make it all go away and leave her alone.

'So what do you think, Detective Constable?' Sadler asked, as he and Joy stood watching one of the divers rising to the surface of the lake. 'Has anything we've heard this morning impressed anything on you?'

Joy drew her coat more tightly around her as the sun disappeared behind a cloud. 'Well, sir,' she replied, 'to me it seems to be bearing out what Vivienne Kane told us last night, that Mr Avery didn't know about his son before now. And if he didn't, well, bang goes his motive.'

'Mm,' Sadler grunted.

She turned to find him looking as uncertain as she felt.

'That particular motive, yes,' he said, still watching the divers, 'but he doesn't deny wanting to end his marriage.' Then with a sigh he added, 'Even if it is true that he didn't know until last night, something was certainly going on in that cottage, or whatever you call it, before we got there. The atmosphere was so tense you could pluck it.'

'Which suggests maybe he had just found out.'

Sadler pursed his lips and nodded slowly.

'The housekeeper obviously didn't know until we told her,' Joy continued. 'No surprise there, I suppose. Shame we can't question his daughter without him being present.'

'I doubt she'd have known. If he was keeping it from the wife, it stands to reason he'd keep it from his daughter too.' He began following the progress of a trio of geese as they paddled across the water towards the opposite bank. 'No word yet from Vivienne Kane about her whereabouts on August 29th?' he asked.

'Not yet. She—'

Sadler turned round as a commotion erupted behind them, his detective's pulses starting to quicken, but it was only one of the sergeants reprimanding a young officer for not looking where he was throwing up mud.

Relaxing again, he said, 'It shouldn't be difficult to find out if Miles Avery and Vivienne Kane have been seeing one another on the quiet. Someone's got to know – family, colleagues, close friends – and one of them will be bound to give it away, if it has been happening.'

Joy nodded agreement.

'Her mother's the obvious first stop,' he continued, 'at which point we'll presumably get to meet the new son and heir.'

'I'll set it up,' she said, taking out her pad to make a note.

Digging his hands into his pockets, he turned to stare up at the house. With its backdrop of cold, grey sky and gloomy trees it appeared much more austere than when the sun was lighting up the creeper and softening the walls. From this distance it was impossible to tell whether anyone was watching from the windows, but he had a feeling Avery might be. He must be expecting them to come and talk to him at any moment, but Sadler was of a mind to let him stew for a while, get a little worked up about what direction the investigation might be taking, before questioning him again.

Taking out his mobile as it started to ring, he listened to the voice at the other end. A moment later he felt his face go slack.

'What is it, sir?' Joy said as he put the phone away.

His eyes went to hers. 'They've found a body,' he told her.

Joy's jaw dropped. 'Where?' she asked.

He turned towards the bottom woods, where the helicopters were buzzing overhead. 'Come on,' he said, 'we'd better get ourselves down there.'

Chapter Eleven

'Have you heard the news?' Linda said as soon as Vivienne walked in the door.

Since she'd been listening to the choreographer's music tape all the way from Devon, Vivienne hadn't.

'They've found a body,' her mother told her.

Vivienne turned cold.

'It's what they're saying,' Linda assured her, looking almost as stunned as Vivienne. 'Apparently it's in some woods, next to the moor.'

Vivienne dropped her bags and took out her phone. 'Miles,' she said shakily into his voicemail. 'I've just heard—' Her voice caught on a wave of resistance. 'You have to call me. Please. I need to speak to you.' Her eyes went back to her mother's as she rang off. 'There has to be a mistake,' she said, her face now totally devoid of colour. 'It can't be her. Are they saying it is?'

'I don't know. Not that I heard, but . . .'

'Where's Rufus?'

'Having his afternoon nap.'

Vivienne started through to the sitting room.

'Vivi,' her mother said anxiously as Vivienne stooped to kiss the softly flushed cheek of her sleeping son, 'the police have been in touch. They want to come here and talk to me.'

Vivienne's heart turned over, and putting her palms to her cheeks she pressed in hard. 'It's all right,' she told her mother, forcing herself to stay calm. 'They'll be trying to find out how long Miles has known about Rufus.'

Linda was taken aback. 'Does that mean you've told him?'

'He found a photograph, last night. He knew straight

away Rufus was his and he's furious that I've kept it from him.'

'But he has to understand why, surely,' Linda protested. 'He knows very well—'

'Of course he understands,' Vivienne cut in, more sharply than she'd intended, 'but that's not going to give him back the first fifteen months of Rufus's life, is it?'

Linda looked at her helplessly. 'I don't know what to say,' she murmured. 'If this body turns out to be Jacqueline's . . .'

'Of course it's not,' Vivienne snapped, and turning abruptly away she went out to the kitchen to switch on the news.

'. . . We're just going over to Dartmoor now,' the studio presenter was saying, 'where our reporter Gavin Havelock is on the scene. Gavin, can you tell us what's happening now?'

A clean-shaven, rosy-cheeked young man appeared on the screen, holding a microphone in one hand and a sheaf of notes in the other. 'Well, Sarah, as we now know, what they've discovered the other side of these woods is the body of a man said to be in a fairly decomposed state . . .'

Vivienne's head started to spin.

'The police haven't made an official statement yet, so we don't know if they've been able to identify the body. If they have, obviously next of kin will have to be informed before— Hang on, I think we're going to an aerial shot now, yes we are.' The screen changed to an overview of the eastern side of the moor, vast and undulating, and forbiddingly bleak. Then the camera made a quick zoom in to a small cluster of activity, partially masked by trees, where men in pale-coloured overalls and others in fluorescent police jackets were moving between randomly parked vehicles and a newly erected incident tent. 'A forensic team arrived about half an hour ago,' the reporter was saying. 'They'll obviously be carrying out a thorough examination of the scene before taking away any evidence they gather . . .'

As he spoke the helicopter camera was panning over to the gardens of Moorlands, where more police officers and sniffer dogs were still much in evidence.

Vivienne's heart tripped as the house came into view. She wondered if Miles was watching this too, if he'd known since its discovery that the body was male, or if he'd had to go through the horror of thinking it might be Jacqueline.

'Has there been any word from Mr Avery at all?' the presenter was asking.

'Nothing so far. In fact there's nothing at this stage to connect him with the body, other than the proximity to his land. However, I've just been told to expect a police statement sometime in the next hour or so.'

Feeling the craziness of it all circling her like a mad merry-go-round, Vivienne clicked off with the remote and stood staring at the blank screen.

Her mobile started to ring and her heart leapt with the hope that it would be Miles, but the number wasn't familiar so she let it go through to messages. She wasn't going to risk speaking to the press right now.

Turning to where her mother was standing in the doorway, she said, 'When are the police coming to see you?'

'Tomorrow morning, at eleven.'

Vivienne nodded distractedly, then picking up the kettle she started to fill it.

'I feel like something a bit stronger than that, don't you?' Linda murmured.

Vivienne took a moment to register the words. 'Mm, yes,' she agreed.

As her mother took a bottle of wine from the fridge and started to open it, Vivienne noticed her shaking fingers and was torn between anger and pity. Clearly Linda was still afraid Miles might be guilty of an appalling crime, and was now terrified, not only of what might happen during the days and weeks to come, but of what it was going to mean to her grandson's future.

'It's not Jacqueline,' she said sharply.

'No, I heard. That's good. Uh, Caroline should be here shortly,' and she passed over a full glass of Sauvignon Blanc.

Vivienne's insides sank. Her sister was about the last person she needed to see right now.

They both started as the phone rang on the counter top. Being the closest, Vivienne picked it up.

'Linda?' a male voice said at the other end.

'No, it's her daughter, Vivienne. Who's speaking please?'

'It's David.'

'David,' she said distractedly to her mother, and passing her the receiver she wandered over to the kitchen door. Suddenly feeling the need to be outside, as though in some strange way it could connect her to Miles, she turned the handle and let herself out.

As she walked along the path, carrying her glass in one hand and trailing the other over the empty washing line, she was gazing down at the fading shrubs and random scattering of autumn leaves. Rufus's baby swing hung from the branch of an acacia, while his see-saw and other toys were tucked away inside his little wooden playhouse. In her mind's eye she imagined Miles on a summer's day rolling around the lawns at Moorlands with his son, swooping him up in the air and laughing as Rufus shrieked and gurgled with delight.

As a terrible foreboding closed around her heart she came to a stop between two yews at the end of the garden, and took a sip of her wine. She wondered what Miles might be doing now, if he was being questioned, or trying to deal with Kelsey, or maybe there had been further developments that had yet to be announced. She could hardly bear to think of what they might be, but no matter what happened, she would never believe him capable of . . . Yet even as she was thinking it her treacherous mind began flashing the horror of an arrest, a trial, prison visits . . . But it wasn't going to happen. The body wasn't even Jacqueline's for heaven's sake, so no matter what insidious tricks her subconscious might play, she knew in her heart that Miles was as innocent of any crime as she was.

With a small shuddering breath she turned around and went back down the path, feeling the damp air starting to seep into her skin. When she reached the kitchen her mother was still on the phone, her cheeks flushed with colour, and her eyes glittering in a way that turned Vivienne cold with dread. A beat later the dread was replaced by puzzlement as her mother said, 'I'm sorry, it's a bit difficult now. Yes. Yes. I understand you're disappointed. So am I, but I can't go with all this . . . Oh David, please don't say that.' She turned away, hunching over the receiver. 'I'll call you back,' she murmured and quickly hung up. When she turned round again Vivienne was watching her with frankly questioning eyes. 'Sorry,' Linda mumbled. 'It was just . . . I was going to . . . Shall we have some more wine?'

'You haven't even started that one yet,' Vivienne pointed out. 'Who were you speaking to?'

'No one. I mean, just a friend.'

'His name's David. Is it someone I know?'

Linda shook her head. 'I – I was going to tell you about him this weekend,' she said hastily, 'but then all this . . . Well, you know now anyway.'

Vivienne's breath was starting to feel short. 'Mum, is he someone you've been seeing, become involved with?' she asked, feeling a ludicrous sense of betrayal that her mother hadn't confided in her.

Linda's only answer was to appear more flustered than ever.

'He is, isn't he?' Vivienne insisted. 'Yes, of course,' she answered for her. 'Mum, it's all right. You don't have to—'

'No it's *not* all right,' her mother interrupted. 'He wants me to go to Italy with him, and I said I would, just as soon as I could work out the timing with you, but now, well . . .' She shrugged and tried to look loyal.

Vivienne's shock was quickly obliterated by a desperate need for her mother right now. She couldn't go away with all this going on. How could she even think it? Then, overcome with shame at her own selfishness, she said, 'You have to go. If it's what you want . . .'

'And leave you to deal with all this alone? Don't be ridiculous. What about Rufus?'

'I can take care of him.'

'How? You're just getting things going again with the agency, and if the worst does come to the worst—'

'It won't,' Vivienne cut in harshly. 'And it shouldn't be an issue, not for you. I've told you before, you have a right to your own life, and I've already taken up too much of it.'

'For heaven's sake, you're my daughter, how can you say something like that?'

'Because it's true. You shouldn't be tied down here with a baby at your age, miles from all your friends and everything you know. I've always hated myself for letting you do it . . .'

'I've settled in here now. I've made new friends.'

'And David's obviously one of them.'

'Yes, but that doesn't mean—' She broke off at the sound of a key turning in the front door, and Vivienne's eyes closed as she braced herself ready to deal with her sister.

'I saw your car outside,' Caroline said sourly as she came into the kitchen. She was as tall as Vivienne, and as dark, but she carried much more weight, and seemed uninterested in tinting the wiry grey strands out of her hair.

'I wasn't hiding it,' Vivienne retorted in like manner.

Caroline pursed the corners of her mouth, then seeing the wine went to help herself to a glass. When she'd finished pouring she stood the other side of the table next to their mother and fixed Vivienne with their father's warm green eyes, except right now hers were chillingly sharp. 'I expect Mum told you I was coming,' she stated.

'Yes,' Vivienne answered.

Caroline's gaze swept her sister's face with ill-disguised contempt. 'I'd decided to speak to you before this outrageous situation blew up,' she told her. 'Now it has—'

'Caro, darling,' Linda interrupted, 'it's not Vivi's fault . . .'

Ignoring her, Caroline said, 'Your association with Miles, Vivienne, has put Mum in a totally invidious—'

'He's Rufus's father,' Linda cut in. 'She can't help the assoc—'

'Let her go on,' Vivienne interrupted, glaring icily at her sister.

Two high spots of colour appeared in Caroline's cheeks. 'Did you know Mum's been seeing someone?' she demanded, clearly expecting Vivienne to say no.

'Yes,' Vivienne responded.

'David just called,' Linda put in.

Caroline glanced at her. 'It's time, Vivienne,' she said, turning back, 'for you to make other arrangements for

Rufus. Mum's taken him on long enough. She's got her own life . . .'

'Vivienne's always saying that herself,' Linda protested, 'but you know that I'm afraid to trust anyone else with him. If Miles's wife should ever know he has a son . . .'

Caroline triumphantly seized the moment. 'Well, I don't think we need worry about that any longer, need we?' she said, witheringly. 'With Jacqueline off the scene, there's absolutely no reason for Vivienne not to start assuming her responsibilities.'

'Maybe you haven't heard the latest news,' Vivienne said through her teeth. 'The body is—'

'. . . male, yes I heard. So, OK, you stay in your fairy-tale world of denial, if that's what you want, but I'm afraid the rest of us need to get on with reality. David's a decent man. He cares a great deal for Mum, and I don't want her bailing out of a trip to Italy because you can't look after your own son.'

'As a matter of fact,' Vivienne seethed, 'I was telling her, as you came in, that she had to go. It's never been my intention to stand in the way of anything she wants to do . . .'

'Oh for God's sake, denial, delusion, where do you get off pretending Vivienne? Never wanted to stand in her way? Like hell. But you've used her for your own ends long enough. It's time to—'

'She really was telling me I had to go,' Linda insisted, 'but I wouldn't feel right, Caro, not with all this going on. Maybe once it's resolved . . .'

'No,' Vivienne declared hotly. 'I'm taking Rufus with me when I leave on Sunday. Caroline's right, it's time I assumed my responsibilities.'

'Vivi, no, you can't,' Linda cried. 'You have to work, and finding the right help—'

'He can come into the office with me,' Vivienne told her, taking no time to think it through. 'You really mustn't cancel anything with David, and I'm sorry if you've had to before this, without my knowing. Now, if you'll excuse me, I think that's my son waking up.'

As she swept out of the kitchen tears were burning her

eyes, though she'd rather have died than let Caroline see. How dare she come in here laying down the law like she had right on her side, when her life was a bigger mess than anyone's? And did Vivienne ever ram it down her throat, or try to humiliate her? Never. The fact her husband was a drunk barely got mentioned, unless it was to blame Miles for making the problem worse. But what the hell was Miles supposed to have done? He'd given Roger more chances than the man even came close to deserving, putting freelance work his way at every opportunity, but nine times out of ten Roger had failed to deliver. In the end he'd left Miles with no choice but to instruct the news desk to stop using him. So for Caroline to carry on holding a grudge the way she was, was just plain stupid. She should have been trying to get her husband off the drink, instead of wreaking some kind of petty revenge on those whose only crime had been to try and help him.

Finding Rufus lying on his back and clutching his feet in his hands as he chattered on in a language of his own, she instantly broke into a tearful smile. 'Hello, darling,' she whispered, going to kneel next to him. 'Did you have a good sleep?'

'Da, da, mum,' he cooed happily and made a quick grab for her face. 'Ink roo ink.'

Laughing as she scooped him up, she pressed her face into the squidgy warm folds of his neck and blew a raspberry. Immediately he started blowing them too, then began jigging up and down chanting, 'Roo ink. Roo ink.'

Suddenly realising what he was saying, she clasped him hard in pride. 'Rufus wants a drink, does he?' she said kissing him. 'You're such a clever boy.'

'Nan, nan, nan,' he cried, and began straining out of Vivienne's arms.

She turned around, and for the first time in Rufus's short life she found herself reluctant to hand him over to her mother. The scene in the kitchen had made her doubly protective, and thinking too of what was happening to Miles she longed desperately to hold their son close, as though any time now it was going to be just the three of them against the world.

Realising how absurd she was being, when no one could love him more than her mother, she forced herself to let him go, saying, 'I'll get him some juice.'

'It's in the fridge door,' her mother told her. 'The organic apple. Vivi, I—'

'Later,' Vivienne interrupted.

Finding Caroline pressing a text into her mobile, Vivienne moved past her to take one of Rufus's beakers from a child-proof cupboard.

'I know it probably won't be easy for you having him back again,' Caroline said, putting her phone away, 'but one of us has to consider Mum . . .'

'Oh, cut the self-righteousness,' Vivienne snapped. 'We both know what's going on here, so either bring it out in the open or damned well shut up.'

Caroline's eyebrows rose sarcastically. 'Isn't that just typical of you to try and grab the moral high ground. Well, let me tell you this, I'd rather be married to a man with a drink problem than hanker after one who's on his way to jail for murdering his wife,' and grabbing her bag she started to leave.

'It *wasn't* Jacqueline!' Vivienne yelled after her, but Caroline was already closing the door.

Snatching up her BlackBerry as it signalled an incoming text, Vivienne clicked through to messages, praying to God it was from Miles, but to her frustration it was a reporter she knew from the *Mirror*, offering a lavish incentive for an exclusive interview.

What about the auction? she wanted to scream. *Is nobody listening? Don't any of you care that a lovely young mother needs your help?*

The instant that rumours of a body had started threading through the press camp, Justine James had leapt into her hire car and driven at top speed back to the Nobody Inn. Time was absolutely of the essence, for the discovery of a body could only mean that within a matter of hours one, or more, of her colleagues would manage to track down Vivienne's mother – and once they found the mother it would be a very short step to finding the child.

She was sorry about breaking her word to Miles, but since she'd never really intended to keep it, the regret was minimal. Besides, he'd be the first to understand that with all that was happening, no journalist in their right mind could be expected to keep this kind of exclusive to themselves, particularly not one who was in such dire need of career rescue. And this would do it in spades, because it wasn't only going to secure her future with the *Mail*, it was going to make that smarmy, loud-mouthed philistine of an editor she had now apoplectic with rage when he realised she'd double-crossed him and delivered to another of his great rivals.

It took no more than thirty minutes to write the piece. It was a pity Figgis hadn't managed to get any shots of the boy yet, but hey, she couldn't have everything, and there were bound to be some library pictures of Sam they could dig out for baby appeal.

After checking her story through, making it as sensational as she could, she sat back for a moment, savouring the triumph. While everyone else ran with the discovery of a body and possible murder, she was going to splash the most powerful motive of all, right across the front page.

Only after she'd clicked to send, and received confirmation that the email and its attachment had gone, did she feel a twinge of trepidation for what it was going to mean having both Miles Avery and Gareth Critchley as lifelong enemies. It wasn't a prospect that thrilled her, especially considering how powerful both men were. However, it was too late to go back now, and picking up the TV remote she tuned to the latest news.

A few minutes later she was still sitting in her chair, staring in disbelief at the screen. The body belonged to a man, not a woman. Everyone had assumed . . . She spun back to her computer, but the email had long gone.

It's OK, she told herself, taking deep breaths. A corpse turning up right next to the Avery land when Jacqueline was still missing was good enough grounds to run with the motive for her murder. Hell, for all she knew there could be half a dozen bodies out there, and even if none of them turned out to be Jacqueline, it still didn't change the fact that the exclusive of Miles and Vivienne's love child was going to be snapped up by someone else if she didn't act now.

Nevertheless, it was with a sick feeling inside that she began to contemplate exactly how Miles might respond to her betrayal, not to mention how badly it was going to go down with the Critch.

'*Nooooo!*' Kelsey screamed, clasping her hands to her head as she shook it from side to side. 'No! No! No!'

White-faced, Miles tried to go to her but she pushed him away, tears of confusion streaming down her cheeks.

'Leave me alone!' she yelled, saliva spraying from her lips. 'I don't want you near me.'

'Darling, it's all right,' he said, keeping his voice gentle.

'You're lying to me. Everyone's lying all the time,' she sobbed. 'Why did you say . . . ? *No!*' she shrieked as he tried to approach her again. 'You have to stop this, all of you,' she raged, turning her stricken face to Sadler and Joy. 'You said it was a woman . . .'

'Kelsey, no one—' Sadler began.

'I can't take any more. Do you hear me? I hate her. I hate you all. Just leave me alone . . .' Rushing past them, she tore open the door and ran out into the bleak afternoon.

Miles was close behind, running across the courtyard to try to stop her, but she was too fast. The kitchen door slammed and locked behind her before she charged up the back stairs to her room.

Feeling the same turmoil of emotions that was tearing her apart, he returned to the sitting room where Sadler and Joy were still waiting. His dark eyes were cold as they took in Sadler's solemn expression. Next to Sadler DC Joy was nervously clutching her mobile, while her pale, anxious face turned repeatedly to the door. He wasn't going to speak. He was only going to fix Sadler with all the contempt the man deserved, and let him damned well squirm in it.

With a gruff clearing of his throat Sadler said, 'We'll be in touch in the morning,' and nodding to Joy he started out of the room.

The instant they'd gone Miles went upstairs to try and talk to Kelsey. There was no reply when he knocked, but she was clearly in there, because the door was locked and when he called out, her music went on to drown him out.

Sighing heavily, he took himself back downstairs and dialled her mobile number. As he'd feared he went straight through to voicemail. 'Kelsey,' he said quietly, but firmly. 'I know today has been hard for you, but it's going to be all right, darling. I promise. Of course it wasn't Mum they found, we knew that even before they told us it was a man . . .' Hearing the emptiness of his reassurance, his eyes closed in despair. How the hell was he going to get her through this when the police weren't bothering to stop false rumours hitting the news, and the press themselves were so keen to make this into a murder, most likely committed by him?

Thunderclouds were drawing a veil over the sun and a sharp wind bowed the trees over the drive as Sadler and Joy walked away from the house. Neither of them spoke, they merely stared grimly ahead, still sobered by Kelsey's understandable explosion.

Feeling the chill in the air, Joy pocketed her mobile and zipped up her coat. She'd like to think she hadn't been a part of what had happened in this valley today, allowing a child to believe her mother was dead and then retracting it, but she had, and now somehow she had to live with it.

Not until they were next to a golden cascade of angel's trumpets where Sadler had left his car did he finally turn to Joy and say with a sigh, 'Well, Detective Constable, that body belongs to someone, so now we need to find out who.'

Joy's eyes were slightly glazed as she turned in the direction of the lower woods where the body had been found. The image of it was staying with her, forlorn and huddled, as though for warmth, in a bed of damp leaves, the exposed skin of its skeletal hands and its sodden clothes smeared with a slimy green sphagnum. As the pathologist had wiped moss and insects from the face she'd looked away, switching her mind from the sad indignity to the rippling song of a hidden curlew. She was a nature lover, so could name many of the grasses and birds around, which was what she'd done, in her mind, to prevent herself from throwing up. 'Whoever he is,' she said, 'do you think he could be connected to Mrs Avery in some way?'

Sadler's weariness showed in the heaviness of his eyes. 'You mean apart from turning up dead right next to her land? Who knows, Elaine? Who knows?'

Looking back at him she gave a small smile and opened the passenger door. She was aware that Sadler had let the rumour float that it was a female body in an effort to wrong-foot Avery, maybe rattle him into making some kind of confession. As a tactic it had spectacularly backfired, and as a decision it stank as badly as the corpse. It just went to prove, she thought dully as they began driving away, that even smart men didn't always get it right.

Miles was sitting in the semi-darkness, his head resting on the back of the sofa, his hands lying loosely beside him. He'd tried several times now to coax Kelsey out of her room, but she still wouldn't come down, in spite of him telling her that they'd identified the body on the moor. It belonged to a forty-eight-year old man by the name of Timothy Grainger, whose alcohol abuse, vagrancy and petty crimes were well known to the police. No one could say yet how he'd come to be in the woods, much less how he'd ended up the way he had.

'Might he be someone your wife knew?' DC Joy had asked doubtfully when she'd called to tell him the news.

'It seems unlikely,' he'd answered, keeping it polite. 'It's not a name I've ever heard her mention.'

'OK, thank you. I'll be back in touch once we've established the cause of death, or if any new information comes to light.'

In a sane world he knew he'd make Sadler pay for the games he'd played today, but with Jacqueline still missing, and a stranger's corpse turning up on the far side of their woods, the world was anything but sane.

Sighing, he glanced at his watch, then closed his eyes as his thoughts drifted out across the stark, misted plains of the moor, down into the clefts, over the harsh granite tors to the rugged uplands, so remote and forbidding. Jacqueline had never been able to feel the romance of the moor, had always failed to see the beauty in its rivers and waterfalls, wooded valleys and colourful heathland. She found everything about it sinister and threatening, detested its folklore and was afraid of its wildlife. To think of her out there on a night like this, alone, lost, maybe even . . .

Sitting forward, he put his head in his hands. Why was he tormenting himself like this when she was no more out there on the moor than she was here in this house? He had to let go of such madness or he'd be no good to himself, never mind anyone else.

Inhaling deeply, he drew his hands down over his unshaven face and let the breath go slowly. Somewhere in the distance thunder was rumbling through the heavens, while rain pattered against the windows of the room. The garden lights were on now, and as far he could make out everyone had gone home. Whether they were planning to continue the search tomorrow he had no idea, nor, at this moment, did he particularly care. He only wanted to go on sitting in this silence, trying to work out what he was going to do about Kelsey. She had to be his priority, he was in no doubt about that, but knowing he had a son who needed him, and whose first fifteen months of life had already been lost to him . . . He didn't want to waste any more time. Even now he was longing to see the boy, hold him in his arms, and feel the energy of his young life.

It couldn't happen yet, though, so at some point he would call Vivienne to tell her that in spite of the way he'd reacted, she was right to protect their son the way she had, and that she should continue to until all this was over. He wouldn't do it tonight. He'd endured enough attacks on his father's conscience for one day, and had neither the energy, nor the will right now, to try dealing with any more.

Chapter Twelve

'Vivi, hi, are you OK?' Alice said, sounding oddly tentative.

Instantly tensing, Vivienne said, 'I'm fine. Just giving Rufus his breakfast.'

'OK. I don't suppose you've seen the *Mail* yet today?'

Vivienne's heart immediately contracted. 'No, Mum takes the *Express*. Why? What's in it?'

'You'd better brace yourself. I'm afraid Rufus – or Miles's love child as they're calling him – has made the front page.'

'Oh my God,' Vivienne murmured, putting down the spoon she was holding.

'The byline belongs to Justine James.'

Vivienne almost reeled. 'But how does she know? She can't . . .' Her eyes closed. 'Miles wouldn't have told her. He just wouldn't.'

'It doesn't seem likely,' Alice agreed.

More dismay sank into Vivienne's heart. 'There's only one other person I can think of,' she said flatly. 'My sister, Caroline.'

Alice didn't comment, showing that her suspicions had already moved in that direction.

'Or her husband,' Vivienne continued. 'One of them has to be the source.'

'But why now, when they've always known?'

'The payout, I imagine. It would have shot up the day Jacqueline disappeared.' A surge of fury tightened her voice. 'To think that my own family could—' She turned round as her mother came into the kitchen. 'Can you pop out and get the *Mail*?' she said. 'Apparently they've found out about Rufus.' Then to Alice, 'Please tell me it's not giving away where we live.'

'Not exactly. It just says that you've got him tucked away in the depths of Berkshire, clearly hoping to protect him from, I quote, "the deranged grief of his father's wife, the tragically bereaved Jacqueline Avery who has been missing from her home—"'

'Stop,' Vivienne interrupted. 'This is exactly what I was afraid of.'

Linda was putting on her coat, her face as ashen as Vivienne's. 'I'll be five minutes,' she called from the front door, and let herself out into the rain.

'The innuendo is brutal,' Alice said. 'It's worse for Miles, but you're not coming out of it too well either.'

'Give me the gist,' Vivienne said, stooping to pick up the spoon that had flown from Rufus's hand.

'You can probably guess at most of it. It's insinuating that you and Miles have conspired to get rid of Jacqueline in order to protect Rufus from any violent reaction she might have to finding out Miles has a son. It's couched in softer terms than that, obviously, to avoid a lawsuit, but the suggestion is, you – and Miles in particular – have a very good reason for wanting his wife out of the way.'

'That woman is *sick*,' Vivienne spat in disgust. 'There's not even anything to say Jacqueline's dead.'

'Sic, sic, sic,' Rufus echoed, bouncing up and down in his high chair.

Vivienne put a hand on his head. 'Doesn't she have any sense of responsibility?' she seethed. 'Or a conscience? I don't even know why I'm asking, when we already know she's devoid of anything approaching human decency.'

'Are you going to call Miles?'

'I've been trying for the past twenty-four hours, but so far he hasn't called back.'

'He's bound to have seen the paper by now.'

'Of course. He has them all delivered first thing, which means he'll be having to deal with Kelsey. Is there any more about the body they found? Does anyone know who it belonged to yet?'

'Yes, apparently it's some homeless guy by the name of, hang on, Timothy Grainger. No one knows how he got there yet, but you can imagine how the clever dicks are trying to concoct some sort of relationship with Jacqueline. It's more thrilling if there is a connection, I suppose, it satisfies the salacious brain cell, which is next door to the other one they have that lets them know when they need food.'

Vivienne's smile was weak. 'I guess it's quite an offering when you're in the business of peddling scandal,' she said.

'I guess it is,' Alice agreed. 'Anyway, I'm afraid I have to love you and leave you now, I've got a meeting in Soho at eleven, but before I go, I think this new turn of events is going to make it extremely difficult for you to continue in Devon, don't you? So let's talk later and discuss a complete swap for you and Pete.'

Vivienne grimaced. 'I've got an added complication now,' she confessed. 'It turns out my mother has a boyfriend who wants her to go to Italy with him, so I have to take care of Rufus. I can't trawl him round the TV circuit that *Belle Amie*'s going to be on, and anyway, I'm not going to let Sharon down.'

'Oh blimey,' Alice murmured. 'Does your mother have to go now?'

'She probably wouldn't if I asked her not to, but there was a bit of a scene here yesterday, which I'll tell you about another time. To be honest, now that witch, Justine James, has splashed Rufus's existence all over the paper, I'd feel better if he was with me. My mother's nervous enough about the police coming this morning, if a bunch of reporters turned up at the door she really wouldn't know how to handle it.'

'Worse still would be if Jacqueline turned up,' Alice murmured.

Vivienne's insides recoiled from the thought. 'At least we'd know she's still alive,' she said, glancing down the hall as her mother came in the front door. 'OK, I'll let you go now. The paper's just arrived, so I can read Justine James's self-serving little exclusive for myself.'

Miles's face was haggard as he stared down at a three-year-old photograph of him and Vivienne, looking light-hearted and very much in love. At any other time the image, and memories it conjured, might have softened him. Today he could only feel fury at finding it emblazoned on a front page under the headline *Avery's Love Child*. Thank God there were no shots of Rufus – or Sam – for which he already knew he had the *Mail*'s editor to thank, since the man himself had called late last night to warn him what to expect from the morning edition.

From the way the article was slanted both boys were clearly meant to be featured, and there was no doubt in Miles's mind that by tomorrow they'd be splashed all over the other papers. Should Jacqueline see them, he hardly dared think about how hard she would find it.

Tossing the paper aside, he reached for the phone. It was no surprise that Justine had run the story; he'd been expecting it ever since she'd told him she knew about Rufus. Nevertheless, the way she'd slanted it was sickening in the extreme. Clearly, she'd presumed the body was Jacqueline's, so hadn't wasted a minute in getting her exclusive to print. After all, if Miles Avery was about to be charged with murder, it was going to be open season for the press. So the fiercely ambitious girl he'd plucked from the ranks of young wannabes and launched on a glittering career, the woman he'd once considered a friend, the colleague who knew how fragile his wife and daughter were, had decided to exact some revenge for being left at *The News* by convicting him before any evidence of a crime even existed.

Having made his connection he spent less than five minutes talking to the the *Mail*'s proprietor, by which time the tightrope Justine was walking had been cut. She was on her way down now, and fast would she fall since her only chance of rescue lay with the Critch, and somehow he couldn't see that happening.

Picking up his mobile he pressed in Kelsey's number. Ignoring the absurdity that they were communicating by phone in the same house, he said, 'Darling, it's Dad again. I'm afraid the press has got hold of . . . Well, there's a front-page story about Rufus. I wanted to let you know . . .' He pressed his fingers into the sockets of his eyes, hearing how different he was when speaking to her than when he spoke to his colleagues. Sometimes he felt like two people inside the same skin, and he wasn't always entirely sure which of them was real.

Registering a knock on his study door, he rang off and looked up as Mrs Davies put her head round. 'Can I get you anything?' she asked, worriedly. 'More coffee? I brought some Cornish pasties with me this morning.'

'Nothing, thank you,' he answered, his smile as strained as his eyes.

She continued to look at him, her ageing face creased with concern. 'Kelsey's all right,' she told him. 'She just let me in to give her some breakfast.'

Feeling a loosening inside at how relieved that made him, he said, 'Did she say anything?'

'Only that she wants to go back to school.'

Sighing, he drew his hands over his face, then after thanking her again he waited until she'd left the room before walking over to the window.

A fine drizzle was spreading like a feathery mist over the lake and trees, making their grey existence seem almost ethereal. However, there was nothing ethereal about the search that had evidently resumed. Not that there was much activity in the garden today, the big effort seeming focused around the ditch where the body had been found.

Sadler had dropped in about an hour ago, for once without Joy, who'd gone to Berkshire to interview Vivienne's mother. Miles hadn't been expecting an apology for what had happened yesterday, but to his surprise he'd received one, grudging though it had been. Clearly, Sadler remained convinced that Mrs Avery's husband knew a great deal more about her disappearance than he was telling, but it seemed that didn't make it any less necessary for the inspector to acknowledge his bad handling of events the day before.

The sudden roar of a chopper engine swooping down over the eastern side of the moor made him look up. The press would be out there again, of course, probably increasing in their numbers and their efforts to reach him. The landlines were switched off, however, so he had no idea how fiercely Moorlands was being bombarded with calls. The only line still open was the one he'd had connected a few months ago for private use, which he assumed hadn't yet been discovered since it hadn't rung. Kelsey knew it, so did Jacqueline, and he guessed at some point he should give it to Vivienne too.

With a sigh that seemed to draw from the very depths of him he returned his gaze to the lake and watched the handful of searchers who were still combing the banks, some up to their thighs in water, others squatting amongst the reeds. The lake's usual residents were grouped in a watchful, nervous mass on the far shore, keeping a safe distance from the invaders.

After a while his eyes glazed as his thoughts began running disjointedly into one another, from Jacqueline, to Kelsey, to the body, to Sadler whose car was still outside, to Joy who might be in Berkshire by now. Evidently Vivienne's mother had moved, because she'd lived in Surrey when he and Vivienne were together. He knew, of course, why she'd uprooted, but he still had no idea of the address, which meant that he didn't actually know where his son might be now.

Feeling those words echoing up from the past, he closed his eyes as though to block the unholy mantra. Where was his son? Who had taken him? What had they done to him? At least in Rufus's case Miles knew he was safe and loved – and alive. What he had no way of knowing, though, was whether any of this was reaching Jacqueline.

Taking a sharp breath he turned back to his desk and was about to pick up his mobile when it started to ring. Seeing it was Justine he clicked on. 'Nothing you have to say is of any interest to me,' he told her. 'If you—'

'Miles, listen! There's—'

'. . . don't already know what your actions have cost you, you will very soon. In the meantime, if you go anywhere near any member of my family – and that includes Vivienne and Rufus – it won't only be your career that's over.'

After ending the call he dialled Vivienne's number, knowing he couldn't put it off any longer, and finding that actually he didn't want to.

'At last,' she said, when she answered. 'I've been so

worried about you. Are you OK? What's happening down there?'

'The search goes on,' he told her. 'Has anyone from the press found you yet?'

'There was a photographer hanging around earlier. No sign of him now, but he's probably bribed one of the neighbours to let him in out of the rain.'

'It can only be a matter of time before Justine, or someone else, turns up,' he said. 'They're going to be after pictures of Rufus. Can you cope? Is there something I can do?'

'I don't think so. To be frank, I'm more worried about Jacqueline. Do you think she knows what's going on?'

'I wish I could answer that. If she does, well . . .' Sighing, he shook his head, not wanting to go any further than that.

'You sound exhausted,' she told him. 'How's Kelsey?'

'Not good. At the moment she won't speak to me at all.'

Her sigh was gentle, making him picture her in a way that stirred a need to hold her. Someone knocked on the door and he turned to see who it was.

'Miles,' she said softly.

The expression on Sadler's face was turning his insides to liquid.

'I'm sorry,' Vivienne was saying, 'it was wrong of me not to tell you about Rufus—'

'This isn't the time,' he interrupted, his eyes still on Sadler.

'But I needed to say it. I want you to know—'

'Not now,' he cut in. 'I'll speak to you later,' and before she could say any more he ended the call.

'I'd like you to come with me, Mr Avery,' Sadler said in a voice that was unnervingly grave.

'Why?' Miles demanded. 'Where are we going?'

Sadler stood aside for him to go ahead.

'Don't tell me you've found her,' Miles said, a charge of adrenalin making him light-headed.

'Not your wife, no,' Sadler answered.

At that Miles swung round, his face so white he seemed about to pass out. 'Not my daughter,' he gasped.

Realising his mistake, Sadler immediately flushed. 'No, it's not your daughter,' he assured him.

Miles's relief was so palpable that he almost staggered. 'Then for God's sake, man,' he growled, 'tell me what it is.'

'Actually, that's what we're hoping you're going to tell us,' Sadler responded, and going out into the rain he opened the passenger door of his Focus for Miles to get in.

'Let me through. Please. Mind out of the way.'

Justine was jostling her colleagues, trying to force her way to the front of the mêlée, but in spite of the driving rain and wind, no one was giving an inch. Up ahead, through a sea of hoods and hoisted cameras, she could see two mounted officers holding back the crowd, and hear several dogs barking.

'What is it?' she growled in frustration. 'Will someone tell me what's going on?'

'Thought you were the one with all the inside gen,' someone close by jeered.

Justine winced as a large man in heavy boots stepped back onto her foot. 'For God's sake,' she seethed, giving him an angry shove.

As he turned round she dived through the space he created and tried to push on to the cordon that had been strung across the narrow country road. It wasn't easy. When a congregated press was after a story they became a pack of starving hyenas: nothing and no one was going to get there first.

'What is it?' she repeated to a BBC cameraman she'd known for years. 'What's all the fuss about?'

As he started to answer she grunted in pain; a photographer had just clunked her head with his camera. It was like a scrum, elbows digging, feet kicking, shoulders shoving, and all the time the rain was coming down like nails. She looked around frantically for the cameraman, spotted him a few feet away and shouted, 'Bill! What is it?'

But Bill wasn't listening. His only focus was the woods behind the phalanx of officers that was holding the media at bay.

Wanting to scream she forced her way towards someone else she knew, ready to claw and scratch like an alley cat if she needed to. 'Alby! Alby! What's going on?'

Albert Finnigan seemed not to hear. He was too busy calling out for a comment from Miles Avery as Miles and Sadler, escorted by two PCs with police issue umbrellas, crossed the corner of a field and disappeared into the shadowy woods the other side.

'Is it another body?' someone yelled.

'Is it her?'

'Why's Avery here?' a reporter next to Justine shouted.

Justine eyed her closely. Miles, here? So that was what all the fuss was about. Her mind went into overdrive. Obviously something had been found, or at least a new development was breaking. Whatever it was, it had to be serious if Miles had been brought to the woods, but hanging around to share the scoop with this bunch of tossers was not what she was about. Exclusives, front pages, new angles, that was what she needed to get back in with the Critch, and like a little epiphany in a world of seething darkness it was occurring to her how she might manage it. No guarantees, but definitely worth a shot, so squirming back through the crowd she made a mad dash along the lane to where she'd left her car.

Minutes later, wipers going like the clappers, she braked hard on the bend before Moorlands, skidded forward on the slippery road, righted the car, then finding the gates unattended, as she'd hoped, she swerved into the drive and sped up to the house. Time wouldn't be on her side, so she had to move swiftly and pray no one else was at home.

Jumping out of the car she ran towards the double front doors, hoping to God she wouldn't have to waste time trying to break in. To her relief one of the doors was unlocked, so pushing it open she stood quietly for a moment, stilling her breath as she listened to the cavernous silence of the hall.

Finally deciding the place was empty she moved quickly across to the study, closed the door behind her and began rifling through drawers and cupboards in search of something, *anything,* that might give her an edge over everyone else. A photograph of Rufus would be great – if nothing else it would suggest Miles had known about his son all along –

or perhaps a letter from Jacqueline begging him not to leave her for Vivienne. Best of all, she was thinking as she moved over to his computer, would be some kind of communication from Vivienne implicating them both in the mysterious disappearance.

Amazed that Miles's password was programmed in for immediate access to his email, she quickly began scrolling through the dozens upon dozens of messages from her colleagues that had come in over the past few days, none of which had even been opened. She couldn't help being impressed by the innovative headings some had used to grab his attention, but there seemed to be no exceptions, as far as the press was concerned nothing had been touched. A few other messages had been checked, it appeared, but none of any consequence, so perhaps she should start looking deeper into the system, even as far as the recycle bin.

She was just scrolling down the left-hand margin to see what special files he'd set up, hoping it might be as easy as finding one marked 'Vivienne' or 'Jacqueline', when a three-word heading in the main inbox happened to catch her eye. Blinking with bemusement, she looked at the sender's ID. A woman, but no one she'd ever heard of. A quick glance at the date and time showed the email had arrived less than ten minutes ago, which meant Miles couldn't have seen it yet.

With a spinning curiosity, and fingers made unsteady by excitement, she clicked on to open the email, half expecting it to be from some kind of nutter, or, more likely, a journo with a particularly sick way of grabbing attention.

However, less than a minute later, having read the carefully phrased sentences and opened the photograph attached to the message, she could only sit staring at the screen, so stunned that she couldn't, as yet, quite grasp the enormity of what she'd discovered.

Taking a split-second decision, she forwarded the email to her own computer and erased it from Miles's. Sweat was beading on her forehead and prickling under her arms. She felt slightly dizzied by what she'd done, as though it wasn't quite real. Her heart was still thudding as she returned to the named files on the left, but whatever they contained couldn't be more explosive than the message she'd just read. Nevertheless, her fingers moved rapidly over the keys as she entered a search for Vivienne.

If she heard the sound of footsteps in the hall she didn't register them, nor did she connect with the door opening as someone came in, all she knew was how violently she started when a voice said, 'What are you doing?'

She spun round to see Kelsey standing at the door.

Kelsey's eyes rounded. 'Oh my God, it's *you*. What are you doing here?'

In spite of how flustered she was, Justine managed a reasonable nonchalance as she said, 'I'm just . . . I was using your dad's computer. He said I could . . .'

'You're snooping,' Kelsey declared, her lip curling in disgust.

'Of course I'm not. I left my laptop at the hotel so your father said I could file from his.'

Kelsey's eyes remained hostile. 'So where is he?' she wanted to know.

'I – I'm not sure. He was here a moment ago.'

Still the girl's suspicion showed no sign of letting up. 'I'm going to call him,' she said, taking out her mobile.

'No! Don't! I mean . . .'

Kelsey stopped in alarm.

'Actually, he's with the police,' Justine told her, surprised by how relieved one small truth could make her feel. 'They're, um . . . They went over to the woods.'

Kelsey looked more scared than ever.

'Oh, it's OK, I don't think it's anything to worry about,' Justine assured her, having no idea if it was, but it seemed the right thing to say.

Kelsey's red-rimmed eyes began darting around the room, as though afraid someone else might be there, then they came to a stop on something on the floor. Justine followed their direction and felt her heart sink with dismay. The front-page story about her new baby brother.

If Justine thought, even for a minute, that Kelsey wouldn't register the headline she was so quickly corrected that her head almost spun.

'That's your name on that story!' Kelsey said savagely.

The girl was definitely her father's daughter.

'You wrote that! You don't care about how my mum—'

'Hang on, hang on,' Justine said, putting out her hands as though they could calm things down. 'Your father knew it was . . . Well, he said himself, it had to come out sooner or later, so . . . so he asked me to do it, before . . . anyone turned it into something . . . Well . . .' With a helpless gesture, she said, 'I have no control over headlines.'

Kelsey seemed more upset than ever. 'He wanted everyone to know?' she said.

Justine was trying to make herself think. 'I guess it's best if it's out there,' she said uneasily. 'Keeping things secret . . . Well, you can see what this has done. It's started people thinking . . . you know, the worst.'

Kelsey's haunted eyes were looking fearfully into hers. 'Have you ever seen him?' she said hoarsely.

It took Justine a moment to realise she meant Rufus. 'No,' she answered. 'Have you?'

Kelsey started, as though shocked by the question, then shook her head. 'Has my dad?' she asked through tightly pinched lips.

Justine's heart did a flip. 'I'm not sure,' she answered cautiously. 'Do you think he has?'

Kelsey shrugged. 'How should I know? He's only just told me about him. Anyway, I couldn't be less interested.'

Justine registered the defensive tone. 'He's your brother,' she said, watching her closely.

Kelsey's eyes sparked. 'No he's not. He's *hers*, not my mother's, so how can he be?'

Encouraged by the vehemence, but realising she was already on borrowed time, Justine said, 'I think we should have a little chat, you and me.'

Kelsey immediately backed off.

'Not now,' Justine persevered. 'I have to go, but if you give me your mobile number . . .'

'What for? It was because of you that my mother tried to kill herself, and me.'

'I had no idea she'd do that,' Justine said awkwardly. 'And I didn't write the whole piece myself.'

Kelsey continued to glare at her.

'Try to think of it this way,' Justine said gently, 'she came back after she read that article. And that was what you wanted. Wasn't it? To have your mum back.'

'I didn't want her to do what she did.'

'Of course not, but remember what else happened?'

Kelsey looked wary.

'To Vivienne?'

It took only a second for comprehension to dawn.

'That's right. It got her out of your life,' Justine said with a reassuring smile.

Now Kelsey was looking puzzled.

'I'll tell you what,' Justine said, reaching for a pad, 'I'll give you the number of my mobile, and if you'd like to talk some more you just give me a call. Any time, day or night, and if you don't want anyone to know, I promise not to mention it to a soul.'

Chapter Thirteen

Rain was streaming down on the umbrella being held over Miles, in a haunting, mesmeric tempo that seemed, oddly, to deaden the horror and even disperse the shock. The ground underfoot was sodden, the trees dripped and creaked in the wind, while the fields that stretched and faded into the moor seemed to sigh and shift in their impenetrable veil of mist.

There was a lot of movement around the edge of the woods, forensic scientists in pale overalls, masks and gloves collecting and bagging evidence; other scene-of-crime officers in issue waterproofs treading carefully about the mire; an Alsatian and a spaniel sniffing eagerly at the base of a sycamore, where crimson-topped funghi were sprouting in profusion amongst the roots. Miles was barely registering it all, though he was aware he was at a possible crime scene where every scrap of substance mattered.

Apparently the dead man, Timothy Grainger, had died from asphyxiation, brought about by choking on his own vomit. A senseless, tragic end, but not in itself suspicious. However, what had turned up since certainly was, though the implications barely registered with Miles, as he stared down at the crumpled, slime-covered coat a member of the forensic team was holding for him to look at. In spite of its condition he was in no doubt it was Jacqueline's. As were the Bali shoes and Hermès scarf which had also been found in the Fendi carry-all buried in another ditch, some fifty metres or so from where Grainger's body had been discovered.

'Over here!' someone suddenly shouted.

Miles looked up. One of the SOCOs was kneeling at the

base of the sycamore, drawing something out from under a blanket of saturated leaves. 'A handbag,' he declared, holding it aloft.

Miles and Sadler walked over to join the small crowd that was gathering around the tree. With gloved hands one of the forensics took the bag and began fishing around for the contents. This time Miles wasn't required to identify the find: the wallet spoke for itself. It was full of Jacqueline's credit cards. Her driving licence was there too, along with a small bundle of store receipts and a slim gold pen inscribed with her initials. A gift from him two Christmases ago.

He watched, as though in a dream, as gloved fingers dug into the bag again and pulled out a set of keys. He knew them instantly; they belonged to Moorlands.

'Got an envelope here, sir,' a young officer called from a few feet away.

Everyone turned round. He was kneeling at the edge of the woods, rain cascading over him as his knees sank into the pulpy earth. 'Nothing in it,' he told them, 'but it's addressed to Mrs Avery.'

Miles watched someone take it from him and insert it in a transparent plastic bag.

Sadler said, 'Do you have any idea how any of this might have got here, Mr Avery?'

Miles swallowed, but when he tried to speak his voice wasn't there.

Sadler waited.

Miles met his eyes, careful to let nothing show in his own. 'I think my wisest course right now,' he said, 'would be to contact my lawyer.'

Sadler continued to regard him, but when Miles said no more he turned away and began trudging back through the autumn debris to his car. As he waited for Miles to join him his eyes moved through the dense, ghostly mists billowing around the moor. 'I'll take you home,' he said, and leaving Miles to open the passenger door for himself, he squeezed past a PSU van to get around to the driver's side.

Neither of them spoke again until they were back at the house, when Sadler, with the engine still idling, said, 'We'll find her, Mr Avery.'

Ignoring the undertone, Miles kept his own voice neutral as he said, 'I certainly hope so,' and pushing open the door he got out of the car.

Vivienne's face was pinched with anger as she hoisted a heavy carrycot up the steps to her sister's front door. Behind her a posse of press was squealing to a halt around her Beetle, having pursued her at dangerous speed from her mother's.

'Vivienne! Vivienne!' they began shouting as they leapt out of their vehicles.

'How old is Rufus?'

'Is it true Miles didn't know about him?'

'Do you know where Jacqueline is?'

As the front door opened Vivienne shoved her way inside and thrust the carrycot at Caroline before storming down the hall into the sitting room.

'What the hell's going on?' Caroline demanded, coming in after her.

'It was you, wasn't it?' Vivienne seethed. 'You, or your damned drunk of a husband, sold your story to Justine James. Well, let me tell you this, Caroline, if anything happens to my son as a result of it, I will hold you fully responsible.'

'Oh, ever the drama queen,' Caroline sneered, throwing down the carrycot. 'They were always going to find out, and only someone as arrogant as you would think—'

'Listen to me,' Vivienne growled, stepping in close. 'There are at least half a dozen reporters out there, so if you don't do as I say, right now, I'm going back out there to tell them who sold me down the river. What a nice headline that's going to make for you, *sister* dearest.'

Though Caroline flinched, her tone was still scathing as she said, 'You don't come round here giving orders . . .'

'Oh yes, I do. You owe me for this, and now you're going to pay. Everyone out there thinks Rufus is with me, and you're going to play along by letting them think it too, at least for the next hour. By then I'll be long gone, in your car, and I'll leave you mine.'

Caroline blinked in confusion.

'Keys,' Vivienne demanded, holding out her hand.

'What the hell makes you think—'

'Give me the damned keys. I take it your car's in its usual place, out the back?'

'Yes, it is, and that's where it's going to stay.'

'Here, take mine,' Roger said, coming into the room and fishing a set of keys out of his trouser pocket.

Vivienne looked at him, and despite her anger felt her heart stir with pity. Her brother-in-law had been an extremely handsome man once, full of confidence and always smiling. Now he was little more than a pathetic shadow of his former self, with bloated features, bloodshot eyes and a personal odour that reeked of booze.

'I've been banned,' he told her, 'so it's no use to me, and it's insured for anyone to drive. We did that so anyone could drive me home.'

Feeling wretched for him, Vivienne took the keys and squeezed his shaking hand. 'Please get yourself some help,' she whispered, as she brushed a kiss to his stubbly cheek.

'If it's any consolation,' he said, turning after her, 'I feel bad about telling Justine.'

Knowing he meant it, Vivienne gave him a reassuring smile. There was no point trying to make him feel any worse, it was done now, so there was no going back. 'Thanks for the car,' she said.

'It's in the second garage at the end of the lane,' he told her. 'The key's on the ring.'

Half an hour later Vivienne was back at her mother's with Roger's battered Polo parked outside, and so far no sign of the press having followed her. She wouldn't have much time though, she needed to be gone from here, with Rufus, before they got wise to her ploy and came back again.

'Vivi, are you sure about this?' her mother was saying, as she came in from loading up the car. 'You don't have to take him now. I mean, I'm not going anywhere yet, and he might be better off staying here until everything blows over.'

Hefting a box of Rufus's toys up into her arms, Vivienne looked at Linda over the top of them. 'He'll be fine with me,' she told her. 'I'm his mother, for heaven's sake . . .'

'I know, I know, it's just that I can't help worrying, especially now—'

'I should think the fact they've found Jacqueline's clothes would make you a lot less worried,' Vivienne cut in, sounding much snappier than she intended.

'I didn't mean that. I just . . . Oh dear, I don't feel right about this, Vivi. Maybe if Miles had called . . .'

'Well, he hasn't. Now, please make yourself useful and bring the other box out to the car.'

As she walked swiftly down the garden path she couldn't help wondering how many of the neighbours might be watching. They obviously knew by now that Linda Kane was the infamous Vivienne's mother, which made 'dear little Rufus' (as the woman next door had dotingly called him the day before as though he were in some way afflicted), the living, breathing son of the suspected uxoricide Miles Avery. She couldn't remember now which of the Sundays had used such a ludicrously pompous word, when wife-murderer would have made the point much more potently. In the end she'd tossed every one of the papers into the bin, unable to stand the scurrilous, hand-rubbing glee that seemed to permeate in every word.

'Here,' her mother said, coming out to hand her another box, 'I'm not sure where you're going to put it . . .'

'I can always come back next weekend for more,' Vivienne told her. 'I'll just take the important stuff for now.'

Linda was still looking as miserable as she obviously felt. 'I wish you'd reconsider,' she said. 'Caroline shouldn't have said what she did . . .'

'Mum, look at you,' Vivienne said, glancing over her shoulder and trying to keep her voice down. 'You've been a nervous wreck ever since that detective came, and the press being out here all day has made you worse.'

Linda's complexion turned even paler.

'Go to Italy with David,' Vivienne said firmly. 'When are you supposed to leave?'

'Nothing's actually booked yet,' Linda replied, 'but he wants to go soon, he says.'

Feeling too many eyes watching them, Vivienne linked her arm and began walking her up the path. 'Get out of here for a while,' she said. 'It'll be much easier for you, and frankly for me too. I won't have to worry about anyone harassing or stressing you.'

'But how am I going to stop worrying about you?' Linda wanted to know. 'And you,' she added, her face softening with love as a bleary-eyed Rufus came crawling out of the sitting room to find them.

'Mum mum,' he said, treating them to a toothy grin.

Vivienne's heart folded at how happy he always seemed. Please God it would stay that way once he was away from her mother.

'You're going to be a good boy for Mummy, aren't you?' Linda smiled tearfully as she swung him up in her arms. 'You're going to show her how clever you are, and how . . .' Her voice wavered and she swallowed. 'I'm going to miss you, sweetheart,' she said hoarsely into his neck.

'Mum, don't,' Vivienne protested, as a lump rose in her throat. 'You're making it sound as though this is the last time you'll see him.'

Linda's watery eyes came to hers. 'I feel so afraid, Vivi,' she confessed in a whisper.

Irritation flashed like a pain in Vivienne's brain. 'What of?' she snapped angrily. 'If Jacqueline's dead, which is what everyone seems to think, then there's no reason to be, is there?'

Linda shook her head, but the anguish didn't fade from her eyes, and Vivienne was still haunted by it an hour and a half later as she steered the Polo into Thames Street towards home.

All the street lamps were on by now, and she noticed several cars parked outside the City Barge as she passed. There didn't seem to be anyone around though, not even a dog-walker, or anyone on their way to the pub. For some odd reason she started to find the darkness between the street lamps unnerving, as though someone might be standing in the shadows watching her drive by.

Glancing in the rear-view mirror to where Rufus was asleep in his car seat, she felt around the passenger seat for the garage remote and indicated to start pulling in. As the up-and-over door yawned open it let a flood of light into the street that fell over the car like a beacon. A moment later it was as though the light had gone mad as it began flicking and flashing, blinding her with its brightness, dazzling her with its glare.

She wasn't sure how many photographers had lain in wait, because they'd gone long before the white mass had faded from her eyes. She guessed it was probably only two or three, but what did it matter how many? They'd got what they'd come for – the elusive shot of Miles Avery's fifteen-month-old son, to feature alongside the one of his missing eleven-month-old half-brother that had made most of the Sundays.

She could only hope now that when Miles saw it, he would finally pick up the phone and call, not only to check that she and Rufus were OK, but to let her know how he was too.

The sun hadn't risen when Justine's mobile rang on the nightstand next to her, waking her up. After taking a moment to remember where she was, she snaked out an arm and brought the phone back under the bedclothes.

'This better be good,' she warned.

'Justine. It's Kelsey.'

Justine blinked, then pushed back the blankets. 'Kelsey?' she said. 'Are you OK?'

'Yes. No. I mean . . .' The girl's voice was broken and nasal. 'I want to see you,' she said, sounding angry.

'Yes, yes, of course,' Justine responded, starting to get up. 'When would—'

'I want you to make my mum come back.'

Justine hesitated, not sure how to reply. 'Well, I . . .'

'You said you could,' Kelsey cried. 'You did it before.'

'Yes, but . . . Well, that was . . .'

'I want her to come back so that everything can be the way it was.'

'Kelsey, I understand why you're upset, but . . .'

'You said I could call,' she shouted. 'Any time, day or night. You said I could talk to you.'

'Yes, of course. It's not a problem. Uh, when do you want to meet?'

'Now. As soon as you can.'

'Where are you?'

'In my room, but I can meet you somewhere. There's a road that goes through the top woods. I can give you directions and meet you there.'

'But aren't the woods cordoned off?'

'That's a different part,' Kelsey snapped. 'Have you got a pen?'

Automatically Justine reached for one. 'OK, go ahead,' she said, poised over a phone pad.

After jotting down Kelsey's instructions, she promised to leave right away, then still feeling vaguely uneasy she rang off.

For several minutes she sat on the edge of the bed staring at the directions, as she tried to think what to do. Something about the girl's voice, or maybe it was her words – in fact it was both – was bothering her. She'd sounded overwrought and panicky, which was understandable with her mother's clothes being found, and everything . . . But the way she'd asked Justine to bring her mother back . . . Well, it was like she was expecting some kind of resurrection or something.

Quickly turning on the news to find out if there had been more developments overnight, she learned there were none, and went to check her computer. The email she'd forwarded the day before was there in her inbox, complete with attachment, so actually, all things considered, great as an exclusive with Kelsey might be . . .

She glanced at the time. This was a hard one. A private chat with Miles's daughter wasn't an opportunity to be passed up lightly. On the other hand, a delusional teenager with issues raging from the past, and a mother who might turn up dead any minute, probably wasn't a species to be messed with. She needed to make a decision, though, the email or Kelsey, because it really couldn't be both.

After the storms through the night the morning had dawned crisply sunny and clear, with a filmy haze rising from the wet earth and sparkling shards of light glinting from the branches of russet and brown leaves. Kelsey's feet were squelching over a slimy groundsheet of leaves as she paced up and down the lay-by where she'd told Justine to meet her. She'd said eight, but it was now eight thirty and Justine still hadn't come. She carried on pacing, her heart full of fear, her mind reeling with images too horrible to bear. They'd found her mum's clothes. Her bag, even her wallet. She couldn't go anywhere without them, so what had happened to her?

A bolt of panic suddenly sent her sprinting along the road as though she could outrun her worst fear. There were no cars around; the track was so narrow that it was hardly ever used. She didn't care where she was going, she only wanted to run and run until no one could find her.

'Daddy, Daddy, Daddy,' she said over and over, until hearing herself she bunched her hands at her mouth as though to push any more words back. He only wanted Vivienne, and if Kelsey didn't get away he might try and do the same to her as— 'No!' she cried, wrapping her head in her arms. 'No, no. He didn't do it. He didn't.'

On she ran, wanting to escape the memory of her dad telling her about the clothes, and the way he'd said she shouldn't be afraid, because it didn't necessarily mean the worst. His voice had been rough and shaky, and his eyes looked sore and dry and full of fear, as though he knew he wasn't telling the truth. But he wouldn't lie to her. He couldn't have done anything wrong, because he was her dad and he didn't do things like that. But what if he had? Her breath caught on a sob. There was no one she could trust. No one in the whole wide world. She wished her brother Sam would come back, because she was sure she'd be able to trust him. It would be just the two of them against the world. He'd take care of her, and she'd never have to be frightened again, because it wouldn't matter about Vivienne or Rufus or anyone else. It would be just them.

After a while, trembling and panting for breath, she began walking along a woodland trail where mulchy puddles edged the path and sunlight streamed in bright misty bands through the trees. She kept her head down, her blonde hair swinging forward masking her face, her hands tucked tightly into the pockets of her parka.

She had to think what to do. She needed to find her mum and Sam and then she could make everything all right again. Her dad would be happy and not want anyone else. They could be a family, the way her mum had always wanted. Just the four of them.

She walked on and on, faster and faster, not hearing the drip of rain in the trees, or the creaks and cracks of branches. She just kept going, because somewhere at the end was an answer. But then there was nowhere else to go. The path had run out, there were no more trees, and she was staring down at the massive gulf of the estuary. The water glimmered and sparkled like a night of fireworks, the wooded valley in front dipping and swelling around wispy shreds of clouds that drifted like gauze across the treetops.

Looking around, she remembered this was where she used to come with her dad when she was small. They used to bring picnics and tell each other their secrets. Sometimes Grandma and Grandpa would come too. She wished they were here now, because she really, really didn't know what to do, and Grandma always used to know the answer to everything.

In the end, as the sky started to blacken overhead, and sharp swathes of light slanted like fans down to the sea, she sank to her knees, sobbing and retching and hating herself for not having the courage to jump.

'Kelsey!'

She froze. Then, terrified, she spun round to find a man coming towards her. The sun was blinding her – she couldn't see who it was.

'It's all right, me old love,' he said, 'it's just me. Tom. No need to be afraid.'

Kelsey blinked, but though she recognised their gardener's voice, she still couldn't make herself register who it was.

She watched him come closer, thinking it might be her grandpa about to emerge from the light, but then she saw who it was and looked up into Tom's crinkly old face.

'There, there,' he said, edging close enough to take her in his arms. 'No need to cry like that now. Old Tom has got you.'

Kelsey was too distraught to speak. She could only let him hold her tight to his earthy-smelling coat and rock her from side to side. It felt good, and safe, and she wanted to stay with him for ever.

'There, you'm all right now,' Tom said, in his throaty burr. 'Wondered where on earth you was off to, I did. That time of the morning. Thought I'd better foller.'

Kelsey tried to reply, but her chest was racked with sobs and her throat was too tight.

'Come on,' he said, starting to lead her back along the trail. 'You'm nice and safe now. Old Tom's got you, so we'll just give yer dad a ring, shall we, and let him know you're all right.'

Miles was waiting at the gate behind the house, barely noticing the icy cut to the wind as he watched Tom bringing Kelsey down through the back field. His failure to shield her from the worst of what was happening was almost tearing him apart. He understood the depths of her fear, he could almost feel it as his own, but while he wanted to rage against a world that was recklessly planting such terrible suspicions, he knew that his anger would only frighten her more.

As they drew closer he could see her face, blotched and swollen and so heart-rendingly unsure. Her eyes were wide and haunted, and as she looked at him he doubted he'd ever felt more impotent or anxious in his life. What was he going to say to try and put her fears to rest? How was he going to explain, or soothe, or make any difference to the dreadful turmoil inside her? He needed desperately to reach her, to return somehow to the place he'd always held in her trust, but if her barriers were still up, if she was still bent on protecting herself . . .

Pushing open the gate he kept his eyes on hers, then to his unutterable relief she broke free of Tom and ran into his arms.

'Daddy,' she sobbed, as he scooped her up and buried his face in her hair. 'Daddy, I'm sorry. I didn't mean to run away. I just got so frightened . . .'

'Sssh, it's all right,' he told her softly, holding her tight and struggling to prevent his own tears. 'Just as long as you're here.'

Her arms and legs stayed round him, clinging to him the way she had as a child, and not wanting to let her go he clung to her too.

After a while his eyes met Tom's and he nodded his thanks for the old man's quick thinking when he'd spotted Kelsey running along the top lane. Wasting no time he'd gone after her, calling Miles on his mobile to let him know what was happening. At that point Miles hadn't even known she'd left her room.

When finally they were back in the house warming themselves next to the Aga, he smoothed the hair back from her face as he said, 'I won't ask where you were going, or what you were doing, I'm just going to swear to you that none of the rumours are true.'

Her shoulders jerked on a sob. 'I know,' she said shakily. 'I mean, in here,' she touched her chest, 'I know, but sometimes I get really scared. It's like everyone's going to leave me, or no one really cares about me . . .'

'Don't *ever* think that,' he said, wrapping her in his arms again. 'You're my world, and if anything should happen to you . . .' His voice cracked with emotion as the mere thought of it overwhelmed him.

She stayed close to him, holding him tight, as though afraid to let go. In the end, with her face still buried in his shoulder she said, 'Can it be just us, Dad? Please. I mean, if Mum's—' She broke off and he felt her tensing ready for his reply.

Knowing she was trying to ask him to turn his back on Vivienne and Rufus he closed his eyes and willed himself to come up with the right words. But there were none she'd want to hear, so for now the best he could do was, 'I think we should run you a nice hot bath, and when you're ready, we can sit down and have a talk . . .'

Pulling abruptly away she said, 'I want to go back to school.'

He watched her turn towards the door, her movements stiff with the pain of being denied his assurance. 'I'm not sure you should, just yet,' he said, worried that letting her go might seem like an even bigger rejection.

She stopped at the door and turned back to look at him,

pale and drawn, and looking so desperately lonely that he came very close to telling her what she wanted to hear.

They both looked at his mobile as it started to ring. It was lying on the table, too far away for either of them to see who it was. Whether she hoped it was her mother he had no way of telling, though he knew that she too would be afraid it was the news they were dreading the most. In the end he walked over to pick it up. 'Miles Avery,' he said quietly.

Hearing the voice at the other end, his eyes went to Kelsey. 'Good morning, Inspector,' he replied. 'What can I do for you?'

As he listened, he continued to look at Kelsey, occasionally glancing towards the window, or nodding, until finally he said, 'I see. Well thank you for letting me know.'

He could feel Kelsey's eyes on him as he put the mobile back on the table, and knew that he'd have to pass on what Sadler had just told him, though heaven only knew how she was going to take any comfort from it.

'They've found her, haven't they?' Kelsey said, her voice rising with panic.

'No,' he answered quickly. 'No, they haven't. What's happened is that someone's come forward who knew the man they found in the woods.'

She waited, her eyes wide with misgiving.

'Apparently this person found Mum's things about a month ago,' he continued. 'They were in a communal bin, close to the station. He and his friend, Timothy Grainger, used the money they found in the purse to buy beer and spirits, and kept the other things to try and sell them. Then, because they had the address of Moorlands and a set of keys, they had the idea of coming here to try and break in. They brought the bag along so they could say they were intending to return it if someone spotted them before they managed to get in. It seems too much alcohol sent their plans awry, and they ended up camping out on the edge of the moor, using some of Mum's clothes to keep themselves warm.'

Kelsey didn't move, or even try to speak.

'The plan, apparently,' he went on, 'was to try again the

next night, once they'd sobered up, but, as we know, Grainger didn't sober up.' He sighed and pressed his fingers into his eyes. 'When his friend found him in the morning he panicked, thinking somehow he would get the blame, so he attempted to bury Mum's things and the body and ran away.'

Kelsey was still staring at him, clearly trying to take it all in.

'I'm afraid all this tells us,' he said gruffly, 'is how her belongings came to be out there in the woods. We don't know how they got into the bin.'

Kelsey took a breath, then looked away, apparently unable or unwilling to speak.

Not knowing what else to say, Miles said, 'How about that bath?'

Her eyes flicked upwards, but didn't come to his, then without uttering a word she turned to leave.

He stood watching her walking out into the hall, wishing with all his might that she was still young enough for him to go and sponge away the mud and huddle her warmly into a towel, the way he used to when she was small. Then he could lie down on the bed with her and try to smooth away her pain. However, at fourteen she could no longer share that kind of intimacy with her father, which he might have found easier to bear if her mother weren't creating, instead of filling, the void.

Chapter Fourteen

'As far as Miles is concerned, I can't tell you anything,' Vivienne was saying as she gazed down at Rufus's sleeping face. 'He still hasn't called.'

'Have you spoken to him since they found her clothes and stuff?' Pete asked, glancing at Alice to make sure he wasn't delving too far.

Vivienne shook her head. 'I heard about it the same way you did, on the news,' she replied, and her eyes moved absently to the window where a mass of white cloud was scudding through a clear blue sky. 'I've left enough messages,' she said. 'I thought he might have called back by now, with Rufus's picture being all over the front page.' She looked down at one of them lying on her desk and felt a swell of love, edged with anxiety.

Drawing a breath, she looked up and found the others watching her so intently that it made her uneasy, as though the world's scrutiny had somehow broken into the sanctuary of their office. 'Enough,' she said, putting the paper aside. 'We have work to do. All of us. Where's Kayla?'

'Should be here any minute,' Alice answered. 'She rang to say she'd be late. When are you two setting off for Devon?'

Vivienne glanced at Pete. 'Hopefully tomorrow afternoon,' she replied. 'Will that work for you?'

He threw out his hands. 'At your disposal, darling,' he assured her. 'La Belle is in New York until the end of next week and though I have to say the English countryside doesn't normally hold much appeal, since we're going to be so *thrillingly* close to—'

'Pete, we're going to need some prelim figures for La

Belle,' Alice cut in quickly. 'You're taking Rufus to Devon, are you?' she said to Vivienne.

Though Vivienne nodded, her attention was now focused on her computer screen, where several flagged emails were still in need of her urgent attention. However, none was from Miles, which was upsetting her much more than it might have a week ago. Surely to God he had to be sparing at least a moment of concern for his son, and she wouldn't mind knowing that she featured in there somewhere too. OK, he had a lot on his mind, but if he'd just communicate once in a while she might find it easier to deal with this situation.

'Maybe he can't,' Alice said when she voiced her frustration. 'I mean we don't actually know what's going on down there, do we?'

'I'm aware of that, but a phone call from my *son's father* to let me know what I might expect to read or hear about him in the next few days surely isn't too much to ask.'

Alice's tone was gentle as she said, 'I'm sure he'll be in touch as soon as he can.'

'If he's not arrested first,' Pete dared to pipe up.

Vivienne shot him a scathing look.

With saucer eyes Pete planted his hands on his hips. 'Well, excuse me for breathing, but there's a body, clothes—'

'Which don't belong to one another.'

'Maybe not, but I read somewhere this morning—'

Stepping in again, Alice said, 'Is anyone up for a brainstorm? I'd like to run some ideas past you for the film, and I have to leave here in half an hour.'

Pete shrugged. 'Count me in,' he said chirpily. 'Shall I put the phones through to voicemail?'

'No way,' Alice replied. 'You drew the short straw to stand in for Kayla, and I'm waiting for at least a dozen calls.'

'Me too,' Vivienne told him. 'Mainly from charities. It's vital we link up with one of them to give us a tax break on the auction. And don't forget, you're supposed to be screening for me. No one gets through who's trying for some kind of statement about Miles.'

'All right, all right,' Pete grumbled.

Ten minutes later, with the brainstorm barely under way, Kayla came bursting in through the door loaded down with toys for Rufus, a supply of assorted sandwiches for lunch and extra biscuits to go with the coffee.

'If we're going to be trapped in here by the press all day, we need supplies,' she informed them, dropping her purchases on her desk. Then, going straight to the pushchair, 'Is he awake? Oh, look at him, he's so adorable. He's smiling at me and he hardly even knows me. Can I pick him up?'

Rolling her eyes, Vivienne gestured for her to go ahead, proud on the one hand of how sociable Rufus was, but worried on the other about how quickly the novelty of having him around was going to wear off.

Minutes later Alice was bouncing him up and down, and Rufus was in raptures, since he adored his crinkly-haired aunt with whom he'd spent many weekends when Vivienne had brought him to London to give her mother a break. Alice and Angus had even come over to the house the night Vivienne had returned from Berkshire, bringing takeaways and wine, and making such a fuss of their godson that it had taken Vivienne until the early hours to get him off to sleep.

Now, as Alice hugged and tickled him, and appeared to forget all about the brainstorm, Pete, who claimed to have an allergic reaction to any human being less than five feet ten inches high, dropped to his knees in a ludicrous game of peekaboo. Vivienne could only shake her head and laugh at how absurdly delighted Pete looked each time Rufus let out a shriek of mirth, then clapped his hands to his own little face to start playing the game too.

Wondering how disruptive she should allow him to be when everyone seemed so much more interested in entertaining him than in the tasks at hand, she turned back to her computer to start answering some emails. As she opened the first one she was dimly aware of Kayla taking a call, but not until Kayla put the caller on hold and said, 'Vivi, it's Al Kohler,' did Vivienne stop what she was doing and turn round.

'He says it's about the auction,' Kayla told her. 'He also says he's going to make your day.'

Vivienne smiled at the kick of pleasure she felt inside. Al Kohler had been Miles's deputy until Miles had resigned from his editorship, at which point Al had departed the same shores and was now one of the senior producers of Sky News. Since he and Miles would almost certainly have remained close friends, Vivienne had little difficulty in trusting him, so if he was saying he wanted to make her day, she was more than ready to take him up on it.

'Al, hi, how are you?' she said, clicking on her extension.

'I'm just great,' he told her, his familiar Scottish brogue coming warmly down the line. 'How are you?'

'Well, I guess I've had better times,' she responded wryly. 'You'll know about Rufus by now . . .'

'A bonnie wee lad, if the pictures I've seen are anything to go by. I'm happy for you, hen. I'll look forward to meeting him one of these days.'

'I have a feeling he'll enjoy meeting you too.' Vivienne smiled as she watched Rufus toddling into the kitchen with Pete. 'Anyway, I've been informed that you're going to make my day – as if hearing from you hasn't done that already.'

'Och, you say the nicest things,' he chuckled. 'But just one word before we go on to the auction, if you speak to Miles tell him not to forget who his friends are. I like to count myself as one, but he's not answering my calls or emails.'

'Nor mine, but don't worry, if I do hear from him, I'll be sure to pass the message on.'

'OK, so now that's out of the way, here's what I'm proposing for your auction. First, we could be interested in televising the whole thing, but I'm not sure the transmission time I'm going to suggest will work for you.'

'Al, we'd stage it at midnight if you'll give us that kind of coverage,' she cried.

'Nothing so drastic,' he laughed. 'Nine on a Saturday morning is what we have in mind.'

'Absolutely no problem. Anything you want—'

'Let me finish,' he interrupted. 'Second, we're going to match what you raise, pound for pound, but before you start cheering, there's a condition attached. We'll want our own people to administer the funds, which isn't to say you, or anyone else you nominate, such as Angus, won't be invited onto the committee, but there could be a lot of dosh coming in if it works well, so our accountants will want to keep an eye on it all.'

Vivienne was smiling all over her face. 'You're right about one thing, Al Kohler,' she said, 'you really have made my day. Thank God someone, somewhere has finally remembered Sharon Goss. I take it it's all down to you.'

'I have to admit it, but it's a damned good cause, and there are a lot of women, or families, in her position who need financial support during times of crisis, and who aren't lucky enough to have the contacts Sharon does. If this auction proves a success, there's no reason not to run more in the future, and those in need can apply for help and we can assess them . . . Well, the administering of it will come later, we don't need to go into it now, but for tax reasons I think we need to be contacting established charities, which I'm sure you're already onto. And we should set a date for lunch sometime soon to go over everything. How's your schedule looking?'

Vivienne quickly reached for her BlackBerry. 'I'm going to Devon tomorrow,' she told him, 'but I'm looking pretty clear for next week. What suits you?'

'Let's say Tuesday. I'll take you to the Rose and Crown on Kew Green. They do great Thai mussels, as you know, since it was you and Miles who introduced me to them. I guess your office is still on the river, in Chiswick?'

'Pier House, Strand on the Green.'

'I'll try to book a table and pick you up at twelve thirty.'

As she rang off Vivienne punched both fists in the air. 'Yes!' she cried. 'Alice, where are you? You've got to hear this.'

'Vivi, another call holding,' Kayla told her, as Alice came out of the kitchen. 'This one's from Stella in Devon. She says it's urgent.'

'You are going to be so impressed,' Vivienne told Alice as she pressed the flashing light on her console. 'Stella? Hi, it's Vivienne. Sorry to have kept you. Is everything all right?'

'Course it is,' Stella laughed, 'everything's always all right with me. Seems like you'm having a bit of a time of it, though. Lovely little boy, I must say. Almost makes me wish me own was that age again. Anyway, not why I'm calling. We've had some news down here, well Sharon has. She's got to go and see her doctor this afternoon, because they think they might have found a donor.'

Vivienne's heart leapt with joy. 'You're not serious,' she cried, though her head was already spinning at the mere thought of how fast they might now have to turn this around.

'Nothing's been confirmed yet,' Stella told her. 'We'll know more later, but I thought you'd like to be kept informed of what was happening. Soon as I has any more news I'll give you a call. Or Sharon will. She asked me to send her love, by the way, and tell you we'm all looking forward to seeing you. And that boy of your'n, if you wants to bring 'im. Got plenty of babysitters in us, don't forget.'

'Thank you,' Vivienne smiled, her heart swelling with their warmth. 'And tell Sharon not to worry, everything'll be all right. We're all rooting for her.'

Stella chortled with pleasure. 'You'm a good girl, Vivienne. Knew that the first time I met you,' and without as much as a toodle-pip she was gone.

'What was all that about?' Alice demanded as Vivienne put the phone down.

'Pete, where are you?' Vivienne shouted.

'Making a Lego car,' he shouted back. Then, carrying his fellow mechanic into the office, 'I heard some of the call, so what's going on?'

As she began filling them in Vivienne was searching for Al Kohler's mobile number. 'I'll have to warn him that we could be up against the clock now,' she said. 'Just pray it doesn't affect their decision. They won't know whether it will, of course, until we can tell them how soon they need to set up the transmission.' Connecting with Al's voicemail she quickly left a message explaining what had happened, and after telling him to get back to her, she said to Pete, 'We should take a camera with us tomorrow to record an interview with Sharon, just in case they admit her before we can get her on air. Or maybe Al will be able to spare a crew to come with us.'

'He'll have to send someone to recce the auction room,' Alice pointed out.

'We need to find out what sort of schedule our firemen are on,' Vivienne continued, glancing at Kayla who was saying into the phone, 'No problem, I can hear you. I'll buzz you in, but make sure no one forces their way in with you,' and pressing a button on the wall behind her she released the downstairs door. 'Theo's arrived,' she announced, an enormous grin lighting up her face.

Vivienne turned to Alice. 'Who arranged for all my prayers to be answered at once?' she demanded.

Laughing, Alice said, 'I'm sure I told you he was coming today, but I should have reminded you.'

'You mean I shouldn't have forgotten.'

'You've had a lot on your mind.'

The door opened and a tall, dark-haired young man with eyes the colour of a tropical sea and a smile to dim the sun strode into the office, wearing a full complement of motorbike leathers, including the boots, with a helmet tucked under one arm and a huge bunch of flowers in the other.

'Oh my God,' Pete murmured, starting to swoon.

Grinning, Theo said, 'Hey Pete, see you've got yourself a new car,' and as the others laughed he dumped the flowers on Alice, kissed her roundly, then went to swing Rufus up in the air. 'Hello, little fellow,' he cooed. 'It's been a while since I've seen you.'

Rufus gurgled with pleasure and tried to reach for the dark lock of hair that fell over Theo's brow. Letting him take it, Theo leaned sideways to plant a kiss on Vivienne's cheek. 'I suppose that lot down there are hanging about for you,' he said, 'but they got me instead. I told them I was your other son.'

Vivienne spluttered with laughter, loving him for being so relaxed. 'Welcome on board,' she said, moving round the desk to give him a proper hug, and enjoying the way he held both her and Rufus in such an encompassing embrace. 'I'm afraid you could find the ship is sailing much sooner than you think,' she warned. 'I've just had a call from Sky, they're going to televise us.'

'Fantastic news!' he declared. 'Apart from a couple of

things I can't get out of, I'm yours for at least the next month. So make use of me in any way you can.'

Behind them Pete whimpered weakly, and slumped down in his chair.

'Sssh,' Kayla said sharply as they laughed, 'they're saying the police are about to make some kind of announcement in the Avery case,' and reaching for the remote control she turned up the sound on the TV.

With trepidation gathering like weights in her heart, Vivienne turned to watch the plasma screen on the wall. DI Sadler, apparently in conversation with someone out of shot, was standing behind a small bank of microphones while the gathered press waited with notebooks, recorders and cameras poised.

'Bet they've found her,' Pete murmured.

As though sensing Vivienne's reaction Theo's arm closed a little more tightly around her shoulders, while he held the bouncing Rufus on his other side.

'OK, right,' DI Sadler said, leaning towards the mikes. 'This is just a short statement to keep you up to date. The search around the area where Timothy Grainger's body was found is continuing, but I should stress that, contrary to some rumours we've been hearing, there has been nothing so far to suggest that Mrs Avery herself was ever at the location. Some of you have been asking for details about the person who came forward with information about Mr Grainger, but I'm afraid the person concerned has asked not to be identified. We are satisfied at this time that neither Mr Grainger, nor the person who was with him at the scene, is in any way connected to the Avery family.' He looked off camera as someone spoke to him, then to the mikes he said, 'Thank you. I think that's about all we can tell you for now.'

A front-row reporter cut in quickly. 'Have you found any fingerprints or DNA that doesn't match Mr Grainger's or his friend's?' he asked.

'At this time there is no evidence to suggest anyone else was at the scene,' Sadler replied affably. His head went up as he pointed to someone close to the back.

'Rob Logan, *News of the World*. Is it true you're reopening the case of Mr Avery's missing son?'

Sadler's expression immediately darkened. 'No, it is not,' he responded shortly and gestured for another reporter to go ahead.

'Julia Green, ITV West. Presumably you've asked Mr Avery if he knows, or knew, Mr Grainger, so can you tell us what he said?'

'Mr Avery denies knowing Mr Grainger,' Sadler replied, looking straight at her.

Vivienne's heart tightened at the cynicism in Sadler's tone, never mind the unspoken message he seemed to send to the reporter. 'Turn it off,' she said to Kayla, and taking Rufus from Theo she carried him back to her desk.

'Hang on, someone's just asked if the search for Jacqueline is happening anywhere else besides Devon,' Alice said.

Vivienne drew Rufus in warmly against her, while her lacklustre eyes returned to the screen.

'The TAG team has spread out further onto the moor now,' Sadler was saying, 'and another house-to-house is being conducted in the area.'

'So you're convinced she never left Devon?' someone pressed.

'No evidence has come to light so far to confirm that she did.'

'Detective Inspector,' someone else piped up, 'do you think she's still alive?'

Sadler fixed the questioner with a gaze that seemed to pass straight through her. 'If she is,' he answered, 'we'd like to know why she hasn't come forward?' He shrugged expressively and let his meaning drift into the room.

As Kayla lowered the sound Vivienne hid her face in Rufus's neck, knowing they were all looking at her now.

'It's a good point,' Pete said quietly. 'If she is still with us, why hasn't she contacted someone?'

Alice wasted no time answering. 'She's not always a rational woman,' she reminded him.

Vivienne sat up, and as her eyes met Alice's she said, 'There's something I'd like you to do for me.'

'Of course,' Alice said. Then added, 'I have a funny feeling I already know what it is.'

Vivienne nodded, as though to confirm her instinct. Then hugging Rufus to her again, she turned back to Theo, whose mere presence was already making everything seem so much easier to handle. There was no doubt in her mind that his participation was going to make a world of difference from here on in, particularly where the press was concerned. Not that the mystery surrounding Jacqueline was likely to disappear from the front pages, but since the nation at large adored this young man, who wasn't only a world-class athlete, but a natural-born entertainer, there was finally a fighting chance of getting some proper coverage for Sharon, the firemen and the auction.

The sound of the Critch's voice made Justine wince as it barked down the phone. 'Were you watching the news?' he demanded.

'Yes,' she answered.

'And you got the same impression I did?'

'They still suspect him.'

The Critch chuckled. 'It's only a matter of time,' he declared confidently. 'As for you, Justie, you can count yourself lucky you found that email, because without it you wouldn't just be toast by now, you'd be the scrapings under my boot.'

She made no comment.

'So, have you followed up on it yet?' he demanded.

'No, I'm just—'

'Well, what the hell are you waiting for? But go careful with it. If it's real, it's dynamite, and we sure as hell don't want it blowing up in your pretty little face now, do we?'

'I'd appreciate knowing I had your full backing before I go any further,' she responded tightly.

'Consider it yours, but you take this anywhere else, Justie, and Avery's wrath is going to look like a pussy lick in comparison to what I'll do to you.'

After ringing off Justine continued to sit on the edge of her bed, letting his words recede like grimy water down a plughole while she reflected on the effect the email's contents had started having on her. At first she'd seen it only as the lifeline she'd needed to rescue herself from a rapid descent into the sad, alcoholic world of Fleet Street has-beens. She'd been as excited and urgent about it then as the Critch was now, but the more she read and considered it, the more it seemed to be sobering her – in fact, it was starting to reach her in a way she wasn't quite sure how to handle.

With a growing sense of trepidation she went to sit down at her computer where the email she'd stolen from Miles was displayed full-screen. As she reread the words, which she could probably recite by heart, she was thinking of what a cruel and senseless tragedy it would be if Jacqueline's body was found on the moor. She really couldn't be sure if she suspected Miles now; she only knew that fate had not been kind to that family, and that Miles was as capable as any man of reaching the end of his tether. He wanted his freedom, had become almost desperate for an escape from the hell of never-ending grief into which Jacqueline had dragged them. He naturally wanted to be with the woman he'd loved – more than that, though, he would want to grasp the second chance life had given him to be a father to his son.

It wasn't a difficult story to tell. Justine had concocted many like it over the years: families torn apart by the wanton vagaries of fate; tragic and understandable crimes of passion; love overcoming all! What she'd never had, however, was such a direct route to the heart of a family in crisis. The father whose background and character was already well known to her, the daughter who'd suffered years of maternal neglect, and the son – the missing son – who, if this email was to be believed, had been killed a long time ago.

She sat back in her chair, feeling the air go out of her. The curious thing was, this really could be the story of her career, yet instead of rushing ahead she was sitting here almost afraid to move on it. Perhaps, if something had come to light about it in her background checks on Sam's disappearance, she'd be feeling less doubtful, but nowhere had she come across a single mention of anyone by the name of Elizabeth Barrett, the sender of the email. Clearly no one else had either, or the story would be out there by now, so what exactly was that telling her? That the email had been sent by a crank? Or from someone Miles had paid to keep silent?

Had she not already shown the message to the Critch she might be approaching this a different way now, but the man had scented blood and blood he would have, whether she got it for him, or he set someone else on the trail – and handing it over simply wasn't an option she was going to allow.

Finally, sitting forward, she began entering a web address to create a new hotmail account. Once her bogus identity was set up, she opened a window and began to type, thinking of Miles and how, as an editor, he might handle this.

Dear Mrs Barrett

As Mr Avery's lawyer, I am in receipt of a copy of your email in which you are making certain claims about his missing son. I'm sure you can imagine how many people have contacted Mr Avery over the years in regard to this matter, often causing the family considerable and unnecessary distress. It is for this reason that Mr Avery has asked me to contact you on his behalf. I shall be happy to arrange a meeting with you if you will be kind enough to furnish some proof of your claim, together with your name, telephone number and address.

With regards, Janette James

Miles's way wasn't the same as the Critch's, and for now, like it or not, she needed to stay close to the Critch.

'You're not still puzzling over that envelope, are you?' DI Sadler demanded, walking into CID with his coat still on and a cup of steaming coffee warming his hands.

'I am, sir,' DC Joy confirmed, turning it over inside its evidence bag. 'It's been bothering me ever since we found it amongst Mrs Avery's effects. Why is it empty? That's what I want to know. What's happened to the letter, or whatever was in it?'

'It might yet turn up,' Sadler reminded her. 'The boys are still out there.'

DC Joy continued to stare down at the badly soiled envelope with its smudged address, roughly torn opening and illegible postmark. Something about it wasn't seeming quite right to her, though she couldn't for the life of her say what, other than the fact that its contents were missing. It was as though, she was thinking, she was holding the key to an important door; the only problem was, she had no idea where to find the door. 'The address is handwritten,' she said, studying the blurred blue ink, 'and most of it's unreadable now, though it's obviously Moorlands and her name is reasonably clear too. The sender's address is missing. It must have come off when she opened the letter, because no little scraps have been found nearby, but there was definitely something, because the letters "mes" are still there on the back. Forensics are working their magic on the postmark, but no luck so far.'

'That might be because it's here on your desk, instead of in the labs with them,' Sadler pointed out. 'Do they know you've taken it?'

DC Joy looked shocked. 'You're surely not suggesting I stole it, sir.'

'Borrowed,' he corrected, and took a mouthful of coffee just as the phone on her desk started to ring.

'Elaine,' a voice said from the other end. 'You might want to get yourself down here.'

'Ryan?' she said.

'That's me. Is Sadler around?'

'Yes, he's right here.'

'Then bring him too.'

Elaine was already getting to her feet as she rang off. 'We're needed in the incident room, sir,' she told him.

'They've found her,' Sadler declared, following her into the corridor.

'I don't think it can be that,' she responded, 'the TAG boys would have called you direct if it was. Your mobile's switched on, is it?'

Sadler checked, then repocketed it as they ran down the stairs.

Minutes later they were entering the incident room, where several uniformed officers were seated at a haphazard arrangement of tables covered in empty coffee cups and an impressive amount of technology. Sergeant Ryan Austin was leaning against one of the white chalkboards, staring down at a recording device that one of the other officers was operating.

'Ah, sir,' he said, as Sadler came in. 'We've received a call that I think you should hear. Play it from the top,' he told the PC.

After the squeal and hum of a rewind the tape began playing, and almost instantly Joy's eyes widened with astonishment, while Sadler's brow started to furrow.

'Hello,' a female voice said softly. 'My name is Jacqueline Avery. I would like you to know that I am perfectly all right. There is no need to go on looking for me—'

'Can you tell us where you are?' an officer's voice cut in.

'I'd rather not,' came the reply. 'I believe I have that right.'

'Of course, but—'

'I urge you not to waste any more time searching for me. I have not been harmed in any way—'

'Can you just tell me—'

There was a click on the line.

'Hello? Hello? Are you still there?'

Silence.

The tape stopped and all eyes went to Sadler.

'We're getting it triangulated,' Austin told him. 'We should have a location any time now.'

Sadler nodded. 'Let me know when you have it,' he said, starting out of the room, 'and get me some copies of the tape.'

'Do you think it was really her?' Joy asked, catching up with him outside the PC's locker rooms.

'Right now,' he replied, still walking, 'I'm reserving judgement.'

Intrigued, Joy glanced at him, but said no more as she followed him back upstairs to CID, where he left her to go into his office.

With the door firmly closed behind him he began running with several theories regarding the call, just in case any coincidence or anomaly managed to fuse itself with something a little more substantial than a mere doubt or suspicion. However, by the time Joy rang to let him know she was putting Sergeant Austin through, he was feeling like a fool who had all the pieces of a jigsaw stuck together the wrong way. The picture was there, he was certain of it, and it might even be complete, but it was as though he had a patch of sky in a field, water flowing upwards, and people with bodies only half their own. Which could only mean, he reflected irritably as he waited for Austin's voice to come down the line, that his perspective on this was shot.

Less than five minutes later he was feeling very differently, for the triangulation had turned up something extremely interesting. 'So what do you make of that?' he asked DC Joy, who'd come to stand in the doorway whilst he took the call.

'I don't know, sir, you weren't on speaker,' she reminded him.

Sadler chuckled and rubbed his hands. 'Well, Detective Constable, it would appear the call was made from the Kew area, using a pay-as-you-go mobile phone registered to someone by the name of Anne Cates.'

'Who?' Joy said, frowning.

'Kew,' Sadler continued, 'as I'm sure you know, Elaine, is not a million miles from Chiswick. Or, to be more precise, a mere stroll across the bridge from Pier House, Strand on the Green.'

Joy still wasn't getting it. 'Are you saying, sir, that you think Anne Cates is really Vivienne Kane? If you are, I'm afraid I can't agree, because we'd have recognised the voice.'

'Certainly we'd have recognised Vivienne Kane's voice, but we've never spoken to her closest friend and business partner, Alice Jackson, who, I believe, happens to work in Chiswick and live in Kew.'

Joy blinked in astonishment. 'You think Vivienne Kane's business partner made the call for her?' she said, afraid he might be losing it.

'It's possible,' Sadler replied. 'As I said, the mobile is registered to Anne Cates, and the address the phone company has is KJA – Kane Jackson Agency? – Pier House, Strand on the Green.'

Joy only stared at him.

'I think we need to speak to Ms Kane, don't you, Detective Constable?'

Joy nodded. 'Yes, sir,' she said, 'I think we do. Shall I get her on the line?'

'No, I want to see her eyes when we turn up unexpectedly. She's in London at the moment, I believe?'

'Certainly according to the papers,' Joy agreed.

'Good. We'll catch the first train in the morning.'

Vivienne was in her upstairs sitting room, sorting through the press interest they'd had so far for the auction, while Rufus entertained himself with some wooden bricks and a hammer. His little face was flushed with pleasure, his dark eyes shining with glee as he banged about noisily, shouting at the top of his voice, or blowing bubbles that burst and ran down his chin. Each time she looked at him she had to fight the urge to scoop him up for a hug, because nothing ever felt so good in her arms as his gorgeously squidgy little limbs.

Finding her eyes drawn to the window as it rattled in the wind, she watched the trees in the courtyard outside swaying wildly in the gusts. Rain sliced down from a dense black sky, drowning the flower beds and devastating the last hardy blooms. Were she to spare it a thought she might almost pity the journalists who were out there somewhere, lying in wait, and certainly she'd be sorry for the tourists huddled into pleasure cruisers making the journey from Kew to Charing Cross. But she was too engrossed in the warmth of having her son near, and the work at hand, even to register the hoot of a whistle as a cruiser passed by.

Since she was expecting Sharon or Stella to call at any minute with news on Sharon's donor, her mobile was right next to her, and when it rang she clicked on without checking who it was.

'Hi, it's me,' a voice said at the other end.

Immediately her heart contracted. 'Miles,' she murmured, sitting back in her chair. 'Thank God. I've been so worried.'

'I'm sorry,' he said. He sounded so tired and hoarse that

she could easily picture his unshaven face and the heaviness of his eyes – and rarely had she wanted to be with him more. 'I don't know if it's wise to call,' he said, 'or just plain stupid not to.'

'What's important is that you stop shutting me out,' she told him.

There was a silence before he spoke again, and the note of defeat that had crept into his voice increased her concern. 'If anything should happen,' he said, 'if this doesn't end the way . . . I want you to know that you and Rufus will be taken care of.'

'Miles, don't say things like that,' she said gently, but firmly. 'We're going to be together, all of us . . .'

'But if things *don't* work out that way . . .'

'They will. Listen to me, please. You haven't done anything wrong.'

'I guess you realise you're the only one who seems to think that.'

'Al Kohler does too. And there will be plenty of others if you'd just let us in. Darling, you're clearly exhausted. You can't go on shouldering this alone.'

'Well, I'm not going to let you do it for me.'

'For heaven's sake! That ludicrously chauvinistic attitude is so typical of you I could scream. You think you have to be the tough guy, always coping alone no matter what life throws at you. Well, for the record, we have a son now, so I get to have a say in what affects him, and his father.'

'I'm not going to argue about this,' he said. 'I just want you to know that no matter how this ends, I've taken steps to—'

'Make sure Rufus is taken care of. Yes, I heard you. So ring off now, if that's all you have to say, because we don't need your charity, or your conscience, we need *you*, and I really don't appreciate the way you're making this sound so final.'

As her voice resonated angrily down the line she immediately wanted to retract the harshness, since her frustration wasn't going to help him at all. 'Look, I know it must seem as though the world is crashing in on you right now,' she went on more gently, 'but you have to remember, your conscience is clear.'

'Even if it is, do you really think it makes a difference? I've been through this before, remember, when they accused me of killing Sam. Now it's Jacqueline, and frankly, if she is alive . . .'

'Of course she is.'

'If you're right then frankly I'd want to wring her neck, not for what she's doing to me, but for what it's doing to Kelsey. I don't think she can take much more. She's either shut up in her bedroom, crying as though her heart's going to break, or she's yelling at me, accusing me . . .' His voice faltered. 'She's got it into her head that she doesn't matter now I have Rufus.'

'Then you have to convince her she does. No matter what she says or believes, you have to keep letting her know you're there, and you won't walk away.'

'Until the police arrest me for murder. What will I tell her then?'

'That's not going to happen.'

'You must know by now that they've found her clothes, her handbag, her credit cards.'

'None of which proves she's dead, and even if she is, do you seriously think I'm going to believe you did it? No, don't even answer that. I'll defend you to the hilt with anyone else, but I'm sure as hell not going to do it with you.'

With a trace of humour in his voice he said, 'I can almost see the way your eyes are flashing.' Then he added in a voice that was both rough and tender, 'God, I miss you.'

'I miss you too,' she said, feeling her heart fold around the words, 'and I can't bear the way you're letting this drag you down. I know it's bringing back too much of the past, but try not to go there, darling. You're no more guilty now than you were then. They can't lock you up for a crime you didn't commit.'

'We both know that's not true, because it happens all the time. Come in,' he said, apparently speaking to someone who'd knocked on his door.

Hearing a woman's voice Vivienne immediately tensed. Surely to God it wasn't Justine James.

Coming back on the line he said, 'Can you hang on a moment, Mrs Davies wants a quick word.'

As she waited, Vivienne turned to watch Rufus crawling towards the French windows that opened onto the balcony. He seemed to be after the ragged plants tumbling from an assortment of pots, but it was still raining too hard for him to go out there. He began banging his fists against the glass and dancing on wobbly legs, so she went to kneel down next to him, turning his attention to her, wishing she could tell him she was speaking to Daddy, but knowing that if he started to shout 'Da da da' it would probably be more than Miles could take.

'Are you still there?' he said.

'Yes,' she answered, her heart tightening at the mere sound of his voice. Sometimes the urgency she felt to touch him was almost overwhelming, and right now was one of those moments.

'The police just called Mrs Davies wanting to know if she's ever heard of someone by the name of Anne Cates.'

Vivienne frowned. 'Did they say who she is?'

'No.' His voice went off the line again as he said, 'It's OK, you can come in.'

Wondering who it was, Vivienne was on the point of asking, when Rufus let out one of his more exuberant shrieks followed by a magnificent gurgle.

Miles said nothing, merely let the silence run, perhaps hoping to hear more, or maybe dreading it. Whichever, all thought of Anne Cates had gone as Vivienne held her breath, imagining the emotions he must now be struggling to contain.

'Wane, wane,' Rufus chanted, hitting the window.

'Yes, darling, it's rain,' Vivienne whispered.

She heard Miles swallow, then in a voice that was barely audible he said, 'I have to go,' and a moment later the line went dead.

Miles was still holding the phone as he rested his head on Kelsey's and inhaled the sweet lemony scent of her hair. The need to see his son, to hear his baby voice again and feel the tenderness of his skin was tearing through him savagely. Yet it felt good to be sitting with his daughter like this after so much trauma and hysteria, knowing she was safe and calm, at least on the surface, and still needful of his reassurance in spite of how hard she'd been trying to resist it.

He tightened his embrace and pressed a kiss to the top of her head. He knew how likely it was that she'd erupt in a fit of rage again at any moment, triggered by an innocent remark of his, or a rogue thought creeping into her mind to create more havoc amongst the confusion. So, for now, he was happy to sit in silence, holding her, listening to the gentle rhythm of her breathing and feeling thankful for the lull in the storm.

'Dad?' she said after a while.

'Mm?'

'How old were you when you first had sex?'

He almost laughed out loud. And there he was thinking how he'd welcome a change of subject from Jacqueline. 'Twenty-nine,' he said, barely missing a beat.

Her gurgle of laughter warmed him all the way through and made him realise how little humour they'd shared lately, when he used to be able to make her laugh all the time.

'Seriously,' she said, sitting up to look at him, 'how old were you?'

Knowing he was probably entering a minefield, but not sure how to avoid it, he said, 'Seventeen. Why?'

She shrugged and looked away, seeming to trail her thoughts along with her. A moment or two later she said, 'How old was Mum?'

He frowned as he tried to remember. 'Eighteen, I think.'

'So you weren't her first or anything?'

'No. She was engaged to someone else before she met me.'

'What, and then like she met you and fell in love so she had to end it with him?'

'Actually, it was already over between them before we met.'

Her bottom lip came out, suggesting she wasn't too pleased with that answer. 'But did you fall in love straight away?' she prompted. 'Did you know she was the right one for you?'

Sensing it was what she wanted to hear, he said, 'I think so, more or less.'

'Was she like the most beautiful woman you'd ever seen?'

He smiled. 'Yes,' he replied.

She nodded, seeming happy with that, then lifting his hand she began twisting her fingers round his. 'So you were seventeen,' she said, keeping her eyes down.

'And now you're going to ask me who she was,' he responded wryly.

She shook her head. 'No, not unless you want to tell me.'

'I'd rather you told me why you're interested.'

She shrugged and continued to stare at their hands. 'No reason,' she said, bending and stretching his thumb.

He waited, wishing he was more up to this, but at the same time glad she felt able to broach it. In the end he said, 'Have you met someone? Is that why you're asking?'

'No,' she replied. 'I just think, like, you know I shouldn't do it while I'm still only fourteen, should I?'

Managing to keep his tone level, he said, 'Well, as it's not even legal until—'

'I know that. I'm just saying.'

When she didn't elaborate any further, he said, 'Is someone asking you to do it?'

'No, but the girls at school . . . Lots of them have already done it, and it's like no big deal, so . . .' She trailed off, leaving him to wonder if it was a big deal or not.

'The time to do it,' he said carefully, 'is when you meet someone special who means a lot to you and thinks you're—'

'That is so old-fashioned,' she cut in. 'It's not like that these days. People just do it because they want to. Anyway, I don't want to talk about it any more,' and turning around she laid her head back on his shoulder.

As he stroked her hair he tried to puzzle out what the conversation had really been about, whether she was undergoing some kind of peer pressure, or perhaps she had met someone but didn't want to admit it.

'You are the coolest dad,' she told him suddenly. 'I can say anything to you.'

'Well, you definitely didn't hold back when you were swearing at me last night,' he reminded her dryly.

She giggled, and cosied in a little closer.

They continued to sit quietly, staring absently into the dying fire, each with their own thoughts, until Mrs Davies brought in some tea and set it down on the desk.

It was a while after she'd gone that Miles started to get up, reluctant to break the closeness but keen to see Kelsey eat something, even if it was only a biscuit.

'You know when I came in just now,' Kelsey said as he poured the tea, 'and you were talking to someone on the phone? Was it her?'

Glad she had no way of seeing his sudden leap in tension, he said, 'Yes, it was.'

She didn't speak again until he turned round to pass her a cup.

'I don't want it,' she said, looking away.

Deciding not to argue, he put it back on the tray and picked up his own.

'So like you had to ring off because I was in the room?' she said, her face becoming pinched.

'Would you have preferred that I carried on talking to her?' he countered calmly.

Her expression turned stonier than ever.

Sighing, he went to sit next to her again. 'I heard Rufus in the background,' he said, 'that was why I rang off. I didn't know what to say in case it upset you.'

'Why would it upset me? I couldn't care less what you say to him.'

'Darling . . .'

'It's *fine*. You can talk to him all you like, and her. It makes no difference to me.'

'I wish you meant that.'

'I do,' but it was clear she didn't.

Taking a breath, he forced himself to say, 'They're going to be in Devon this week. I'd like it very much—'

She was on her feet. 'I'm going back to school tomorrow,' she told him, her voice shaking with anger.

Knowing it would be wrong to try and talk her out of it, but not wanting her to go like this, he said, 'Why don't you come and sit down? We need to talk—'

'I am so not interested. What you do with her—'

'Kelsey, please try to understand why it's important that

you and Rufus meet. You're both my children . . .'

'He might be, but you don't have to worry about me any more. I'll go back to school and then you can be with him.'

'That's not what I want. You're creating a difficulty where there doesn't need to be one.'

'It's you who's creating the difficulty just by having him,' she cried. 'Anyway, I don't care what you do, because I won't be here.'

As the door closed behind her he put his head in his hands, despairing of what to do, or even say, to try and get through to her. Then quite suddenly she was back.

'You couldn't give a damn where Mum is now, could you?' she accused furiously. 'You're not interested in anything about her, because all that matters to you is your *son*.'

'Kelsey—'

'And that's all that matters to her too,' she shouted over him. 'So you're both the same and I'm sick to death of you. I hate this house and this family and I wish you were all dead.'

As she went thundering up the stairs he reached for his phone and did something he hadn't done in days. He called Jacqueline's mobile which hadn't turned up with her other things and left yet another message reminding her she had a daughter and asking her to spare a thought for what this silence was doing to her.

'If you're checking your voicemail,' he said, 'you'll know by now how desperate she is, and if you're up to date with the news perhaps you'll understand how much she needs you while she tries to adjust to what's happening.' He was about to ring off when he suddenly added, 'It might be over between us, Jacqueline, but she's still a child, for God's sake. She doesn't deserve this. As her mother you should stop being so damned selfish and put her first for once in your life.'

Chapter Fifteen

The church clock on Kew Green was striking midday as a dark-haired woman in a camel coat passed by. She was counting the chimes absently in her mind: *one, two, three . . .* through to *eleven, twelve, thirteen, fourteen.* She halted. Her eyes came up from the pavement to look around. Had anyone else noticed? It didn't seem so, because the world was continuing on its way, cars speeding in either direction, dog-owners and their pets roaming the green, early lunchers heading for the pubs. She was certain she hadn't made a mistake, so perhaps she was the only one who'd bothered to count.

She glanced up at the tall bell tower with its elegant green dome and intricate arches. Both golden hands of the clock were pointing to twelve. There was no fourteen, but how could there be? Her gaze lost some focus as her thoughts became blurred by curiosity and a little amusement. Then it occurred to her that maybe only she had heard the final two chimes, because only she was supposed to. At the suggestion of a coded message, a hidden sign, her heart gave a jolt. She wished it was possible to have the last two minutes over again, to be certain she'd heard right. Then, as though surging up from a bottomless well, the chilling echo of the same refrain – *please let me have the last two minutes over again* – made her turn from the church and walk on.

It was an ordinary day; a dullish sky, with an occasional skip of wind, and leaves gently falling. She paid it no attention, because the weather held no more interest for her than nature, or people, or places. She and the world were strangers now, passing one another by like ships in the night, or hands on a clock. There was no desire to renew their acquaintance; they only had old animosities and an uncrushable spectre of hope to bind them together.

Life, on the other hand, was her enemy. She detested its trickery as much as its extravagant promises and barefaced artifice. It had dealt so cruelly with her that to punish it she had simply withdrawn from its game. Never again would she be seduced by its persuasive glimpses of a rosy future or believe in its ability to come good in the end. She had no heart to engage with it anyway, no blood left to shed, or even tears to cry. Now, when she cut herself, guilt ran from her veins, and when she cried shame rolled from her eyes.

If only she could have those few minutes over again. Life didn't allow that though, did it? It delivered its blows then left the defenceless to the harrowing torment of their own minds, and the insupportable burden of a conscience that could never be salved. The screaming in the night had never been her baby crying for his mother, it had always been her. Wild, plaintive howls of grief and despair to break the harshest of hearts and soften the coldest of souls. Miles would find her in the garden, begging the moon and stars to take pity on her in a way the sun never did. *Please, night, bring him back before another day dawns without him.* But night never did. It was unmoved by her plight; it had no interest in filling her empty arms, or easing her pain. Like God and fate, it blessed the people who'd crept out of nowhere to devastate her world, while it cursed her for the two minutes of negligence that had allowed them to steal her son.

She was still walking, approaching the roundabout at Richmond now. The garage that used to be there no longer was; it had become an estate agent's a while ago, though she didn't know when. She stood on the far side of the busy interchange, staring through the traffic to the benign-looking building opposite with its glossy white facade and black timber frames. Never a day went by when she didn't stand here, not really seeing, just thinking, about Sam, and who he might be now. And the person, or people, who'd taken him. Had it been a kind, gentle woman who'd gone on to love him and treat him well? Or an evil, sadistic monster who'd— She shut that down abruptly, as she'd finally learned how. Over the years the person, or people, who'd devastated her life had acquired a thousand different faces and even more names. She saw them in shops and on buses, outside schools and in playgrounds. She never spoke to them, she only watched their children and felt the emptiness inside her growing deeper and blacker until sometimes it was all there was left of her.

In the early days she'd been drugged in an effort to silence the nightmares and keep her calm. It had turned her into a zombie, but it hadn't stopped her thinking about stealing a child – if life could take from her, she could take from it. Not that she wanted someone else's child, she only wanted her own, but sometimes she felt an urge to punish the world for what it was doing to her. She'd never done it, because even in her grief-demented state she'd had enough compassion to care about the woman who'd suffer.

With her eyes still focused on the building opposite, she wondered if those responsible had ever returned to the scene of their crime. Did they know it was no longer a garage? Why would they care? Had they spared a thought for her that day, or any day since? Surely they must have read or heard the news, so they'd have known that the police, and even some of their friends, had started to suspect her and Miles of killing their son? It hadn't made those who'd taken him come forward, but it had brought others into the light, people who had opinions and theories, others who'd suffered similar fates, and a woman who'd stepped from the shadows to claim that she knew for a fact Sam Avery had never been in the car when his mother had driven into the garage.

She blinked reflexively as a driver sped past, angrily blasting his horn. She didn't look to see what had prompted it. She wasn't interested. She merely continued to stare at what used to be the garage, unaware of time or space, or even sound. Her breath was shallow, and her nerves taut and frayed like thin copper wires. Sam's laughter was pushing up from the past to blend with Miles's frustration and Kelsey's angry confusion. He wanted to be heard, but his sister's voice was louder, drowning him out with her sobbing and pleading, desperate to be seen and loved. The need moved past her like a breeze. She knew it was there, and even fleetingly felt it, but it didn't penetrate far or remain. It had no place with her, she wouldn't accept it, because it belonged to a world she had no part in.

Life wasn't going to touch her again, and if it thought it had made amends by giving her a daughter, it must realise by now she had proved it wrong. It could keep its little tokens of mercy and false bundles of joy. She'd been cheated of one child, she wasn't going to be tricked again. Miles could nurture and bond with their daughter if he chose to, the risk was his to take. For her there was no forgiveness – life hadn't returned her son, so she wouldn't accept what it had given her in his place. Nor would she allow it to toss her another son, a substitute, a salve, as though Sam had never really mattered. Oh no. She wouldn't conceive again until her firstborn was back in her arms.

Her head went down and she bunched her hands more tightly in her pockets as she turned to walk on. Anne Cates needed to return to the house she had rented, which she'd paid for in cash, in advance, so no one bothered her at all, not even her landlord who lived in Spain. To her neighbours she was merely the dark-haired woman at number fourteen who kept herself to herself. One or two mumbled good morning and passed on by, heads down, hurrying to the station where they bought various newspapers on their way to work. The headlines would be of momentary interest before they turned the page, moving on to the next. They'd never connect them with the woman who occasionally walked around the green, or stood on a roundabout staring at something that didn't exist any more. They'd have no idea of the shock she'd received on picking up the paper two days ago, or of the emotions that had followed since like shadows, trailing behind for a while, then suddenly looming large and dark at the front of her mind.

It wasn't her intention to go to the river, but when next she registered her surroundings she was standing in the small, squelchy pools that muddied the shore when the tide went out. Her footprints were fading like ghosts behind her, while seagulls swooped in to peck at flotsam discarded on the desolate banks. Several times these past weeks she'd imagined letting the water close over her, cold and comforting, embracing her like sleep until she was no more. She wouldn't do it, because if Sam came back she had to be waiting.

Out of nowhere, names began floating up from the past, rising to the surface like small pockets of air, bursting. Anne Cates. Elizabeth Barrett. Vivienne Kane. Then they vanished, dispersed, disintegrating, blending back into the river like tears, perhaps to be washed up again, but on other shores, not here.

Finally she began retracing her steps, remembering where she was going, but having no interest in arriving. Since leaving home she'd walked a lot, around Richmond and Kew, often as far as Chiswick and back. During her journeys she'd often thought about Miles and Kelsey, hearing their voices in her mind, and even caring in a way, but whenever she felt their pain she quickly shut it out. She didn't want any part of it, even though she understood now, in a way she hadn't before, that the years of rejection she'd subjected them to had, perversely, bound them to her so tightly that she'd stifled all the love Miles had felt, and created a need in Kelsey that could never be fulfilled. She should have left them a long time ago, or stayed in America. It had been a mistake to come back, but it was one she wouldn't make again.

You want to kill me for this, Miles, don't you? she murmured inside her head.

She could hear him saying yes. *Yes, yes and yes.*

You don't know who I am any more, she told him.

I never did. Not since . . . but between them they didn't say Sam's name any more.

Now he had another son, Rufus, whose name he could speak all the time.

Vivienne was speeding down the M4 in her brother-in-law's Polo with Rufus asleep in his baby seat behind her, while Pete followed on in his Audi. They'd set out early for Devon, and so far seemed to have escaped the press. In fact there was surprisingly little traffic around, which was why, as they passed the Leigh Delamere services close to

Chippenham, she recognised Theo as he roared past on his motorbike. Knowing he'd arrive long before them, he'd already arranged to meet Stella and Sharon at the Smugglers, where they were going to give an interview to one of the local papers. At some point later in the day, or perhaps tomorrow if the firemen were free for a photocall this afternoon, Theo was due to embark on his first session with the choreographer.

'Dancing!' he'd cried in mock horror when Vivienne had first put it to him. 'I have to gyrate my body in front of the cameras? Everyone's going to think I'm like him.'

She'd had to laugh at that, not only because he was well known for camping it up in front of the cameras, but because Pete had let out a little whimper of 'Yes please.'

They were going to have a riot, those two, entertaining the WI ladies with all their teasing and flirting, while pulling together with Sky to stage a memorable event. Naturally she'd be there to oversee things, but with Rufus to take care of and the mounting need to sort something out with Miles, she wasn't foolish enough to think she could do without their front-line assistance.

Hearing the jingle of her phone in her earpiece she glanced down at the mobile on the seat next to her, and seeing it was Alice clicked on right away.

'Are you sitting down?' Alice demanded.

'As I'm driving I'd find it hard not to be.'

'OK, get ready for this. The police have just been here looking for you. They're trying to find out if you – actually *we* – know anyone by the name of Anne Cates.'

Vivienne's initial alarm was already turning to confusion. 'Miles mentioned that name yesterday,' she said. 'Did they tell you who she is?'

'Just that she has a phone registered at our address.'

'At *our* address?'

'Right here at Pier House.'

Vivienne wasn't liking the sound of this. 'And the police actually came in person to ask if we knew her?'

'They did indeed, and they were pretty pissed off to find you'd already left for Devon. I almost told them, more fool them for not checking before coming, but I didn't think it would go down too well. Anyway, I thought I'd better warn you that they're going to be in touch.'

'Thanks,' Vivienne murmured, and after ringing off she gave a voice command to her phone which connected her to Miles's mobile. To her surprise and relief he answered straight away.

'Hi, are you OK?' he asked.

'Fine,' she assured him. 'At least I think so. Apparently the police have just been to my office asking about this Anne Cates. Isn't that who they asked Mrs Davies about?'

'Yes,' he responded, sounding surprised. 'Did they throw any light on who she is?'

'No, but apparently she has a phone registered at the Pier House address.'

Miles fell silent.

Feeling a beat of unease, Vivienne said, 'Are you thinking what I'm thinking?'

'Probably,' he replied, 'but if it is Jacqueline, why would she do that? It doesn't make any sense.' Then, without waiting for an answer, 'When you speak to the police ask them *when* the phone was registered. They must know – in fact, they must have received a call from it to have been able to trace it. So what did this woman have to say?'

'I guess we can't know that until the police decide to tell us, so I'll call you back once I've spoken to them,' and checking to make sure Pete was still behind she pulled out to overtake a slow-moving lorry.

Seconds after disconnecting, her earpiece rang again. Since it wasn't a number she recognised she took a chance it might be the police, and wasn't disappointed.

'Ms Kane? Detective Inspector Sadler here.' His voice resonated authority and no little annoyance, reminding her that he'd had a wasted journey to London.

'Hello, Inspector,' she said amicably.

'I've been trying to get through,' he told her, 'so I imagine Mrs Jackson beat me to it.'

There was no point denying it, so she didn't. 'You want to know if I've ever heard of someone called Anne Cates,' she said, glancing in the mirror as Rufus started to wake up.

'The answer is, I haven't, but perhaps you wouldn't mind telling me why you're asking.'

Sounding as if he minded a great deal, he said, 'Someone claiming to be Jacqueline Avery contacted the incident room in Exeter yesterday afternoon, asking us to call off the search. The call was made from a pay-as-you-go phone that has been registered in the name of Anne Cates at your office address. I wonder if you can explain any of that?'

Vivienne's pulse had started to race at the mention of Jacqueline. 'No, Inspector, I can't,' she told him as Rufus started to mutter and kick. 'I've never heard the name Anne Cates before. Do you know *where* the call came from?'

'Kew. You were in the area yesterday, I believe.'

Kew! 'I drove through, on my way to the supermarket,' she said, her mind starting to spin. Did he seriously think she'd set herself up with an alias in order to sabotage the search? Worse was the fact that someone really had registered that phone at her office address, and the call had come from as close to home as Kew. 'Out of interest, Inspector,' she said, remembering Miles's instruction, 'do you know *when* the phone was registered?'

'On September 19th, eight days before Mrs Avery disappeared.'

Meaning? For the moment she could come up with no clear idea. 'Do you have a recording of the call?' she asked, having to speak up to make herself heard above Rufus's demands for attention. 'If so, maybe you should ask someone who knows Mrs Avery's voice if it's her.'

In a tone that could have cut glass he said, 'Thank you for your advice, Ms Kane. I'll be sure to bear it in mind.'

Resisting the urge to bite back, she hit the indicator to take the approaching slip road. 'If you'll forgive me, Inspector, I'm driving at the moment, and as you can no doubt hear, my son is in need of a drink.'

'Before you go, Ms Kane,' he came in quickly, 'I'd like to know where you can be contacted in Devon.'

Realising he was expecting to be told Moorlands, she took some pleasure in saying, 'I'll be on this number,' and after wishing him a good day she cut the connection.

Minutes later she was standing in a truckers' lay-by on the

A46, trying to comfort Rufus as she told Pete about the call. Thankfully, since Alice had taken Pete aside to tell him to stop with the negative comments about Miles, he'd been treating the matter much more seriously. However, she could have wished for a slightly different answer when she suggested that Anne Cates could be Justine James up to some kind of mischief again.

'I think the date rules out that possibility,' he said gravely, stepping in closer as a lorry thundered past. 'No, I definitely think it's Jacqueline and in *Kew*.'

'I have to speak to Miles,' she said, and handing Rufus over she reached back into the car for her phone. 'There are toys in the box, and his bottle's down the side of his chair,' she instructed, starting to dial.

A few minutes later, having listened to what she was telling him, Miles said, 'It has to be her. On the one hand it's a great relief to know she's alive, but we have to ask ourselves, why haven't the police contacted me?'

'I think they have it in their heads that *I'm* responsible for the call. It might explain why they tried to see me in person.'

'That's preposterous,' he declared. 'Sadler's an idiot. He's so convinced we've been up to no good that he's lost the ability to see straight.'

Deciding not to pursue that, she said, 'What would she be doing in Kew?'

'It's right next to Richmond, which was where we were living when Sam was taken.'

Knowing he was trying to stop her thinking exactly what she was thinking, she said, 'If she knew about Rufus before she disappeared, she might not have realised he wasn't living with me.'

'*If* she knew, and I'm finding it hard to believe she did. It's not something she'd have kept to herself.'

Unless she was planning to snatch him, Vivienne was thinking, trying not to panic. 'We have to assume she knows now,' she stated.

'Of course. It would be foolish not to. Where are you?'

'On my way to Devon.'

'Is Rufus with you?'

'Of course.'

'Then I think you should bring him here.'

She blinked with shock.

'Call me when you get as far as Exeter, and I'll go up through the top woods to open the gate.'

'But how is that going to help?' she cried. 'If Jacqueline finds out . . .' She put a hand to her head, turning towards the car. 'And what about Kelsey?' she demanded. 'She doesn't want him there.'

'She keeps saying she wants to go back to school.'

'But you can't send her away to make room for Rufus. It'd be the worst thing you could do right now. No, I'll continue on as I am.'

'He'll be safer here with me.'

'Miles, you have to be realistic,' she said desperately. 'In Jacqueline's mind . . . Well, God knows what's going on in her mind. No, I can't bring him to you. I won't stop you seeing him, I'll never do that, but I have to protect him.' Hearing her own words, she said, 'Oh God, I'm sorry, I'm not trying to accuse Jacqueline or Kelsey of wanting to harm him, but to me Jacqueline feels like a frighteningly loose cannon, and Kelsey's already got too many problems. Miles, please don't take offence, but he's my son so I have—'

'He's mine too,' he reminded her, 'but it's OK, I understand why you're nervous so I'm not going to force you. Are you going back to Richard and Susie's?'

'I'd intended to.'

'Good. Their grounds are pretty secure, but there's a lot of press around at the moment, so can someone stay with you?'

Thinking of Theo, she said, 'Absolutely.' Then, after taking a breath, 'I'm sorry, I don't mean to overreact, it's just . . .'

'Don't apologise. It's been a shock, finding out about the phone, and realising it could be Jacqueline. But remember, we still don't know for certain that it was.'

'Who else would tell the police to call off the search? Anne Cates? Who is she?'

'I keep feeling as though the name should mean something.'

'Nothing's meaning anything right now,' she said shakily, 'except the fact that I feel so afraid for my son that I can't think straight.'

'He's going to be fine,' Miles said firmly. 'I'm always at the end of the line, and I have every intention of doing better than that just as soon as I can.'

Realising she had to calm down, she said, 'I'm sorry, you're right. It's just the thought of her being so close all this time . . .'

'If she was, then she's proved she doesn't mean you any harm,' he pointed out. 'I feel it's far more likely that she's in the area because of the link the place has to Sam.'

'Then why use my address?' Knowing he wouldn't have an answer for that, she went on heatedly, 'If only we could communicate with her in some way, let her know—'

'Can you hang on for a moment?' he interrupted.

As she waited she went to check on Rufus and Pete, who seemed to be getting along fine with a biscuit and tumbler of juice in the back of the car.

'What did he say?' Pete wanted to know, keeping his voice down.

'He thinks it's her too.'

He pulled a face. 'Spooky. Bet it makes you glad we're on our way out of London.'

Unable to deny it, she said, 'Nevertheless, we mustn't let Rufus out of our sight.'

'You can count on me. Does Daddy want to see him?'

Before she could answer Miles's voice came back on the line. 'Kelsey's going back to school,' he told her. 'She's all packed, but she doesn't want me to drive her. Mrs Davies is going to do it.'

'Why doesn't she want you?'

'She's not speaking to me at the moment. Don't ask, it changes from hour to hour. It does mean she won't be here, though.'

'I still don't think it's a good idea for me to come.'

'No, you're probably right,' he agreed with a sigh. 'But I do want to see you, so call me when you arrive – and drive safely.'

'Of course,' she whispered, and after ringing off she

inhaled deeply of the cold, fuel-fumed air, before turning back to the car.

'Why are you taking so much?' Miles wanted to know, as Kelsey carried her laptop down the stairs to join the holdalls and boxes already stacked in the hall.

'It's the same stuff I brought home,' she replied tartly.

'But do you need all that when you'll be back at the weekend, and half-term's coming up?'

With a supercilious toss of her head she said, 'You wouldn't even begin to understand what I need. Anyway, I'm going to Martha's for the weekend.'

'I see,' he responded slowly. He wanted to tell her she couldn't, but was reluctant to make the situation any worse by starting a row. 'I wish you'd let me drive you,' he said.

'It's fine, Mrs Davies is happy to do it. Can I have some money?'

Bristling at her tone, he said, 'Is that any way to ask?'

With a surly impatience she shifted her weight to one leg and rolled her eyes. 'Please,' she said, drawing out the word.

Not wanting them to part on bad terms, he swallowed his frustration and said, 'How much do you need?'

'A hundred quid should be enough.'

His eyes widened.

'Don't look at me like that!' she cried. 'Martha and I are going shopping at the weekend, so I've got to have something.'

'Even so . . .'

'Oh fine, keep your money.'

'I'm not saying you can't have it . . .'

'Yes you are. Well, that's OK. I can manage.'

'Kelsey, for heaven's sake, you're creating an issue where—'

'*I* am?' she cut in furiously. 'It's you who won't part with the money.'

'All right, you can have it, but I'd appreciate less of the attitude, if you don't mind.'

'Yeah, and I would appreciate being made to feel like I

matter around here, but hey, we can't have everything, can we? Except you, of course. You get to have it all.'

'What on earth are you talking about?'

'I heard you on the phone just now, telling her to come here. Well that's absolutely fine, because I am like gone, OK? I won't be in your life any more.'

'I'm not letting you walk out of here like this,' he said angrily. 'You need to listen to what I'm saying—'

'No, you need to listen to me! I'm making my own decisions from now on and one of them is to leave this house. You've never wanted me here anyway, so I'll happily make room for your son. I'm just sorry his name isn't Sam—'

'Kelsey, for God's sake, you're twisting this round and hurting yourself as much as me— Come back here!' he shouted as she started to leave. 'You're not going anywhere until we've sorted this out, even if I have to lock you in.'

'Just try it,' she challenged. 'I'll scream child abuse quicker than any of them out there can cry murder.'

At that his eyes closed, until realising she was opening the door he reached out and put a hand against it. 'I wish I knew how to make you believe that you matter more to me than anyone else,' he said sadly.

'That is so not true,' she cried. 'You can't wait for me to go so you can get her moved in here. Well, this is me going, OK? You don't need to worry about me any more. Just enjoy your son.'

'Vivienne is not coming here,' he told her. 'She understands how difficult it is for you, which is why she turned me down.'

'Well, she's free to do what she likes now. I've got all my stuff—'

'You are not setting foot outside this house until I know where you're going.'

'To *school*,' she almost screamed. 'The place you always send me when you want me out of the way.'

'Then let me take you. We can talk on the way.'

'There's nothing else to say, now if you'll excuse me, Mrs Davies is waiting in the car.'

Certain he shouldn't let her go, but not quite knowing

how to stop her, he said, 'I want you back here at the weekend. I'll come to pick you up—'

'I'm going to Martha's. It's all arranged.'

'Kelsey . . .'

'Would you mind carrying my suitcase?'

Sighing with exasperation, he picked it up and followed her outside. 'Here,' he said, taking out his wallet once her luggage was in the boot. 'I've only got sixty in cash. If you want more, you'll have to come back before you go shopping.'

'Nice try,' she muttered, and grabbing the money she stuffed it into her belt bag while striding round to the passenger seat.

'Don't I get a proper goodbye?' he said softly.

She stopped, keeping her face averted.

'Please don't let's part bad friends.'

'I'm not,' she retorted. 'I'm just saying, you can do what you want now.'

Realising there was a small space opening up, he walked round the car and drew her into his arms. 'I've already spoken to the headmistress to let her know what's going on . . .'

'Oh, like they don't already know.'

'. . . so if you get there and decide you want to come back, or if in a couple of days . . .'

'I'll be fine,' she assured him, sounding less hostile now.

'Call if you need anything. Call anyway.'

'I always do.'

He smiled, because she did, even when she had nothing particular to say. He hoped that was going to continue – in fact he was going to make sure it did by ringing her.

After opening the door for her to get in, he stood watching the car going off down the drive. Letting her go troubled him as much as forcing her to stay would have done.

Dear Ms James, thank you for your prompt response. You will find my address and telephone number below. Please call any time to make an arrangement for us to meet. I will show you the spot where Mr Avery's son is buried. Mr Avery `might now wish for the remains to be removed and given a proper burial. Yours, Elizabeth J. Barrett`

Justine sat staring at the email, feeling herself moving between horror and a very necessary caution. If – and it was a big if – this woman was on the level, then Miles Avery *had known all along that his son was dead*, and might even . . .

Getting briskly up from her chair, she walked to the window. She had to think this through very carefully now, because the possible repercussions, if she came right out and accused Miles of being involved in his son's death, or at least knowing about it, were already making her head spin in a way that could see much more disaster ahead than glory.

As things stood, she had no idea whether or not Elizabeth Barrett was a nutcase, so no way would she run the risk of going to print with anything – at least, not in her name – until she knew for certain who the woman really was. She'd already opened up several lines of investigation, but as yet nothing useful was coming back. There was no mention of her in the press cuttings, national or local, from the time Sam went missing, nor had anything come to light to connect her to the Averys at any time since. However, a few contacts had yet to get back to her, one of whom had access to the archives of the Richmond Division of the Metropolitan Police. If Elizabeth Barrett didn't turn up in those files, then Justine would be much more inclined to believe that she'd unearthed something truly sinister. If she had, she'd be duty bound to go public with it. If she hadn't . . . Well, she had a fairly good idea what she'd do next, but for now she was content to wait until the remaining contacts, including the police archivist, got back to her.

Chapter Sixteen

DC Joy was turning off her mobile as Sadler carried two steaming hot mochas out onto the station concourse and set them down on the bistro table where she was sitting. They were waiting for the next train back to Exeter, having more or less wasted their time in London, and she suspected the text she'd just received wasn't going to do much to improve Sadler's mood, since it wasn't lending itself at all well to his suspicions about Miles Avery.

'I've just heard from Dotty in forensics,' she told him, as he sat down. 'The postmark on the envelope – the one we found in the woods addressed to Jacqueline Avery?'

He nodded.

'It's Twickenham, which covers Richmond on Thames.'

His hand stopped before the mocha reached his mouth.

'It would account for the "mes" that hadn't been torn off the back,' she said blandly, judging it tactful for him to state the more obvious connection.

'It's also,' he said, 'right next to Kew, where the call came from, and where the Averys were living when the boy went missing.'

She nodded.

His eyes flicked upwards as a booming announcement began flooding the station with an unintelligible explanation for a delay. 'That wasn't ours, was it?' he asked.

'I don't think so.'

He took a sip of his mocha, then narrowing his eyes thoughtfully, he said, 'So someone was writing to her from Richmond. Do we know the date of the postmark?'

'August 18th.'

He pondered that for a moment. 'Well over a month before she disappeared. So what was in that envelope?'

Refraining from reminding him that she'd been asking that very question since the envelope had turned up, she said, 'I have some theories, sir. Can I run them past you?'

His eyebrows rose, but not unkindly. 'I'm all ears,' he informed her, and shot a menacing look at a rowdy pair of pierced, tattooed and shaven-headed youths who were playfully punching and kicking each other as they headed for a platform.

'Well, sir,' she began, wresting back his attention, 'first of all we're agreed, aren't we, that Jacqueline Avery could have dumped her own bag and clothes in the bin that Grainger and his mate found them in?'

Sadler's expression began to sour. 'Are you about to suggest that she disguised herself, threw away everything that would identify her, then took off to . . . Well, Richmond? Is that where you're going with this, Detective Constable?'

She nodded eagerly. 'More or less, sir,' she confirmed, a glimmer of excitement appearing in her eyes. 'You see, it would tie in with the money too. She withdrew a large amount of cash because she didn't want her movements to be traced through her bank account or credit cards. She swapped the clothes she wore to the station that morning for those she had inside the bag; she might also have had a wig to cover her blonde hair, or she's dyed it since, or whatever, and then, having more or less "disposed" of Jacqueline Avery, she became Anne Cates.'

Though this all seemed a little too pat for Sadler's taste, he wasn't going to deny that it had some merit. 'Why Anne Cates?' he asked.

'No idea, but I suppose it's as good a name as any if you want to become somebody else.'

'Why would she want to be somebody else?'

Joy grimaced and shrugged. 'Only she can tell us the answer to that,' she replied. 'But I do think we need to take another look at those CCTV tapes to see if we can spot someone who *might* be Jacqueline Avery. Up to now we've been looking for a blonde woman dressed in black and leaving around ten in the morning. I know we've checked every train that day, and the next, but if she did change her appearance . . .'

Sadler cleared his throat gruffly, and drank more of his mocha. 'You mentioned theories in the plural,' he reminded her as she began spooning the foamy chocolate from the top of her drink.

'Mm, well, I think that's kind of it,' she admitted, after licking the spoon, 'because you're going to ask me now why she might have gone to Richmond, and on that I'm drawing a blank. As you say, it's where she and her husband lived when the baby was snatched, but that was fifteen years ago, so I've no idea why she'd go back there now.'

Sadler's gaze drifted off across the concourse, focusing on nothing as he thought.

'Thanks to the envelope,' Joy went on, 'we know Mrs Avery has been in touch with someone in Richmond during the past couple of months. I think that in itself means we should contact the local police to get them fully up to speed on the case.'

Sadler didn't disagree.

'We also know – and this is probably the most disturbing part of it so far – that Anne Cates has used Vivienne Kane's address for her pay-as-you-go.'

'Ah, so we're now presuming that Vivienne Kane was telling the truth when she claimed never to have heard of Anne Cates?'

Joy looked a little sheepish. 'I'm afraid so, sir,' she replied.

'Which means, in a nutshell, Detective Constable, that you're telling me I've got this all wrong. Miles Avery had nothing to do with his wife's disappearance and therefore I've been persecuting an innocent man.'

'I wouldn't put it quite like that, sir,' she protested. 'And we've no idea yet how right or wrong I am. I just wanted to float my thoughts past you.'

'Well, they've anchored, Elaine, because I think you've made some very valid deductions. I might not like them, but I'm certainly not going to allow my own ego to get in the way of the truth.'

Feeling a flood of fondness for the old fart, Joy smiled and drank some more mocha. 'So what do we do now, sir?' she asked, already having her own ideas, but judging it time to take a back seat to experience.

'As we're in London, I think we should change these tickets, and take a trip out to Richmond to introduce ourselves to the local police. Then, when we get back to Devon, we'll have the Avery housekeeper in to listen to the phone call.'

Joy looked surprised. 'Why the housekeeper, and not Avery himself?'

Asserting himself fully, he said, 'Everything you've come up with makes perfect sense, Elaine, but none of it's been substantiated yet. We still have a missing woman, a motive for wanting her out of the way, and enough evidence to suggest it's happened. So I'm afraid until we've made a few more enquiries Mr Avery's ID on the voice isn't the first one I'd trust.'

Stella Coombes's ready laughter and warming good nature was proving as irrepressible as ever. The woman was like an inextinguishable ray of sunlight, a rose that never stopped blooming. With her nothing seemed to be a problem, and even if it was it would be dealt with 'pretty swift, so no glum faces round 'ere thank you very much, everything's under control.'

Of course she was talking about Sharon when she'd said that, but her positive attitude combined with her bustling air of competence was putting Vivienne's anxieties into a far healthier perspective. Almost from the moment she'd pulled up outside the auction room – or spanking new barn as it actually was – she'd felt so much lighter in her mood that her unease about Jacqueline had, at least for the moment, melded into the background.

'Now, I wants you to know,' Stella was saying as she and Vivienne walked over to the stables, with Rufus propped on one of Stella's solid arms while happily tugging on her strange New Age pendant, 'that a couple of the women have gone and backed out since all this business came up about you being involved with the Avery thing and all. Now I'm sorry if that offends you,' she went on quickly, 'but I believe in speaking bluntly. Not so's to hurt anyone, you understand, but to make sure we all knows where we are. Anyway, it's not a problem, because I've already found some others what are happy to take their places, you know, manning the phones and serving drinks and stuff, so I think we'm all going to have a lovely time come the day. Course, me, I'm going to be mortgaging our farm to get some action out of that young Theo. I told him that and do you know what he said, saucy monkey? He said, "You're such a little cupcake, Stella, it would be my pleasure to be any kind of slave your heart desires."' She laughed delightedly, and planted a noisy kiss on Rufus's cold, silky cheek.

Laughing too, Vivienne reached over to dab the drool from Stella's necklace, then stood aside to watch her introducing Rufus to the old nags who were standing patiently in their stalls, watching their visitors approach. For his part, Rufus, who'd never seen a horse before, was beside himself with excitement, and didn't hold back from clasping their soft grey muzzles in his fat little arms and rubbing his face all over theirs. Not for the first time Vivienne reflected on the mixed blessing of how fearless he was, but she couldn't help smiling at the gentleness of the horses. What a wonderful thing Susie Blake was doing here, she was thinking, providing a comfortable and dignified end for these ageing beasts.

'Well, I suppose we better get down to some business now, young man,' Stella informed Rufus. 'We'll come back and check on the old girls again later. We might even arrange to put you on one of the ponies what you 'aven't seen yet. Got a couple of Shetlands tucked away round the back 'ere. Belongs to the couple what runs the place. Anyway, we'll see,' and hiking him higher in her arms she turned towards the barn.

'Is Sharon joining us?' Vivienne asked, as they walked into the cavernous space that was now devoid of everything bar sawdust on the floor and stacks of chairs near the back. 'There's a TV crew due to turn up any minute, hoping to get an interview in the can.'

'Oh, yeah, yeah, she's on her way, don't you worry about that. Theo went and took her young lad for a ride on his motorbike while she was at the doctor's.' Seeing Vivienne's alarm, she gave her a mischievous wink. 'I know what you'm thinking, the boy's only three, but Theo's not daft. He didn't turn the engine on. He just been wheeling him about the village saying hello to everyone, and making that little boy's eyes sparkle.'

Loving Theo for immersing himself so readily into the community, not to mention what he was doing for Sharon's children, Vivienne started over to join Pete, who was already busy with Reg Thomas, the auctioneer.

'Petey,' she said, 'this is Stella who I've told you so much about. Stella, Pete, who's going to be running things with me. Having said that, once the TV people get here we'll all be royally bossed around by them, but try not to let it bother you, we need them. We also need an answer from the firemen. Can they make a photo shoot this afternoon?'

'It's all in hand, darling,' Pete assured her, while kissing Stella on both cheeks. 'Photographer and studio booked, eight of them can make it, and Theo's going to join them. Once the public at large, or should I say oestrogen at large, gets a glimpse of all that testosterone, we can start looking at six figures for our fund.'

'Oooh, here, you'm one of them fairies,' Stella announced merrily. 'My son's one of you lot, but don't tell his father. Be all hell to pay if Sid found out. He thinks the only extra use for a bum is parking a pushbike,' and though it was a crude old joke everyone laughed, simply because she did.

'This woman is priceless,' Pete pronounced, fluffing up Stella's carroty hair, 'you're going to look just scrumptious on camera, darling. In fact, I can see you becoming a cult.'

'Reckon we got enough of them round here already,' she chortled. 'What with all the bloody witches and Satanists and spiritualists. Place is rife with 'em. But now here's someone whose cult I definitely wouldn't mind joining.'

They all turned as Theo and his two-litre Honda swerved into the yard, with a helmeted Sharon riding pillion and clinging tightly to his waist.

Going over to greet them, Vivienne smiled to see Sharon's flush of pleasure as she struggled to hold her wig in place while removing her helmet.

'Wow, that was something else,' Sharon declared, giving

Vivienne a hug. 'First time I've ever been on a motorbike. Lovely to see you. We was half afraid you might not come.'

'I told you before, I've no intention of letting you down,' Vivienne reassured her. Then in an undertone to Theo, as Sharon began unwinding her bobbly scarf and unzipping her coat, 'I need a word with you.'

With a wink to let her know he'd heard, he informed everyone that they'd just passed a Sky TV crew car, so they probably ought to get down to some sort of rehearsal.

'Did Stella tell you about the women who've dropped out?' Sharon whispered to Vivienne as they started towards the barn.

'Yes. I can't say I'm surprised. It's a pity, though, because this should be about you, not me.'

'That's as may be, but I'm disgusted with them myself. Anyway, it's not going to be long before the press find out you're here, at the refuge, so I was thinking, why don't we see if we can rope in a few of the local lads to try and keep them away, you know, like bouncers? They're all itching to do something, and they're feeling a bit left out at the minute, so I bet they'd jump at the chance to get involved, those who're free to do it. Trouble is, they might want paying, but we could always settle up with them after the auction, if there's enough money in the pot.'

'That's for you, and women in your position,' Vivienne reminded her, 'but it's a good idea, so I'll work out a way to pay them.'

'Actually, it shouldn't be all that difficult to make the place secure,' Sharon went on, clearly thrilled that she'd hit on a useful suggestion. 'There's only one way in by car, so they can easily block the road down by Ingall's farm, and even if someone manages to get across the fields, we'd see them coming, so we could send someone to see them off.'

Inwardly Vivienne was smiling to herself, but as naive as the plan was, it was certainly one way of sorting out the invited from the intruders. 'So who do we talk to to round up our heavies?' she asked.

Sharon laughed mischievously. 'Who do you think? Stella. She'll get them on the case in no time at all. I was thinking you might need someone to help keep them out of Sir Richard's place too, if you're still staying there.'

'I am, but it's pretty secure, and Theo will be with me, so let the press make of that what they will. Now, down to more important matters, any news yet on when they're likely to admit you?'

'No. There's still some things going on with the donor, apparently, but I promise to let you know what's happening the minute they tell me.'

As Vivienne looked into her girlish blue eyes that were doing such a valiant job of hiding how afraid she must be, she felt such a surge of admiration for her courage, not to mention affection for the selflessness that made her so special, that tears filled her eyes.

'Oh blimey, looks to me like you'm going to start getting all soppy on me,' Sharon chided. 'Can't be having that now. Too much to do. So where's this Pete Theo's been telling me about? Ooooh look, that must be your kiddie what Stella's holding. I got to go and see 'im. He's just a baby, dear little thing.'

As she took off across the barn Vivienne turned to Theo, who was strolling up behind them, apparently engrossed in sending a text.

When he'd finished, she said, 'I know you're planning to stay with friends on Dartmoor.'

'Cousins, actually,' he corrected. 'On my dad's side. They've got a place close to Dunstone. I'm sure you'd be welcome to join us, they've got plenty of room.'

'Actually,' she said, 'I was going to ask you to join me at the cider press.'

He looked at her in surprise.

After explaining about the call the police had received from someone claiming to be Jacqueline, she said, 'We've no idea yet if it was actually her, but it seems highly likely, and as we've no way of knowing exactly where she is . . . The call was made in Kew, but there's nothing to say she's still there—'

'You don't have to explain any further,' he interrupted, with a chivalrous twinkle. 'I'll call my cousins and let them know there's been a change of plan. I might have to go up there for dinner later, though, because I think they've already arranged for some other friends to come over, but I can't see any problem in you and Rufus joining us if you'd like to.'

She smiled. 'I need to speak to Miles first,' she said, 'but if we're free, we'd love to. Now, that looks very like a camera crew arriving, so bang goes our rehearsal, looks like we're about to go straight for it.'

'No problem,' he whispered, 'I have everything under control,' and after treating her to a reassuring peck on the cheek, he sauntered over to join Sharon and Stella, his fellow interviewees.

Thrilled by what an asset he was already proving, Vivienne took off back across the stable yard to greet the crew, half hoping Al Kohler might be with them, though knowing it was unlikely for someone in his position to come out to location.

'Al's going to try and get down for the auction,' the producer told her as they shook hands. 'Meanwhile, we're here to recce the place for the OB guys, and shoot an interview with . . .' He checked his clipboard. 'Sharon, Stella and, of course Theo Kenwood-South. He's here, is he?'

'Over there,' Vivienne said, pointing the way. 'I'll let you decide where you want to set up, but I should warn you neither Sharon nor Stella has had any time to prepare.'

'Don't worry about that. We'll take good care of them. At some point I need to talk to you about doing a live link with the studio tomorrow morning. They'd like it to be from Sharon's home, with her kids around, if possible. And Theo.'

'I'm sure they'll both be amenable,' Vivienne responded, heartened by how much thought was already going into setting it all up. 'This is Pete Alexander who I believe you've already spoken to,' she said, as Pete came to meet them. 'Now, if you'll excuse me, I need to take this call,' and leaving them to it, she clicked on to answer her phone.

'Hi, are you OK?' she asked softly as she turned back outside.

'Fine,' Miles replied. 'Where are you?'

'At Susie's horse sanctuary. We're using the barn here for our auction. What's happening with Kelsey?'

'She's gone back to school. Relations were restored somewhat before she went, but not completely, so I'm still worried.'

'Of course, but maybe it's good for you to have a little time apart. It's been pretty intense this past couple of weeks.'

'You're right about that,' he said dryly. 'Anyway, I guess you're busy so I'd better not keep you. I was just wondering if it would be convenient for me to come over later?'

Feeling a swell of love, she said, 'Of course it would. I'll stand Theo down, so come whenever you like. We'll be at the cider press from about five.'

'Thank you.' His voice was deep and soft. 'I'm afraid it has to be conditional on Kelsey,' he added. 'If she calls and wants me to go and get her . . .'

'Don't worry. Just come if you can. We'll both be looking forward to seeing you.'

Justine was regarding the Critch with barely a trace of the contempt that generally seethed at her insides when she was near him. Her predominant emotion was triumph for how effectively she'd just managed to silence the egotistical moron.

As she waited the incessant hubbub of the newsroom outside swirled on around the glassed-in pod that was his, an urgent river flowing around the immutable rocks of his brain. For him the world had stopped with the words she'd just spoken, and wouldn't move again until he'd fully grasped what it could mean.

'Let me get this straight,' he said finally, his gingery whiskers sparking in the funnelled glow of his desk lamp. 'This woman is not only suggesting that Miles Avery's known all along his son was dead, but she can even show you where the body is buried?'

'She said remains, which is all there would be now, obviously,' Justine responded, feeling like putting her feet up on his desk.

He got up, walked to the door then turned back again. His

round, hairy belly was straining to make an appearance through the buttons of a pale pink shirt that was only half-tucked into his low-slung trousers. Sartorial elegance had never been his strong point, any more than subtlety had ever played a part in his chequered career.

'So what next?' he asked, and could hardly have looked more excited if saliva had started to drool from his lips. 'Have you set up a meet with her yet?'

In a gratifyingly condescending tone – that was very likely to bypass him completely – she said, 'Actually, before I go any further with this I think we need to discuss a return to a full-page column every Sunday that allows me to contribute to other – non-rival – publications where I choose.'

He appeared neither shaken nor surprised – why would he, when she was talking his language? 'You failed to mention moolah,' he reminded her. 'It has to be part of the deal, so let's have it all on the table.'

'You can make me an offer. I'm not greedy, but I do need a new car.'

'Just don't make it a Merc.' Then, hardly pausing for breath, 'Don't piss about with this, Justine. Make doubly sure that woman's on the level, because we really don't want you burying yourself along with those bones, now do we?'

No, we most certainly don't, she was thinking to herself as she started to leave. *But I'm sure as hell going to enjoy shovelling the dirt over yours.*

Jacqueline came to a stop beside a weeping willow whose branches hung like knotted hair down to the river. For a while she gazed at its reflection in the grey light of dusk, shimmering and ethereal, sinking to a murky, invisible depth. Was there a world beyond, hiding behind the impenetrable darkness? Somewhere bright and tranquil that would welcome her to the golden pastures of a painless existence, if she yielded herself to it?

Turning her back on the unanswerable questions she stared in through the gate in front of her, across a small, triangular courtyard with neat beds and golden trees, to a row of town houses on the far side. She knew which was Vivienne Kane's because she'd seen her there two days ago, moving about the kitchen on the ground floor, setting a table in the dining room and answering the phone. She hadn't caught a glimpse of the child, but a buggy had been outside the back door, so she'd supposed he was in there, snug and safe, the very essence of his mother's *raison d'être*.

She hadn't hung around long, and she didn't now. People hurrying home from the station were noticing her, having to walk around her to get past, and throwing her strange or irritated glances.

The air was dampened by a fine drizzle as she started back along the towpath, passing elegant river-fronted homes and inhaling the sour stench of the exposed shore below. The tide was low, sucked back to the centre of its bed, a dull, uneven ribbon of liquid that gleamed like metal in the lamplight.

Soon she came to the grassy banks and park benches in front of Pier House. She walked on by, not stopping, but not hastening either. She kept her eyes ahead, glancing only once at the windows of Vivienne's office where Vivienne's partner, Alice Jackson, was sitting at her desk, talking on the phone. *Kane and Jackson, PR Consultants, Pier House, Strand on the Green* . . . She could even recite the postcode by heart.

Yesterday when she'd come she'd got only as far as Kew Bridge before spotting a clutch of reporters outside the building. Their presence had told her Vivienne was inside, so the fact they weren't in evidence this evening must mean Vivienne wasn't there.

As she climbed the steps to the bridge the roar of traffic began thrumming a wild tattoo in her head, humming and honking, stopping and starting. It was jammed in both directions, four strips of loudly impatient vehicles with bicycles skimming along the sides like militarised flies. She quickened her pace, until halfway across she stopped beneath one of the Victorian lamp posts to stare back at Pier House. No one was visible now, but the lights in the office were still on.

A few minutes later she was crossing Kew Green, moving south with the traffic towards Richmond. She wondered if the clock at St Anne's would chime the right hour if she waited for the time to come round. She walked on, counting her steps, murmuring the numbers aloud, only falling silent if someone passed by. The rhythmic chant of the words pulled her into a kind of trance, fixing her on nothing, sealing her from the world outside her cocoon of sound.

Tomorrow she'd go back in the hope of finding Vivienne and her son at home.

It was long past five o'clock, and there was still no sign of Miles. However, there had been no call or text to say he couldn't make it, so Vivienne was far from giving up hope yet.

Earlier, she'd found it both curious and pleasing to discover how like home the cider press had felt when she'd carried Rufus in through the door. Laura, the housekeeper, had already lit the small wood burner, so the place had even smelt welcoming with its smoky pine scent and lingering fragrance of beeswax polish.

Now, having settled Rufus on a rug in front of the fire and surrounded him with cushions and toys, it was cosier than ever, and more romantic, since she'd closed the curtains against the wintry dusk, and the candles she'd found under the sink were flickering warmly over the whitewashed walls. A bottle of champagne was in the freezer compartment undergoing a rapid chill, and just in case Miles was able to stay for dinner, she'd driven to Bovey Tracey as soon as the crew had finished filming to buy two steaks from the butcher. At the same time, Sharon and Stella had popped into a local farm to pick up all the fresh veg she'd need to concoct Stella's very own recipe for ratatouille.

Confiding in them had been almost impossible to avoid when she'd felt such a sense of elation after speaking to Miles. It had been written all over her face, and once they knew, it had become debatable who was more excited about Rufus meeting his daddy for the first time, them or her. Theo had to be told too, of course, so he was going to his cousin's from the photo shoot, as arranged, where she'd promised to join him later if Miles was unable to stay. As for

Pete, as soon as the crew was ready to depart, apparently thrilled with the interview, he had led the way over to the Smugglers in Kenleigh where they were all spending the night before setting up early the next morning for the live link from Sharon's house.

So everything was running smoothly to date. Sharon's camera-shyness was hardly noticeable in Pete's and Theo's capable hands, while an embarrassing tendency to overact on Stella's part perhaps wasn't a wholly bad thing. Most importantly, though, in amongst the teasing and humour, they'd managed to get the point of the auction across in a way that was both moving and compelling.

So now Vivienne was free to relax for the evening, and she would just as soon as Miles turned up.

Looking down at Rufus she felt a surge of pride rise up in her simply to see the way he was sitting on the rug, his little legs spread wide to keep himself balanced as he waved about his toddle-along tortoise and chattered on in his earnest baby way. Just thank God he had no idea what was supposed to be happening now; he felt no nervous anticipation, not to mention the crushing disappointment she could sense looming if Miles failed to come.

Deciding to wait until six before ringing, she lay down next to Rufus and put her arms behind her head. Almost instantly she started to laugh as, taking his cue, he launched himself onto her.

'Hello,' she murmured as his face appeared over hers.

'Mum, mum,' he muttered, making her wince as he dug a foot into her side.

'I love you, Rufus Avery,' she declared, swinging him up in the air.

'Pane, pane, pane,' he cried in excitement.

'Aeroplanes?' she teased. 'You want to play aeroplanes?'

'Brrrrm, brrrrm,' he responded, kicking out his limbs and dribbling into her face.

Laughing, she tilted him towards the sofa, before quickly jerking him back again.

He gurgled happily and bunched his fists to his mouth.

'Boom, boom,' she reminded him.

'Buh, buh,' he echoed, clapping his hands together.

She set him off on another dive, then lowered him onto her chest so his face was almost touching hers. 'Love you, love you, love you,' she whispered.

He blew a wet raspberry through his lips and tried to bite her chin.

'Kiss?' she asked, but he was much more interested in one of her earrings, which he'd just spotted and was trying to eat.

Beside them the logs glowed red inside the wood burner, while the candlelight flickered and danced around the walls and the air filled with the heady scent of melting wax and burning pine. She was straining her ears for the sound of a car arriving, but all she could hear was the incessant flow of the stream outside, and the grunting of a belligerent stag, probably not too far away. There seemed to be no wind now, nor any hint of rain. The press was a cosy cocoon of warmth, protecting them from the chill, dark night, but not, alas, from the anxiety of what might be delaying Miles.

'Mrs Davies the housekeeper is here, sir,' DC Joy said, going into Sadler's office. 'And guess who brought her.'

Sadler finished his email to Richmond CID confirming details of their meeting earlier, clicked send, then said, 'I don't need to guess, I know.'

Joy watched him spin round in his chair. 'Are you going to let him listen to the tape too?' she asked.

Sadler scratched his chin thoughtfully. 'That depends whether or not the housekeeper's able to identify the voice. If she confirms it's Mrs Avery . . .' His eyes came up to Joy's. 'Well, we still won't know for certain, because we've already established the housekeeper's loyalty to Mr Avery, so if he's told her to say the voice is his wife's, for all we know she's willing to go along with it.'

Joy wasn't looking convinced. 'She doesn't strike me as the kind of woman who'd be an accomplice to a crime,' she said.

Sadler threw her a meaningful glance. 'Our prisons are full of people who look like butter wouldn't melt,' he reminded her, 'but on your advice, Detective Constable, I'm trying to keep an open mind. Is everything set up down there?'

'We've got an interview room in the custody area,' she told him. 'I'll ask Mr Avery to wait in reception, shall I?'

Sadler nodded, and picking up his mobile he followed her out into the corridor.

Several minutes later Joy was watching the housekeeper's soft, crumpled face as Sadler, having explained what was about to happen, leaned forward to start the tape.

'Hello. My name is Jacqueline Avery . . .'

'Oh my goodness,' Mrs Davies exclaimed, clasping her hands to her cheeks. 'Yes, that's her.' She looked up in shock, her eyes darting anxiously between Sadler and Joy as Sadler stopped the tape. 'It's her,' she repeated, as though afraid he might doubt her.

Joy glanced at Sadler, expecting him to challenge the old woman, but for the moment he appeared to have nothing to say.

'Are you sure?' Joy asked.

'Positive,' Mrs Davies answered.

'Would you like to listen to the rest of the tape, just to be certain?'

'I don't need to, but I will if you want me to.'

Sadler nodded the go-ahead, so Joy restarted the tape.

At the end of it tears were shining in Mrs Davies's eyes. 'I always knew he'd never done nothing wrong,' she said, searching for a Kleenex. 'See, she's not dead at all. She's there, speaking on that machine, telling you she's all right so you can stop that blooming nonsense around his house now, turning up his garden, and having helicopters flying all over the place. Frankly, if you don't mind me saying, I think you owes him an apology—'

'Thank you for coming in, Mrs Davies,' Sadler interrupted. 'You've been extremely helpful.'

She looked uncertainly at Joy, clearly not knowing whether that was a dismissal or not.

Smiling, Joy put a hand on her arm and walked her to the door.

'Just one thing before you go,' Sadler said.

Mrs Davies turned back.

'Are you sure you've never heard the name Anne Cates before?'

The old lady's face was blank. 'I don't think so,' she said. 'I mean, not so's I can remember.'

'OK, thank you,' Sadler replied, and with a wave of his hand he gestured for Joy to take her out.

A few moments later Joy popped her head back round. 'Do you want Mr Avery to hear it?' she asked.

Sadler looked up from under lowered brows. 'Yes,' he said slowly. 'Yes, I think I do.'

As Miles listened to the tape he was aware of DC Joy's scrutiny, her dark, amber eyes watching his, her readiness to interpret his slightest movement as an indication of relief, or surprise, remorse, even anger. He felt all those things and more, but he had no intention of showing them, much less discussing them with a detective. He merely continued to listen to his wife telling the police she was all right so there was no need to go on looking for her.

As DC Joy turned off the machine, Miles felt Sadler's scepticism like a chill in the air. He didn't look at the man, instead focusing on Joy as he said, 'I believe Mrs Davies has already identified the voice, so if I'm free to go . . .'

With a quick glance at Sadler, Joy asked, 'Are you confirming Mrs Davies's opinion?'

'I doubt it will make any difference whether I do or don't,' Miles responded, 'so if you'll excuse me. There's somewhere I have to be.'

After receiving a nod from Sadler, Joy walked Avery back through the station to where Mrs Davies was waiting. Before opening the door to reception she said, 'Are you still worried about your wife, sir?'

'What do you think, Detective?'

She continued to regard him. 'I expect the search will be called off now,' she said.

Knowing she was still hoping for a reaction, he kept his expressionless eyes on hers. What she wouldn't know was how painfully those words resonated with him. *The search will be called off now.* The echo might be coming from a distance of fifteen years, but he would never be free of their memory, or their meaning.

She dropped her gaze. 'I'm sorry,' she said quietly, suggesting that perhaps she'd realised after all.

'So am I,' he replied, and pushing the door open into reception, he took Mrs Davies by the arm to walk her back to the car.

'I have to call Kelsey,' he said as they joined the traffic on Heavitree Road.

'Here, let me,' Mrs Davies offered, and taking his phone from the speaker clamp she pressed in the number.

After three rings Kelsey's voice came chirpily down the line. 'Hey Dad,' she said. 'Everything OK?'

Relieved to hear her sounding upbeat, he said, 'Everything's fine, but I have some news. It's good,' he added quickly.

'Great, lay it on me.'

'Mum has been in touch with the police.'

Kelsey fell silent.

Realising too late that he should have driven over there, instead of doing this by phone, he said, 'She told them she's all right, and she wants them to call off the search.'

'Do they know where she is?' Kelsey asked, sounding a long way from chirpy now.

'Apparently she made the call from Kew, but it was a couple of days ago. The phone she used is registered to someone called Anne Cates. Do you know that name?'

There was a pause before Kelsey said, 'I feel like I should.'

'Mm, me too, but I can't place it.'

'Oh, I know, isn't that what her great-aunt was called? The one who did the paintings she sold?'

'Of course,' he said. 'Of course.'

'So that was it?' Kelsey demanded. 'That's all she said? I'm all right, stop looking for me?'

'Apparently.'

'Then fuck her, is all I can say! I mean, what about everyone else? Don't we matter? Like, does she have any idea what she's put us through? All that crap the police and press have been laying on you?'

'I doubt she's—'

'Well she can stay wherever the hell she is as far as I'm concerned, and I hope she never comes back.'

Taking a breath, Miles said, 'Would you like me to come and take you for dinner?'

'No thanks! You're as bad as she is, you just dress it up differently.'

'Kelsey, I think you—'

'I don't care what you think. Just get off my case, all right? I don't need you, and I definitely don't need her, so leave me alone, both of you.'

As the line went dead Mrs Davies reached forward to turn off the phone. 'This isn't easy for her,' she said quietly.

'No,' he responded. Then, after a pause, 'Do you think I should drive over there anyway?'

Afer giving it some thought she shook her head. 'I doubt it'd do any good right now. If I was you, I'd give her a bit of time to calm down and call her again in the morning.'

Chapter Seventeen

Vivienne picked up her BlackBerry and scrolled to Miles's number, ready to dial. Once it was there, she found herself hesitating, as though something inside her had caught on an instinct she didn't quite understand. She tried to ignore it, but her reluctance to connect persisted. Whilst she and Rufus were here, tucked inside the thick stone walls of the cider press, it was as though nothing bad could reach them. Once she made contact with the world outside it would be like opening the door for all the demons to come in.

Disturbed by the thought, she put a hand to her throat and continued to look down at Miles's number. Not for a moment did she consider him one of the demons, nor was she shrinking from defeating those he'd inevitably bring with him. What she dreaded, she realised, was learning that his lateness meant more difficulties had arisen. Already he was dealing with too much, and now here she was postponing the awful moment of discovering there was more. It was a cowardly form of denial for which she detested herself, since it meant that as long as she put off knowing what might have happened, it wouldn't be real, and therefore she wouldn't have to feel unable to cope.

Her eyes drifted to Rufus, who was playing with his toys again, but her thoughts were moving to the sprawling black shadow of the moor outside. She could almost feel it swelling from the other side of the trees, a jumble of arable fields and forests and deadly quagmires they said could swallow a man whole. She pictured the tucked-away villages, tiny pinpricks of light in the vast swathe of night, rivers gushing wildly through the desolate landscape, and the hostile, barren terrain that stretched endlessly over the crown of the moor, peppered with curious stone circles and rife with impenetrable mysteries and their restless ghouls.

'Mum, mum,' Rufus muttered to himself, while trying to shove one of his his toy maracas into the mouth of his drop-and-roar dinosaur.

As her eyes drew focus she tried to shake the strange presentiment that had her in its grip, but it was like being in a dream from which she couldn't awake. The power of the moor seemed omnipresent, swirling around the cider press like a cyclone with her and Rufus in its eye.

The sudden sound of a car's wheels crunching the gravel outside made her heart beat faster. Her eyes darted to the glass-panelled door, where the glow of headlights was illuminating the terrace and giant gunnera behind it. She noticed tiny insects and moths flitting and perching on the leaves, then everything returned to black as the headlights went off. Moments later a car door slammed and footsteps started towards the stone bridge. It could only be Miles, she knew that, yet she was trying to remember if she'd locked the door.

A figure appeared in the shaft of light that fell from the kitchen door, and even as she gasped she started to smile with relief. It was Miles. He'd come at last.

As he entered a draught of damp air came in with him, and she saw immediately how gaunt and tired he looked, but there was a softness in his eyes as they came to hers that reached far down inside her.

'I'm sorry I'm late,' he said.

'It doesn't matter. You're here now.'

He continued to look at her, as if almost afraid to let go, or move on. Though Rufus had fallen silent Miles would know he was there, if only because of the baby scent in the air. She understood his delay of the inevitable, the pause before the immensity of something from which he could never retreat. Not that he would want to, but how could he not be mindful of what life had done to him before?

Finally his eyes moved past her, and for a long, breathless moment he merely stood there, taking him in. His son, his own flesh and blood. She saw the emotions cross his face as the treasured memories of Sam melded with the reality of now. She noticed the tremble at the corner of his mouth, and the movement in his throat as he swallowed, but most of all she felt the tremendous wave that must be engulfing his chest.

She turned to look at Rufus, and her own emotions began to rise. He'd stopped playing to look up at the stranger who'd come into the room, as though he knew this man was different to the other strangers he'd met. She guessed he'd picked up on the atmosphere surrounding his parents, but he didn't seem afraid, only hesitant, and in a way expectant. Then his hands jerked upwards and his maraca flew across the room. He looked at it, as though perplexed as to how it had got there, then he gazed in fascination as Miles went to pick it up.

Vivienne's heart was in her mouth as she watched the precious moments unfold.

With the maraca in his hand Miles stooped down as close to Rufus's height as he could get, and held it out for him to take. Rufus's eyes and mouth were three perfect little Os as he looked uncertainly from Miles to the toy and back again.

'Is this yours?' Miles asked softly.

Rufus merely continued to stare at him, his creamy baby skin flushed by firelight, his whorls of dark hair springing randomly up from his head. Then quite suddenly he broke into an enormous grin, and began bouncing noisily up and down.

Vivienne almost sobbed with pride as Miles put the maraca into Rufus's fist and lowered himself to a sitting position. 'So you're Rufus,' he said, so quietly she barely heard. 'Do you know who I am?'

'Mum! Mum! Mum!' Rufus cried gleefully, while waving his maraca about.

'Not Mum, no,' he said, putting a large finger into Rufus's other fist.

'This is Daddy,' Vivienne said shakily, going to kneel down with them. 'Are you going to say hello to Daddy?'

Rufus's eyes moved curiously to her, before venturing back to Miles. Then without warning he threw himself forward, making a grab for Miles's nose. Laughing, Miles caught him, growling and pretending to eat him all up, while Rufus shrieked with delight and rattled his maraca. Miles turned him upside down, buried his face in his belly, then swung him high in the air.

'Pane! Pane! Pane!' Rufus demanded.

'Aeroplanes,' Vivienne whispered, biting her lip to try and stop the tears.

Miles swooped and whisked him around, laughing at so much exuberance while blinking back his own tears, until finally he set him down on the rug and reached into his pocket.

'I have something here for you,' he said.

Baffled, Rufus continued to watch his father's face until his hand emerged holding a small, oddly shaped package with a squashed blue bow. Rufus pounced, but Miles was too quick and swung it out of the way.

'Say thank you, darling,' Vivienne reminded him.

Rufus looked at her, then at Miles and tried to pounce again.

'Rufus,' she warned.

He grinned cheekily. 'Me, me, me, ta,' he trilled.

Miles gave him the package and the bow was instantly treated as a chew.

Laughing, Miles detached the bow then began carefully tearing the paper. Intrigued, Rufus watched, until deciding it wasn't happening fast enough he plunged in with his own fists, ripping the paper apart and rescuing an extremely cute, curly-furred teddy.

'Ted, ted,' he shouted.

Vivienne laughed, hardly able to contain her happiness. Then suddenly it was all too much and she started to sob. 'I'm sorry,' she gasped. 'Oh God, I'm sorry. What a fool.'

Rufus frowned in disapproval as Miles put an arm around her and pulled her head onto his shoulder.

'We've got the most beautiful son,' he whispered into her hair.

'I knew you'd love him,' she said brokenly, and as she lifted her head to look into his face she saw how the tiredness and angst had been smoothed away. It would only be temporary, she understood that, but she could be in no doubt now of how desperately he had needed this, or of how wrong she had been to make him wait.

'I'm not sure how long you can stay,' she said, 'but I delayed his bath, just in case . . .'

Miles turned back to his son. 'What do you say, Rufus?' he asked. 'You and ted in the tub?'

'Ted,' Rufus answered, waving the bear at him.

'I'll pour some champagne and bring it up,' Vivienne said.

'Champagne too,' Miles responded, clearly impressed. 'Now why didn't I think of that?'

Not wanting to remind him that he had many other things to be thinking about, she lowered her eyes to his mouth, letting him know she'd like a kiss.

When it came, tender and loving, so much sensation began pouring through her that there was nothing she could do to stop her lips parting and her tongue moving to find his. He held her firmly while deepening the kiss, and as the desire that had lain dormant in her for too long began to awaken she sank weakly into him.

A moment later they were laughing as Rufus's little face peered up from under theirs, as though trying to work out what was happening.

'There are plenty of towels already up there,' Vivienne said hoarsely. 'I'll join you in a minute.'

Tucking Rufus under one arm, Miles got to his feet then helped her up too. Before letting her go he lowered his face to hers and kissed her again.

'I guess this could come off now,' she said, sliding her hands under the shoulders of his coat.

After allowing her to help him, while swinging the apparently contented Rufus from one arm to the other, he smiled at the way she held the coat against her.

'Before you go up, tell me what news on Kelsey?' she said. 'Have you spoken to her since she went back to school?'

A cloud passed over his eyes. 'Yes,' he answered. Then, looking down at Rufus, his expression softened again. 'There's more to tell, but it can wait. Let's try to make tonight all about him.'

Knowing they both deserved it, Vivienne let it go and

stood watching as he carried Rufus over to the narrow staircase that rose against the back wall. He glanced at her and winked. 'Don't be long,' he whispered. 'And if you look in the other pocket you might find something for you.'

Surprised, and intrigued, she slid a hand down over the soft black cashmere, and finding a small box in one of the pockets she pulled it out, feeling like a child at Christmas.

The instant she saw the wrapping her heart turned over. 'Miles?' she murmured.

There was no response; he was already upstairs.

With shaking fingers she untied the black silk bow, peeled back the matching paper and found herself staring down at a dark red leather box, too big for a ring, the wrong shape for a necklace, but the perfect size for something she'd always wanted.

Easing off the lid, she unfurled the black tissue and her heart leapt as she saw the slender platinum band. It was a Cartier love bangle. She knew he couldn't possibly have bought it today, because it would only be available in London, so he must have had it for some time.

Suppressing her initial instinct to run upstairs and throw her arms around him, she went to place the open box on a tray, added two glasses filled with champagne and one of the candles, then carried it all up to the vaulted mezzanine bedroom, where she pushed aside a pile of books to rest the tray on an old pine chest.

The bathroom door was closed, but she could hear Rufus yelling and splashing as Miles played ducks and submarines. She wondered how he was coping with all the memories and emotions this must be evoking, but knowing him as she did she understood it wouldn't be something he'd want to discuss. Then, hearing a huge splash followed by a cough and splutter from Rufus and a laugh from Miles, she pushed open the door to find out what was going on.

Miles was kneeling next to the bath, sleeves rolled up over his elbows and a towel draped round his neck, while a naked Rufus clung to the edge and bounced merrily up and down.

'I should go and get my camera,' she said, 'but I don't want to miss another moment.'

Circling Rufus's little body with his big, dark hands, Miles said, 'Didn't you mention something about champagne?'

'It's right here,' Vivienne assured him. 'Along with my bracelet.'

Keeping hold of Rufus he turned to look at her, and his eyes stayed with her as she came to kneel beside him. 'Thank you,' she whispered, putting her mouth to his. 'It's beautiful.'

'I bought it for your birthday two years ago,' he told her. 'I'm just sorry it's taken so long to get to you.'

'It doesn't matter. I have it now and I hope you're going to fasten it for me.'

'The screwdriver should be at the bottom of the . . .' He gasped as Rufus almost slipped from his grasp. '. . . box,' he finished, giving Rufus a playful shake.

Half an hour later they were all three lying on the bed, Rufus in the middle sucking noisily at his bottle while his parents sipped champagne and admired their son.

'You've made me the happiest man in the world,' he told her softly.

Feeling her throat tightening, she said, 'I knew you two would fall instantly in love.'

He looked down at Rufus, whose big eyes were starting to droop. 'There are no words to describe this,' he whispered, and from the tremble in his voice she knew how close his feelings were to the edge.

She put her glass down and cupped her hand round his face. It was some time before he was able to look at her, and when he did his eyes were wet and full of love. Yet she could sense the spectre of reality hovering.

'What is it?' she whispered.

He looked at her, then away again, clearly not wanting his problems to trespass on this precious time. In the end, seeming to accept that they wouldn't simply go away, he said, 'I drove Mrs Davies into Exeter. It's why I was late. The police wanted her to listen to the phone call they'd received.'

Vivienne waited, watching him and already knowing.

'They played it to me too,' he said, and in the silence that followed she became aware of the same foreboding that had seemed to seep down from the moor earlier. It made her shiver and want to reach for his hand, not because she was afraid, but because she was concerned for the terrible toll this was taking on him. 'And was it . . .?' she said quietly.

His eyes continued to gaze at nothing, until eventually he nodded. 'Yes,' he said huskily, 'it was Jacqueline. Alive and well and apparently not wanting to be found.'

Realising what issues this created, not only for him and Kelsey, but for her too, she said, 'What are you going to do?'

'I don't know. If the police call off the search . . .'

'Is that what they're saying?'

He nodded. 'I'm relieved she's safe, of course, but I'm worried about when or how she's going to turn up again.'

Not to mention where, she added in her mind. 'Have you told Kelsey?'

'Yes. She's as hurt as you'd expect her to be. Jacqueline doesn't seem to have considered her at all.'

Vivienne looked down at Rufus's sleeping face, unable to imagine him not featuring in her every decision. Yet how would she be behaving if someone snatched him away and she never saw him again? Would she understand her priorities then? Would she even know what they were any more? The hell of Jacqueline's position could never be imagined, or explained, much less endured, yet she'd been forced to live with it for the past fifteen years. So was it any wonder she'd lost sight of everything else?

If only someone could give her an answer, no matter what it was, for surely even finding out her son was dead had to be better than this unending torment.

Overnight strong winds across the south coast had blown away the clouds, leaving a clear, sparkling blue sky and a sun that streamed down on a spectacular array of crimson and tawny leaves that either still clung to their branches, or lay like piles of felt in the gutters and banks at the edge of the road.

The air, Justine was thinking, as she turned out of West Worthing station towards the address Elizabeth Barrett had given her, was brisk and exhilarating, tinged with salt from the sea and the pungent earthiness of a damp, sun-baked ground. It was the kind of air that carried nostalgia in its breezes and expectancy in its warmth. It was making her feel excited about being here, and charged with the promise of where it could lead.

The sensible heels of her lawyer's shoes clicked on the pavement as she skirted puddles and avoided uneven cracks, while her unbuttoned raincoat swished quietly over the formal navy suit she'd bought in Debenhams the day before. It was stereotypical attire for a solicitor, to which she'd added a borrowed briefcase, a plain black handbag, and dark-rimmed glasses with plain lenses for good measure.

A few minutes later, still following directions, she turned into a shady street where the terraced houses were as uniformly ordered, neglected, or meticulously polished as those on any other Victorian street in the country. Each house had a porch around the front door, a large bay window next to it, and two sash windows above. In front a small garden with a narrow path led from a gate to the house.

Then she rounded a corner, crossed diagonally and found herself walking through a much more eclectic arrangement of cottages and semis and a few grander-looking residences behind high stone walls. Elizabeth Barrett's house turned out to be a bungalow tucked away at the end of a cul-de-sac, behind a large sycamore tree and a leaf-strewn lawn. The net curtains at the windows all matched and were scooped up each side to allow a view through, while the front door was painted dark green and cream, with an oval stained-glass pane above a gleaming brass knocker. There was no sign of a car, nor of anyone waiting to greet her, but she presumed a press on the bell would remedy that.

It was only after she'd rung that she spotted a neat white envelope Sellotaped to an inside wall of the porch. To her dismay she saw the name Ms J. James handwritten in careful script across the front, and taking it down she tore it open.

Dear Ms James, I am very sorry not to be here on your arrival. As I had no phone number for you I was unable to contact you, except by email, but I fear you might already have set out from London before it reached you.

I'm afraid a family emergency has called me away from home. My sister, who lives in Tunbridge Wells, has been taken to hospital with a suspected stroke. Naturally I had to go immediately, but as soon as I have established the seriousness of her condition and how long I shall be required to stay, I will be in touch again to make another arrangement.

Please accept my sincere apologies if you are reading this note, as it will mean you have had a wasted journey. Perhaps you will be kind enough to contact me with your telephone number in order to avoid anything like this happening again.

With regards, Elizabeth J. Barrett.

PS: Please give my best wishes to Mr Avery and assure him that everything is still very well taken care of.

Slightly shaken by the postscript, she read it again, then deciding to avoid any obvious deductions, she tucked the note away and called Elizabeth Barrett's mobile. She wasn't surprised to find herself diverted through to voicemail, so she was ready with the right amount of sympathy over the sister, before leaving her own mobile number and expressing a hope that they would be able to meet soon.

'Are you sure someone's not dicking you around?' Critchley growled when she called to update him.

'I can't be sure of anything right now,' she responded smoothly. 'I'll try ringing her again in a couple of hours, or she might ring me.'

'I don't like the sound of it,' he said belligerently. 'Too much of a coincidence, her sister taken ill the very morning you're supposed to meet her.'

'You're pointing out the obvious,' Justine informed him, 'so what do you want me to do? Give up on it? Or take it to the next step?'

'What do you think? You've got to stick with it now. Any idea where Avery is?'

Her eyebrows rose at the question. 'Moorlands, at a guess.' Then, realising what was on his mind, 'You can't seriously be thinking he's set me up? He didn't even know the email had arrived.'

'What about the daughter? You said she came in while you were there.'

'After I'd erased it.'

'But she could have told her father you were in his study.'

'Even if she did, it still doesn't mean they know about the email.'

Critchley grunted at the other end, a kind of reluctant acquiescence. 'OK, set up another meet with the woman as soon as you can, but I've got to tell you, I'm not liking the way this is looking.'

Sadler's eyes were on Joy as he sipped his coffee and listened to her report back from Richmond CID. When she'd finished he left the kitchenette and crossed the corridor to his office. 'Did we really expect to find Mrs Avery staying at her old house in Richmond?' he asked, as she followed him in.

'I'm not sure,' she replied, 'but it had to be checked. Apparently the current owners didn't even know she'd ever lived there.'

Sadler nodded and drank more coffee. 'You realise we're in a very difficult position here, don't you, Detective Constable?' he said.

'How so, sir?'

'If we're agreed that it was Mrs Avery who made the call, and I believe we are, then we have no grounds for continuing the search.' He put his cup down and folded his arms. 'I'd just like to know why Mr Avery wouldn't come right out and say it was her.'

'That's easy, sir. He has a history with the police that he obviously hasn't forgotten, and considering what it is no one can really blame him for not wanting to be helpful.'

Sadler cocked an eyebrow. 'Plus he might not be that eager to find his wife,' he added. 'So the question now, Elaine, is on what grounds can we keep the search going?'

Joy waited for him to answer his own question, until

realising he was expecting her to, she started and said, 'Well, sir, um . . . Do we have any grounds, if Mrs Avery wants us to call it off?'

Sadler waited.

Moments later Joy's eyes showed her comprehension. 'Of course, sir, the mobile phone,' she exclaimed. 'It's registered at Vivienne Kane's work address, and there can't be any doubt that she knows about Rufus Avery by now, so we've got to make sure she's not stalking them.'

'To date we've got nothing to say that's happening,' he reminded her. 'There have been no sightings, no threatening calls that we know of, or attempted break-ins.'

'Or complaints from Vivienne Kane,' Joy added. 'But Mrs Avery's obviously in the area for a reason, presuming she's still in Kew or thereabouts—' She stopped as Sadler's phone started to ring.

'Sadler,' he said into the receiver.

'Sir, it's PC Yolland,' the voice at the other end announced. 'I'm working with the SOCOs out at Moorlands. Well, we're on Dartmoor, actually, but you know, close to . . .'

'I know where you are, son. What can I do for you?'

'We've made another discovery, sir. Actually, one of the dogs did. He found it about a quarter of a mile from where the body was, buried in the long grass—'

'Just tell me what it is,' Sadler cut in.

As he listened to the answer his eyebrows rose with interest. To Joy he said, 'Seems a mobile phone's turned up, Detective Constable.' Then to PC Yolland, 'Any idea who it belongs to?'

'Not yet, sir. Forensics have got it charging in one of the PSUs, but we can't find the number.'

Joy was already using Sadler's computer to bring up Jacqueline Avery's details. A few minutes later, after dialling the number Miles Avery had given them for her mobile when he'd reported her missing, she put the call on speaker and they listened to the phone at the other end starting to ring.

'Bingo,' Sadler murmured. 'I'll expect a call log on my desk by mid afternoon,' he told Yolland.

'We've already checked,' Yolland told him, 'everything's been erased up to the date she disappeared. Incoming and outgoing. There are text messages after, and voicemails, but we can't access them without the code.'

'Who's the provider?'

'O2.'

'OK, we'll get onto it,' and ringing off he said to Joy, 'What are you up to?'

'I was about to go and watch more of the station's CCTV tapes,' she answered. 'No one even remotely like Mrs Avery got on a train going in any direction that morning, but there's still the afternoon to be got through, and even the next day, and the day after that . . .'

'Right, stay with it,' he said, 'I'll get someone else to prise the records out of O2.'

Vivienne was lying beside Miles on the bed, watching him clear a text from Kelsey.

'At least she's in regular contact,' she said soothingly as he dropped the mobile on the bedside table. 'OK, some of her messages can be a bit curt, but that one wasn't bad.'

'Curt?' he laughed. 'They're downright rude.'

'Except when she's telling you you're the best dad in the world and she's really missing you.'

'And wants some money.' He shook his head in despair. 'Were you like that as a teenager? She's so unpredictable, actually *irrational*, she makes my head spin.'

'I was probably worse,' she assured him, and pushing aside the duvet she rolled onto him.

This was the third morning they'd woken up together in the cider press, though the previous two they'd been allowed no luxuriating in the pleasure of finding one another there, since Rufus had demanded to be rescued from his travel crib at six and hadn't gone back again. Now, it was after eight and Rufus, miraculously, was still sleeping.

Gazing down into Miles's unshaven face, she wondered how she'd stood being without him for so long, because now he was here, his eyes full of love as he looked back at her, she could hardly get enough of him.

'What are you thinking?' he asked softly.

'How much you mean to me,' she replied, loving the feel of his hands running over her body.

'Oh no,' he groaned as his mobile started to vibrate again.

Knowing he wouldn't ignore it in case it was Kelsey, she reached over to pick it up. Seeing Kelsey's name, for the second time that morning, she handed it to him.

'Sorry,' he said, looking up at her.

She merely kissed him, then rolled back to her side of the bed as he clicked on to take it.

'You haven't answered my text yet,' Kelsey accused angrily. 'Did you get it?'

'Yes, of course,' he said, 'but I didn't realise it needed a reply.'

'Well, like, I was saying good morning, so maybe you could say good morning back. Or is that too much to ask?'

'No, of course not. I'm sorry, it was thoughtless. Good morning, darling. How are you?'

'As if you care.'

'Clearly not in a good mood,' he responded smoothly.

'Actually, I'm great. In fact, I've never been happier.'

'Now why am I finding that difficult to believe?'

'It makes no difference to me what you believe. I just did the polite thing in saying good morning, but you're clearly too busy . . .'

'Kelsey, this is becoming childish. I've apologised for not texting back, I've said good morning, now what more do you want?'

'Don't bother,' she snapped and the line went dead.

Sighing wearily, he clicked his phone off and closed his eyes. 'Did you hear any of that?' he asked.

'All of it,' Vivienne confessed. 'She's lonely and afraid, but she doesn't want to admit it.'

He turned to look at her, his eyes gazing far into hers as though still not quite able to believe she was there.

'Has she mentioned Jacqueline since you told her about the call to the police?' she asked, brushing the backs of her fingers over his cheek.

He shook his head. 'She hasn't mentioned you either, and I told her you were going to be in Devon.'

'She's got a lot to be dealing with.'

He continued to look at her, leaving her in no doubt of how deeply his feelings ran. 'She'll have to start coming to terms with the fact that you're in my life,' he said gruffly, 'because I'm not letting you go again.'

Smiling, she moved forward to kiss him.

'I've been thinking,' he said, 'if she's going to Martha's for the weekend, I should come to London with you. Apart from not wanting to let either of you out of my sight, I'd like to check the house in Richmond where we used to live, find out who's there now, and if anyone might have seen Jacqueline.'

'Haven't the police already done that?'

'If they have they haven't told me. But being in the area might trigger something for me that's not coming to mind now.'

'Will you stay with us?' she asked, snuggling in closer.

'I'm not sure. I want to, but if there's any press hanging around . . .' He let the sentence drift as he ran his fingers up into her hair.

'They seem to have backed off a little since Jacqueline contacted the police,' she reminded him.

'No more mystery, so no more scandal,' he commented dryly. Then, 'I'm sorry for bringing all this chaos into your life.'

She was about to protest when Rufus let out a sudden wail. 'Not for that chaos, though,' she teased.

'No, definitely not for him,' he said, and turning over he scooped Rufus out of the crib to bring him into bed with them. 'Good morning, little fellow,' he murmured. 'I was wondering when you were going to join us.'

'Mum, mum,' Rufus chanted, waving his fists and kicking out his feet.

'You do realise your timing isn't great, don't you?' Miles asked him.

Rufus yawned, then gave a loud burp that made them both laugh.

'My mother doesn't go to Italy until next Monday,' Vivienne said, putting a finger into Rufus's hand. 'I could ask her to have him for the weekend.'

Miles didn't even hesitate. 'I'd rather he was with us,' he said, 'or you, if I end up staying in Kensington.'

She smiled. As disruptive and demanding as Rufus could be, she understood perfectly Miles's need to make up for lost time, as well as the overprotectiveness that was only to be expected, considering his past.

'I guess I should go and make his lordship some breakfast,' she said, starting a luxurious stretch then losing it to a laugh as Miles poked her in the ribs.

'At last,' he said. 'I'll have coffee and toast, no butter, just marmalade. Two slices should be enough.'

Eyes twinkling, she said, 'And what would his lordship's son be requiring?'

'What do you say, Rufus?' he asked, swinging him up in the air. 'Soldiers and a boiled egg? Yes? Good man. Then that's what it shall be.'

Reluctantly sliding out of bed she reached for her robe, sorry to be dressing when they'd come so close to making love, but happy just for this precious time together.

After kissing them both she started down the stairs, wondering what the weather was doing, if it was hampering or helping work at the stables, where over the past couple of days everyone had swung into action to turn the barn into a studio-cum-saleroom. Luckily, the uninvited press was much less in evidence now, which made coming and going a great deal easier. The local lads who'd been called in to act as security were lending a hand with anything that needed doing, from driving, to building, to getting Theo and the firemen to sign photographs. The lads themselves were intending to sell these on the big day – and then on the Internet – to contribute to the cause.

Sighing to herself, Vivienne put on the kettle and slotted two slices of bread into the toaster. She was thinking about Kelsey now and how, under any other circumstances, she'd probably have loved to be involved in the auction too, and Vivienne would have loved to invite her. However, with the way things stood Kelsey would almost certainly reject out of hand even the merest suggestion of coming anywhere near it, simply because of Vivienne's part in it all. It was such a pity, but Vivienne had to concede that for the moment at least there was nothing to be done about it, particularly as Miles hadn't yet told Kelsey about how much time he was spending with Rufus.

Chapter Eighteen

More laughter was ringing out around the stable yard than hammering, sawing and drilling as the vast wooden barn underwent its transformation. Camera platforms and catwalks were being crafted from locally donated plywood, a bank of split-screen TV monitors was already covering the back wall, and crudely knocked-together bench tables were starting to line up all along one side. These were for the two dozen phone lines that a small team of BT engineers was already installing, while the catwalks were for Theo and the firemen to strut their stuff.

It was still too early for rehearsals of any kind to take place on set – they were being fitted in at the fire station, between shifts and emergency calls. However, it wasn't stopping the construction crew from mincing about the barn like dancers, teasing the WI ladies who dropped in either to help, or deliver freshly baked cakes and pies, and generally whipping up the kind of saucy hilarity that TV crews were famous for.

Stella was in her element, having set up a small canteen area where she served the food and flirted shamelessly with her customers. She was particularly outrageous when the camera was on her, which was often, as a daily update of the project's progress was being screened each morning on Sky News. The TV package was always presented by Theo, whom Vivienne had made official spokesperson for the auction, and regularly featured interviews with Sharon, who was still waiting to hear when her transplant could happen (so the nation was experiencing her tension). The firemen, whose dance rehearsals were hilarious, also appeared regularly, together with reminders of how the audience could already start making their bids – or straight donations, if they preferred.

'Please tell me,' Pete demanded as Vivienne pulled up in the stable yard around eleven, 'that I'm the one going to London for when Theo and the firemen do a calendar shoot in the buff?'

Vivienne laughed, and grimaced an apology. 'Sorry,' she said, turning to lift Rufus from the car. 'I have to meet with Al Kohler and a charity rep on Tuesday, so I have to be in London anyway – and you're needed here.'

With a flamboyant toss of his head Pete stuck out his arms to take Rufus, and wiggled off over the puddled courtyard with him, leaving Vivienne to follow on with her files and clipboard.

By midday she was seated at a table she'd requisitioned as a desk, either dealing with phone calls, or running through an ever-changing procedure with Sky's production manager. Rufus had been whisked off to the manège by Stella and Theo, who were also taking charge of Sharon's children for the day, and as they trotted around on the Shetlands, even with all the noise in the barn Vivienne could hear the children's shrieks of delight.

As one particularly piercing yell travelled into the barn she paused for a moment to listen, and found her thoughts drifting to Miles and how happy she was that he was finally in Rufus's life. From there it was a short step to wishing they were in private together somewhere right now, finishing what they'd hardly even started this morning.

'Al Kohler wants to talk to you,' Pete said, interrupting her reverie as he brought his mobile over.

Taking it, Vivienne said, 'Al, when are you coming down this way?'

'Sooner than you think,' he replied. 'We've got an earlier transmission slot if you want it. It's just come up and is yours if you can be ready.'

Gulping with dread, and excitement, she said, 'When is it?'

'Saturday week at ten in the morning.'

'Oh my God!' she cried. 'That really doesn't give us much time, but how can I possibly turn it down?'

'Thought it might work for you,' he said drolly. 'We'll give it plenty of oomph between now and then. I hear you've got a calendar shoot next week, so we'll be there for that, and I'm about to line up a director to work on the promos. With stuff coming in all the time, he won't have a problem.'

'Al, you're an angel,' she told him. 'If we can pull this off the way we're hoping, you're going to be making a lot of difference to a lot of people's lives.'

'And I'm the only one with a halo?' he teased.

'But you look so much cuter in it.'

Laughing, he said, 'Got to go now. Call if there's anything, and don't forget our meeting on Tuesday.'

As she rang off and handed Pete back his phone her own started to ring. Seeing it was Miles she clicked on right away.

'I've just had a call from Kelsey's headmistress,' he told her, 'wanting to know how Kelsey is, and if she's going to return to school before half-term.'

Vivienne's heart sank to a horrible depth. 'But Mrs Davies took her back,' she protested.

'Yes, but apparently Kelsey left again the day after I told her about Jacqueline's call. The headmistress thought I'd come to pick her up.'

'So where can she be? You've spoken to her since, so we have to assume she's all right . . . Obviously you've tried calling her?'

'Of course. I was diverted through to voicemail. The last time I actually spoke to her was first thing this morning.'

'What about her friend, Martha? She has to know where she is.'

'The headmistress is going to talk to her and get back to me.'

'What can I do?'

'For the moment nothing, apart from take care of our son. I'm going upstairs to check Kelsey's room, and if need be I'll drive to the school. I'll call as soon as I have some news.'

After ringing off Vivienne walked over to the manège, where Rufus and Sharon's children were still riding round in circles on the Shetlands, with Stella and Theo as guides.

Seeing her coming, Theo handed the reins he was holding to Stella, and walked to the fence. 'Is something the matter?' he asked, responding to the worried look on Vivienne's face.

'Kelsey's not at school, where she's supposed to be,' she told him, smiling faintly at Rufus's unfailing exuberance.

'Ah, not good,' Theo responded. 'Have you any idea where she might be?'

She shook her head, and her eyes glazed as she stared out across the fields. 'She's been calling regularly, but from her mobile, so heaven only knows where she is.'

Theo was starting to look troubled. 'One of her friends must know,' he said.

'That's what Miles is trying to find out. I'm sure she can't be far.'

Theo turned as Stella came to join them, with the children and Shetlands in tow.

'Hello you,' Vivienne said, catching Rufus as he hurled himself at her.

'Mum,' he cried gleefully. 'Ross.'

'Yes, it's a horse,' she agreed. 'And you're a very good rider.'

'You'm looking a bit glum, you two,' Stella told them. 'Has somethin' 'appened?'

Vivienne handed Rufus to Theo and went to scoop Sharon's children from their ponies, while Theo told Stella about Kelsey.

When he'd finished Stella filled her cheeks with air and blew it out in an exasperated sigh. 'Bloody kids, pardon my language,' she said. 'They'm more trouble than they'm worth half the time.' She looked at Vivienne with a meaningful expression. 'If you asks me, she's either out there trying to find her mother, or just as likely, she's doing it to get attention from her father.'

'Which he gives her all the time,' Vivienne assured her.

'Ah, but it's a bit different now this little rascal's on the scene, innit?' she said, chucking Rufus under the chin. 'Her position as apple of Daddy's eye is being threatened.'

'That's what worries me,' Vivienne said.

'Oh, she won't be far,' Stella said, squeezing her arm. 'Believe me, they never are.'

'Wherever she is,' Vivienne muttered, 'I could brain her for doing this to her father. Considering what's happening with her mother, the last thing he needs is his daughter getting him caught up in some ludicrous game of hide-and-seek as well.'

'Tha's probably what it's all about,' Stella told her. 'Kids that age don't think about what they'm doing to their parents. And after all that poor girl's been through, it'd be a miracle if she ever thought about anyone but herself. Bet I wouldn't if I was her. What about you, Theo?'

'I'm no expert,' he responded, 'but if she really has run away, I bet she's feeling pretty lonely right now.'

As Kelsey's headmistress showed Miles into her study Martha Barnes got quickly to her feet, looking nervous, guilty and very much as though she'd like to bolt.

'I'll leave you to it, Mr Avery,' the headmistress said, and lancing Martha with a look that made the girl shrink, she added, 'If you need me I'll be next door, in the office.'

After thanking her and waiting until she'd gone, Miles gently told Martha to sit down, and took the other guest chair in front of the desk.

Regarding her bowed head, he cut the preamble and said, 'You told me on the phone that you don't know where Kelsey is, but I think you do, Martha, so please, I need you to tell me.'

'I don't know,' she wailed, keeping her head down. 'Honestly, I don't.'

'I'd like you to look at me and say that.'

Her head stayed down as she shook it.

'Martha, do you realise, if you don't cooperate with me, I'll have to contact the police?'

She stiffened, but all she said was, 'I swear she didn't tell me where she was going.'

'But you saw her, when she came back to school?'

She nodded.

'What happened?'

'Nothing, I mean like she came back, and then you rang to say her mum had been in touch with the police . . . I didn't mean to upset her. It was like a really dumb thing to say, I know that now—'

'What did you say?' he broke in, his pulses starting to quicken.

Her eyes stayed on her tightly bunched hands. 'Only that I thought her mum was mean for not calling her . . .' Her head came up. 'I didn't expect her to go off on one,' she cried defensively. 'She's always saying how her mum never thinks about anyone but herself, or her brother that went, well, you know . . .' She stopped again, apparently afraid she was stumbling onto forbidden ground.

'What happened after she lost her temper?' he prompted.

She shrugged. 'She said she thought I was her friend, but now she knew I wasn't she was going to ask to be moved from our room. But that's not true!' she protested. 'I am her friend. I really like her, and I always stick up for her when the others get on her case about you and being a daddy's girl and all that.'

Having had no idea Kelsey was being teased or taunted, Miles put it aside for the moment, saying, 'What did she take with her?'

'Not much, actually. A lot of her stuff is still here.'

'Where did she go?'

'I don't *know*. She just went, and like, none of us know where she is now.'

'Is she texting or calling you?'

She nodded.

'What does she say?'

'Just that she's sorry she shouted at me, and she hopes I'm still her friend.'

'You must have asked her where she is.'

She shook her head. 'I mean, yes, I have, but she won't tell me.'

Not at all certain she was being truthful, he said, 'Can you suggest somewhere she might be?'

She shrugged. 'Not really. I mean, I thought she'd gone home, to you, but then . . . Well, she's all upset about, you know . . .' Her eyes flicked to him anxiously.

'Vivienne?' he said for her.

She nodded. 'Like she's always been . . . Well, you know,

she thinks you don't want her any more, and I can understand why that's hard for her, because when she first came here, she used to tell everyone about how you know all these important people . . . She was dead proud of you. It was why everyone started calling you the ledge – that's legend – and they called her daddy's girl, because every time we were talking about boys all she used to talk about was you.'

Feeling the painful conflict of Kelsey's hero-worship and unhappiness, he said, 'If you really don't know where she is, will you help me to find her?'

Her eyes started to dart about the floor. 'Well, uh, I mean yes,' she said, and her manner as well as her tone left him in little doubt that she already knew.

'OK. If you speak to her before I do,' he said carefully, 'will you tell her how worried I am?'

She nodded. 'I think she knows that,' she confessed. 'I mean, she knew you would be.'

Understanding that was exactly what Kelsey wanted, he said, 'When did you last speak to her?'

She hesitated. 'Um, I think it was this morning.'

'Before or after you and I spoke on the phone?'

She took a breath. 'Before, I think. Yes, it was before.'

Certain she was lying, and that she'd already told Kelsey her absence was starting to cause a fuss, he said, 'I'll give you my mobile number. Please call me the minute you hear from her again, or have any idea where she is.'

Taking the piece of paper he handed her, she read it and said, 'Can I go now?'

'Of course,' and resisting the urge to shake the truth out of her, he went to open the door. 'You've been very helpful,' he told her as she passed into the adjoining office. 'Thank you. I hope you won't mind telling the police everything you've told me.'

She visibly paled. 'Have you reported it to them already?' she asked.

'No, but I'll have to. Kelsey's only fourteen.'

Her eyes flitted over to the headmistress, who was clearly listening, then putting her head down again she scuttled across the office and out into the corridor.

'I'm sure she knows where Kelsey is,' Miles told the head.

Mrs Ferndale pursed her lips. 'Girls of that age,' she said tersely. 'They think themselves exceedingly clever at times, when they're anything but. I'll talk to her again, and contact you as soon as I have anything to report.'

'Kelsey, it's me,' Martha whispered into her mobile. 'Your dad's just been to the school. He's really, really worried. You have to tell him where you are, or I'm going to be in big trouble.'

'No, I'm not doing that,' Kelsey protested. 'And don't you either.'

'He says he's going to contact the police. If he does, I'll have to tell them . . .'

'He won't!'

'How do you know?'

'Because I'll tell him not to.'

'Like that's going to stop him.'

'It will—'

'Oh my God, I have to go,' Martha said quickly. 'Someone's coming. I'll call you back as soon as I can.'

Miles was speeding along the dual carriageway towards Exeter when his mobile started to ring. It didn't surprise him to see it was Kelsey, though it had taken her a little longer to call than he'd expected.

'I don't know what kind of game you think you're playing,' he said sternly, 'but I want you to come home right now.'

'No way!' she cried angrily. 'If Mum can go off saying she doesn't want to be found, then I can too. See how she likes it.'

Stifling his exasperation, he said, 'Kelsey, the only way she's going to know is if I contact the police and it gets in the papers. Is that what you want?'

Silence.

'Is that what you want?' he repeated.

'Maybe,' she replied sulkily.

'I don't think so, because I don't think you've thought this through. Now where the hell are you?'

'I'm not telling you, but I'm perfectly safe so you don't have to worry.'

'You're being absurd. Of course I'm worried. You're fourteen years old . . .'

'I can take care of myself.'

'By running away from school? A very responsible action. And from what Martha tells me you've been having problems there that you've never mentioned to me, so we need to talk.'

'Forget it. I'm staying right here until you make *that woman* go away.'

Biting down on his anger, he said, 'She isn't at the house, and I won't be held to blackmail like this. You're being selfish and immature—'

'Oh, like and you aren't? You're the one who doesn't have time for anyone else now you—'

'Kelsey, I'm not getting into an argument with you over something you're making up. Of course I have time for you. I always have, and always will, but I won't tolerate this kind of manipulation.'

'Well that's just tough, isn't it, because I'm not coming back until she's gone, and that's that.'

Having to accept they were getting nowhere like this, he forced himself to sound conciliatory, and said, 'She's going back to London later today. Will you come home then?'

Silence.

'Are you there?'

'Yeah, I'm here.'

'Will you please answer my question.'

'I might come. Then again, I might not.'

Barely suppressing his frustration, he said, 'Where are you sleeping at night?'

'In a bed.'

'Where?'

'None of your business.'

'Do I need to remind you of your age again?'

'I'm safe, all *right*!' she shouted. 'No one's going to do anything, because no one knows I'm here.'

'Where?'

'In my— Oh, very clever. I'm going now. Goodbye.'

Hearing the line go dead, he turned off his own phone and pressed down harder on the accelerator. In my what? Friend's house? Dormitory? Could she still be at the school, hiding somewhere? It was certainly possible, so he called the headmistress to ask her to mount a thorough search.

'If she's not there, then my guess is she's at a friend's house,' he said when finally he spoke to Vivienne.

'But wouldn't their parents wonder why she isn't at school?'

'Not if they're away and the house is empty. Anyway, it's the best I can come up with right now. I don't know whether to contact the police or not. Maybe I'll try talking to her again first. Whatever, I'm afraid this means I'll have to stay in Devon for the weekend.'

'Of course,' she said without hesitation. 'Will we see you before we go?'

'If there's no press around I'll come over to the stables now, if you're still there?'

'We are. The Sky TV crew's here, but no journalists at the end of the road. How far away are you?'

'About twenty minutes.'

'OK. I'll see you when you get here. Have to go now, someone's trying to get through.'

'At last, Mrs Avery's mobile phone records,' Sadler announced, striding into CID with his chest pumped up. 'It seems she called a number in Richmond on Thames three times during the week before she disappeared.'

Joy swivelled away from her computer. 'Who does it belong to?' she dutifully asked.

'An estate agent,' he replied. 'And unless I'm gravely mistaken, it's the one on the roundabout at the junction with Kew Road.'

Immediately understanding the significance, Joy reached for the report. 'That's it,' she confirmed, recognising the estate agent's name. 'Fifteen years ago it was a garage – the one her little boy was snatched from. But why would she be calling them? Surely no one there would know what had happened during its previous existence.'

'I could hazard a guess or two,' he responded, 'but you have the number, so off you go. I'll be in my office when you've finished.'

Ten minutes later Joy wandered in with a bewildered expression on her face. 'No one's ever heard of her,' she informed him. 'I even tried the name Anne Cates, but that didn't trigger anything either.'

'Mm,' Sadler grunted. 'Did you send her photographs over to Richmond CID?'

'Did it as soon as we got back,' she assured him.

'Then maybe a photograph will jog someone's memory better than the name.' His eyes came to hers. 'Unless your theory about her changing her appearance holds good. If it does, the shots we have might not be of much use.'

'It's still worth a try,' she said gravely. 'I'll get onto Richmond right away, and see how soon they can send someone over.'

There was no one else in the church of St Anne's; no vicar, no flower-arranger or stray tourist. Jacqueline was alone in a pew close to the altar, observed by the eyes of Christ on his cross, along with angels, saints, and Mary with the son she'd been allowed to watch growing into a man before he was taken. They gazed down at her from colourful windows and embroidered mantles, impervious, unmoving, silent witnesses to a solitary woman's need for understanding. They who had known suffering, who had endured pain and cried out in torment, watched her with wide, unblinking eyes, showing no mercy or compassion, no feeling at all.

A couple of days ago, when she was passing at midday, the clock had stopped chiming at six. She'd stared up at it, waiting, even willing it to complete its task, but six was as far as it went. She didn't really believe in signs, but she'd decided to go into the church anyway, simply to find out if there really was a problem with the clock, or if she was imagining it.

She'd found herself in a bright, welcoming nave with exquisite white Tuscan pillars and lovingly polished pews. No one was around, so she'd walked on down the aisle, encouraged by the quiet, content to be out of the wind. It was the first time in many years that she'd stepped into the house of God. After all the ranting and raging at his cruelty he'd become nothing to her, because he had proved that he had no existence.

She still didn't believe, but she'd started dropping into the church regularly now, breaking her journeys between Richmond and Chiswick. She didn't pray, or read, she simply sat with her thoughts, letting them drift back over the years, like a breeze over water, moving the surface, but disturbing nothing beneath. Sometimes there were more stirring sensations, and she might even, on occasion, feel as though she could become submerged in sadness, or regret, or even elation, but then her journey would swirl round full circle, to arrive back at the wall she was facing. There was no way over or around it, there was only it, and her, at the journey's end – and an understanding that had been dawning in her heart, perhaps for a very long time, but much more clearly over the last few days.

Lifting her head, she gazed up into the marble eyes of the Madonna and felt the pull of the years that stretched behind her, taking her back and back, and showing her how she'd allowed herself to fall into the deepest, darkest pit, too afraid to come out, and too terrified to let anyone in. It was as though an army of demons had found its way through the fractures in her heart to the very essence of who she was. She fought to keep herself safe, tried everything to push them away, because if she didn't she knew Sam would never come back. No one had ever understood how vital it was to keep everything the same, not even Miles. It was wrong to move forward without Sam, because he wouldn't know where to find them, but Miles had made her, and though for a while she'd been able to cope, in the end everything – life, destiny, hope, even despair – had drawn her back to where she had lost him.

It wasn't as though she could start again from the time he'd disappeared, but lately the struggle hadn't seemed so great, nor the fears so intense. She could think more clearly now and see what lay ahead, in a way that made her heart beat more steadily and her eyes take on a penetrating glow. It was as though she was reaching out to an answer that might, eventually, lead her from the darkness into light.

She had never thought to find solace this way, yet it seemed to be happening. One of her greatest fears, that Miles might have another son, was now a reality, and instead of becoming overwhelmed by denial and rage, as she'd expected, she was only aware of a growing sense of calm and curiosity – and a feeling of hope that seemed to soothe the turbulence inside her.

She wasn't afraid any more. She was only eager, she realised, to embrace the son that had come to Miles, to feel the comfort of his small body in her arms and smell the sweet baby scent of him. Surely no one would begrudge her that when her need was so great – not even his mother.

'Hey, Vivi,' a perky voice chirruped down the line.

'Hey, Kayla,' Vivienne chirruped back, turning at the sound of a car coming into the stable yard. Seeing the grey BMW, she felt her heart warm and started to smile. 'Here's Daddy,' she whispered to Rufus, who was half asleep in her arms.

'Where?' Kayla whispered back. 'I can't see him.'

'Very funny. How are things your end?'

'Great news from Sky. Apparently their finance bods have struck a deal with a major cancer trust, so we can use their charity status for the auction. So tax deductions, here we come.'

'That's fantastic!' Vivienne cried. 'People are much more likely to be generous if they know that.'

'Exactly. Also, Angus wants me to tell you that he can make lunch with Al Kohler and team next Tuesday. He reckons you'll form a kind of committee which he's happy to be part of, and wants to know if you're interested in chairing it, because he'll put you forward if you are.'

'I think our role is to publicise the auction,' Vivienne replied, tucking the phone under her chin in order to shift Rufus onto the other arm. 'But I'll give it some thought, because maybe I would like to be more involved. Anything else?' she asked, her eyes connecting with Miles's as she walked over to the car. Was it really possible to love him more every time she saw him, because that was certainly how it felt?

'No, I think that's about it,' Kayla responded.

'Hi,' Miles murmured, putting his mouth to hers as he took Rufus from her.

'Hi,' she murmured back.

'Hi yourself,' Kayla put in. 'Can I go now? Are we done here?'

'I think so,' Vivienne replied, smoothing a hand over Rufus's cheek as he snuggled up to his father. 'Get Alice to call me when she has a minute. I'll be back in Chiswick tomorrow and I need to see her.' As she clicked off she said to Miles, 'Any news from the school? Has she turned up there?'

'Not yet. I've spoken to her again, though, and I get the impression she could be ready to come out of hiding.'

'Well, that's a relief. What did she say?'

'That she's sorry and realises she's being selfish, and because she doesn't want me to worry she'll come home but only on the condition . . .' He grimaced. 'I'm sorry about this, but the condition is that you're not there.'

'It's all right,' Vivienne assured him. 'I wouldn't be at Moorlands anyway, and it's important that you make her feel as secure as you can, particularly while she's going through all this with her mother.'

He nodded gravely. 'I just hope she decides to turn up tonight. What time are you leaving?'

'In about an hour. I'll collect some things from the cider press first, then start making tracks.'

Gazing down at Rufus's sleep-flushed cheeks, he said, 'I'm loathe to part with him.'

'It'll only be until Wednesday,' she reminded him.

'Still too long,' he murmured. 'Kelsey's friend told me a couple of things today about some kind of bullying or teasing at school—'

Turning to find out what had stopped him, Vivienne saw Stella coming towards them, a very troubled expression on her face. Immediately she was concerned, for she'd never seen Stella without at least the beginnings of a smile, nor did she appear at all surprised, or even curious, that Miles was at the refuge. 'What is it?' Vivienne asked. 'Has something happened?'

'Yes, it has,' Stella said bleakly. 'Or maybe I should say it's not going to. Oh dear, it's a terrible bit of news. Not what we was expecting at all. It shouldn't 'appen like this. It's mean, is what it is. Getting someone's hopes up then letting them down . . .'

'You need to tell us what it is,' Vivienne prompted gently.

Stella nodded grimly. 'It's our little Sharon. Turns out her donor in't up for it after all, so she can't have the transplant.'

'Oh no.' Vivienne reached for Stella's hands. 'That's awful. Where's Sharon now?'

'She's at 'ome with the kids. All shook up she is, by the sound of her. I ought to get meself over there, but my hubby's in having his cataracts done this afternoon, so I have to go and pick him up.'

'Don't worry, I'll go,' Vivienne assured her. And, turning to Miles, 'She shouldn't be on her own now.'

'No, of course not,' he agreed.

'I reckon she'll like that, if you goes,' Stella said. 'It'll make her feel a bit special. But what are we going to do about this auction now? I mean, if she . . .'

Hugging her, Vivienne said, 'It'll go ahead as planned, because we still need the financial support for when she does get a donor.'

'Yeah, yeah, course you're right.'

Spotting a camera pointing in their direction, Stella turned into full frame as she said, 'Our poor girl. You got to help her. Someone out there, please,' and with her eyes full of tears, she put her head down and trundled off to her car.

Vivienne turned to Miles. 'I'll call you later, when I'm on my way back to London. If you hear anything from Kelsey in that time, don't forget to let me know.'

'Are you sure that's her?' Sadler growled as Joy replayed a section of CCTV footage. 'I can't see how she looks like anyone with all that hair and sunglasses.'

'That's what caught my attention,' she told him. 'It's a classic disguise.'

'What's to say it's a disguise? It looks perfectly normal to me.'

'Maybe it is. I'm just saying, sir, it *could* be Mrs Avery and if it is she boarded a London-bound train at four twenty on the day she disappeared. Six hours after she was supposed to be travelling. That gives her ample time to change her hair and clothes, dump the bag containing everything of her real identity, and even to shop for any last-minute items she might need.'

'Mm,' Sadler grunted.

'What's more,' she continued, 'while you were down at the pub having lunch with the boys, *sir*, I had a very interesting chat with DC Ball in Richmond. Apparently he went round to the estate agent's this morning, and it turns out that someone there *does* know the name Anne Cates.'

Sadler scowled.

'The agent in question wasn't in the office when I called yesterday,' she explained, 'but he's been quite helpful today. Apparently, Anne Cates got in touch with him a couple of months ago about renting a house or apartment in Richmond. She wanted a short-term let, which she was prepared to pay for up front and in cash. He showed her quite a few, he says, and was certain she was going to take one close to the green, but then at the last minute she called to say she'd found somewhere else.'

'Did she tell him where?'

Joy deflated slightly as she shook her head. 'But I don't think we'd go far wrong in assuming it's in Richmond, or possibly Kew, since that's where the call came from.'

'Mm,' Sadler mumbled ponderously.

'I've taken the liberty,' Joy went on, 'of asking DC Ball to contact all the estate agents in Richmond to find out if they've rented a place to an Anne Cates sometime during the past two months. It could be that the envelope we found contained a letter from one of them.'

Sadler nodded approval. 'Good thinking. Have you mentioned any of this to Mr Avery?'

'No, sir. My last contact with him was yesterday when he called to ask if anyone had checked the house he and his wife used to own in Richmond.'

'And you told him someone had?'

'Of course.'

He sat quietly thinking for a moment, his expression creased with concentration. 'Has that pay-as-you-go phone been used again since the call came in?' he asked.

She shook her head. 'Not that anyone's mentioned, and they've got instructions to let us know the minute it is.'

'OK, so we don't know if she's still in the Kew area . . . Are Ms Kane and her son still in Devon?'

'They were earlier today, sir. I couldn't be sure now.'

'Then get onto it, Detective Constable, and I'll speak to DC Ball's superiors. I think we need to ratchet it up a little around there.'

Chapter Nineteen

It was after nine in the morning when Vivienne finally woke up to find bright shafts of sunlight streaming through the skylights above her bed. Since she hadn't got back to Chiswick until after eleven the night before she wasn't surprised to find Rufus was sleeping in too, particularly after he'd used up so much energy playing with Sharon's children before they'd left Devon. As usual, Sharon had tried to put a brave face on what she was going through, but it was clear that her hopes had been devastated by the donor's withdrawal. Now all she could see looming was the horror of leaving her children with no mother or father.

Vivienne had stayed with her until Stella had turned up and the children were asleep, doing her best to comfort and reassure her, but nothing she could say would ever ease the fear in Sharon's heart – only another donor could do that. Considering Sharon's rare tissue type, the chances of finding a replacement in time now were almost non-existent, but Vivienne was refusing to give up hope. They were generating a lot of publicity for the auction, so maybe someone with the right match might yet come forward.

After checking on Rufus, she padded downstairs to the kitchen, where she turned on the TV and filled the kettle to make tea. She was about to call Sharon to find out how she'd slept, when she noticed there was a text on her BlackBerry from Miles.

Don't want to wake you. Kelsey at London house, on way there now. M.

Heaving a sigh of relief, Vivienne checked the time he'd

sent the message, and seeing it was about half an hour ago, she tried his mobile first.

'I'm just joining the M5 at Exeter,' he told her, when she got through.

'What happened? How did you find out where she was?'

'I guessed, and she admitted it when I called first thing. She wants to come back, but doesn't have any money for a ticket, so I'm going to get her. How are you, this morning?'

'Fine. Rufus is still sleeping, and one of our promos is going out on Sky as we speak. In fact, they're showing Stella's plea after we found out about Sharon's donor yesterday.'

'Then let's hope it has the desired effect. Have you spoken to—'

'Hang on,' Vivienne said, starting to turn cold. 'Oh God, you're not going to like this. You and I are in the back of shot, with Rufus, and guess what, when Stella clears frame, it seems the cameraman zoomed in on us before he cut.'

'You're not serious,' Miles groaned. 'I hope to God Kelsey isn't watching. Or Jacqueline.'

'I thought the camera panned with Stella,' Vivienne said helplessly.

'So did I. Christ, before we know it that image is going to be all over the place.' He sighed irritably. 'I guess it was just naive to think interest was going to die down now Jacqueline's made contact. Hang on, someone's trying to get through. And no prizes for guessing who.'

'Kelsey?'

'I'll call you back.'

At his end, Miles slowed up a little as he switched to the incoming call.

'I am like so never, *ever* coming home again,' Kelsey seethed through her teeth. 'I just saw you on TV with your *son and her*—'

'I'm sorry, it—'

'*Sorry*! What good's that? Have you thought how Mum's going to feel if she sees it? Hasn't she suffered enough?'

'What matters—'

'How could you shove it in her face like that? You're mean and selfish and you don't deserve us.'

'It wasn't a deliberate—'

'I don't blame her for running away. She's had a life of hell being married to you. Well, I'm going to find her and when I do you'll never see either of us again, because we hate you.'

'Kelsey, don't hang up—' It was too late; she already had.

Wasting no time he hit the call-back, but wasn't surprised to find himself diverted through to voicemail, so after leaving a forceful message telling her to stay put, he reconnected to Vivienne.

'God knows what she's going to do,' he said angrily. 'She's got no idea where Jacqueline is, so she doesn't even know where to start looking and it'll be at least another two hours before I get there.'

'I'd go over myself, but we know that won't help. Here's a thought, though, Theo's on his way here. Maybe he'll go over on his motorbike. If she's still there, he might be able to stop her from leaving.'

'But she doesn't even know him.'

'She knows who he is, and do you have any better suggestions?'

Miles heaved a sigh of frustration. 'If he'll do it, I'll be deeply in his debt.'

'I can only ask. Once I have his answer I'll call and let you know.'

Minutes later, when Theo arrived, expecting to be briefed on the coming week, Vivienne explained what was happening. She could have kissed him when, in typical Theo fashion, he took the request in his stride and turned right around to go over to Kensington.

'Success has never gone to that boy's head,' she said to Miles when she called back. 'I guess that's why we all love him so much. I'd love to see Kelsey's face when he turns up.'

'So would I,' Miles responded dryly. 'Let's hope she's still there.'

'I told him to call you as soon as he knows. Now I have to go, your son has just woken up.'

After ringing off she ran upstairs to find Rufus chuntering away to his toes, but as she made to scoop him up in her arms the phone rang again.

'Vivi, darling, it's Mum. I've been trying to get through . . .'

Vivienne's eyes closed. 'Because you've been watching Sky?'

'You've seen it?'

'I have. It wasn't supposed to happen like that, but let's try not to forget who this is really about.'

There was a blank silence from the other end.

'Sharon, the girl who's dying,' Vivienne reminded her angrily. 'For God's sake, Mum, it's bad enough when the press cuts her out . . .'

'I'm sorry, I'm sorry,' Linda cried. 'Of course it's about that dear girl. But Vivi, I think I should cancel my holiday.'

'Why? Look, I really appreciate how concerned you are, but I swear, Rufus and I are fine. You need this holiday— Hang on a moment, someone's trying to get through.'

'Hi it's me,' Alice said breezily. 'Angus thought you might like to know that we've just received a cheque from *La Belle Amie* which we're giving straight to you to make your mortgage arrears history. Also to tell you that we're leaving home in about half an hour, so we'll be with you soon after.'

More relieved than she could express about the payment, and thankful that someone at least had apparently not seen the recent Sky broadcast, Vivienne said, 'I'll make sure the coffee's on. Theo might not join us, I'll explain when you get here.' Then, going back to her mother, 'That was Alice. I can pay off my mortgage arrears.'

'Well, that's extremely good news,' her mother declared. 'I'm delighted, but now getting back to—'

'Mum, I know you mean well, but you're making me tense when I probably don't need to be. So please, just tell me you're flying off to Italy tomorrow to have a good time.'

'All right, but you know where I am . . .'

'I do, and I'll call every day while you're away so you'll know there's nothing to worry about.'

'OK,' Linda agreed reluctantly. 'Give Rufus a big kiss from me and tell him I miss him.'

'Of course,' Vivienne promised, and they both laughed as Rufus let out a jubilant shriek. 'I think that's his way of letting you know he's all right,' she said, and after ringing off she swept him up in her arms to bury her face in his fat little belly.

'Mum, mum,' he gurgled, clutching her hair.

'Oh Rufus,' she groaned with a laugh, 'you really don't smell too good.'

'Mm, mm,' he replied, dribbling down his chin and kicking out his legs.

'Come on, let's run a quick bath for us both, and once you're all nice and fresh you can watch a cartoon while you have your breakfast.'

It was turning into such a beautiful autumn morning that the corner café on Thames Road had pushed open its large glass doors to let the sun's warmth stream in over the round glass-topped tables and copious green foliage that spread amongst them. There were even a few customers sitting outside on the pavement, sipping coffee and reading the papers, apparently oblivious to the light flow of traffic passing by.

From where she was sitting Jacqueline could hear the sounds of a nearby playground as small children swayed back and forth on the swings, or whooped down the slides, or chased a ball. Occasionally a dog barked, or an adult shouted, and a constant twittering, warbling chorus of birdsong carried through the gently moving air. She was remembering how she used to wander parks and playgrounds in the early years, searching, longing and feeling certain that today she would find him. She'd sit on benches watching other women with their children, wondering what they would do if they were to lose them. Would they haunt parks and playgrounds as she did, stand outside schools and public swimming pools hoping against hope that their child would come out? Or would they manage to do what she never had and put their lives back together again? Perhaps they would feel that they could no longer continue with such a cruel partner as hope, lighting each morning with promise and darkening each night with yet more despair.

No woman could ever be the same after losing a child.

Even if she were able to seal off the emptiness as though it were no longer there, and ignore the aching heart, even somehow stifle the guilt, something fundamental inside her would be gone. It was worse than losing a limb, or sight or speech, because it was as though something had been taken from every part of her. Nothing functioned the same way any more, it had neither the power nor the desire to do so, because all her senses were dulled, and each thought was tormented by a guilt that was almost as hard to bear as the loss.

Folding the paper she'd brought with her, she put it down on the table and picked up her cup. A while ago a young man had come out of Vivienne's garage and roared away on his motorbike. He could have been Sam's age, she'd thought, but in his helmet and leathers it had been hard to tell. Once she might have convinced herself it was Sam, but lately she'd stopped doing that. He was no longer there in every teenage boy she saw, or somewhere just out of sight if she could only find the right corner to turn. She was coming closer all the time now to realising that her world was not a place he was ever going to exist in again.

With a small, strangled sigh, she cast her mind back sixteen years to the day he was born. It was where she'd like to go now, deeply, safely into the past, pulling it up around her like a blanket, losing herself in its warmth and protection. She'd be sealed in a time when his tiny body was hers to hold, and his life was just beginning. She'd had so much to live for then, so many reasons to love and dreams to believe in. Sam's sixteenth birthday and her fortieth had been a long way in the future, a day only to be imagined, but never like this.

She looked down at her cup. The coffee had become lukewarm, but she drank it anyway. She'd had no breakfast; food didn't matter much to her any more. There weren't many things left of importance, they'd faded over time along with her hopes and dreams. It was as though she was being slowly erased from the world, growing fainter and fainter, colourless, ghostlike, until soon she would be nothing at all. Even so, deep down inside her a small light continued to burn, not for her, or Sam, but for Kelsey. She'd turned away from it for years, but had never really been able to extinguish it. She recognised it now, and around it was an aura of warmth that seemed to radiate contentment and send waves of understanding into her heart.

She knew what she had to do, and wasn't afraid of it any more. The fear had left her several days ago, but it wasn't until she'd seen Miles with his son and Vivienne on TV this morning that she'd become fully aware of the emptiness inside her where panic had always reigned before. It had confused her at first, as though the ground had vanished from underfoot, leaving her suspended in mid-air. She should fall and crash, but for some reason she hadn't. She had been left staring into the vacuum, seeing and feeling nothing until finally the darkness began to fill with words, and through the words she could see vague and distant lights. *Though I walk through the valley of the shadow of death . . .* Walk through . . . Don't stop . . . No need even to linger . . . Yet she'd abandoned herself in its very depths, had become so immersed in her loss and at one with the guilt that she'd long ago stopped looking for a way out. Instead, she'd tried to draw everyone in with her.

She was moving on now, though, taking tentative, but occasionally confident steps forward as the next stage of the journey became more focused in her mind. She could see Miles and Kelsey, and wanted to reassure them, but mostly she was aware of Vivienne. It was as though Vivienne had become the woman she'd once been, young, vital, burning with love and unafraid of life. She had no tragedy to hold her back, no sickened conscience to torment her. She was free and blameless, with a baby boy to adore and hold and watch grow. Jacqueline wanted to reach her, and connect with her, not to be her, but to pass on the torch that would light the way from the valley of the shadow of death. Vivienne could be trusted to carry it for Miles and Kelsey, because Vivienne was able to live and love in a way Jacqueline never could now.

Picking up a paper napkin she dabbed the corners of her mouth, then reached into her bag for her purse. She wondered if Kelsey had met her new brother yet. Rufus. It was a good name. Jacqueline liked it and hoped Kelsey did too.

*

Vivienne was attempting to read through the documents Angus had dropped off the night before, while clearing the sitting-room floor of some of Rufus's toys, when the phone started to ring. As she reached for it she quickly put out a foot to stop an exultant Rufus from hurtling headlong out through the open French windows. 'Careful,' she warned. 'You're going too fast.'

He went down with a plop, and looked up at her with wide, indignant eyes.

'Hello,' she laughed into the phone.

'It's me,' Miles told her. 'Theo just rang. He's at the house with Kelsey.'

Vivienne's eyes closed with relief. Thank God Kelsey had still been there. 'Is she OK?' she asked, going to the entryphone to buzz Alice and Angus in.

'So he says. She wouldn't speak to me herself, but he assured me she's agreeing to stay where she is until I get there.'

'Where are you now?'

'I'd say midway between Bath and Swindon, so about an hour and a half from Kensington. Do you have company? Wasn't that the doorbell I just heard?'

'Yes. Alice and Angus are here. We're meeting about the auction, then we'll probably stroll along to the City Barge for lunch.'

'Sounds good. How's my son today?'

Smiling down at Rufus, who was still sitting close to the windows, his little legs splayed while he chewed on the corner of a plastic brick, she said, 'He's on great form.'

'Then give him a hug from me. I'll call you again when I'm closer to London.'

'Before you go, are you staying for the weekend, or will you take her straight back to Devon?'

'I'll have a better idea once I've spoken to her, but she ought to return to school on Monday. It'll only be until Thursday, when half-term starts, but she's missed enough time already.'

After ringing off Vivienne was about to shout down for Alice and Angus to come up when the sitting-room door opened, and to her surprise a total stranger came in. A beat later she froze in horror.

'Oh my God,' she murmured, moving instinctively towards Rufus, then stopping as though not to draw attention to him.

Jacqueline's pale, piercing eyes dropped to Rufus, then came back to regard Vivienne. Her face appeared sallow in its unflattering frame of dark hair, while her mouth seemed to bleed into a feathery nimbus of lines. 'Hello Vivienne,' she said quietly. 'I hope you don't mind—'

'What are you doing here?' Vivienne suddenly blurted, shock reverberating through her so violently that she'd started to shake.

Jacqueline looked apologetic. 'I had to come,' she said. 'I knew you wouldn't welcome it, but since I read about you and your little boy in the papers . . .' Her eyes drifted to Rufus again, who was watching her with interest.

Trying to swallow her panic, Vivienne glanced at Rufus too, then back to Jacqueline as she said, 'I won't stay long. I'd just like . . .' She smiled awkwardly. 'Would you mind if I sat down?'

Vivienne drew back, as though to resist. Then, hardly knowing what she was doing, she gestured towards the sofa, and watched as Jacqueline came further into the room and put her bag on the floor before perching on the edge of the cushions. She was wearing a short camel coat over black jeans and a polo-neck sweater, and her hair, which was hanging loosely around her collar, was obviously false.

'Won't you sit down too?' she said, waving a hand towards a chair. She looked at Vivienne with eyes that seemed vacant, yet fleetingly unsure. 'Please,' she added.

Still in shock, Vivienne sank down on the chair's arm, then watched in alarm as Jacqueline peeled off her wig as though it were a hat, and dropped it on the seat beside her. Beneath was her more familiar, slightly mussed blonde hair clasped, as usual, in a velvet slide. Vivienne's eyes went back to hers, searching for a glint of malice, or anger, or worse, derangement, and found herself more unnerved than ever by the air of perfect calm.

'You must know,' Vivienne said, attempting to take control, 'that everyone's been looking for you.'

Jacqueline nodded.

'So where have you been?'

'Actually, not far from here.'

Vivienne's mind was racing; she was finding it hard to think straight. 'Why haven't you been in touch?' she asked. 'Miles has been so worried.'

The corners of Jacqueline's lips tilted upwards, as though to smile, but it didn't reach her eyes.

'You seem not to believe me,' Vivienne said.

Jacqueline still didn't speak, only turned to look at Rufus.

With her heart in her mouth Vivienne's eyes moved to him too, and she almost shouted in protest as he began crawling towards Jacqueline's bag. 'No darling, it's not yours,' she said, starting to get up.

'It's OK,' Jacqueline said, putting up a hand to stop her. 'He can play with it.'

'But he might . . .'

'Please, leave him. He's just a baby, he can't do any harm.'

Vivienne sat down again, and willed Alice and Angus to turn up right now. 'I'm expecting some friends,' she said, hoping it would unsettle Jacqueline enough to make her leave, but Jacqueline merely continued to watch Rufus as he beat a clumsy tattoo on her bag.

'You know, I've lived in such fear of Miles having another son,' she said softly. 'It's one of the reasons I couldn't let him go. It would have seemed so wrong, so dismissive of Sam, yet now it's happened . . .' Her eyebrows rose as she shook her head in bewilderment. 'I never needed to be afraid,' she said, almost to herself. 'If only I'd known.' Then, looking at Vivienne, 'You should take good care of him. He's very precious.'

'Yes, of course,' Vivienne said hoarsely. And, clearing her throat, 'Jacqueline, why – why are you here?'

Jacqueline's eyes returned to Rufus. 'It's occurred to me a few times this past week,' she said, not answering the question, 'that if Sam is dead, your son could be his little spirit returned.'

Vivienne's heart turned cold.

Jacqueline looked up and smiled sympathetically. 'You don't want to think that, do you?' she said. 'I don't blame you, I'm sure I wouldn't either, in your shoes.'

Vivienne said nothing. All she knew was a desperate urge to grab Rufus and run, but Jacqueline was closer to both him and the door.

'Do you know St Anne's, in Kew?' Jacqueline asked.

Confused, Vivienne said, 'Do you mean the church?'

Jacqueline nodded. 'The clock sometimes strikes odd hours, did you realise that? Four chimes at three o'clock, or fourteen at midday. It's all quite random. They've been trying to get it repaired for years, the vicar told me. I find it rather amusing, myself. It's as though it's out of step with the world. I keep wondering if that's why I feel so at home there.'

Vivienne stared at her, not knowing what to say. Then the phone rang on the table behind her and she started violently.

'Please don't answer,' Jacqueline said.

Vivienne's eyes grew wider.

'I won't take up much of your time,' Jacqueline promised.

They sat in silence listening to Alice's voice chirping into the answering machine. 'Hey, it's me. You're probably in the loo, or garage or somewhere. Sorry we're not there yet. Angus got caught up with a client on the phone, and I've just realised I need to call in at the office on the way over, so we'll probably be at least another half an hour to an hour. Hope that's OK. Call me if it's a problem, otherwise see you then. Bye.'

Vivienne's eyes stayed on Jacqueline. Her heart was like a fist in her chest, clenched with dread. No interruption imminent, and she couldn't risk leaving the room to make a call.

'Do you go to church?' Jacqueline asked, as if there had been no break in the conversation.

Vivienne shook her head. 'No,' she answered.

'But you believe?'

Vivienne only looked at her. What did she want her to say? 'I'm not sure,' she answered. 'Sometimes, yes, I guess I do.'

'I didn't, for years. I had no reason to. I'm not sure I do now, but I like that church, so I go inside and sit there for a while.'

'Do you – do you find it a comfort?' Vivienne ventured after a pause.

Jacqueline nodded. 'Mm, though it's hard to say why. Perhaps because no one there expects anything of me. I don't think they're even very interested in who I am. No one's ever asked my name.'

'Would you tell them, if they did?'

Jacqueline's hands tightened their hold on each other. 'I'd probably say I was Anne Cates,' she confessed. 'It's a name I've been using. It belonged to a great-aunt of mine on my mother's side. I never knew her. She was an artist and some of her works were passed down to me. A couple of them were quite good, actually, but I've let them go now. Everything has to go in the end.'

Wondering what lay beneath the final words, Vivienne said, unsteadily, 'Your – your phone. The one you used to call the police. They said it's registered under that name at my office address.'

Jacqueline seemed surprised, then vaguely contrite. 'I'm afraid it was the only one I could come up with at the time,' she said, 'and I felt sure you wouldn't mind. There's no harm done, is there?' she asked.

'No, no,' Vivienne assured her. 'I just . . . Well, it was . . . Actually,' she said, gesturing towards Rufus, 'I need to go and change him.'

Jacqueline looked down at him. 'He seems fine to me,' she said, and lifting a hand she rested it gently on his head. 'I think he can wait a while longer, can't you, little fellow?'

Rufus gazed up at her with wide blue eyes.

She laughed softly. 'You know, I'm trying to work out who he's most like, you or Miles,' she said. 'With you both being dark it's hard to tell, but perhaps his father has the edge. What do you think?' Before Vivienne could answer she made a humorous tutting sound. 'Of course you'll see Miles in him much more than yourself. It was a silly question. Please ignore it.'

Vivienne's gaze returned to the slim hand on Rufus's

head. What was she intending to do? How much longer before she became angry or vengeful or even violent? 'I think we need to let Kelsey know you're safe,' she suddenly suggested, praying it was the right thing to say.

Jacqueline's eyes came up from Rufus.

'She's been extremely worried,' Vivienne told her. 'She's even run away . . . I mean, she's here in London, actually. At your house. I'm sure it would help her a lot to hear your voice.'

Though Jacqueline's expression softened in a smile, behind it she seemed agitated and upset. 'I can't help her,' she said quietly.

'But you're her mother.'

'She's better off without me. I'm just messing up her life. It's all I've ever done, since the day she was born.'

Eager to keep the subject off Rufus, Vivienne said, 'If you'd engage with her, let her know that she matters every bit as much as Sam . . . Doesn't she at least deserve to be given a chance?'

Jacqueline returned her gaze to Rufus. 'He's not as much like Sam as I expected,' she said, stroking his cheek. 'Probably because he's dark and Sam was fair, like me.' She swallowed and took a breath that trembled in her throat. 'Why do you think such a terrible thing happened?' she asked, keeping her head down.

Vivienne's heart folded around the bewilderment in her voice. 'I don't know,' she answered gently. 'I'm just so sorry that it did.'

'No one knows, and everyone's sorry. It hasn't brought him back, though, has it?'

'Any one of us would if we knew how.'

When Jacqueline's eyes came up they showed a light of gratitude. 'But we're restricted by the hand of destiny,' she said. 'We can't change what's meant to be, no matter how awful it is. Do you believe that?'

Again Vivienne was unsure how to answer.

'Some would say that it was my destiny to lose a child; that it is the only reason I came to this world, to suffer in order to make myself at one with God. Would you say that?'

Vivienne tentatively shook her head.

'But you have to agree it's an answer of sorts.'

'I guess it could be. Is it one you accept?'

Jacqueline swallowed and looked away. 'I can think of no good reason to lose a child,' she said, 'so I understand why some find it helpful to go to a bigger picture, or a nebulous creation that might have some hidden meaning in its complexities, or even a purpose in its random strokes. If nothing else it absolves you of responsibility, because you can't be to blame for things over which you have no control.' She paused for a moment. 'At what point was it decided that our lives, yours and mine, would intersect, and by whom?' she asked, and smiled sadly. 'Don't worry, I'm not expecting you to answer, or even to engage with my ramblings, I'm just giving you an example of what goes through my head, and how impossible I find it to make any sense of my life.' She looked up. 'I see myself in you, the way I used to be,' she said. 'I had everything worked out; I knew where we were going, Miles and I – we had a son with another child on the way; he was already doing well and I believed in him the way you do now. It never occurred to me that anything could go wrong, because like you, I had faith in people and trust in life. It's a good way to be, even though it's an illusion, because things rarely turn out the way we expect.' She took a deep breath and brushed her fingers lightly over Rufus's cheek.

Taut with misgiving Vivienne watched her movements, while praying that this wasn't leading up to something terrible and calamitous.

'If I were to get to know you, I think I'd like you,' Jacqueline told her with a curious smile. 'I have an instinct about you that makes me think you're as genuine as I used to be, and as caring. You do care, don't you?'

Vivienne's eyes were wary as she nodded.

'Yes of course. You care about your son, your mother, your friends, the girl you're trying to help, Miles . . . What about Kelsey, do you care about her?'

Not knowing whether the answer should be yes or no, Vivienne decided to go with the truth. 'Very much,' she answered softly.

'But only because of Miles?'

Vivienne swallowed. 'If it weren't for him I wouldn't know her.'

'So you mind about Kelsey as Miles's daughter, not as a person in her own right?'

'I've hardly had the chance to get to know her, but I'm sure, if I did—'

'I'm not trying to trick you,' Jacqueline cut in. 'I'm merely trying to find out if you'll take good care of her.'

Vivienne stiffened. 'I can never replace you,' she said. 'You're her mother. It's you she wants to have a—'

'But it's you she's going to get – or are you hoping I'll take custody of her so you and Miles can be alone with your son?'

'No, that's not . . .' Oh God, which was the best way to answer that?

'I'm afraid she wouldn't come to me, even if I suggested it,' Jacqueline went on. 'It would be wrong of me to, anyway, I'd only carry on hurting her, which is all I've ever done. Has she met Rufus yet?'

Vivienne shook her head. 'She's not . . . Well, she hasn't taken too well to the idea of him.'

Jacqueline nodded, and her face showed her inner strain. 'I'm sure she'll come round, in time,' she said. Then she started to laugh as Rufus grabbed the hem of her coat to pull himself up. 'How clever you are,' she told him as he began bouncing up and down in front of her. 'Is he walking?'

'Oh, yes,' Vivienne answered.

'Mum, mum, brrrrrsssst!' he gurgled, ending with a shower of bubbles.

'May I?' Jacqueline said, putting her hands under Rufus's arms to lift him.

Vivienne's heart rose to her mouth. The answer was *no, no, no,* but she was already picking him up.

'There you are,' Jacqueline cooed, settling him on her lap. 'Is that nice?'

Spotting the wig, Rufus made a dive for it.

Jacqueline passed it to him, and seemed to enjoy the way he began tearing it apart. 'He's very sociable,' she commented.

'Yes,' Vivienne said, the word seeming to skim across the top of her lungs.

'That's not always a good thing, as I found to my cost,' and leaning forward she touched her lips to Rufus's cheek. 'You know, this is the first time I've held a baby since Sam was taken.'

Vivienne's tension grew. 'What about Kelsey?' she reminded her.

Jacqueline frowned, and once again Vivienne glimpsed an inner struggle behind the mask. 'What I should have said,' she corrected, 'is it's the first time I've held a baby boy since Sam.' Then to Rufus, 'I can imagine how proud your daddy must be of you. He's very lucky to have you.'

Vivienne could barely move. Her head was spinning, her chest was tight with fear.

'He deserves you,' Jacqueline continued, smiling down into Rufus's watchful eyes. 'He's a good man. Difficult, but good. And loyal.' She looked at Vivienne. 'Wouldn't you agree, Miles is loyal?'

Vivienne only looked at her.

'He never told me about Rufus, you know?'

'He didn't know. He only found out recently.'

Jacqueline was puzzled. 'You didn't tell him he had a son?'

Vivienne was mute. What could she say that wasn't going to offend her? 'You two had only just got back together,' she managed. 'It would have complicated things . . .'

As understanding dawned in Jacqueline's eyes Vivienne braced herself ready to snatch Rufus from her lap, but Jacqueline merely looked away and continued to play with him as though it was something she did every day. 'Round and round the garden, like a teddy bear, one step, two step, tickle you under there,' and she laughed along with Rufus, hugging him to her as though she'd known him since birth.

Unsure whether she was more confused or afraid, Vivienne struggled for something to say that might take Jacqueline's mind off Rufus, or even prompt her to put him down. In the end, she said, 'Jacqueline, why did you disappear the way you did? What was the point of alarming everyone like that?'

With a tremulous sigh, Jacqueline rested her chin on Rufus's head as she gazed thoughtfully at nothing for a while. 'I couldn't tell Miles where I was going when I left,' she said, finally, 'because at the time I believed, or hoped, that if I disappeared the way Sam did it might lead me to wherever Sam is.' She smiled indulgently at the notion. 'That sounds crazy, doesn't it? Well, of course it is, but sometimes I think if I can step away from the world, into some kind of parallel universe, I might find the place people go to when they vanish.' She grimaced at her fancifulness and kissed Rufus's mass of dark curls. 'I've spent years creating that world for myself,' she said. 'I've given it people and towns, all kinds of things, including Sam, of course, because this world was too hard to be in. I'd have lost my mind entirely if I'd gone on living with the fear of what he might be suffering. For years I used to wake up at night certain I'd heard him screaming, that he was with people who were doing things to him . . . Terrible things, and he was screaming for me . . .' She broke off, biting her lip to stop it trembling. 'So I came up with this other world . . .'

She was lost inside her thoughts now, seeming hardly to notice that Rufus was trying to eat one of the buttons on her coat.

'I suppose you could say I became caught between the two worlds,' she went on sadly, 'so I wasn't able to be a mother to either of my children. Nor a wife. I'm just . . .' She stopped and let the words die in her throat.

Torn between pity and the need to take Rufus from her, Vivienne looked on helplessly.

'I was always so afraid of Miles having another son,' Jacqueline continued, 'and now I realise what a blessing it is. He's been given a second chance, which is only right, because he wasn't to blame for losing Sam. His punishment has never been just, and now it's over. A beautiful infant spirit has come to bring him the joy that should always have been his. A son he can watch grow into a man.'

She swallowed and turned her eyes towards the sky outside. 'For me the punishment will never end, and nor should it. There's no redemption or forgiveness waiting in the future for me, no second chance, there's only the eternal hell of never knowing where he is, and how shamefully I failed.'

'But it wasn't your fault,' Vivienne said softly.

'Not only with him, but with Kelsey too,' she said, as though Vivienne hadn't spoken. Then her eyes focused and she started to smile. 'It's a beautiful day, isn't it?' she said. 'It almost feels like spring. The weather was like this the day Sam was taken.'

As she stood up Vivienne stood too, her arms going instinctively to take Rufus, but Jacqueline seemed not to notice as she carried him across the room to the balcony.

Vivienne watched, fraught with horror, as Jacqueline stepped outside and leaned over to look down at the courtyard below. 'No!' she heard herself gasp. 'Please . . .'

'It's very pretty here,' Jacqueline commented. 'I expect you enjoy being close to the river.'

'Jacqueline . . . Please . . .'

Seeming not to hear, Jacqueline hiked Rufus higher in her arms and gazed up into his face. Apparently liking the look of her, he clasped his hands to her cheeks and gave an excited squeal as he squeezed.

Jacqueline murmured something Vivienne couldn't hear, and sat him on the railing.

Vivienne's panic erupted. 'No, stop, please!' she shouted, dashing forward.

Jacqueline spun round. 'What is it?' she cried, clutching Rufus to her.

Vivienne halted.

'Oh my goodness. You're afraid,' Jacqueline gasped. 'You think . . .' Appalled, she looked at Rufus, then turning her head away she thrust him at Vivienne. 'Please take him,' she said, her voice strangled with pain.

Grabbing him, Vivienne wrapped him tightly in her arms, her breath coming so fast it was hard to speak. 'I'm sorry,' she choked. 'I didn't mean . . . It's just that he was so close . . .'

Jacqueline's hands were over her face. 'You thought I'd harm him,' she said brokenly. 'You thought . . .' She lifted her head, and registering how Vivienne was shaking, she said, 'Yes, of course you did. Look at you. It's why you didn't tell Miles you'd had him, you were afraid of me.' Her eyes were swimming in tears. 'I can't be trusted with my own children, so why would you trust me with yours?'

'I'm sorry,' Vivienne said sincerely. 'I just . . . Oh God, Jacqueline, I'm sorry.'

'It's all right, I don't blame you. You're not the first.'

Feeling even worse, Vivienne said, 'Why don't we go downstairs? I'll – I'll make some tea.'

Jacqueline took a breath, attempting to pull herself together. 'I'm sure you'd rather I left,' she said, and walking past her she went to pick up her bag.

'No, please have some tea,' Vivienne heard herself say.

Jacqueline turned round. 'I don't need your pity.'

'That's not what I'm offering.'

'Then what? Friendship?' She smiled, almost mockingly. 'You already have everything that should be mine . . .'

'No, I have what you turned your back on,' Vivienne told her. 'Miles loved you. Kelsey still does.'

At the mention of Kelsey, Jacqueline's eyes turned away. 'You'll take better care of them than I can,' she said. 'Time has proved how incapable I am.'

'Don't turn your back on Kelsey,' Vivienne implored. 'She's fourteen years old . . .'

'You'll be a much better influence on her than I can . . .'

'How can you say that when you don't even know me?'

Jacqueline's eyes were sad yet ironic as she said, 'Almost anyone would do a better job than I have, and if Miles trusts you, there doesn't seem any reason for me not to.'

'But you're her mother.'

'And not the kind she deserves. She needs a good role model, someone she can confide in, who takes an interest in who she is and what she does in a way I never have. Tell me you won't do that.'

'What I will or won't do isn't the point . . .'

'Oh yes it is. Knowing Kelsey will be taken good care of, and not only by her father, is what's setting us all free. Surely you realise that.'

Afraid of how final this was starting to sound, Vivienne's voice rang with anger as she said, 'She doesn't want me! She wants you. For heaven's sake, at least speak to her on the phone, and tell her you're all right.'

Jacqueline only shook her head.

'Please,' Vivienne urged, fighting to keep Rufus from springing out of her arms.

Jacqueline watched him, appearing both amused and troubled. 'He's getting hungry,' she said. 'I shouldn't keep you any longer.'

'No,' Vivienne protested, as she began walking towards the stairs. 'I can't let you leave here without at least knowing where you're going.'

Jacqueline stopped. 'I chose to disappear,' she said, 'because I didn't want to be me any more. For the past fifteen years I've been the woman who lost her son; who never stopped looking for him; who refused to give up the hope of finding him. I've been pitied, laughed at, scorned, shunned . . . I've even been accused of killing him.' She dropped her head for a moment as though too tired to go on. Then, hooking her bag higher, she started down the stairs.

Going after her, Vivienne said, 'Do you still have the mobile phone you registered at my address? Can we contact you on that?'

'I don't want to be contacted.'

'Then why come here?'

When she reached the bottom Jacqueline looked up, her eyes stopping at Rufus. 'To see you and him,' she said simply, and leaning forward she kissed Rufus on the cheek. 'You're a very special little boy,' she whispered.

As she started to open the door Vivienne darted forward to cover her hand. 'No!' she cried, more determined than ever. 'I'm not letting you go anywhere until you've spoken to Kelsey.'

Jacqueline turned to her. 'You see, you're already looking out for her,' she said.

'Then help me. Don't just walk out on her. Please talk to her. Tell her she matters. Every child deserves that from their mother.'

Jacqueline's eyes were untroubled as she said, 'It's good to know I'm leaving her in capable hands.'

'I don't want her,' Vivienne insisted. 'She's yours. Why would I care what happens to her?'

'You just do.'

'You owe her, Jacqueline.'

Jacqueline's head went to one side.

'She didn't ask for any of this. She's just a child, about to become a woman. You must realise how much she needs you.'

'She'll do much better—'

'Stop making excuses and hiding behind your pain. You can do this, Jacqueline. You can speak to her, and at least try to explain why you find everything so hard.'

'She knows.'

'No, she guesses, because you've never talked to her about it. She needs to hear it from you, why you're so afraid to be a mother, but that you love her anyway.'

'She wouldn't believe me . . .'

'For God's sake, at least *try*. She's going through a terrible time and you're the only one who can really help her. Miles does his best—'

'OK, you're right.'

Thrown by the sudden turnaround, Vivienne gasped on the breath she'd taken, and rested her head against Rufus. 'Does that mean . . . ?' she whispered, daring to hope.

She heard Jacqueline swallow. 'Yes, I'll talk to her,' she said.

'Thank you,' Vivienne breathed. 'Not for me, for Kelsey.'

Jacqueline's smile was edged in sadness. 'I hope she'll thank you,' she said, 'but I don't think she will.'

'She doesn't need to know it was my suggestion.'

'No, it's probably best she doesn't.'

Vivienne stood aside. 'You can use the phone upstairs in the sitting room,' she said. 'It'll be more private,' and holding tightly to Rufus she watched Jacqueline start back up the stairs, still hardly able to believe that any of this was actually happening.

Sounding as stunned as Vivienne had expected on being told about Jacqueline's visit, Miles said, 'Where is she now?'

'Upstairs talking to Kelsey on the phone,' she replied.

'Please tell me I did the right thing in persuading her to call.'

'I'm sure you did. I've no idea what the outcome will be, but Kelsey needs to hear her, if only to feel satisfied her mother's really still with us.'

Deciding not to tell him how uneasy Jacqueline had made her about that, at least not yet, Vivienne said, 'Will you contact the police? Or shall I?'

'I'll do it, but they'll want to speak to you – and her. Do you think you can keep her there?'

'I don't know.' She looked up at the sound of voices approaching the front gate. 'Alice and Angus have just arrived,' she told him, opening the door before they could ring.

'Good, because if Kelsey lays into her mother the way only Kelsey can,' Miles was saying, 'there's no knowing what kind of state she might be in after. Incidentally, do you realise it's Jacqueline's birthday today?'

Vivienne's heart contracted. 'How could I have forgotten?' she murmured, knowing it was because so much else was going on, but nevertheless . . . 'That means it's Sam's sixteenth. Do you think it's connected to why she came here?'

'I've no idea. I gave up trying to work out what's in her head a long time ago.'

After handing Rufus to Angus, she pointed him and Alice through to the kitchen, saying to Miles, 'Where are you now?'

'The London side of Reading. I spoke to Theo a few minutes ago, he's still with Kelsey, so if you can keep Jacqueline there for another half an hour I'll come straight to you.'

'I'll try.'

'If she insists on leaving, at least get her to tell you where she's going.'

'I'll do my best. Is it a good idea to let her know you're on your way, or will that . . .'

'No, don't mention it. You say she seemed calm, but we've no idea how long that will last, or how it might change, and knowing I'm about to arrive might trigger something you won't want to deal with.'

Unsettled by the warning, she said, 'I'll leave you to contact the police now, and unless you hear from me again to say she's left, I'll see you in half an hour.'

At that Alice turned round, a picture of astonishment.

Vivienne held up a hand to stop her and put a finger to her lips. 'Jacqueline's up there,' she whispered, pointing to the ceiling as she clicked off the phone.

Alice's jaw dropped as she gave a slow blink, while Angus stopped cuddling Rufus to stare at her.

With an apologetic grimace Vivienne said, 'I'm afraid the explanation will have to wait, in case she comes down.'

'But what's she doing up there?' Alice demanded under her breath.

'Phoning Kelsey.'

This time Alice turned to Angus, as though expecting him to step into the breach, but he appeared equally bereft of words.

'Coffee?' Vivienne offered. 'I'll make some fresh.'

Alice sank down at the dining table. 'How long's she been here?' she asked, keeping her voice low.

'Half an hour or so.'

Alice glanced at Angus again, still not quite able to take it in. 'So where's she been all this time?' she asked.

'I'm still not sure exactly.'

'Is she all right? I mean, stable?'

'She seems it. At the moment, anyway. Miles is on his way. He left Devon early, because Kelsey's in Kensington . . . Ah, that could be the police,' she said as her mobile started to ring.

'Ms Kane? It's DI Sadler,' the voice at the other end told her. 'Mr Avery's just informed me that his wife is with you.'

'That's right, Inspector. She's still speaking to her daughter at the moment. Can I ask her to ring you back?'

'I'd be more obliged if you could keep her there,' he retorted dryly. 'We're contacting the police in Richmond to let them know where she is. Do you have any idea yet where she's been all this time?'

'Not really, but I think mainly around this area.'

'Is she all right?'

'She seems to be, but I've only met her once before, so I

don't have much to go on. Certainly she doesn't seem very like the woman I've heard so much about. She was very gentle with my son, and there's been nothing aggressive in her manner—' She glanced up at a noise on the stairs, and seeing Jacqueline coming she was about to say she'd pass him over when she realised it might not be a good thing for Jacqueline to know the police were on their way. So putting a formal note into her voice she said to Sadler, 'Thank you for your call. If you text me your number that would be very helpful,' and ringing off without saying goodbye she gave Jacqueline a smile of reassurance as she reached the foot of the stairs, and beckoned her into the kitchen.

'How did it go?' she asked, the bizarreness of the situation making her slightly light-headed as Jacqueline came towards her, carrying the wig in one hand and her bag in the other.

Jacqueline was about to answer when she spotted Angus and Alice. 'I'm sorry, I'm intruding,' she said, taking a step back.

'Not at all,' Vivienne assured her. 'Let me introduce you. Alice and Angus Jackson, this is Jacqueline Avery.'

Angus came forward to shake Jacqueline's hand, while Alice remained utterly flummoxed. 'Pleased to meet you,' Angus said, still holding onto Rufus.

'Thank you,' Jacqueline replied, and smiled as Rufus made a lunge towards her.

'I'm making coffee,' Vivienne told her. 'Will you have some?'

'Actually,' Jacqueline replied, 'I've just told Kelsey I'll go over there.'

Amazed – and then alarmed, considering what had happened the last time Jacqueline staged a reappearance in Kelsey's life – Vivienne blurted, 'Are you sure? I mean . . .'

Jacqueline nodded. 'I've said I will, so I think I should.'

'Why not have a drink, or some lunch before you go?'

'No thanks. I'm not hungry and I should leave you to your friends.'

'Oh, we don't mind if you stay,' Vivienne told her hurriedly, knowing she was making a complete mess of this.

'And I have plenty of food in.' Thank God she couldn't see the empty fridge.

'No, really. I'd rather be going,' Jacqueline said quietly. 'It's a long walk to the tube—'

'Then let me drive you,' Vivienne jumped in.

Alice was staring at her as if she'd gone mad.

'You don't need to,' Jacqueline replied. 'I enjoy walking.'

'No, I insist,' Vivienne said, earning herself another bemused blink from Alice. 'My friends will stay with Rufus, won't you?'

It was left to Angus to assure her they would.

'You just have to heat up his bottle,' Vivienne told them, reaching for her keys, 'and help yourselves to anything else. You know where everything is. Oh, you'll need to give him his lunch, so I should write down what he has,' and quickly pulling a Post-it towards her, she scribbled the words *Call Miles on his mobile*, before turning back to Jacqueline and saying, 'Are you ready?'

Appearing slightly dazed, Jacqueline nodded, and after an awkward glance at Alice she went to give Rufus a kiss before following Vivienne out to the car.

Chapter Twenty

'How long ago did they leave?' Miles asked Alice when she got through to him.

'About ten minutes,' she replied. 'I've been trying to reach you, but kept going straight to voicemail.'

'I must have been in a down area. If you can, call Vivienne and tell her to take the long route via Cromwell Road. It'll give me a chance to get there first.'

'Where are you now?'

'Just coming off the Chiswick flyover, so probably not too far behind. I'll call Theo now and ask him not to leave should Jacqueline show up before I do.'

'Theo?' Alice repeated blankly.

'He's with Kelsey.'

Alice had no words.

Accelerating hard through a set of amber lights, Miles said, 'Is Rufus OK?'

'He's fine,' she assured him, her eyes softening as she turned to look at him. 'Angus is giving him some milk, which he's making a lot of noise about. I mean Rufus, not my husband. Is there anything else we can do?'

'I don't think so. Just try to speak to Vivienne without alerting Jacqueline.'

After disconnecting, Miles sped on towards a set of red lights, and coming to an abrupt halt began searching for Theo's number. 'Is Kelsey in earshot?' he asked when Theo answered.

'Yes,' came the reply.

'She's told you her mother's on the way?'

'She has.'

'OK. I should be there in the next five to ten minutes,

hopefully before Jacqueline, but just in case, please, whatever you do, don't leave Kelsey alone with her.'

'No problem.'

'Is Kelsey all right?'

'Seems it.'

'I really owe you for this.'

'It's cool.'

After ringing off Miles sped away from the lights, swallowing the next stretch of road in a matter of seconds, before veering off towards the Hammersmith roundabout. Barring accidents, breakdowns or demonstrations, there was a good chance he'd arrive at the house before Vivienne – provided she'd taken the long route – but he wasn't going to relax, or even take much notice of red lights, until he was in through the door, with Kelsey under his protection.

'I've already done it,' Vivienne was saying in response to Alice's message from Miles.

'So you're taking the long way round?' Alice said, needing to be certain.

'Yep.'

'Good. Now, you'd better tell me what to give Rufus for dessert to make this seem about him.'

Aware of Jacqueline's quiet presence beside her, Vivienne said, 'He can have one of the apricot crumbles. They're in the cupboard next to the fridge.'

'Great. Now remember, take it nice and slow, and call me as soon as you can.'

After disconnecting via her earpiece, Vivienne cast a quick glance at Jacqueline before turning off the Cromwell Road to start heading up Marloes Road towards Kensington High Street. 'I think the other way might have been quicker,' she said, 'but we're not far. How are you feeling?'

Jacqueline nodded distractedly and continued to stare out at the crowded arrangement of town houses they were passing.

'Would you like me to wait while you go in?' Vivienne offered. 'I can always drive you back to where you're staying.'

It was a while before Jacqueline responded. When she did

it seemed she hadn't heard the question. 'I remember when Miles and I first moved here,' she said still watching the elegant houses with their varying facades and gardens given over to parking. 'I really didn't want to come. Richmond was Sam's home, so we needed to stay there until he came back. That's what I used to tell myself,' she added in a whisper. Then, in a stronger voice, 'It was an awful day when they carried me out of that house. They had to drug me.' She looked down at the wig bunched in her hands. 'It must have been terrible for Miles,' she said quietly. 'Actually, I knew it was, but I couldn't help myself. Moving house was like giving up hope.' She swallowed and took a small gasp of air. 'He's sixteen today,' she said, twisting the wiry hair around her fingers.

Vivienne could only feel the wretchedness of having no words to offer, either of comfort or any real understanding.

Jacqueline sat staring blankly at the wig, until finally she said, 'I wonder what you'll be doing on Rufus's sixteenth. Do you ever imagine how you might celebrate? Whether it'll be at home, or in a restaurant, or perhaps he'd prefer to be off with his friends? I don't expect you ever consider that he might not be there any more.' She sighed raggedly. 'It's not the kind of thing you plan for, is it? Only destiny, or fate, or God, makes those kinds of plans and you know nothing about it until it's happened, and by then it's too late.'

Vivienne swallowed as she glanced over at her.

'Did you know that some people doubt that Sam was even with me that day?' Jacqueline said. 'They think I, or Miles, did something to him . . .' Her voice faltered as her fingers tightened on the wig. 'It's extraordinary, the things people think, even those that know you. Everyone has their suspicions. Friends of years standing start looking at you differently, or trying to avoid you, or . . .' She took a breath in an effort to steady her voice. 'Has Miles ever told you about a woman called Elizabeth Barrett?'

Vivienne shook her head. 'I don't think so. Who is she?'

Jacqueline's head came up and she sucked in her lips as though forcing back more words. Then, looking around at where they were she said, 'We're almost there. I wonder if Kelsey's as nervous as I am.'

*

'Dad!' Kelsey cried, coming out of the kitchen as he let himself in the front door. 'You got here fast.' Her eyes were shining. 'You'll never guess who's here.'

'Theo Kenwood-South – and Mum's on her way,' he replied, dropping his keys on the hall table.

Kelsey's jaw dropped. Then, pushing past her surprise that he knew this, she protested, 'She might not come in if she knows you're here.'

'I parked around the corner so she won't see the car,' he told her. 'Hi,' he said, stepping forward to shake hands with Theo. 'Thanks for waiting.'

'No problem,' Theo assured him. 'Kelsey and I have had a good chat.'

As Kelsey glanced up at him Miles noticed how flushed her cheeks became. 'Theo's recording an episode of *Sports Quiz* this evening,' she told him. 'He said we can go if we want to.'

Miles put a hand on her head. 'We'll see,' he responded. 'It's a lovely offer,' he added, to Theo.

'It stands if you want it,' Theo assured him, reaching for his helmet. 'I guess I should be going now.'

'I can't thank you enough for coming,' Miles said, going to open the door. 'I'll hope to catch up with you in Devon sometime next week?'

'You can count on it,' Theo replied, his handsome face breaking into a grin. 'Next Saturday's the big day.'

Kelsey giggled. 'Theo's been telling me all about what's happening behind the scenes,' she informed Miles.

Miles smiled fleetingly. He didn't want to appear rude, particularly in light of how helpful Theo had been, but he was keen to talk to Kelsey before Jacqueline arrived and he wasn't sure how much time they might have.

'You have my number if you need it,' Theo reminded Miles as he went past him. 'You too,' he added to Kelsey.

Kelsey blushed to the roots of her hair as her eyes flicked to her father. 'Thanks,' she said in a whisper.

Following Theo out to the gate, Miles kept his voice low as he said, 'Can you call Vivienne to let her know I've arrived, and tell her it'll probably be best if Kelsey doesn't see her, so she should drop Jacqueline around the corner in the square.'

'Will do,' Theo assured him, and planting the helmet on his head, he sat astride his motorbike and revved up the engine.

Even before he'd reached the end of the road Miles was back inside, going into the kitchen to join Kelsey. 'What did Mum say when you spoke to her?' he wanted to know.

'Nothing much really. Just that she's sorry if she worried us, and she's been doing a lot of thinking. She's going to tell me about it when she gets here.'

'Is she intending to stay?'

'You mean, is she coming back to us? I don't know, I didn't ask. Are you going to let her, if she wants to?'

Seeing how worried she was, he said, 'We've a lot to discuss.'

Her face darkened. 'You mean about *Rufus* and *her*. Well they've got no right coming into our lives—'

'Kelsey, this isn't the time for us to start arguing. Did Mum tell you where she's been since she left?'

'She said here, in London. I don't know where exactly.'

'You realise what today is, don't you?' he asked bluntly.

She looked pinched as she nodded.

'So you understand why I'm anxious?'

Again she nodded. 'You're not going to stop me seeing her,' she told him angrily.

'That's not my intention, but—' He broke off at the sound of a key going into the front door, and turned to look down the hall. 'She's here,' he said, seeing her silhouette through the opaque glass panel.

Kelsey's face had already paled, and seeming far less confident all of a sudden she moved in closer to her father.

As Jacqueline came in she closed the door quietly behind her, then stopped as her eyes connected with Miles.

For a long time neither of them spoke, though Miles could sense how unsettled she was to find him there. For his part, he was aware of a tightness in his chest, and the unbridgeable gulf that separated who they were now from the young couple who had once been so deeply in love. He still cared for her, in spite of how hard she made it, but all the closeness they'd shared had bled through the cracks a long time ago.

'I didn't realise you were here,' she said finally.

'I've just arrived,' he told her. Then, after a beat, 'So how are you?' He'd sounded sharper than he intended, and saw her flinch. It was her vulnerability that had made it impossible for him to leave her; her need for protection, from others as well as herself. It formed the rim of the gulf that, perversely, bound them together as irrevocably as it kept them apart.

'I'm fine,' she said.

'Are you going to tell me where you've been for the past six weeks?'

She took a breath, and looked at Kelsey. 'I came here so we could talk,' she said. 'Do you still want to?'

Kelsey nodded and shrugged, trying to appear nonchalant, but not quite making it.

Jacqueline's eyes returned to Miles. 'I don't suppose you trust me to be alone with her,' she said.

'Do you blame me?'

'No, but I promise it's not why I'm here.'

Kelsey looked up at her father as he said, 'How long are you staying?'

'I suppose . . . I guess that depends on how much time you'll allow me.'

'This is your home.'

She seemed surprised by that, but didn't make any comment.

'Why don't you take off your coat?' Kelsey suggested. 'It's really dumb us all standing around here like this.'

Jacqueline glanced at Miles as though expecting him to object. When he didn't, she started to unfasten her buttons. 'Are you going to insist on staying while Kelsey and I talk?' she asked.

Before Miles could answer, Kelsey said, 'Dad, I'm not going to do anything I don't want to. I'm fourteen now, I can take care of myself.'

Looking down at her, Miles said, 'I'm not arguing about this. You can go into the drawing room, the two of you, but I'll be right here.'

'I'll leave my bag,' Jacqueline said, putting it on the

bottom stair. 'Just in case you think I have something hidden inside.'

Kelsey rolled her eyes, but neither she nor Miles objected to the bag being left. 'Maybe you want to give her a body search,' Kelsey muttered sarcastically to her father.

Knowing the rudeness was to cover her embarrassment Miles let it go, and stood aside as she started into the hall where Jacqueline was already opening the drawing-room door. When they were standing together he suddenly felt the tragedy of their relationship squeezing his heart. They were mother and daughter, yet Jacqueline could be a stranger in an unfamiliar house with a child she barely knew for how comfortable she appeared. It was how it had always been with her, never really seeming to belong, doing everything she could to avoid a connection.

Watching the door close behind them, he took a deep, unsteady breath. Was he right to let this happen? Even if Jacqueline didn't attempt to hurt Kelsey physically, there was no knowing what she might inflict emotionally, and God knew she'd already done enough damage on that front.

In the end, not liking himself much for it, he moved silently down the hall to stand outside the door. If things started to get out of hand he wanted to know in time to stop it, not only for Kelsey's sake, but for Jacqueline's too. No matter what armour his wife used to protect herself, he knew Kelsey had the ability to get through at times and when she did, she could provoke a reaction in Jacqueline that even he would have trouble controlling.

Kelsey was curling into a corner of one of the large, rust-coloured sofas that flanked the hearth, looking anywhere but at her mother. As Jacqueline sat on the other sofa, she was aware of the anxiety churning her heart, but only as a faraway sensation, a discomfort once removed, like the echo of a scream, or the residue of pain. Her mind was a jumble of disjointed thoughts: memories that rose up from the past, visions that stole in from the future. She might be a hundred miles away, or several years – or in this room, watching herself from the corners. She tried to imagine what was happening inside Kelsey, whether she felt resentful or afraid, curious, or perhaps even relieved to know her mother was safe. It was probably a combination of all those things, but on a deeper, more critical level, Jacqueline wondered if Kelsey was as driven by hope as her mother had once been. Had she allowed herself to believe that one day things would come good between them? Did she ever think about how it would be if her brother had never been born, or stolen, or perhaps returned? In her way she must hate Sam, Jacqueline realised, but maybe she longed for him too.

Looking at her now, all silky blonde hair and teenage attitude, no outsider would ever guess how deeply her insecurities were rooted, gnawing at her self-worth, eroding her confidence. She had a beautiful face and a composure that exuded as much nonchalance as arrogance – and a considerable amount of anxiety, did she but know it. Nevertheless, Jacqueline felt certain that whatever mistakes she'd made with Kelsey – and she knew they far outweighed any good she might have done – Kelsey had it in her to survive. She'd been blessed with enough courage and inner strength to overcome the demons planted by her mother, but most of all she had the right father to smooth the way, as he always had throughout her young life. Were it not for Miles . . . But there was no point going there. It was too late to undo her neglect as a mother, or her failure as a wife, or her obsession with Sam. She needed to focus on the present now, and how she was going to try and feel, even transmit, some affection and concern for her daughter.

'Why are you looking at me like that?' Kelsey suddenly demanded, using belligerence to disguise her unease.

Jacqueline bunched her hands and glanced briefly down at them. 'I'm not sure how I'm looking,' she replied.

Kelsey's eyes flickered with surprise. She was used to her mother responding in like tone, not sounding all . . . Well, she wasn't sure how she was sounding. Her jaw tightened as she tried again. 'So where have you been all this time?' she said rudely. 'I suppose you know people actually thought Dad had offed you?'

Used to Kelsey's bluntness, as well as her hostility, Jacqueline only said, 'It's why I called the police to let them know I was all right.'

Kelsey's expression became more pinched. 'So why didn't you call us?' she wanted to know.

'Because I needed some time alone – apart from you and Dad.'

'Yeah, well, you didn't have to go off without saying anything, did you? And you could have answered my messages. Not that I care,' she quickly added. 'It makes no difference to me.'

'I didn't get your messages,' Jacqueline told her. 'I threw my old mobile away the day I left. I knew you'd try calling me and . . . I'm sorry, I should have been more considerate.'

Kelsey's eyes widened. Something was really different here, and it was making her nervous. 'Well, that would be a first,' she snapped. 'And, by the way, if you think Dad's going to take you back, then you've got some serious making up to do, because you know *she's* around again, don't you?'

Understanding the challenge, while surprised by the intimation that Kelsey might want her back, Jacqueline said, 'You mean Vivienne? Yes, I know Dad's seeing her again.'

Kelsey stared at her with shocked, then big, angry eyes. 'You *never* use her name,' she cried accusingly. 'Or not like that, anyway.'

'No,' Jacqueline agreed, 'but things have changed.'

Kelsey drew back. 'How?' she demanded, suspiciously.

Jacqueline took a breath, and envisaging the candles on the altar at St Anne's with the eyes of icons gazing down at her, she said, 'Well, that would be a little hard to explain in a simple sense . . . It's more esoteric . . .'

'Oh puhleeze . . .'

'All right. Let's just say that I don't feel the same way about Vivienne as I used to, and there's no reason for you to either.'

Kelsey was beginning to flounder badly in this unfamiliar world. This woman wasn't her mother – she might look the same, and it was definitely her voice, but the things she was saying were weird and nothing like the way she used to be. 'You've never even been able to think about her without going ballistic!' Her voice shook with anguish. 'I've even heard you threaten to kill her if she goes anywhere near Dad.'

Jacqueline nodded and glanced down at her hands. 'That's because I was afraid,' she explained steadily. 'We all say and do things we don't mean when we feel threatened or out of control.'

More unnerved than ever, Kelsey got to her feet and went to stand in front of the hearth. 'You're starting to freak me out,' she told her angrily. 'Normally we're rowing by now, or not speaking or . . . This is so not you.'

Saddened by Kelsey's need for the fierce and rancorous showdowns she was used to, Jacqueline held onto her resolve to remain calm as she said, 'I'm just trying to get rid of all the negative feelings I've planted in you.'

Kelsey's mouth opened, then her hands shot up. 'OK. That is it!' she cried. 'You don't say things like that. You don't care what's going on with me, so *what is wrong with you*?'

Jacqueline took a breath that was shaky and thin, while focusing on the light that flowed from the image of candles. 'I know I've been a dreadful mother,' she said evenly, 'that I haven't been there for you the way Dad has. I've never told you how special, or beautiful you are . . .'

Kelsey started to turn away, then suddenly spun back, her eyes bright with fury. 'You've got to start acting normal or I'm going to call Dad in to sort you out,' she warned.

'It is normal for a mother to praise her daughter.'

'But you're not like other mothers. You're all wrapped up in yourself and Sam . . . I've never mattered to you, so you can't start behaving as though I do now.'

'Actually, you've always mattered,' Jacqueline told her, 'I was just too afraid to show it.'

'And what, suddenly you're not and that's supposed to make it all right?'

'No, I probably still am, but I want to try to make you understand why I've been the way I have.'

Kelsey stared at her with helpless incomprehension.

Lowering her eyes, Jacqueline gazed down at her hands again as they tightened around one another. 'It's too late now for me to be the mother you deserve,' she said quietly.

'What I've done . . . The terrible confusion and doubts I've sown inside you . . . It can be healed, I hope, but it's going to take a lot of patience and understanding on the part of those who love you. Your father's always been there for you, you know that. He'll never let you down the way I have. I believe Vivienne will be a good friend to you too.'

Kelsey's eyes flashed. 'I am *so* not interested in that woman.'

'That's me talking, not you,' Jacqueline told her. 'You don't hate her, you hardly even know her. You're simply afraid of the changes she's going to make in your life, but you don't need to be.'

Kelsey gaped at her, too bewildered to respond.

'I'm trying to free you from my prejudices,' Jacqueline explained, 'because they were wrong. I've—'

'No. I'm not listening to any more,' Kelsey cut in, clapping her hands over her ears, 'it's all too weird.'

Jacqueline waited for her to put her hands down again.

'See!' Kelsey cried in frustration. 'Normally you'd shout at me for saying something like that, or send me to my room, or tell me I can't come home next weekend, so stop acting weird. It's doing my head in.'

Jacqueline swallowed and touched a finger to a small twitch at the corner of her eye. 'What matters,' she said, 'is that you understand how much you are loved and wanted. I know you don't doubt that where Dad's concerned . . .'

Abruptly switching attack, Kelsey said, 'He's got a son now, I hope you know that.'

'Yes, I do. Rufus.'

Kelsey stared at her. Then, in a tone clearly meant to offend, 'That is such a stupid name.'

Jacqueline said, 'He's an adorable little boy, and I think you're going to become very fond of him.'

Kelsey's jaw dropped. 'Are you telling me you've met him?' she said incredulously.

'I went to Vivienne's this morning.'

'Oh my God.' Kelsey's hands went up as though she couldn't take any more. 'You have to stop now, because it's so not funny . . .'

'No, it's not funny. It's real, and it's hard, I understand that.'

Kelsey regarded her warily.

Jacqueline looked back, waiting for the storm to settle inside her.

'So, is she still in one piece?' Kelsey snapped. 'I mean . . .'

'Yes of course she is.'

'Does Dad know you went?'

'I imagine he does by now.'

Kelsey swallowed as she tried desperately to make some sense of this. She looked at the window, the door, all around the room, taking a breath now and then, but no words came out.

Wishing she knew how to help her, Jacqueline sat quietly, wondering if Miles was listening outside and feeling certain he was.

'Why did you go?' Kelsey suddenly demanded.

'To Vivienne's? I needed to talk to her, to find out what she's like. I wanted to meet Rufus too.'

Though still profoundly confused, Kelsey was starting to feel a tentative fascination now. 'So what happened?' she asked, genuinely wanting to know.

'I think, at least I hope,' Jacqueline said, 'I've managed to put her mind at rest.'

'About what?'

'Me, and the fact that I'm not going to go on trying to come between her and Dad.'

Kelsey stared at her, misery darkening her eyes as she struggled to understand.

'It's time for me to let go,' Jacqueline told her gently. 'Not only of Dad, but of a lot of things. During these last few weeks I've come to realise how far down the wrong path I've gone, how I've allowed my . . . issues . . . to cause all sorts of problems for our family, when they should only ever have been mine. Now I can see the way forward and I'm going to take it.'

Kelsey was hardly breathing, but a new suspicion was dawning in her eyes. 'You're going back to the States,' she said. Then, before Jacqueline could answer, 'Well, I suppose I should be grateful you're telling me this time.'

'I'm not going to the States,' Jacqueline said quietly.

Kelsey blinked, seemed to think about it for a moment, then abruptly shutting it down she summoned as much nastiness as she could muster as she said, 'Actually, I really don't want to know what you're going to do. It's of no interest to me because *you are not my mother*.'

As the words resounded around the room, Miles could only wonder if they had hurt Jacqueline as much as intended. He pictured her face, impassive and lined, her eyes probably watching Kelsey from a place no one could reach. He wanted to go in there and shake her, make her see that in spite of what she was saying she still wasn't connecting with her daughter. But he knew he had to give her more time, because it was going to take many more hours, days, weeks, even years, to win Kelsey over when the rift between them was so wide. However, at least this was a start.

Hearing his mobile ringing in the kitchen, he moved quickly back down the hall to go and pick it up.

'Miles, it's Alice. I'm still at Vivienne's and the police are downstairs wanting to know where Jacqueline is. What shall I tell them?'

'Oh hell,' he groaned, glancing back down the hall. He was thinking fast, and coming to a snap decision, he said, 'I don't think it's a good idea for them to turn up here now, so let me speak to them.'

A few minutes later, after explaining that Jacqueline was trying to communicate with her daughter in a way she never had before, and assuring the police he'd bring her to them in Richmond sometime later in the day, Miles rang off and returned to the sitting-room door. The role of eavesdropper was still sitting ill with him, but he had little choice when he was afraid of what Jacqueline might do or say.

Though it was difficult to make out everything that was being said, he was relieved to hear Kelsey sounding less angry now, while Jacqueline apparently remained as measured, and detached as before. Then he tensed as he heard her say, 'Dad will marry Vivienne as soon as he's able . . .'

Kelsey turned her head sharply away.

'I know you're afraid they'll push you out,' Jacqueline went on gently, 'but Dad loves you too much to let that happen. And it'll be good for you to be part of a family that's normal and uncomplicated – if families can ever be that.'

'But *we're* a family, you me and Dad,' Kelsey protested.

'And look what bad shape we're in. It's my fault, of course . . .'

'Not necessarily. It's Sam's. Or the people who took him. And you can get help.'

Seeming surprised by the answer, Jacqueline gazed searchingly into her eyes as though seeing, or understanding something she hadn't realised before.

Kelsey looked back, waiting for her mother to respond, to reveal something of what was happening in her mind, but as the seconds ticked by Jacqueline still said nothing. In the end, Kelsey dared to say, 'I wish you'd tell me about him. I mean, I know he was just a baby when he went, but it's like I've got this brother that I've never known and no one ever really talks about, except he's there all the time.'

Jacqueline took a breath and held it deeply inside her.

Kelsey's eyes were showing how afraid she was now, while in the hall Miles struggled with the urge to go and sweep her into his arms in an effort to protect her from the rejection he knew was coming.

'Not now,' Jacqueline finally replied. 'Another time.'

Miles's eyes closed in despair. If he thought he could force something out of Jacqueline he'd go in there right now and do it, but he knew from bitter experience that it was useless even to try. She'd lost the ability to discuss her feelings not long after she'd lost her son, and it was going to take a lot more than this period alone to bring it back.

'So where have you been since you left?' Kelsey suddenly asked, the stiffness in her tone hiding the hurt of being rebuffed. 'You still haven't told me.'

Jacqueline swallowed hard and brought her head up. 'I'm renting a house in Richmond,' she said, on a shuddering breath.

Seeming surprised to have received an answer, Kelsey regarded her coldly. 'So are you going to like, stay there, or are you coming home?' she went on, her expression saying she couldn't care less either way, when Miles knew very well that she could.

'It is my home now,' Jacqueline said.

Kelsey flinched, and tightened her jaw as she turned to stare at the window. 'Can I come to see it?' she asked shortly.

Outside Miles felt his hands clench. If Jacqueline turned her down he was going in there to shake the damned woman back to her senses, because surely to God she must realise by now how desperate Kelsey was for them to have some kind of relationship – and how willing she was to try, in spite of how little her mother deserved it.

The silence dragged on until finally Jacqueline said, 'Yes, if you'd like to.'

Miles unravelled with relief.

'Really?' Kelsey asked, clearly amazed. 'When?'

'Uh – soon.'

'Why not now?'

'Well, I'm not sure Dad will want you to, and I think this might already have been enough for you for one day.'

'I'm not a child.'

'I know, but this isn't easy for me either. In fact, I should probably be going—' She broke off as the door opened and Miles came into the room.

'Talk to her,' he said angrily. 'Tell her why you've been the way you have all these years. Explain how you've felt. For God's sake, give her something.'

Kelsey's eyes went from her father back to her mother.

Jacqueline was staring at Miles, but in her mind's eye she was seeing the candles. The flames were liquid and white with golden halos and dripping stems. She could feel their warmth, even smell their scent. It was all right, she told herself, it wasn't difficult. She could do this – and wasn't it why she'd come?

When finally she turned to Kelsey she looked into her eyes and felt the words starting to form, like rain in mist. Kelsey appeared worried and kept glancing at her father, but neither of them said anything, only waiting for Jacqueline to speak. 'After what happened to Sam,' she began quietly, 'I felt I didn't deserve you, or that if I allowed you to come close I'd lose you the way I lost him. I was terrified of it happening again. I thought perhaps there was something in me that would make it happen.'

She swallowed and inhaled shakily, but her resolve held firm. 'I've spent years being afraid of something that it turns out I had no need to fear at all,' she said, and the focus of her eyes became blurred as her gaze started to drift. 'I've always been terrified of Dad finding someone else and having a son,' she confessed. 'I thought if he did then Sam wouldn't matter to him any more, that he might not even want him to come back. I just couldn't bear . . . I couldn't allow it to happen, and I was prepared to go to any lengths to stop it.' She paused and took a breath. 'But now it has happened, and I . . . It's not anything like I expected.'

Miles met Kelsey's eyes, and seeing how anxious she was, he gave her a look of reassurance.

'At first, I kept waiting for the anger to kick in,' Jacqueline continued, 'but it didn't. Instead, it was as though a terrible weight was being lifted from me. It was strange. I didn't understand it, so I put it down to shock, or denial, and felt certain that once it passed I'd be as angry and afraid as I'd always expected to be. Then it finally dawned on me that it wasn't going to happen, and more than that, I started to realise that the reason I seemed lighter inside was because I wasn't feeling guilty any more for depriving Dad of his son, and you of your brother.' Her eyes refocused as she returned them to Kelsey. 'Not that Rufus can ever take Sam's place,' she said earnestly, 'it would be wrong even to think it, but he's a new life, an innocent child you'll both love and cherish in a way that will help to put the past where it belongs, and bring you a lot of happiness in the future. It's what you both deserve, and I'm not going to stand in the way of it any longer.'

Not knowing what to say, Kelsey looked at her father again. He was watching Jacqueline and realising, in a way which she possibly didn't, that as comforting and sincere as the words might have been, she had effectively put Rufus between Kelsey and Sam. She still couldn't share her lost son with her daughter, and he wondered if a day would ever come when she might.

'Dad and I should have gone our separate ways a long time ago,' Jacqueline told Kelsey. 'He's more than ready to let go of the past, but I can't, and actually I don't want to.'

Kelsey was staring hard into her face. 'So what,' she said, 'you're going to live on your own from now on, pretending, like you always have, that Sam will come back?'

Jacqueline shook her head. 'No, that's not what I'm going to do. As I said, I've seen the way forward and I don't think it's going to be anywhere near as hard a path to take as I'd feared.'

Miles's face darkened as Kelsey shifted uncomfortably. 'So what about if I want to come and live with you?' Kelsey challenged.

Jacqueline looked surprised. 'What, and leave Dad?' she said. 'I don't think that's what you want.'

'He's going to have Vivienne. And *Rufus*.'

'But I've already told you, they won't shut you out.'

'And you will, is that what you're saying?'

Jacqueline's voice faltered as she started to answer. 'No, I just know that deep down inside you don't really want to leave Dad.'

'That's not good enough,' Miles growled.

Jacqueline looked at him, and after a moment she nodded, seeming to accept he was right. 'You can come and see me whenever you like,' she told Kelsey. 'We might . . . Well, who knows, we could even become friends—' She broke off as Kelsey's eyes suddenly filled with tears. 'What is it?' she said, thrown by the unexpectedness of it.

'I don't want you to leave us,' Kelsey cried, using anger to cover her despair. 'I want you to come home. I don't even care if you go on being mean to me . . .'

'Oh, Kelsey,' Jacqueline murmured, and going to her she drew her into the first embrace they'd shared in years. 'I've caused you far too much pain in your short life,' she said. 'All I want now is for you to be happy.'

'Well, I can't if you're not going to be there, can I? I mean like I hate you and everything, but . . .'

'This is just fear of change that you're feeling,' Jacqueline told her, cupping her face between her hands so she could look into her eyes. 'But I promise it'll all be much easier than you think. No more rows between me and Dad, or me and you. You—'

'No!' Kelsey cried, slapping her away. 'You're my mother. You can't just walk out on me, it's not fair.'

Catching her hands between her own, Jacqueline held them tightly to her chest. 'I told you, you can come to see me whenever you like,' she said gently. Then, with a smile, 'We can start doing all the things we should have been doing.'

'Such as?' Kelsey sniffed suspiciously.

'Well . . . We could begin by getting to know one another, finding out the kinds of things we like to do . . .'

'Too weird,' Kelsey told her.

'OK, then maybe we could explore Richmond together. It's changed quite a bit since I last lived there.'

Kelsey looked at Miles, seeming to need reassurance, and as he nodded she said, in a tone that made her words sound less friendly than they might, 'Actually, Martha's gran lives there. It's supposed to be really cool.'

Jacqueline was smiling past the tears in her heart. 'It is,' she told her. 'And think how much nicer it'll be, if we're not arguing any more.'

'Yeah, well, I expect we still will sometimes, because that's like only normal.'

'Of course, but it won't be the way it was before.'

Still seeming uncertain, Kelsey broke out of the embrace and went to stand with her father.

Turning to them, Jacqueline looked at Miles as though seeking approval, which he gave in the briefest of nods. Her eyes went to Kelsey, drinking in her young face. She couldn't help wondering how like Sam she might be, but unless a miracle happened that was something none of them would ever know.

'Would you like something to drink?' Miles offered.

She shook her head. 'I think I should be going,' she replied.

He didn't argue, because Kelsey had probably had enough for now.

'We don't have your address or phone number,' Kelsey reminded her as she went to pick up her bag.

Jacqueline's eyes went to Miles as she said, 'I'll write it down for you.'

'I'd like to have a word before you go,' Miles told her, and after checking to make sure Kelsey was holding together, he started down the hall.

Going to Kelsey, Jacqueline gazed directly into her eyes and made to touch her cheek, but at the last minute she drew her hand away. 'We'll talk again,' she said softly.

'Do you promise?'

'I promise.'

As she followed Miles into the kitchen Jacqueline saw the notepad and pen he'd put out for her, so went to write down her address and telephone number.

'The police want to talk to you,' Miles told her quietly. 'They need to know you're safe.'

Jacqueline frowned. 'But I've already told them . . .'

'They need to see you, and I've said I'll drive you there.'

She almost bristled. 'I can go alone,' she protested.

He shook his head. 'I'm taking you.'

'But you don't have to. Vivienne's waiting outside. She offered to drive me home after I'd spoken to Kelsey.'

His eyes held firmly to hers.

'Are you really going to leave Kelsey on her own now?' she challenged.

'She can come with us.'

'What's the point, when Vivienne can take me?'

Picking up the address and phone number she'd written on the pad he read it through, before saying, 'OK. Just make sure she takes you to Richmond police station on the way. In fact, I'll call to let her know she has to do that.'

Jacqueline nodded agreement, then hoisting her bag onto her shoulder she went into the hall to put on her coat. To her surprise, as she slipped in her arms, the phone in her pocket started to ring. She began fishing for it until, realising who it was likely to be, she looked back down the hall.

Miles was watching her, his own mobile in his hand. 'I wanted to be sure,' he told her, and as Kelsey came out of the sitting room he cut the call.

'I was thinking,' Kelsey said, 'why don't we give Mum a lift home? Then we can see her house.'

'Someone's waiting outside for me,' Jacqueline told her.

Kelsey looked puzzled. Her mother didn't have any friends, or none that she knew about.

'I'll call you later,' Jacqueline told her as she pulled open the front door. 'Dad's got my number, and the address.'

Kelsey watched her go out, then, unable to hold back her tears, she said, 'But this is where you live.'

Either Jacqueline didn't hear, or she wasn't willing to respond, because the door closed quietly behind her, followed a moment later by the sound of the gate.

Going to take Kelsey in his arms Miles held her tight, resting his head on hers as she sobbed.

'I didn't wish her a happy birthday,' Kelsey said, looking up at him.

Glad she couldn't see the coldness that crept into his heart at the reminder of the date, Miles smoothed back her hair, saying, 'You can give her a call.'

Kelsey nodded. 'I know,' she said, pausing halfway up the stairs, 'I'll send her a birthday text.'

Vivienne was on the point of taking Rufus for an early bath when her mobile started to ring. Seeing it was Miles she quickly clicked on. 'Hi, how's it going?' she asked.

There was a pause before he said, 'Please tell me Jacqueline's with you.'

She blinked in surprise. 'I thought she was with you.'

'Damn,' he muttered. 'Damn. Damn. Damn. Where are you?'

'At home. I dropped her in the square, like you said, then . . . What's wrong? What's happened?'

'She left here a few minutes ago, saying you were waiting to drive her home. I knew I should have gone with her to check, but Kelsey was upset . . . I don't suppose the police are still with you?'

'No. They'd already left by the time I got back.'

'Did they leave any names, numbers to contact them?'

'Yes, I have them right here,' Vivienne replied, grabbing the phone pad.

After jotting them down he said, 'I'll call you back,' and the line went dead.

A few minutes later the phone rang again. 'The police are sending someone to check the address she gave me,' Miles told her. 'I know the phone number works because I've tried it. She's not answering now, though.'

'How did she seem when she left?'

'It's hard to say. Not her normal self, that's for sure. No hysterics, no scenes or threats, but she could be taking a different medication that's keeping her calm. What's bothering me is that she talked about wrong paths and seeing the way forward . . . Were it any other day of the year I might be willing to believe she'd done some adjusting to losing Sam . . .' He took a breath and let it go slowly. 'How did she seem to you?'

Wishing she could reassure him, Vivienne said, 'To be honest, she gave me the same impression as I think she gave you. Did you tell the police how worried you are?'

'Of course.' Then, in a tone that was almost angry, 'She can't come back into Kelsey's life just to go and do something stupid now. If she has, I'll . . . Damn it, I'll kill her myself.'

Vivienne's smile was weak. 'How's Kelsey now?' she asked.

'A bit dazed, and upset. I'll tell you more when I see you. Remind me when you're back in Devon?'

'Wednesday. When are you going?'

'I'd planned to go in the morning, and right now I don't see any reason to change that. Theo's invited us to a TV recording this evening, which we might go to. Kelsey could probably do with some light relief after the past couple of hours. How's my boy?'

'Right now, plastered in Play-Doh and about to have a bath.'

He sighed in a way that told her how stressed he was feeling. 'I'm sorry about all this,' he said. 'Not being there for you and Rufus, Jacqueline turning up the way she did—'

'Miles, there's nothing to apologise for,' she interrupted.

'All that matters is that they find her before she tries celebrating her birthday the way we're afraid of.'

At his end, after assuring Vivienne he'd call again if there was any news, Miles rang off and went upstairs to check on Kelsey. 'Did you text Mum?' he asked, going in through her open bedroom door.

She nodded, and held out her mobile for him to take. 'She's just texted back.'

As he read the message he felt a cold fist closing round his heart.

> Thank you. 40 is a milestone, so is 16. Did you remember it's Sam's birthday too?

'Have you answered?' he wanted to know.

'Yeah. I told her I did remember, and asked if she was celebrating tonight.'

'And?'

'Nothing, but I only sent it a couple of minutes ago.' Looking up at him she said, 'Who do you think her friend is, the one she said was waiting to give her a lift home? Do you think she's met someone? Would you mind, if she had?'

'Actually,' he said gently, 'the friend was Vivienne,' and he was about to add that Vivienne hadn't been waiting outside, when he cut the words off. She didn't need to hear that right now.

'Vivienne?' she echoed, looking flustered and angry again. 'I don't understand how she can go from hating someone so much one minute, to behaving like she's her best friend the next.'

As he started to answer her mobile bleeped with a message, and hoping it was Jacqueline he waited as she clicked it open to read.

When she'd finished she passed the phone over. 'It doesn't sound as though she's having a rave-up,' she commented.

> Just a quiet night. Lots to think about. Glad we talked today.

Having no idea whether he could take comfort from that, or if he should feel more worried than ever, he handed the phone back and went downstairs to speak to the police again. Still no report back from the officers who'd gone to the address Jacqueline had given.

An hour later they all knew that Jacqueline had provided a false address. 'The people there have heard of her,' the policeman told him, 'but through the news, not because she's living there, or anywhere close, according to the residents I spoke to. No one remembers seeing her.'

'I've told you what today is,' Miles reminded him, 'so we have to find her.'

'Of course. We're mounting a house-to-house search of the area, starting right now. The problem is, it's Saturday, so a lot of people are out, or away for the weekend, but that's no reason not to try. We'll get back to you as soon as there's any news.'

After ringing off Miles closed his study door and tried Jacqueline's number again. Finding himself diverted to voicemail, he resorted to texting instead.

`We know address you gave is false. Police are looking for you. Imperative you call as soon as you get this.`

When the message had gone, he ran back upstairs to find out if Kelsey had received any more texts.

'You're starting to spook me now,' Kelsey accused. 'Why are you so keen to keep hearing from her?'

She had to know, but for the moment he was prepared to play along with the denial. 'I need to speak to her,' he replied, 'and she's not taking my calls. Send a message asking her to ring you, then you can pass the phone to me.'

Feigning irritation, Kelsey pressed in a text, then in an attempt not to look bothered as they waited for a response she began flipping through a magazine.

Five long minutes later the phone signalled an incoming message.

Battery low, but promise to call in morning. Goodnight. Tell Dad not to worry, will contact police.

Handing the phone back, Miles returned to his study to call the police, then Vivienne.

'The trouble is,' he said, after updating Vivienne on what had happened since they'd last spoken, 'I don't know whether to believe her or not. On the one hand I can't see her being so cruel as to tell Kelsey she'll call tomorrow, if she knows Kelsey's going to receive some entirely different news, but on the other we have no reason to trust her – particularly given the date.'

'You say the police are doing a house-to-house.'

'Apparently, and they're working with the phone company to try and trace where the texts are coming from, but no word on that yet. I just wish to God there was something I could do, but I can't leave Kelsey, and I sure as hell don't want to worry her any more than she is already.'

Acutely aware of how painful this must be for him, another search in the very same area as the one that had been mounted for his son, Vivienne was about to respond when he said, 'Hang on, someone's trying to get through. I'll call you back,' and after switching lines, 'Hello. Miles Avery speaking.'

'Mr Avery, it's DC Ball. I thought you might like to know that your wife has just rung in to the station.'

Miles's surprise was so profound that he actually stopped breathing.

'I spoke to her myself, and she admitted the address she gave you was incorrect, but she's saying she wants to keep her whereabouts secret for the time being.'

'And you just accepted that?'

'She assured me she's not intending to harm herself in any way.'

'But she won't tell you where she is. Doesn't that sound just a little bit suspicious to you?' Frustration was making him unreasonable, but for God's sake, they couldn't just accept her word for it. 'Is anyone still out there looking?' he demanded.

'Of course. I'm just letting you know that she's made contact.'

Biting back an angry retort, since it was hardly the detective's fault Jacqueline was playing games, Miles thanked him and after abruptly cutting the call he dialled Jacqueline's number again. To his amazement she answered.

'Miles, you're making a fuss about nothing,' she informed him. 'I've spoken to the police, I've told Kelsey I'll call tomorrow, what more do you want?'

'How about your address?' he snapped back.

'You'll have it when I'm ready. For the time being, I want to be left alone.'

'I've no intention of visiting you.'

'Kelsey has, but there are things I still have to sort out. Meanwhile, I'll speak to her, and send texts.'

'That's not good enough.'

'All right, if it makes you happy I'll text her my address,' and without saying goodbye she ended the call.

'Actually, I don't feel quite as worried now I've spoken to her,' he admitted, when he got through to Vivienne again, 'but I still don't like what she's doing, and I can't imagine I'm going to get much sleep tonight.'

Vivienne said, 'I wonder what things she has to sort out.' Then, in a slightly different tone, 'Actually, I don't know if it's relevant, but I've just remembered something she asked me when I was driving her to Kensington earlier: she wanted to know if you'd told me about someone called Elizabeth Barrett.'

Miles's eyes closed in dismay. 'Please don't tell me that woman's been in touch with her,' he groaned.

'If she has she didn't say so. Why? Who is she?'

'Believe me, you really don't want to know.'

'Maybe I do.'

'Another time,' he told her, hearing Kelsey coming down the stairs. 'Give my son a goodnight kiss from me. I'll call tomorrow before we set off for Devon, and hopefully *after* Kelsey or I have spoken to Jacqueline.'

Chapter Twenty-one

'Sir, I've just heard from the guys in Richmond again,' DC Joy said as Sadler walked into CID on Monday morning. 'Still no word on Mrs Avery's whereabouts. They want to know if they should go on looking.'

Sadler glanced at his watch.

'She called her daughter three times yesterday,' Joy reminded him, 'so we know she's still with us.'

Sighing, he said, 'Then I don't suppose we can go on using up valuable police resources. Any word yet from the estate agents about letting out a house or a flat?'

Joy shook her head. 'She might have answered an ad in the paper,' she suggested.

'If she did then it could prove almost impossible to find her.' Throwing up his hands in frustration, he said, 'Why doesn't she give her daughter the damned address, the way she promised? Is that so hard to do?'

'No, but she's within her rights to keep—'

'I don't care. And frankly, until I clap eyes on that woman, or at least speak to her myself, I'm not going to sleep easy at night.'

'And we really can't have that, sir.'

'No, Elaine, we can't. So, now we have to ask ourselves, has the daughter been persuaded to keep the address a secret, or does she really not have it?'

'Mr Avery says she's keener than anyone to find out where her mother's actually living.'

Sadler shook his head impatiently. 'They're back in Devon, are they? Father and daughter.'

Joy nodded. 'He's taking the daughter back to school this morning.'

'OK. Call Richmond and let them off the hook, but I want you to keep on it, Elaine. It could be not all the agents have been contacted yet, and the press are all over it again, so someone might come up with something. I think we'd *all* sleep a lot easier if we actually knew where that woman was staying.'

'When we get there,' Miles was saying to Kelsey as he indicated to join the main road that cut across the north-east corner of the moor, 'we're going straight in to see the headmistress.'

Kelsey turned to look at him. 'What for?' she demanded.

'Do I need to remind you that you ran away last week while you were under her care? If nothing else you owe her an apology. Whether she hands out a punishment will be up to her.'

Kelsey looked mutinous. 'I wish I wasn't going back now,' she said sulkily. 'I mean, I'm supposed to be traumatised and upset, so putting me in detention is really going to help, isn't it?'

'I'm sure she won't do that once we've had a chat with her, but you still owe her an apology.'

Kelsey turned to stare out of the window.

After a while Miles reached out a hand, and when hers eventually slid into it he glanced over and gave her a smile. 'I'm sure you've told everyone by now that you've met Theo Kenwood-South,' he teased. 'So everyone's going to be waiting to see you.'

Blushing and rolling her eyes, she said, 'That was really cool, going to the recording and going to the green room after.' Then, after a beat, 'He's really nice, isn't he? Like, down to earth, and normal.' Smiling, she brought his hand to her cheek to rest against it. 'Yesterday was really cool too,' she told him, 'just me and you, you know, making lunch together and going for a walk. It was like we always used to.'

Having enjoyed their day together too, he gave her hand a squeeze before easing his own free to change down as they approached a slow-moving tour bus. They'd spent a lot of time talking about Jacqueline during the past thirty-six hours, going over what had been said and how Kelsey was feeling about it now. For the moment she seemed to be handling things reasonably well, but he knew that could change at any moment, particularly if Jacqueline went on ignoring her promise to give Kelsey her address.

Still, at least she'd been in touch, three times yesterday and once already this morning, so, thank God, she hadn't marked her and Sam's birthday the way he'd dreaded. He'd prefer to know where she was, however, or exactly what she was up to, but for the time being he could breathe a little more easily. Kelsey, too, seemed noticeably more relaxed, and her new crush on Theo was something of a godsend, not only for the limelight it was going to afford her at school, but for Theo's connection to Vivienne.

In fact, the subject of Vivienne and Rufus was about the only one he and Kelsey hadn't touched on during their long talk yesterday, and when he'd tried to broach it last night she'd disappeared to run a bath. Since he wanted to discuss it before she came home again on Thursday, he'd decided to take advantage of their drive back to school to attempt this. The question now was how to bring it up in a way that wasn't going to make her feel threatened, or pushed into a situation over which she had no control.

In the end, daring to hope that Jacqueline's change of heart over Vivienne might have had a positive effect on Kelsey, he said, 'We've been talking quite a lot since Saturday about Theo and his role in the slave auction . . . Well, obviously you know who's behind it all, so it stands to reason that Vivienne will be coming back to Devon this week. Yes?'

Kelsey turned to stare out at the passing scenery.

Not quite sure what that meant, he said, very gently, 'While she's here I would like you to meet Rufus. I know right now you'd rather not think of him as your brother, but that's who he is, and he's just a baby, darling. He can't hurt you, and he certainly can't ever take your place in my heart, because that's always going to be yours.' He held his breath, waiting for the explosion, but Kelsey only kept her head averted.

Choosing to feel encouraged by her silence, he pressed on

carefully. 'I was hoping,' he said, starting to tense now, 'to invite Vivienne and Rufus to stay at Moorlands when they come to Devon on Wednesday.'

To his amazement there was still no response.

'Of course that means,' he went on, bravely, 'that they'll be there when you come home on Thursday.'

By now her silence was starting to unnerve him.

'Will you have a problem with that?' he probed gently.

Turning to stare straight ahead, she said tartly, 'It's your house. You can do what you like.'

He was about to remind her that it was her house too, when he realised that her answer could, possibly, be construed as a breakthrough of sorts. Deciding to leave it there for now, he allowed a few minutes to pass before glancing in the rear-view mirror and saying, 'Luckily, no sign of the press following us.'

The tension in the car immediately evaporated as Kelsey sighed and rolled her eyes. 'That was so annoying, the way they were waiting when we left the house this morning,' she declared. 'What do they think we're going to do, stop the car and have a chat like they were our relatives, or something? I hate being in the papers about something like this, it's embarrassing.'

'But the upside is that one of them might find out where Mum is,' he pointed out, 'if he or she does their job well, especially now the police have called off the door-to-door search.'

'I hadn't thought of that,' she said, turning to look at him. 'And it's not like they haven't got a clue where to start any more, because we know she's in Richmond. So why don't you *ask* someone to do it? Not that Justine James, though,' she added quickly. 'I can't stand her.'

'I don't think anyone's going to need asking,' he remarked dryly.

Realising the truth of that, she sat quietly for a moment, then said, 'Actually, I forgot to tell you this, but you know the day they discovered Mum's bag and stuff on the moor?'

'Mm,' he responded, wondering where this could be going.

'Well, I found Justine James in your study.'

He glanced over at her in surprise.

'She said you'd given her permission to use your computer.'

Knowing full well he never had, Miles frowned.

'She was lying, wasn't she?' Kelsey prompted.

He nodded. 'Yes, she was. Did she say anything else?'

'Not really,' she answered, in a way that left him wondering if she were being completely truthful. However, he couldn't imagine her covering up to protect Justine, so guessing she and Justine had had words he turned his mind to what Justine might have found, or planted, on his computer. A few suggestions started presenting themselves, and already he could feel himself growing cold at the thought of how she might use them.

A weak mid-morning sun was slanting into the untidy garden where Justine James was standing, staring curiously down at what lay at her feet. The soil was viscous and dark, specked with grit and leaves, and bound by a hairy tangle of old roots. The hole was no more than a foot deep, scooped from beneath a hedge where wild mushrooms clustered and weeds sprouted with limited hope. The bones inside were like small sticks, lying quietly, unobtrusively, in their hollowed niche, inert tokens of a small body that had once lived and breathed, a lively spirit that had infused its magic into flesh and blood.

Beside her, Elizabeth Barrett, a short, homely woman of around sixty, waited patiently, respectfully; no sighs or shifting of weight, not even a question or comment.

As she took it all in, Justine was hearing the Critch's voice before she'd left. 'We don't want any screw-ups with this,' he'd growled. 'If the woman turns out to be a fruitcake you'd better find out now, or it'll be your funeral we're going to, not Avery's, and neither of us wants that, now do we?'

His grin had made her itch to slap his face, but she'd merely seethed behind her smile, knowing she'd already discovered much more about Mrs Barrett than she was prepared to reveal – at least for now.

'Would you like to go in again?' Elizabeth Barrett asked.

Justine inhaled sharply, then started back down a narrow path that had been trodden into the grass, gazing, as she had on the way out, at an old swing that hung crookedly from a rusty frame, the seat planks rotten, the chains ready to snap.

Once back inside the bungalow's narrow kitchen where the smell of old gravy mingled with polish and mould, she turned to look into Elizabeth Barrett's cautious eyes.

'Would you like some more tea?' Mrs Barrett offered.

'That would be nice,' Justine replied, having to cough the scratchiness from her throat.

Mrs Barrett refilled the kettle and began to rinse out the pot. 'I've kept all the cuttings from back then,' she said. 'They're in a book. I pasted them in myself, after my husband died. He didn't know I kept them, of course. He'd have made me throw them away.'

Doubting there would be anything there she hadn't already seen, Justine said, politely, 'Would I be able to take a look at them?'

'I'll get them down, when we've had our tea.'

Justine smiled her thanks and passed over the caddy Mrs Barrett was reaching for. 'So how, exactly, did you first meet Mr Avery?' she asked chattily.

Mrs Barrett blinked once or twice, then prised open the lid of the decorated tin. 'It was my husband who met him,' she replied. 'He was a security guard in the building where Mr Avery worked. They used to say good morning to one another, and pass the time of day now and then, you know how you do. Three spoons, one for each person and one for the pot.'

Justine watched the tea go in, noticing how steady the woman's fingers were, in spite of the shakiness in her voice.

'We were living in Mortlake then,' Mrs Barrett went on, passing the caddy back, 'only a couple of miles from the Averys in Richmond. Not that we ever saw them, or anything – we didn't even know it was where they lived until it all came out in the papers about their son going missing.' She blinked again, quite rapidly, as though uncertain whether she'd said what she'd meant to, then she began staring fixedly at the kettle.

Justine waited, wondering what was in her mind now, if

it was whirling like a kaleidoscope, or remaining still like a painting that faded over years, but never changed shape.

'Of course he wasn't in the car when Mrs Avery drove into the garage,' Elizabeth Barrett went on, her gaze still focused on the kettle. 'He was never there, that's why no one was seen taking him. He was at home with me. Safe and sound.' Her eyes flickered and a quick, self-conscious smile twitched her lips. 'I did my best with him,' she said. 'Mr Avery made the right choice when he brought him to me. He wanted me to take care of him, you see, so I said I would. He was afraid, he told me, of what his wife would do to him.'

While impressed by how convincing Mrs Barrett was sounding, Justine knew that it was all the tormented fabrication of a woman with a tragic past. According to police archives Elizabeth Barrett had lost her own son to a cot death, and had been imprisoned for five years before being released on appeal.

The report had gone on to detail how the investigating officers in the Avery case had checked into Elizabeth Barrett's claims when Sam had gone missing, and after establishing her background and the fact that her mental health had been affected as a result of it, they'd hushed the matter up in the hope of sparing Jacqueline Avery any more unpleasant press speculation.

Though Justine could have concocted a story from the file alone, she'd wanted to meet Mrs Barrett in person, and now she had she was forming a much clearer idea of how she was going to treat this exclusive. However, there was still a way to go, and the Critch was nobody's fool, so she knew she must tread extremely carefully now, and watch her back at all times.

The kettle began whistling, startling Mrs Barrett from her reverie, and as she poured hot water onto the tea she started talking again. 'My husband and me, we came here quite soon after we had the baby,' she said, possibly meaning her own child, but there again it could have been Sam. 'It was a bit of a tumbledown place then that Jim had inherited when his mother died. No central heating, the roof leaked, the garden was like a jungle . . . We really had our work cut out, but Mr Avery gave us a bit of money to get started, which was very nice of him.'

Justine frowned. There had been no mention of money in the police report. 'How much did he give you?' she prompted.

Mrs Barrett's head twitched slightly as she thought. 'I forget now,' she answered. 'It was a long time ago.'

Justine nodded sympathetically. 'So what actually happened to Sam?' she asked, taking two teaspoons from the drawer next to her.

Mrs Barrett gave her a quick glance. 'Sam,' she said, as though reminding herself. 'He wasn't with us nearly long enough. But they never are, are they? They come, take over your world and then they go again.' She began setting cups and saucers on a tray, followed by a packet of custard creams, a milk jug and a sugar bowl, then finally the pot. 'Shall we go and sit down?' she suggested. 'It's a bit more comfortable in the front room, next to the fire.'

Justine followed her into the sitting room, where she put the tray on top of a fireguard that caged in a small hearth of buttery-coloured tiles and glowing fake coals.

Choosing a threadbare armchair, Justine watched her hold a strainer over each cup as she poured. 'So what actually happened when . . . ?'

'Milk and sugar?'

'Just milk, thank you. When you said—'

'Biscuit?'

To be polite she took one and nibbled a piece off one corner.

Holding her cup and saucer in both hands, Mrs Barrett sat down in a facing chair and looked at Justine. 'I don't know how Mrs Avery found out where we were,' she said evenly. 'She just turned up one day when my husband was out, and I was here on my own with the baby.'

Knowing they were going deep into the realms of fantasy now, Justine said, 'What did she do when she arrived?'

At that Mrs Barrett's head went down, and for a long time she watched the tea swirling around a tiny patch of bubbles in her cup. Then, picking it up, she took a sip. 'Mr Avery said I was never to tell anyone what happened,' she answered finally. 'He came here after, with some other people, and . . . Actually, I think that was when he gave us the money, not when we moved here. It's been a long time, so it's all a bit muddled in my head now.'

'Of course,' Justine murmured.

'Anyway, as Mr Avery's lawyer, I expect you know what she did.'

Justine nodded slowly, aware that Mrs Barrett had never met Jacqueline Avery in her life. Only Miles had ever come here, with the police, after this tragically deluded woman whose dead husband had indeed once been a security guard at *The News* had begun to confuse the loss of her own child with the abduction of Sam.

Tears rose in Mrs Barrett's eyes. 'Mr Avery told me that if I accused his wife of murder again he would have to take some action against me,' she said raggedly. 'He was a powerful man, and I didn't want to go to prison or anything, so I hid the baby in the garden and never told anyone about him.'

Knowing that the bones she'd been shown belonged to a dog, Justine looked at the woman and felt vaguely fascinated by how convincing she might sound to anyone who didn't know her background. Using a gentle tone, she said, 'Are you hoping Mr Avery will give you some more money? Is that your real reason for being in touch again now?'

Mrs Barrett's gaze stayed vacantly on the fire. 'His wife's gone missing, hasn't she?' she said. 'Poor thing. I understand how she feels,' and giving a little sigh she raised her cup to drink some more tea. 'I'll go and get my albums now, shall I?' she suggested, suddenly getting to her feet. 'I won't be long. You stay there, and help yourself to another biscuit. I made them myself.'

Justine looked at the Tesco packet and started to wonder how soon she could leave. Maybe she should take a look at the albums first, she decided, out of politeness if nothing else.

Jacqueline was wearing an auburn wig now, cut boyishly short with a sixties style full fringe. Her navy gaberdine was belted at the waist, and her glasses had a neutral frame with rose-tinted lenses. She realised it was only a matter of time before someone saw through her disguise, or her landlord was tracked down to his villa in Spain, or someone from the press discovered where she was living, but she wasn't especially perturbed by this. She barely even thought about it, because her mind was in another place now, somewhere behind the candles, apart from this world.

As she walked away from St Anne's church she was listening to a message from Miles on her mobile. When it was over she turned the phone off and continued to walk, feeling the drizzle on her face, and the chill air moving about her trying to steal its way in. Nothing was getting through, however, because it was no longer possible for her to be touched by the weather, or disturbed by the noise of traffic, or moved by a conscience that might once have reacted to the anger in Miles's voice. She could feel for him if she allowed it, but she wouldn't, because all she wanted was to stay with the sense of peace that was growing all the time inside her, soothing and healing, while a golden halo of light seemed to protect her from anything that might prolong the end to her old life and confuse her purpose for the days to come.

The only connection she felt to this world now was through Kelsey. Though she didn't want to see her, she welcomed the contact between them, because they both still needed it. It was all a part of the process, a journey through forgiveness and understanding that might help Kelsey during the darkest hours ahead. *Yea, though I walk through the valley of the shadow of death* – Kelsey would only be walking through, she must not stop. Jacqueline wanted her to understand that. It was why, since Kelsey had returned to school two days ago, she'd texted her each morning and spoken with her both evenings. For now it was enough; they didn't need to go into any more detail yet.

Last night Kelsey had been chatty, as though talking to one of her friends – or even a mother with whom she'd always had a close and easy relationship. It was a fantasy in which Jacqueline had been willing to play her part, and she would continue to do so, until Kelsey understood that she could no longer be there for her. Being a good mother wasn't something to be switched on and off, dabbled around with and summoned at will. It took a lifetime's practice, and Jacqueline had made too many mistakes to be able to erase them at this late stage. Instead she was letting them go, shedding them like a skin, to emerge cleansed and whole for a new beginning.

So the separation between her and Kelsey would soon become permanent – and silent – with only the natural bond they shared holding them together. No matter how distanced they became by time or space, or how angry and alone Kelsey might sometimes feel, they would always be a part of one another. Jacqueline knew that, because of Sam. Wherever he was now, whatever had happened to him, she would always be his mother, and he would never stop being her son.

It didn't hurt to think that now, because nothing hurt any more – except how she felt about Kelsey, and Jacqueline was only waiting for that to stop hurting too.

Chapter Twenty-two

Miles was waiting at the front door as Vivienne eased her car gently over the humpback bridge that joined Moorlands' drive to the courtyard. Even before she'd turned off the Polo's engine Rufus was yelling with excitement, and Miles was laughing as he yanked open the door to scoop his son out of the baby seat into an enveloping hug.

'Welcome back,' he murmured to Vivienne, as she joined in the embrace.

'It's good to be here,' she told him, looking up into his eyes. And it truly was, to the point that emotion was tightening her throat. It was like a dream coming true, but even better than she'd imagined. She looked around at the trees and shrubs that climbed the slopes towards a pergola; the jumble of wellington boots that cluttered the back porch; the arched and leaded windows that must belong to the new kitchen extension they'd designed together. Already she was feeling the same tender attachment to the place that she'd known throughout their year together. 'Everything's looking wonderful,' she said, noticing how the pineapple sage she'd planted herself had grown to more than twice the size and was now ablaze with red flowers, while the tobacco plant next to it with its long white trumpets and huge floppy green leaves must, she knew, fill the evening air with an exquisite perfume.

Meeting his eyes, she put a hand to his face, and would have kissed him had Rufus not decided to get there first. Laughing, she said, 'Sorry we're so late. I called in to see Sharon on the way.'

'I thought you might have,' he replied, trying to avoid Rufus grabbing his mouth. 'Come inside and tell me about it. I'll unload the car after you've had something to eat.'

Vivienne grimaced. 'I'm afraid I don't have time for lunch,' she confessed. 'I have to be at the barn – or auction room as I should call it – in half an hour for a meeting with Sky. Incidentally, did Theo drop in this morning on his way to the refuge?'

'He did, and the brochures he brought with him are on my desk. What am I supposed to do with them?'

'Nothing. They're for me to add to a press release, which I'll probably have to leave until tomorrow, which is fine, because they don't need to be given out until Saturday.'

'OK. Then let Mrs Davies prepare a sandwich for you to take with you now. Are you leaving Rufus here?'

'If you don't mind.'

Miles eyed Rufus warningly. 'You'd just better behave yourself, young man,' he said gravely, 'and let's get it straight now, I'm the boss around here.'

'Mum, mum, mum,' Rufus cried delightedly.

'That's right, Rufus,' Vivienne told him. 'At least you understand.'

'Me, me,' Rufus answered, and flashed a grin that almost suggested he knew what he was saying.

Laughing, Miles said, 'I'll need instructions on what I have to do to keep him fed, watered, entertained and out of mischief while you're gone.'

Going round to open the boot, Vivienne said, 'His favourite toys are here, in this box. We've also brought a good supply of nappies – he probably needs changing right away, so I hope you're up to it – and there's plenty of food in the Tupperwares, as well as juice, milk, in fact everything any self-respecting one-year-old could wish for.'

'Oh my, what a handsome lad you are,' Mrs Davies declared, coming out of the front door. 'You must be Rufus. I've been looking forward to meeting you.'

Intrigued, Rufus's eyes widened, then in an exuberant surge he tried to throw himself at her.

Chuckling with pleasure, Mrs Davies turned to Vivienne. 'Hello, I'm Emily,' she said, holding out a hand to shake.

'Really?' Miles chipped in. 'I never knew that.'

Mrs Davies raised her eyebrows. 'I expect there's a lot about me you don't know. Probably don't want to, either,' she added to Vivienne.

Warming to the twinkly-eyed housekeeper, Vivienne clasped her hand in both of hers. 'It's lovely to meet you,' she said. 'I hope Rufus and I aren't going to add too much to your workload—'

'Pfft,' Mrs Davies interrupted. 'I've brought up four of me own, so this little fellow won't be no bother for me. Let's get you all inside now, shall we? It's turning a bit chilly out here.'

The instant Vivienne stepped across the threshold she was assailed by the familiar smell of the place, and closed her eyes to inhale deeply. It was part Miles, part woodsmoke and part something that was uniquely its own, a mix of candlewax, old wood and a vague hint of mould, and as the memories came flooding back she felt Miles's arm go around her. How could she even begin to express how happy she was to be here? She only wished it could all be as perfect as it felt.

'Any word from Jacqueline?' she asked, as Mrs Davies bustled off back to the kitchen.

'No, but she's still in regular contact with Kelsey, so I'm not feeling quite as worried any more. On the other hand, I won't relax completely until I know where she is, and what the heck her future plans might be.'

Fully understanding that, she said, 'Have you spoken to Kelsey again about me being here?'

'Not since Sunday, but I'll remind her when I call later.'

Vivienne nodded and tried to swallow her nerves as she turned to gaze around the entrance hall again, taking in its impressive collection of postmodernist paintings and the high arched window at the far end which allowed an uninterrupted view of the terraces and lawns beyond, right down to the lake. She started to smile. 'So you had it put in,' she said.

'As you can see,' he responded. 'And the window's not the only one of your ideas that I followed through. You'll find them all over the place, but if you're about to take off again the tour will have to wait. Do you have any idea what time you'll be back?'

'My guess is, it'll be late. If Rufus starts playing up, though, just call and I'll try to get back sooner.'

'I'm sure we can manage. Before you go, tell me about Sharon.'

Sighing despondently, she shook her head. 'To be truthful, I was a bit taken aback by the change in her after just a few days,' she answered. 'She's determined to try and keep her spirits up, but the effort's taking its toll, you can see that in how tired and grey she's looking. And it's not going to get any easier, because she's just told me that she has to start another course of chemo next week.'

'Oh no, I'm sorry to hear that. Still nothing positive about a donor?'

'No, but at least the auction's coming in time to provide some financial help with transport to and from the hospital, and taking care of the children. I just hope we can get it to her by next Wednesday, when her treatment's due to begin.'

'I can always bridge the gap, if necessary,' he offered. 'In fact, I'd intended to make a straight donation, so why don't I give it to you, instead of going through the official channels?'

'That would be great if Sky hadn't offered to double what we make, so we need your funds in the pot. Bridging the gap would be wonderful, though, if we need it, and we can pay you back as soon as the money's released. Now,' she went on, checking her watch, 'crash course in Rufus about to begin, then I'll have to go like the clappers if I don't want to be late.'

Half an hour later, still munching on the smoked-salmon sandwich Mrs Davies had prepared for her, she drove into the stable yard and came to a halt next to a gigantic trailer that hadn't been there before. She soon discovered it was divided into dressing rooms for the 'auction lots', while the smaller vehicle behind it was for make-up. The place was a frenzy of activity with crew and the construction team still working on the barn, the WI setting out rows of chairs or decorating their telephone tables, and Pete bossing about

Theo and six of the firemen, who were being photographed for one of the local papers.

Finding the Sky producer, Vivienne went straight into a meeting that didn't end until long after five. At that point she took a moment to call Miles, who assured her he and Rufus were getting along famously, and after being blown a couple of raspberries down the line and treated to a shriek or two, she rang off to start on the dozen or more phone calls she needed to make or return. By seven thirty, fortified by one of Stella's home-baked pasties and a glass of the production manager's Sauvignon Blanc, she shut herself up in one of the dressing rooms to begin ploughing into the emails that required attention before the morning, while Theo and the firemen took over the barn to rehearse their routines.

It was close to ten o'clock by the time she eventually turned into the drive at Moorlands, feeling exhausted, but exhilarated, as much by the hilarity she'd just left behind as to be coming home to Miles.

'Ah, at last,' Miles yawned, when she found him half asleep on the bed with a spark-out Rufus in dinosaur pyjamas beside him. 'Have you eaten? Mrs Davies made a lasagne—'

'I'm fine,' Vivienne interrupted, kicking off her shoes to lie down with him. 'Did you speak to Kelsey again?'

'Mm, I did,' he confirmed, pulling her against him. 'She still didn't have anything to say about your visit, but I've had an idea that I think might work rather well.'

'Oh? Are you going to enlighten me?'

'Absolutely, but not right now, because with his lordship out cold, I was hoping we might take advantage of this rare opportunity to spend some time focusing on us.'

'Dad, it's me,' Kelsey cried into her mobile. 'What time are you coming to pick me up?'

'Actually, I'm not,' he told her.

'Yeah, yeah, very funny. I came back for four days—' Her face suddenly froze as she realised he might not be joking. 'Oh, yeah, *she's* there, isn't she?' she said, her heart turning over as she looked across their shared room at Martha.

'Yes, Vivienne and Rufus are here,' he replied evenly. 'I told you last night they'd arrived, and I'm hoping you'll be here soon too, once Theo has collected you.'

Kelsey blinked, then her eyes rounded with awe. 'Oh my God, Dad! Are you serious?' she demanded, a rush of blood flooding her cheeks. 'Theo's coming to get me?'

Martha's mouth fell open.

'He's already on his way,' Miles informed her.

'On his motorbike?'

'On his motorbike.'

'Oh my God, oh my God, why didn't you tell me? I have to get changed. What time will he be here? Dad, you are like so dead for not telling me. What if he'd turned up and I was still in my uniform?'

'You've still got plenty of time,' Miles responded dryly, 'he only left a few minutes ago.'

Kelsey's excitement was already turning to panic. 'I have to go,' she said urgently, and without as much as a goodbye she tossed the phone onto the bed and clasped her hands to her face. 'Did you hear that?' she said to Martha. 'TKS is coming to get me. You are going to die when you see him. He is sooo fit. I mean, I know you've seen him on TV, but in real life . . . Oh my God, I think I'm going to be sick.'

Martha was laughing. Since half the school was seething with envy that Kelsey actually knew TKS, she had no problem understanding what a big deal this was for her friend. 'What are you going to wear?' she demanded. 'It'll have to be jeans if you're going on his motorbike. Shit, what about all your stuff? How are you going to get it home?'

Kelsey stared at her in horror. 'I know, I'll get Dad to bring me back tomorrow,' she declared, and overcome with excitement again she began squealing and jumping up and down. 'He is so lush, Martha. You just wait. I mean he's too old for me, I know that . . . Actually, I think he just sees me like a sister, which is OK, because I don't mind having a brother. I mean one that's older, not *Rufus*, who's apparently there at the house. I am so pissed off about that. Just because Mum suddenly thinks Vivienne's all cool and wonderful doesn't mean the rest of us have to think so too.'

'He's dead cute, though,' Martha said. 'You know, in the photos I've seen.'

Kelsey slanted her a look, then remembering Theo she started to grin again. 'I'm going to call Mum and tell her,' she suddenly decided.

Still finding Kelsey's new relationship with her mother a bit weird, Martha said, 'I'm going to make sure everyone's around when TKS turns up. They've got to see you go off on his motorbike. It's going to like so do Poppy's and Sadie's heads in, I can hardly wait.'

'Mum!' Kelsey said into the phone as she gave Martha the thumbs up. 'It's me. Guess what, you know Theo Kenwood-South, well he's only coming to pick me up from school. Isn't that amazing? It's all right, you don't have to call me back or anything, because I'll probably be on my way home. I just wanted you to know. Um, I'll speak to you later, OK? Uh – hope everything's cool with you.'

As she rang off she felt an odd sort of feeling starting to creep over her, like a chill mist coming out of nowhere. Well, maybe not nowhere, because she knew it was to do with still not knowing what was going on with her mum, or even where she was, exactly. It was odd the way she wouldn't tell anyone, a bit spooky even, except Mum did listen to her messages now, and usually she rang back within an hour, or less. So it was all right really. There was nothing to worry about, and feeling herself being scooped up by another wave of euphoria she tore open her recently packed suitcase to begin rummaging around for her new Seven jeans, and the black top with cut-out shoulders that she could wear under the leather jacket her dad had bought her in Italy last year. It had only been the two of them, because her mum hadn't wanted to come . . .

'Word's going round faster than Lynette Howard can grow spots,' Martha informed her, bouncing back into the room. 'Everyone's like, *oh my God.*'

Kelsey's eyes sparkled. 'You know what, I don't even really care that *she's* going to be there when I get home,' she declared rashly. Then, after considering that for a moment, 'Actually, it's going to be a bit weird seeing Dad with Rufus the dufus, knowing he's like his and all that.'

'Oh it'll be fine,' Martha told her. 'He's just a baby. Theo's the one you need to be worrying about. Have you decided what you're going to wear yet?'

Kelsey was back in her suitcase. 'Oh look, I'd forgotten all about this red top,' she cried, holding it up. 'It is soooo lush. I have to wear it. Or maybe I should save it for Saturday. You're definitely coming to the auction, aren't you? Dad's reserved us places right in the front row, he said.'

'Are you kidding? I'm definitely going to be there. But what about *her*? Won't she be there too?'

'Oh, we'll just ignore her. With any luck she might go away.'

Martha giggled, more because she was expected to than because it was funny. 'You know what,' she said, getting on with her own packing, 'I hope you don't mind me saying, but I'm still finding it a bit freaky the way you're suddenly OK with your mum. I mean, like she was always really cool with me and my parents, but you two were always at one another . . .'

'Actually, I think she's got God,' Kelsey informed her, whilst wriggling out of her old jeans. 'Or they've put her on new medication or something. Anyway, whatever, she'll probably go nutso again any time now, so don't get too worried. I know I'm not.'

Martha glanced up at her but she didn't say anything, even though she knew that Kelsey really was worried about her mum. However, Martha could understand why she wouldn't want to talk about it now. Who would, when Theo Kenwood-South was on his way to pick her up?

Until the moment she sauntered out of the school's ancient front doors to find Theo waiting next to his motorbike, surrounded by younger girls clamouring for his autograph, Kelsey had never really understood what a true high was. It was like floating on air, she found. She was a movie star, a pop idol, the most important person in the world. Her heart was tripping and she was finding it nearly impossible to stop smiling and stay cool, though she was shaking and still felt a bit sick inside. It wasn't only the way a path started opening up for her to go through, it was knowing that apart from the girls already stumbling towards their parents' cars, and those who'd come out purposely to get near him, every window in the school had faces pressed to it not wanting to miss the big event.

Being too shy to look at him, Kelsey kept her head down as she walked, glancing out occasionally, but hardly registering a thing. When she reached him her elation soared to new heights as he took the small bag she was carrying, before handing her a helmet to put on.

Seconds later they were roaring out through the school gates, her arms clasped around his waist, her head resting against his back and her heart just about ready to burst.

Having thoroughly approved of Miles's idea of Theo going to collect Kelsey, Vivienne was now daring to hope that when Kelsey came in she might be distracted, or even bedazzled enough, not to care about anyone or anything besides her new crush. And even if she did, while Theo was around surely the worst Kelsey would be was sulky and silent rather than downright rude.

That was Vivienne's hope . . .

Nevertheless, she couldn't remember when she'd last felt this nervous. There had been so much discussion about how and where to greet Kelsey, which room, who should be there and who shouldn't, that by the time they heard the motorbike coming up the drive Vivienne was about ready to bolt back to the refuge. She was by now under no illusion: no matter how warm or carefully planned this homecoming might be, Kelsey still wouldn't accept her. This didn't mean she, Vivienne, wasn't going to try to make the next few minutes go as smoothly as possible, she'd just rather, given the choice, be almost anywhere else in the world.

'It's going to be fine,' Miles whispered, putting an arm around her.

'Easy for you to say when you're the hero on her pedestal,' Vivienne murmured through yet another fluttering of nerves. 'Still, at least she's not getting me and Rufus all in one go.'

'Maybe that would have been too much,' Miles conceded,

'but it's going to happen, and sooner rather than later, especially if he wakes up in the next ten minutes.'

'He wouldn't,' Vivienne said. 'He's my son, he knows when he needs to give his mother a break.'

Miles laughed and touched his mouth to hers. 'No running back to the cider press,' he warned.

Vivienne's eyes came guiltily to his.

'I can read your mind,' he informed her. 'But you've promised the place to Alice and Angus for the weekend now, and besides, this is where you belong.'

'Try telling your daughter that.'

'I'm about to, if forced.'

At the sound of the front door opening, Vivienne's face visibly paled. 'Our father who art in heaven,' she began, making both herself and Miles laugh.

'She's a fourteen-year-old girl,' he reminded her.

'And you don't get how much worse that makes it?'

'You can handle it,' he whispered, and letting her go, he turned round ready to greet his daughter. He knew he was probably every bit as anxious as Vivienne, but was, for the moment anyway, doing a better job of hiding it.

Outside in the hall Kelsey was saying to Theo, 'If she's in there I'm sorry, but I'm just walking out again.'

'No you're not,' Theo informed her firmly. 'You're going to be polite and charming and give your dad the kind of hug you normally do.'

'I am so not hugging her.'

'No one's asking you to, least of all her.'

Kelsey's eyes flashed. 'Like she gets a choice?'

'Will you just go in there?'

Kelsey turned towards the door, but moved no further. 'You first,' she said. 'No, hang on, what am I supposed to do if Rufus the dufus is there? There's like no way I can pretend he's my brother.'

'Where's the pretence?'

'You know what I mean.'

'You understand me too, now get yourself in there and at least say hello.'

*

As the door opened Vivienne's heart felt as though it was ducking for cover. *Just remember she's fourteen and you're an adult,* she willed herself silently, *and it's not as though you've never met before. OK, she didn't like you then, but there were occasional moments when she was less hostile.* Not that Vivienne could think of a single one offhand, but she knew they'd happened, so hanging onto that thought she summoned a warm, welcoming smile and managed to sustain it until the moment Kelsey came into the room behind Theo. That was when she knew, beyond a shadow of doubt, that it was going to be all uphill from here.

Still struggling with her smile, she watched Miles embrace his daughter as though she were a prodigal returned. It was overdone and they all knew it, but everyone was on edge. Vivienne's eyes flicked hopefully to Theo, but though his expression was eloquent, she couldn't work out what he was trying to tell her.

'You've met Vivienne before,' Miles was saying as he eased Kelsey in Vivienne's direction. 'She's in charge of Theo's auction at the moment, as you know, so all I can say is Theo better watch out.'

It was such an astonishing banality for Miles that Vivienne could only blink, while Kelsey rolled her eyes and turned her head aside with a superior sigh.

Collecting herself quickly, Vivienne said, 'Hello Kelsey, it's lovely to see you again.'

Kelsey pursed a corner of her mouth and looked everywhere but at Vivienne.

'Kelsey?' Miles prompted.

'Oh sorry, like you want me to pretend,' she said, as though just getting it. 'OK, fine. If that's what I have to do, hello Vivienne, it's nice to see you – *not*.'

Vivienne coloured, but as Miles drew breath she quickly stepped forward. 'No don't, it's all right,' she told him.

'No it isn't,' he corrected. 'Kelsey, I'm not going to tolerate that kind of rudeness—'

'So don't! See if I care. I'll just go and live with Mum.'

'Actually, you'll go to your room, is what you'll do,' he told her sharply.

'Great,' but as she made to flounce off Miles grabbed her arm.

'You'll apologise before you go,' he said furiously.

'No way,' she spat.

Theo said, 'Kelsey, why don't you just give her a break? She hasn't done—'

Vivienne cut in. 'Kelsey's obviously upset, so why shouldn't she show it? I'd rather that than have you pretend to like me,' she said directly to Kelsey. 'At least this way we know where we stand.'

Kelsey's face was a mask of insolence.

'Just so's it's clear,' Vivienne said pedantically, 'my position is that I'd like us to be friends, while yours is to make sure we're enemies.'

'What-*ever*.'

'OK. You realise that's going to hurt your dad a lot more than—'

'He's made his choice. I didn't ask you to come here—'

'That's enough,' Miles growled angrily. 'Kelsey, leave the room now, and don't even think about coming back until you're ready to apologise.'

'Well that won't be any time soon,' she snarled, and spinning on her heel she stormed out of the door.

Looking helplessly at Vivienne, Theo said, 'I'm sorry, I did my best—'

'It's not for you to be sorry,' Miles interrupted tightly. 'I thought she might behave a little more courteously with you around, but apparently I was wrong. So it's for me to offer you an apology.'

'It's cool,' Theo assured him. 'Shall I go and see if I can reason with her?'

Miles shook his head. 'I'll go when she's had a few minutes to stew,' he said. Then to Vivienne, 'I didn't expect it to be quite that bad. I'm sorry.'

'It's just going to take time,' she assured him, trying to play it down despite now being horribly torn about whether it was wise for her and Rufus to stay any longer. Then, remembering Rufus asleep upstairs, 'She won't go into your room, will she?' she asked anxiously.

'I doubt it.'

'Maybe I should go and check on him anyway.'

After closing the door behind her she stood in the hall taking a deep, steadying breath, not having realised until then quite how shaken she was. Clearly Kelsey was terrified of anyone coming between her and her father, but though Vivienne could understand it, she didn't, for the moment, have a clue how to handle it.

As she began climbing the stairs she was wondering how Miles would take it if she told him she and Rufus were moving out. The trouble was, it might create even more tension between him and Kelsey, and maybe it wasn't a good idea to let Kelsey think she could rule her father's life with tantrums and rudeness. However, while she was going through this difficult period with her mother . . .

She'd arrived on the landing and was passing Kelsey's room as quietly as possible when the door suddenly opened and Kelsey came out.

'Oh my God, what are *you* doing here?' Kelsey spat, recoiling as though she'd just walked into a snake. 'I so don't have anything to say to you. In fact I can't even believe you've got the nerve to come up here.'

'Kelsey, I'm not—'

'Just when Mum's starting to get herself together, you have to turn up again. Well, we don't want you here, OK? So why don't you just go, and take that stupid kid of yours with his stupid name with you. In fact, I bet he's not even Dad's, you're just saying that—' She gasped and turned white as Miles came charging up the stairs. 'Don't touch me,' she cried, shrinking back as he came across the landing.

'Get in that room now,' he raged. 'I've had as much as I'm going to take from you, young lady—'

'Well that's good because I'm leaving.'

'In that room now,' he seethed, and moving straight past Vivienne he slammed a hand into the door before Kelsey could bang it shut. 'Oh no, you're going to listen to me,' he told her, and pushing her out of the way he closed the door behind him and marched her over to the bed. 'Sit there,' he barked furiously.

'I am not—'

'Do as you are told, or you can forget going to camera rehearsals with Theo tonight.'

Startled, since she hadn't even known she was invited, she said, 'You can't threaten me—'

'I can, I will and I just have. Now sit there and calm down.'

'*Me* calm down, what about you?'

'You'll learn to curb your tongue or your privileges will be whipped away so fast it'll make your head spin.'

'If I'm living with Mum it won't be up to you. In fact, I'm going to call her right now and tell her you're abusing me.'

'*Think* before you use words like that,' he snapped. 'They're dangerous and could cause a whole lot more trouble than either of us could handle.'

'Well, you are! Look at you, standing there shouting at me.' Her face started to crumple. 'It's not fair. You always blame me for everything, and it's not my fault. I didn't ask her to come here, and I didn't ask you to have any more children, but now you're making me live with them and I don't want to. This is my house, and Mum's, not theirs.'

'Of course it's yours,' he said, his temper dissolving as he went to sit beside her. 'No one's ever going to dispute that.'

'So why do they have to come here?'

'You know why.'

'No I don't.'

He took a breath, and putting an arm around her, he said, 'Look, I understand this is difficult for you . . .'

'No you don't. You're not thinking about me at all. You're taking her side all the time.'

'You make it hard to take yours when you're being rude and offensive. So tell me how I can defend that.'

Her jaw clenched as she jerked her head away.

'At least Vivienne's prepared to give it a try,' he coaxed gently. 'I wish you would too.'

'I don't want to.'

'Not even for my sake?'

'No, because you'll just keep picking on me, no matter what I do.'

'You know that's not true.'

'Yes it is.'

'Have I ever treated you unfairly before?'

'All the time.'

At that he smiled, and saw her mouth twitch too before she turned away.

'It's not funny,' she growled.

'No, it's not. It's actually quite serious, because we have to find a way to live together, all of us, and for that to happen we've got to make some extra effort.'

'Yeah, and like *Rufus* is going to do that.'

'Darling, try not to make stupid remarks. They're not helpful and—'

'See, when *I* say something it's stupid—'

'If you're asking me to point out the obvious, that he's a baby and you're practically an adult, then there you have it. Frankly, I'd prefer you to act your age, but for the moment you seem to have other ideas. Let's hope it changes when you go to the rehearsal with Theo tonight, because you've already shown him a side of you I think he'd rather not have seen.'

'I told him I didn't want to see her,' she retorted, flushing angrily, 'but he made me go in.'

'Ah, so now you're trying to make your bad behaviour his fault?'

'That's not what I said.'

'It's what it sounded like, so once again, think before you speak. There's only one person who bears responsibility for the way you spoke to Vivienne and that's *you*.'

'There you go again, sticking up for her and making me in the wrong,' she wailed, tears filling her eyes.

'Then explain to me how you were in the right.'

'*No*! I don't want to talk about it any more. You always twist things round to make them my fault so what's the point. Anyway, I'm going to call Mum now because I know you don't want me here, so I'm going to ask if I can go to live with her, then I'll see if Theo will take me up to London on his motorbike.'

'Call Mum by all means, but even if you can find out where she is, Theo has other commitments tonight.'

'So I'll get the train.'

He stood up and walked across the room.

'What are you doing?' she asked uneasily.

'Here's the phone,' he said, holding out her extension.

Her eyes came up to his. 'Is that like, because you really want me to go?' she said, a little less cocky now.

'No, it's because I want to find out where your mother is, and I think we stand a better chance of her telling you than me. Then you can go off to the rehearsal with Theo, as planned.'

She swallowed her tears, and wiped her face with the back of a hand. 'Her number's in my mobile,' she said.

'Which is where?'

'Downstairs in my bag, with my make-up. Dad, I can't go down there like this. My mascara's bound to have run and anyway, I don't want to bump into *her*.'

Taking a deep breath rather than argue any more, he said, 'OK, I'll go, but don't think you've got away with not apologising, Kelsey, because you're actually not going anywhere until you have.'

'No, Miles,' Vivienne said, when he came into the bedroom to find her. 'Forcing her to say sorry will just make things worse. Let her go off with Theo for now. They're having so much fun over there that she'll probably be in a much better frame of mind by the time she comes back.'

'Aren't you going?' he asked, taking Rufus from her.

'There's nothing for me to do tonight, and it would ruin it for her if I did.'

Sighing, he gazed down at Rufus's sleepy face and said, 'Promise me, young man, that when you get to be a teenager, you'll be easier.'

Rufus yawned and burped, making him smile.

'So what happened when she tried calling Jacqueline?' Vivienne said, keeping her voice down even though Kelsey was across the landing behind the closed door of her own room.

'She got flipped through to voicemail, but she says that's normal and Jacqueline usually rings straight back. I just wish she'd damned well call *me* back, because God knows I've left enough messages.' He sighed again, and hoisted Rufus onto one shoulder. 'What is she playing at?' he growled quietly. 'If she wants to set up home in Richmond I'm hardly going to stand in her way. In fact, I'll help her, if she needs it.'

Dabbing some drool from his collar, Vivienne said, 'Has it occurred to you that we could be handling this all wrong with Kelsey? We should be giving her more time to get used to the idea of me and Rufus, especially while her relationship with Jacqueline is going through this . . . well, new phase.'

His face was inscrutable as he turned to stare down at the lake.

'If she got to know Rufus more gradually,' Vivienne continued, 'and in a different environment, rather than her own home, she might not feel quite so threatened.'

'She's away all week,' he reminded her, 'and you're in London, so are you suggesting you don't come here at weekends? We'd never see one another.'

'You'll be in London some of the time, and if things work out between her and Jacqueline, she'll probably go there at least every other weekend.'

Turning to look at her, he said, 'She doesn't deserve how considerate you're being, but I'm thanking you for it anyway.'

'I just want it all to work out,' she told him softly. 'Now, why don't you go and find out if Jacqueline's called back yet, while I manoeuvre his lordship into a fresher-smelling nappy?'

A few minutes later Miles returned, looking slightly less strained as he closed the door behind him. 'Yes, she's spoken to her,' he said, and started to laugh as a little fountain sprang up from the semi-naked Rufus. 'Apparently Jacqueline's still in Richmond, and she says Kelsey can go there whenever she likes, just not yet.'

'Mm,' Vivienne responded, searching for the baby wipes. 'So what are we to conclude from that?'

'You tell me.'

'Well, she could be having some kind of counselling, or therapy, which needs to reach a certain stage, or even completion, before she'll be ready to interact with her family again.'

He shrugged. 'It's one explanation, but if it is the case, why not say so?'

Unable to answer that, Vivienne decided to voice what she knew was in both their minds. 'You're still afraid she has something else planned, aren't you?' she said. 'Even though the joint birthdays have passed.'

Miles nodded gravely. 'I can't think of any other reason for her to be so secretive about where she is.' Then, with a sigh, 'I felt sure someone from the press would have tracked her down by now.'

'Are the police still looking?'

'Not with the same urgency as at the weekend. She's been in touch, assured them she's not intending to harm herself, and asked to be left alone. So what can they do?'

Vivienne shook her head, and not wanting to point out that even if they knew where Jacqueline was, they couldn't keep a twenty-four-hour watch on her, she said, 'How was Kelsey after she'd spoken to her?'

'She seemed OK, but to have behaved the way she did earlier tells us she's feeling more anxious and insecure than ever.'

'Which is hardly surprising. What's she doing now?'

'Getting ready to go off with Theo, but not, she tells me, before she's fed the ducks and introduced him to Henrietta.'

'Who?' Then, remembering the abandoned goose, 'Oh yes, I'd forgotten all about Henrietta. Did the Canadas ever come back?'

'No,' Miles replied, coming to kneel down next to the bed, 'but I don't think we've given up hope yet, have we Rufus?'

As she sat back on her heels to let him take over the clean-up, Vivienne was recalling the rare moment of closeness she and Kelsey had shared the day they'd watched the heart-rending spectacle of a little gosling being left behind by its mother. No, she thought to herself, we certainly won't give up hope yet.

Chapter Twenty-three

It was late on Friday evening when Miles returned to Moorlands with Kelsey, having just collected her luggage from school, and Martha from her parents' house near Dawlish. No one else was at home, as Vivienne had taken Rufus over to the refuge where final rehearsals were under way before the next morning's live transmission, and Mrs Davies had gone with them.

Though there had been no more unpleasant scenes that day, it was mainly because Kelsey was doing her level best to avoid seeing or speaking to Vivienne. However, Miles had spotted her at her bedroom window in the afternoon, watching him kicking a ball about with Rufus, and though she'd shaken her head when he'd beckoned her down to join them, she hadn't disappeared from view. Nor had she rebuffed him when he'd gone to her room later, needing to make sure she wasn't feeling neglected. True, her mood had been prickly, but she hadn't seemed quite as hostile as the day before, even if her tone was meant to convey that she had no intention of being friends.

'I've told Mum they're here,' she'd said, as though throwing out a challenge.

'Really?' he'd responded affably. 'What did she say?'

'That she wasn't surprised.'

'Oh.' Then, after a beat, 'Is that all?'

The way she shrugged suggested to him that Jacqueline might have urged her to try and make friends, but if she had, Kelsey obviously wasn't going to admit it.

'How is she?' he asked, as Kelsey had started to get ready to go out with him.

'OK. Actually, she's going to watch the auction tomorrow, just in case I'm in shot.'

'Well, you're in the front row, so you could be.'

She carried on applying her mascara. 'Does that mean I'm going to be near *her*?' she asked sourly.

'If you mean Vivienne, then I believe you won't be far away.'

'Where are you?'

'Actually, in between the two of you, and I'm still trying to work out whether that's the wisest, or most dangerous place to be.'

Though she'd tried not to laugh she hadn't succeeded, but before he could get through any further, she'd punched his arm and disappeared into the bathroom. He'd known then that she really didn't want the bad feeling to continue, she just needed to find a way to back down without losing too much face.

Now, as they got out of the car, Kelsey clearly had other things on her mind for she and Martha could barely contain their excitement over tomorrow's big event.

'Theo looks so cool in his trunks and goggles,' Kelsey was whispering as they followed him into the hall. 'And he's a fantastic dancer, I saw him at rehearsals last night. Actually, they all are, and there's this one fireman, Percy, he—'

'*Percy!*'

'I know, wild isn't it, but honestly, he is sooo fit. He's good at electrics apparently, so if you need rewiring . . .'

Martha smothered a snort of laughter. 'Light me up, baby,' she sniggered, and they went off into paroxysms.

'Go on up to my room,' Kelsey said, 'I just need to sort out about later,' and following Miles into his study where he was playing back his messages, she said, 'Dad, is it OK if Martha and I go to the Nobody after rehearsals, with the others? Everyone's going and I expect we can get a lift from—' She stopped as his hand went up. 'What?' she said, feeling suddenly nervous at the look on his face.

After hitting the button he replayed the last message.

'Miles, it's Justine. There's something you need to know. You'd better call me back as soon as you can.'

Stopping the machine, he picked up the phone.

Uppermost in his mind was the fact that Justine had accessed his computer – or perhaps she'd found Jacqueline . . . 'It's Miles,' he said when she answered.

'Hang on, I'll pull over.' Then, a few moments later, 'You got my message?'

'I did.'

'OK. So does the name Elizabeth Barrett mean anything to you?'

Miles became very still. His eyes went to Kelsey as he said, 'I'd rather ask why it means something to you.'

'She's the focus of the Critch's front page on Sunday.'

Miles's heart skipped a beat. 'But how . . .?' Then, not bothering to go there, since they obviously knew who the woman was, 'It was established at the time that she wasn't creditable . . .'

'She's saying you gave her money to keep quiet.'

Shock reverberated through him. 'That's absolutely untrue,' he said. 'Now let me ask you this, how did you find out about Elizabeth Barrett? It was never made public.'

'The Critch has a police source.'

'I'm sure he has, but you need to know the right questions to ask. So answer me this, did you seriously think Kelsey wouldn't tell me she found you using my computer?'

There was a fraction of a pause, but it was enough to tell him how she'd first learned about Elizabeth Barrett.

'Spare me the lies, Justine,' he said, cutting off whatever she'd been about to say. 'The timing is too much of a coincidence. You were *trespassing* in my house, going through my personal files, and probably thought you'd hit gold when you stumbled upon something from that woman. Well, you must know by now that she isn't sane, so perhaps you'd like to tell me how you and the Critch are proposing to handle a story that has neither substance nor newsworthiness.'

'The story's all his,' she insisted.

'Just answer the question.'

She took an audible breath. 'OK, he's running it as a kind of sympathy piece. You know, what families like yours have to go through when a child is abducted . . .'

'And that's a front page? Try again.'

'All right. He's going to run her allegations and accusations, not as truth, but, like I said, as an example of what can happen when families are traumatised by the loss of a child. Elizabeth Barrett and Jacqueline have both suffered mentally since losing their sons . . .'

By now Miles's face was taut with fury, but with Kelsey there he had to try and hold onto his temper.

'He's also going to be asking questions,' Justine continued.

'What kind of questions?'

'You'll have heard them before. Was Sam really in the car when Jacqueline drove into the garage? Why were there no witnesses when it was on a busy roundabout? How come there's never been any sign of him since?'

'You do realise what this could do to her, don't you?'

'I have pointed it out, but you know the Critch. He's going to use the cover-up over Elizabeth Barrett's allegations to ask if it's connected in any way to the fact that Jacqueline's missing now.'

'But she isn't.'

'You don't know where she is, and actually, the police have confirmed that she's still considered a missing person.'

'The fact that they haven't seen her might be distorting their view,' he retorted, 'but as I've seen her myself and she's in regular contact with Kelsey . . . Actually, I'm not getting into this with you. I'll just tell you this, Justine, if that story goes to print my lawyers will hit you and your editor so damned hard you'll be lucky not to end up behind bars.'

As he banged down the phone he tried to keep his voice even as he said to Kelsey, 'Call your mother. If she doesn't answer, tell her she has to ring you straight back.'

'Why?' Kelsey asked, sounding as worried as she looked.

'Just do it,' he snapped.

Obediently Kelsey took out her mobile and pressed in the number. After going through to voicemail she said, 'Mum, it's me. Please call me back.' She jumped as Miles grabbed the phone. 'Jacqueline, I have to speak to you,' he said urgently. 'Gareth Critchley has found Elizabeth Barrett. I don't know if I can stop the article, but I'm going to do my best.'

Taking the phone back, Kelsey said, 'Dad, what's happening? You're scaring me.'

Sighing, he dragged his hands over his face. 'It'll be all right,' he said. 'Go on upstairs and get ready now. I'll order a taxi to take you and Martha to the barn.'

'I thought you were coming?'

'I need to make some calls. If it's not too late by the time I've finished I'll join you there.'

After she'd left the room he immediately picked up the phone again, not bothering to try his lawyer's office at this time on a Friday, but going straight to Stefan's mobile. He got the voicemail, so left a brief message explaining the urgency, then rang off and called Vivienne.

'What's wrong?' she said, picking up straight away on the tone of his voice.

After telling her about the call from Justine, he said, 'I'm going to try to get an injunction, but the man's no fool. It's the weekend, so it'll be next to impossible, even if I had grounds, and it's not likely he's left me any.'

'You've tried calling Jacqueline to warn her?'

'Kelsey has. We're waiting for her to ring back.' Suddenly aware of how tense he was, he said, 'It was bad enough when that damned woman dragged it all up again, years after Sam was taken. It didn't make the papers, but we saw it all . . . The claims she made that Sam was never in the car; that I'd taken him to her to keep him safe from his mother; that Jacqueline tracked him down and smothered him . . . It was crazy, but the police had to check it out. Once they established the woman's history they hushed it all up, which, frankly, they more than owed us after what they'd put us through.' He fought back a surge of anger as he pictured Sunday's front page. 'And now, all these years later, it's coming to light,' he said bitterly. 'There must have been an email on my computer the day Justine broke in here that even I hadn't seen, and she's got the nerve to call and tip me off, as though it's all down to the Critch.'

'Which means she has to be playing a double game,' Vivienne pointed out. 'The Critch has the story, you have the tip-off . . .'

'Whatever she's doing, my only concern now is

Jacqueline. If that story runs, then however it's worded, I don't really want to think about the kind of effect it might have on her.'

By the following morning Miles's lawyer was busy trying to obtain an injunction, while Miles himself pulled what strings he could in an effort to get hold of an advance copy of the story. So far neither of them was having much success, but at least Jacqueline had been in touch the night before, by text to Kelsey.

```
Tell Dad not to worry. Will be looking out for
you on TV tomorrow. Mum x
```

'I suppose it's gone some way to putting my mind at rest,' Miles was saying as he drove Vivienne and Rufus over to the barn. 'At least it won't come as a shock now. She knows it's happening and can avoid the paper if she chooses.'

'Which I'm sure she will,' Vivienne responded, turning to hand Rufus back the plastic hammer he'd just flung into her lap. 'Did you call the police before we left?'

'Yes, I spoke to Sadler. He can't order another house-to-house now she's asked for privacy, but he assures me they're still on the case, talking to estate agents, local traders, taxi firms. All by phone, of course, which isn't very satisfactory, but it's better than nothing. Actually, he knew about Elizabeth Barrett already, because he's seen the files, so he understood why I'm so worried.'

'Did you mention you're thinking of calling in a private detective?'

'No, I'm still waiting to hear back from Stefan on that, but even if he manages to hire someone today, the chances of them finding her before tomorrow have to be virtually non-existent.'

Vivienne glanced over at him, knowing he was far more concerned than he was prepared to admit. 'If you want to drop me and Rufus at the refuge and go on to London to try and find her . . .'

'Believe me, I've considered it, but what good will it do?

I'm in the same boat as everyone else, I don't actually know where to start, apart from Richmond, of course, and it's a big place. Not to mention that we don't even know for certain that that's where she is.'

Sighing, Vivienne reached into her bag for a tissue to wipe Rufus's mouth. 'Well, like you said, at least she's prepared, and she doesn't have to read it. In fact I feel certain she won't now you've forewarned her.'

Hoping she was right, he let the subject drop as he indicated to turn into the horse sanctuary, where the courtyard was already as crowded with vehicles as it was with people.

'You'll have to park over there,' Vivienne said, pointing him past the chaos to a patch of wasteland next to an enormous fire engine. It had been brought in for the children's entertainment, to be supervised by the firemen not taking part in the auction, while their wives and girlfriends organised sedate trots around the manège on the ageing horses. 'I wonder if Sharon and Stella are here yet?' she said, looking around.

'Did Sharon make the camera rehearsal last night?' he asked, bringing the car to a stop.

'She did, but she was exhausted by the end of it. Stella started threatening to organise a wheelchair for today, but the last I heard Sharon was refusing to have anything to do with it. "I'm turning up on me own two pins," she said, "or I'm not turning up at all."'

With a smile Miles went to lift Rufus from the back seat, while Vivienne retrieved her briefcase and a pile of brochures from the boot. After making sure they had everything they needed, she kissed them both and left them to their own devices, while she hurried off to join the frenetic build-up to transmission.

The barn's interior turned out to be an even bigger mêlée of activity than the area outside as it underwent its spectacular transformation into a TV studio-cum-saleroom. Lights, cables, cranes and scaffolding were scattered about all over the place, while the auctioneer's stand was being miked up, and tracks were laid either side of the catwalk for the cameras. Even though it was still early many excited punters were already bustling into their seats, determined not to have them stolen, while representatives of the bone-marrow trust that was lending its charitable status were setting up a stand at the back of the room.

After leaving some of her brochures with them, Vivienne deposited the rest with the volunteers who'd offered to hand them out, then went over to join Pete in the area designated for manning the phones. He was listening closely as the WI ladies, who were already at their stations, received a last-minute briefing from two experts provided by Sotheby's.

'Did Alice and Angus manage to get here last night?' Vivienne whispered in his ear.

'Yep, but it was after midnight,' he replied. 'They've gone to collect Kayla from the station now.'

Smiling her thanks Vivienne left him to it, and went to make sure the seating area set aside for the invited press was stocked with brochures, photographs and all the necessary contact information.

By the time Stella and Sharon arrived at nine, minus a wheelchair, the refuge was teeming with so many people it seemed doubtful everyone would fit in.

'What a blooming turnout,' Stella chuckled, after forcing a path through the crowd to Vivienne. 'And look at our girl, in't she a treat? Had her hair done specially at eight o'clock this morning, she did.'

Though Sharon's wig seemed larger than ever, it had been prettily styled, and to Vivienne's relief her cheeks had regained some colour, after being chalk-white by the time she'd left rehearsals last night. Nevertheless, she was still sunken-eyed and very fragile-looking, and, Vivienne noted, she wasn't letting go of Stella's arm.

'Don't you start thinking I was at the hairdresser's at that time,' Sharon said, her tone conveying mischief, 'it was just me wig what went. Eileen took it over, and Stella brought it back. Now how's that for a bit of slavery?'

'Nothing like what we'm hoping to get here today,' Stella chuckled, rubbing her big hands together as she looked around.

'I hope you brought your chequebook,' Vivienne teased. 'The opening bids are already high, and going up all the time, from what I hear. Apparently they're starting at five thousand for Theo.'

Stella gave a squawk of merry protest. 'How the bleedin' 'ell am I going to afford the gorgeous bugger now?' she demanded. 'I was buying him for our Sharon, I was.'

'Pfff,' Sharon retorted. 'You was after him for yourself, everyone knows that. Anyway, you can't even swim.'

Laughing, Vivienne said, 'Where are your children? Didn't they come?'

'They was whisked off by the firemen, soon as I got here,' she answered, stumbling against Stella as someone barged past.

'Blimey, it's a squash in 'ere,' Stella grumbled. 'I s'pose we ought to find out where they wants us to sit. They changed it half a dozen times during last night's rehearsal, so for all I know we could be up on the catwalk with the crumpet by now.'

'You should probably go through to make-up,' Vivienne advised. 'They might want to fluff you up and powder you down before you go on air. It's in the green trailer at the back of the car park.'

'What about wardrobe?' Stella asked, winking at Miles as he pushed his way through with Rufus to join them. 'I've brought me thong for a spot of pole-dancing, if they wants it. I've already got it on if you're up for a quick butcher's.'

Vivienne gave a choke of laughter as Miles blanched.

'Come on, you wicked old tart,' Sharon said, tugging Stella's arm. 'I needs a bit of make-up even if you don't.'

As they merged back into the crowd Vivienne took an electrified Rufus from Miles and treated him to a resounding kiss on the cheek. 'Looks like you're enjoying yourself, young man,' she laughed, squeezing him hard. Then to Miles, 'Any news from Stefan?'

'No injunction,' Miles responded.

Knowing how disappointed he must be, even though he hadn't really expected one, Vivienne reached for his hand. 'It'll be OK,' she said softly.

He nodded and attempted a smile. 'If we were talking

about any other editor,' he said, 'I might try appealing to his better nature, but as the Critch doesn't have one, there's not a lot of point. Incidentally, Kelsey and Martha have just arrived with Mrs Davies and her husband.'

Experiencing a flutter of anxiety, Vivienne said, 'Then maybe I'd better hang onto Rufus for now. You don't want to be bumping into Kelsey when you're holding him.'

Miles's expression became droll as he said, 'Don't worry, she's going to be far too interested in what's happening on stage to notice anyone else, but he's all yours for the moment. I've just spotted Al Kohler over at the catering truck.'

As he disappeared into the crowd Vivienne turned to find Reg, the auctioneer, heading her way, and immediately started to grin. His whiskers had clearly been waxed and curled for the big occasion, while his outfit might have come from a Tyrolean drag museum.

'Where on earth did you get the lederhosen?' she laughed, giving him a good lookover. 'Do you have a hat to go with it?'

'Course I do,' he answered, sweeping it up onto his head. 'Got the feather fresh from one of me own pheasants this morning, I did. Anyway, I keeps meaning to tell you about them paintings Mrs Avery brought in. You know, the ones her great-aunt did, and my missus bought one. Well, that's where the name Anne Cates came from, because it's there, large as life in the corner of our landscape.'

Not having the heart to let on that they already knew, Vivienne said, 'I'll be sure to tell Miles. Great piece of detective work, Reg, and I hear you're an even better auctioneer.'

'Christie's are going to be head-hunting him after today,' Pete declared, as he came to join them, 'if the pheasant you plucked that feather from doesn't get in first. What do you look like, Reg?'

'Good, innit?' Reg beamed, running his hands down over the frills around his bib front. 'The director said he'd never seen anything like it.'

'I doubt any of us has,' Pete muttered. 'Anyway, you're wanted in position now, so if you're ready, maestro . . . Got your hammer?'

'It's on me podium, unless some bugger's nicked it.'

As they squeezed off through the crowd Vivienne turned round to search for Alice and Angus, and to her alarm almost collided with Kelsey. 'Oh, hi,' she said awkwardly, clutching Rufus more tightly to her and praying Kelsey wouldn't start creating a scene.

Kelsey's eyes flicked to Rufus, then grabbing Martha's arm she dragged her off in another direction.

'Goodness, that went well,' Alice commented, coming up behind her. 'Hello my darling,' she cooed at Rufus. 'Are you enjoying all the fun?'

'Nan, nan, brrrrr,' Rufus bubbled, clapping his fists.

'No, not your nana, your godma,' Alice corrected. 'And godpop,' she added, as Angus turned up.

'Gopopop,' Rufus shouted.

'I hope you've reserved us some good seats,' Alice said, casting an eye over the audience.

'Front row left of stage,' Vivienne informed her. 'Right next to Kelsey, in fact.'

'Oh goodee. You know, I really don't understand why you have such a problem with her. She was a perfect delight when Angus and I were introduced to her just now, wasn't she, darling?'

'I don't think she quite realised who you were,' Angus replied disloyally.

Alice rolled her eyes, and continued to take in the sea of rustic, polished and mostly laughing faces. 'It's like a party,' she declared, 'which I suppose it is in a way. Just a pity we don't have any champagne.'

'There'll be plenty after, courtesy of Sir Richard and his gorgeous wife Susie,' Vivienne told her. 'They called from Australia late last night to make a very handsome donation too, no strings attached.'

'Ah! Don't you just love them? And Angus has told me how many donations you've already had like that. It's amazing. Brilliant. So how much is in the kitty so far?'

'The last I heard it's approaching twenty-four thousand, and the auction, as it stands, is expected to raise somewhere in the region of forty thousand.'

Alice's eyes boggled. 'My God, you're surpassing yourself, my angel.'

'Personally, I haven't given anything yet,' Vivienne laughed, 'or not in a monetary sense. But it's wonderful how generous everyone's been since we got our charitable status. Now it's tax-deductible there's an even bigger incentive to cough up. Where's Kayla, by the way?'

'Would you believe, in the firemen's dressing rooms?' Alice replied with no little irony. 'Making sure she has all their details was how she put it to me.' Then, as someone started shepherding them towards the seating, 'Oh, yippee, looks like we're being asked to take our places. Angus, bring our paddle, darling, we're going to win ourselves a fireman's lift.'

Laughing, Vivienne turned to see if Miles was anywhere in sight, and spotting him coming her way with Al Kohler, she moved forward to meet them.

'So here's the bonnie wee lad,' Kohler chuckled, his deeply lined features and shiny bald head looking rather hot under the lights. 'I can see why your daddy's very proud of you, young man.'

Clearly thrilled to be making yet another new friend, Rufus gurgled loudly and started banging his hands together.

Laughing, Kohler waited as Vivienne handed Rufus to Miles, then embraced her warmly. 'Looks like we've quite an event on our hands,' he said, smiling around him.

'Thanks to you,' she reminded him.

'I don't take other people's credit,' he said with a wink. 'It's all down to you.' Then, as Miles turned away with Rufus, responding to one of the TV assistants who was trying to make them sit down, 'Miles told me about tomorrow's edition of *The News*.'

'What do you think?' she asked, glancing at Miles, but he obviously couldn't hear.

'What I *know*,' Kohler replied, 'is that the Critch has gone too far this time, and Justine has successfully dug her own grave. What matters, though, is Jacqueline.'

Vivienne regarded him soberly. 'Of course,' she said, 'but she might not read it, and anyway, I keep thinking, if she was going to do anything, well, like that, she'd have done it by now.' She paused as he leant nearer to hear her better.

'She's had ample opportunity these past six weeks,' she said, 'and since the birthdays have come and gone . . .'

He was nodding. 'Precisely,' he agreed. 'So the question is, why won't she tell anyone where she is, or what she's doing?'

'Or,' Vivienne added, 'what she's hiding from.'

On the small dining table that was pushed up against a flowery-papered wall was a copy of that morning's newspaper, opened to a centre-page spread of the 'boys up for bids', as the paper was calling them. Next to it was a large notepad covered in neatly handwritten lines and a mobile phone. In the same room, set at an angle beside an original Edwardian fireplace, was a TV where a programme announcer was informing viewers that the much anticipated Slave Auction would begin after the commercial break.

The screen filled with an improbable happy family at breakfast, but Jacqueline's thoughts remained with Kelsey and how excited she probably was now, not only to be there, at the auction, but to be so close to the event itself that she might even appear in shot.

She was glad for Kelsey, but her eyes were starting to glaze as her mind drifted on, like a restless spirit, to Miles, then Rufus, the church of St Anne, the Virgin Mary, and finally to the woman who'd resurfaced from the past, Elizabeth Barrett. Tomorrow her delusions would be released from obscurity to cover the front page of *The News on Sunday*. Her story would be told in a way to shock and unsettle, or there would be no point in running it. Once again people would start asking, what really happened to Sam Avery? Had he actually been in his mother's car that day? How come no one saw him?

None of it had the power to hurt her any more. She only minded because it was prompting Miles to step up the search for her again. She didn't want to be found yet. She had chosen her time and until it came she wanted to remain where she was, safe, in this place called missing. At her core there was only warmth and stillness; in her heart there was simply the memory of pain. The scars were fading like stars at dawn, blending with the light to become invisible, free of the darkness.

Her mobile started to ring. She looked down at it, already knowing it would be Kelsey making sure she was keeping her promise to watch. She let the call go through to messages. She'd speak to her when the auction was over, and assure her she'd seen every minute. She hoped Kelsey would be in shot. She hoped Miles, Vivienne and Rufus would be too. She'd like to see them all together before she turned off her phone and finished her letter.

That was when she would be ready to leave this place called missing.

'Thought I might find you here, sir,' DC Joy murmured as she came up behind Sadler at the back of the TV room, where practically the entire station was gathered to watch the auction. 'I brought you a paddle in case you want to make a bid.'

Sadler cast her a sidelong glance.

Her eyes were all innocence. 'Oh, your Christmas bonus already spoken for?'

Unable to suppress a smile, he said, 'If my bonus came even close to where those bids began I'd be buying myself a DC with answers, instead of cheek.'

'Sssssh,' someone hissed from the front.

'Oh my God. There's Jamie Murray,' a female voice cried out. 'He was with the fire crew at my DUI in Marsh Barton last Wednesday.'

DC Joy looked at the dusty monitor where a delicious blond hunk with Herculean muscles, a fireman's helmet, and salopette bracers over his bare chest was swaggering up and down the catwalk in time to 'Come on Baby Light My Fire'. The audience was responding wildly to his gyrations, while across the bottom of the screen the bids for his skills as gardener-cum-chauffeur – or Mellors, as he was letting himself be known – flipped up and up and up with the speed of Third World inflation.

'Do you think that's real?' Joy whispered to Sadler. 'I mean, are that many people really ringing in?'

'Thankfully that is a mystery we're not here to solve,'

Sadler responded dryly. 'What news on Mrs Avery?'

'DC Ball in Richmond says they've contacted all the agents now, and there's still nothing coming up under the names of Avery or Cates.'

Sadler shook his head, more bothered than ever since Miles Avery had been in touch, worried about the possible effects of Sunday's paper. 'I take it they've tried Jacqueline Cates and Anne Avery,' he said, knowing already this would have been done.

Joy gave him a look to confirm it.

'What about her maiden name?' he said, knowing it was idiocy even to go there at this stage.

Joy appeared slightly disconcerted. 'I didn't think of that, sir,' she confessed.

'Then think about it now, Elaine, there's a good girl,' he said. 'Probably they're ahead of you in Richmond, but we never know.'

Her eyes strayed back to the screen.

'Scoot,' he growled in her ear.

'On my way, sir,' she said with a cheeky salute. 'Just please don't blow the entire annual on TKS, because I don't earn as much as you and I want him for me.'

One by one the firemen were dancing down the catwalk, each of them in various states of dress – or undress – as they performed to such numbers as 'Wheels on Fire', 'Start the Fire', and 'Great Balls of Fire'. The female members of the audience were lapping it up, applauding and laughing delightedly as someone rotated a cheekily exposed shoulder, or gyrated his hips, or pouted winsomely into camera.

Reg was doing a valiant job, in spite of the noise, encouraging the audience – and viewers at home – to up the bidding for the firemen's 'back-room skills' as he was calling them. His innuendos and double entendres were rife and hilarious, while the performances became raunchier and more expansive all the time. Most importantly, though, the bids were very quickly showing signs of surpassing everyone's dreams. Twelve hundred pounds for a private chauffeur for a week; fifteen hundred for Spanish lessons;

eighteen hundred for a gardener for a month; a whopping eight thousand for Percy to rewire a house; two thousand for Pete the plumber who roused the audience to a frenzy with his plunger, and another two thousand for Rick the DIY enthusiast whose bag of tools got Reg into an hysterical tangle of puns, alliterations and promises.

By the time the amateur weight-lifter – a huge, bald-headed man in skimpy trunks, protective boots and a yellow standard-issue helmet – had brought the house down with his mincing and flexing, the amount raised from the auction was already standing at close to thirty thousand pounds.

'It's amazing!' Vivienne cried to Alice, applauding wildly along with everyone else, and catching the choreographer's eye across the catwalk, she gave her two robust thumbs up. 'Fabulous,' she mouthed. 'Sensational.'

The choreographer was beaming, while Reg laughed heartily as he waited for the applause to die down behind the weight-lifter. 'And now, ladies and gentlemen,' he announced like an end-of-pier compère, 'please get those paddles waving and pound notes flying for our very own golden boy, the free-styler extraordinaire, the fastest man in Speedos, and hottest hunk in a hairy chest, Mr Theo Kenwood-South.'

'Who's writing his script?' Alice demanded as the place erupted with a rapturous welcome for Theo.

'I think he's making it up as he goes along,' Vivienne answered, laughing as Theo came swaggering onto the catwalk in luminous silver shorts and an enormous pair of madly glittering goggles. The music paused as he struck his opening pose. Everyone fell silent. Then up came the opening bars of 'Hey Big Spender' and the audience exploded into laughter.

His routine was so camp and outrageous that before long it became virtually impossible to hear Reg over the din, as everyone whooped and cheered him on. However, the production team was keeping a close watch on the bids, relaying information to relevant sources, signalling to Reg and urging everyone to dig deeper and deeper. Then suddenly, like a stripper, Theo tore off his Velcro-held shorts, swirled them a few times round his head, and sent them sailing into the audience. Wild shrieks filled the air as literally hundreds of eager hands rose up to grab the trophy. He was now in gold sparkly trunks and dollar-sign goggles that someone tossed in from the wings, dancing up and down the catwalk to 'Money, Money, Money'.

'It must be like this at a Chippendale show,' Alice shouted into Vivienne's ear, as Kelsey and Martha leapt up to join those who were already dancing on their chairs. 'Someone's going to throw their knickers in any minute. You wait.'

'Just don't let it be you,' Vivienne warned, struggling to hold onto a delirious Rufus.

'Not wearing any, darling.'

With a gurgle of laughter Vivienne released Rufus into Miles's stronger grasp, then promptly jumped up with Alice and Kayla to join in the dancing.

'Look at how high the bids are going,' she shouted, pointing to the off-air monitor. 'It's already at nine thousand.'

At that moment the screen changed to a shot of a WI lady receiving a call which upped the figure to ten thousand. 'I wonder who's on the other end?' Alice yelled as a massive cheer went up and Theo gave an exaggerated bow, followed by a couple of bicep flexes.

'Probably his mother,' Vivienne replied and they burst out laughing.

'Oh my God, he's shameless,' Alice shrieked, as Theo began a very suggestive simulated swim.

'Ladies and gentlemen,' Reg boomed into his microphone, 'do we have any advances on ten thousand for private time with this swimmer sublime?'

'Oh God,' Vivienne groaned, as a hundred paddles rose up and as many voices yelled, 'Eleven, twelve, fifteen, *twenty*.'

'Come on now, ladies,' Reg cautioned, 'don't start what you can't finish.'

As they screamed with laughter, Mrs Kent, a local businesswoman known to have a penchant for young men, upped the bidding to ten thousand five hundred.

'Thank you, Mrs Kent,' Reg shouted above the crowd,

and as everyone cheered the monitor switched back to a shot of the WI lady, whose caller took little time to increase the figure to eleven.

'Eleven thousand,' Reg cried ecstatically. 'Friends, we are making history today. I have eleven thousand so far for private coaching and a day using the fantastic facilities in Bath with Britain's very own Olympic gold-medallist. Now, do I hear twelve? Come on, ladies, let TKS help ease the PMS.'

'Please tell me he didn't just say that,' Vivienne winced as a stream of voices yelled, 'Me, me, me.'

'Don't knock it,' Alice laughed, 'he could end up with his own show at this rate and he'll be our client.'

Theo was boogieing forward, twirling and teasing, urging the audience to clap and dance along with him until, to a rousing cheer, he reached out to haul Stella up onto the catwalk. The brazen old eccentric immediately began stealing the show with an hilarious freak-out not at all in time to the music, while Theo pirouetted around her before turning to grab Kelsey's and Martha's hands to pull them up too.

Vivienne swung round to Miles and burst out laughing at the look on his face.

'That's my daughter,' he stated indignantly, but his eyes were shining, and seeming to decide that his son could no longer be stopped from joining in, he stood up so Rufus could try and clap his hands as high as everyone else.

'This is amazing,' Vivienne cried, as Reg announced that the redoubtable Mrs Kent had taken the bids up to twelve thousand.

Before Miles could respond Rufus gave such an almighty leap that he almost broke free. 'My God, that could have been expensive,' Miles laughed, grabbing him more securely.

'Look, look, the phone caller's just taken it to thirteen,' Alice shrieked excitedly. 'You're right, Vivi, it has to be his mother. Angus, try your sister's number, I'll bet it's busy.'

For the hell of it Angus did so, and when the engaged signal came down the line they dissolved into laughter.

Seconds later the place was in uproar again as the music changed to the cancan and all eleven firemen, in black fishnet stockings, frou-frou skirts and feather boas, came high-kicking back onto the stage. On the catwalk Theo, surrounded by his impromptu troupe, created another line, while Reg informed whoever could hear that the bids had now gone up to 'an incredible fourteen thousand'.

'What are we going to do if Mrs Kent wins?' Vivienne shouted to Alice. 'The woman's a sex maniac by all accounts.'

Though Alice laughed she saw the problem right away – for Theo it would be a horrible embarrassment, for them it would be a PR disaster. As she started to answer, the phone caller took the figure up to fifteen thousand.

'Oh my God!' Vivienne cried. 'Where is this going to end?'

The camera swung back to Mrs Kent. 'Don't do it, don't do it,' Vivienne pleaded.

'Do I hear sixteen thousand?' Reg sang out.

'No, no,' Vivienne muttered.

'Sixteen thousand?'

Vivienne was holding her breath.

'I have fifteen thousand for the fetching fellow in faux lamé trunks,' Reg informed them.

Vivienne and Alice groaned at Reg's unstoppable corniness.

'Fifteen thousand. Going once. Going twice . . .'

Vivienne willed the hammer to go down before Mrs Kent's libido got the better of her again.

'Sold to our mystery caller,' Reg announced, with a resounding thump, and Vivienne's breath came out in a rush of relief.

'Of course, it could be another sex maniac for all we know,' Alice shouted above the applause.

'Don't even think it,' Vivienne shouted back.

When the cheering eventually died down and transmission switched back to the studio, Miles said, 'Unless my maths is out, we have a grand total of forty-three thousand from the auction, with a further twenty-four already pledged, so the kitty's standing at somewhere around sixty-seven thousand.'

'That's brilliant,' Vivienne replied, 'but not enough, because some high-flyer in the City has promised to double it if we get to a hundred.'

'We still don't know how many straight pledges came in while we were on air,' Alice reminded her. 'So we might have made it.'

They looked round in search of Al Kohler, and spotting him climbing up on stage to take over the mike, Vivienne struggled her way through to Sharon, whose cheeks were glowing.

'This is a long way beyond what we were hoping,' Vivienne beamed as she hugged her. 'You're going to be so well taken care of now, you'll think you're a princess.'

Sharon was smiling all over her face as she swallowed the lump in her throat. 'It's been brilliant,' she declared. 'And will you just look at that old trollop up there dancing. What is she like?'

Vivienne laughed as Stella gave them a wave. By now the catwalk and stage was crowded with frilly-frocked firemen, as Reg was calling them, and as many of the audience as could fit themselves on.

Suddenly the music dipped and Al Kohler could be heard asking for everyone's attention.

A camera tracked in to get a better angle on him as the studio switched back to the auction, and when the noise had completely died down, he said into the mike, 'Good morning, everyone. My name is Al Kohler, I'm the executive producer, and it's my great pleasure to be able to tell you that in addition to the sixty-seven thousand pounds raised by the auction and private donations before we went on air, we have received further pledges amounting to just over twenty-seven thousand. This makes a grand total of almost ninety-five thousand pounds, which I know far surpasses the dreams of Sharon's WI friends, who came up with the idea of this auction in the first place. So congratulations to you all, ladies, you must feel very proud of what you've achieved here today.'

As everyone whooped and cheered Miles murmured to Vivienne, 'I'll make it up to a hundred.'

Her eyes were shining. 'Do you realise that means the

figure will rise to three hundred thousand, because Sky is doubling the amount too?'

'Really,' he said dryly, 'well, that's the best return I've ever known on five grand. Now all we need is a suitable donor for Sharon.'

As soon as transmission was over the party began in earnest. Champagne corks started popping faster than fireworks, while the choreographer's music tape was played all over again, and, still in their fancy costumes, the firemen twirled and jived their new fans up and down the catwalk. Theo made a hasty return to a pair of ripped jeans and body-hugging T-shirt, and since there was still no prising Stella from him, or Martha from Percy, Kelsey grabbed her phone and took it outside where the crew was packing up, and half a dozen long-suffering horses were trundling around the manège carrying small children on their backs.

'Mum! Great, you answered,' she cried breathlessly when she made the connection. Her elation was so great that it took a moment for her natural caution to kick in. 'You didn't watch, did you?' she accused, only too aware of how her mother rarely failed to disappoint her. 'Well, it's OK . . .'

'I watched,' Jacqueline assured her. 'I didn't realise you were such a good dancer.'

Kelsey's eyes lit up. 'Yeah, but not like Martha,' she said modestly. 'She's amazing. Did you see how much TKS raised? Everyone's teasing him now, saying it was his mother on the phone.'

There was a note of humour in Jacqueline's voice as she said, 'Whoever it was, they've got themselves a great deal, even at fifteen thousand.'

'That's exactly what Dad said. Actually he really wants to speak to you, shall I go and get him?'

'No, darling, don't do that.'

Kelsey's smile started to fade. 'Did you get his messages?' she asked. 'He left one last night and again this morning.'

'Yes, I got them.'

'So you know what he wants to talk to you about?'

'I do, but there's nothing to be said.'

Kelsey looked round as someone set off the fire engine's siren, then stopped it again.

'I've already told him not to worry,' Jacqueline reminded her. 'It won't be a problem.'

Kelsey wasn't sure what to say.

'It sounds as though you're having a wonderful time down there,' Jacqueline commented.

'Yeah, we are.'

'I expect you want to get back to it.'

'Um, yes, I suppose I should. I'm glad you watched. It was really cool, wasn't it?'

'Very.'

After a beat Kelsey said, 'I'm going now then.'

'OK.'

'Bye then.'

'Goodbye, my darling. God bless.'

Kelsey didn't ring off, but in the end Jacqueline did, and as the line went dead a horrible feeling started to come over Kelsey. It was all kind of grainy and weird and seemed to be pulling her down and down into a place that was dark and scary. *God bless.* The words were making her head seem clogged, and she felt sort of sick. She wanted to call her mother back to find out if that was why she'd changed, because she'd got God, but then Martha came out looking for her, carrying two more glasses of champagne.

'What's up?' Martha hiccuped, her cheeks flushed like a pair of poppies

'Nothing,' Kelsey answered.

'Come on, you're missing all the fun.'

Kelsey's eyes came up to hers. Her face was pale with worry, but then the music inside changed to one of her favourite bands, and the bad feeling evaporated in the urge to dance. 'So have you managed to pull Percy's plug yet?' she teased, grabbing a glass, and laughing uproariously they plunged back into the swirling mass of Devonshire revellers.

Chapter Twenty-four

'Ah, there you are, Just*ine*,' Critchley drawled, as his rotund frame in grubby shirt and low-slung pants drew up alongside her desk. 'I was wondering when you might grace us with your presence again.'

Justine glanced up. As usual he looked as though he should stink, but amazingly didn't. Then, returning her eyes to the computer screen, she continued to type.

'I don't suppose,' he said, resting his stumpy, freckled hands on her desk, 'it was you who gave Avery the tip-off about tomorrow's front page, was it? No, of course not. Why would you want to risk having an injunction slapped on your very own exclusive?'

In spite of the prickling in her armpits, Justine carried on with what she was doing.

'On the other hand,' the Critch continued chattily, 'it would appear that you've had your name removed from *your very own exclusive*. Oh yes, I know about that. You have to be stupider than I already had you down for if you thought it wouldn't get back to me before tomorrow.'

'No, I knew it would,' she told him.

'OK. So let's look at this again, shall we? We know there's nothing anyone can do to stop that front page, because everything checks out. We're not breaking any laws, and it's not accusing anyone of anything. It's simply telling a sad story of what it can be like to lose a child, and regurgitating a few questions that were asked fifteen years ago – and guess what, Justie, they still need answers.'

Without looking up, she said, 'And you think you're going to get them?'

Critchley chuckled. 'Who cares? You did a good job. In

spite of your duplicity Avery's going to squirm on the end of my line tomorrow, and then he's going to remember what it's like when the sharks come along to feed. He's been there before, let's see if he can survive it again.'

Justine clicked on to print, then rose to her feet. 'It's not a question of whether he can,' she said, pushing past him, 'it's whether his wife can – oh, and by the way, that's my resignation.'

The Critch laughed loudly. 'If you think that's going to save you from Avery's wrath, Justie,' he said, evidently enjoying himself, 'then you're more deluded than sad old Jacqueline.'

Spinning round, she said, 'No, it probably won't save me, but it's going to bury you, you asshole,' and flinging her bag onto her shoulder she stalked across the office, triumphant in having the last word – until she reached the lift, which started to descend before she could stop it.

'Next time you speak to Avery,' the Critch called after her, 'make sure he knows, just in case he's under any illusion, that this is payback time for *The Grunt*.' Still chuckling at her desperate jabbing on the button, he wandered back into his office and was just sitting down when his secretary rang through to announce another call from Avery's lawyer.

'Put him on,' Critchley responded, rubbing his hands.

A moment later Stefan Harding's voice came down the line. 'Mr Critchley, I'm calling to inform you that my client will be pressing charges against Justine James for the theft of an email from his computer, and for false representation when approaching Mrs Barrett.'

The Critch gave a snort of pleasure. 'Please tell your client that if he thinks that's going to stop tomorrow's front page then he's even dumber than the Justine.'

'You should also be made aware,' Harding went on smoothly, 'that the charges against Ms James will extend to you as an accomplice.'

Critchley barked a laugh. 'You can try, Mr Lawyer, but it won't stick, and you know it.'

Harding's tone remained affable as he said, 'Good day, Mr Critchley.'

As the line went dead Critchley leaned forward to replace

the receiver, the smirk on his lips taking longer to fade than the gleam in his eyes. There was more to that call than was immediately evident, he was certain of it, he just wasn't managing to figure out what – yet. However, the very fact that Avery was riled enough to start suing meant he was under the man's skin, which was exactly where the Critch wanted to be. In fact, he could hardly wait for tomorrow, when Avery's discomfort was going to be every bit as public as the cartoon he'd commissioned, and that his old paper still ran, ridiculing the Critch every damned, fucking day of the week.

Vivienne was kneeling on the floor with Rufus when Miles brought the papers in the next morning and tossed them on the bed.

'It's there,' he told her shortly. 'Not that I thought he'd back off.'

Reaching over, Vivienne picked up *The News on Sunday* and turned it over to see the glaring headline in giant black letters. ***AVERY CHILD WAS NEVER IN CAR*** followed in much smaller print by *claims woman who has dogged family for years.*

After glancing at Miles with an expression that showed her dismay, she began reading.

'After fifteen years the unanswered question of whether or not Samuel Avery was in his mother's car the day she claims he was abducted, arises again following Mrs Avery's own recent disappearance. We are told by a family member that Mrs Avery has been in touch with them, but at the time of going to press the police still had no knowledge of her whereabouts. It is believed that since the alleged abduction . . .'

Alleged, she repeated harshly in her mind.

'. . . of her son, Mrs Avery, wife of prominent Fleet Street editor Miles Avery, has suffered several breakdowns. Suspicion of her own, and her husband's involvement in their son's disappearance arose at the time, and has never completely gone away. Avery was taken in for questioning six weeks after Sam was supposedly taken, but was eventually released without charge. Mrs Avery is said to have suffered a severe nervous collapse following an accusation of murder by Mrs Elizabeth Barrett, whose husband worked with Avery at the time the mystery occurred.'

Rigid with contempt, Vivienne turned to an inside page.

'Mrs Barrett is now claiming that Avery paid her to leave his family alone, a claim Avery denies. However, highly significant questions still remain unanswered: **Was Sam in the car when Jacqueline Avery drove into the garage? Why were there no witnesses when she was on a busy roundabout? Why has there been no sign of Sam since? Where is Mrs Avery now?'**

Having read enough, Vivienne looked up at Miles.

His face was pale, but his voice was steady as he said, 'At least it seems to be more damaging to me than to Jacqueline. Whether she'll see it like that . . .' His eyes closed in despair. 'That damned Barrett woman came out of the woodwork six years ago, just when Jacqueline was finally getting it together and the next thing I knew she was right back where we started. Worse, in fact, so I don't even want to think about how she might handle it now.'

'Has Kelsey spoken to her since yesterday?' Vivienne said, wincing as Rufus grabbed her hair to pull himself up.

'Not that she's mentioned. It was bedlam for most of the day, though, and she'd had more than enough to drink. I think I'll—' He stopped as a loud crash came from downstairs, followed by gales of girlish giggling. 'Well, I guess that means they're up,' he said dryly. 'Now I'd better go and find out what damage they've done.'

He arrived in the kitchen to find Kelsey on her knees making a bad job of shoving pots and pans back into a cupboard, while Martha attempted to crack eggs into the skillet they'd presumably been looking for.

'Oh, sorry, did we wake you?' Martha gasped when she saw him. 'We couldn't find . . .'

'Dad, you're here – *ouch*!' Kelsey grunted, banging her head as she backed out of the cupboard, and she and Martha promptly dissolved into laughter again. 'Sorry,' she said, trying to make herself stop, 'we felt like a cooked breakfast. Is that OK?'

'Of course,' he answered, going to fill the kettle. After

placing it on the Aga he said, 'Have you spoken to your mother again since yesterday morning?'

Kelsey suddenly clapped her hands to her face. 'Oh my God, the paper!' she cried. 'Has it arrived? Is it bad?'

'It's not good.'

'Can I see it?'

'I'd rather you didn't.'

'But I can't go back to school with everyone having seen it except me,' she protested.

Conceding the point, he said, 'First I'd like an answer to my question, have you spoken to your mother since yesterday morning?'

Kelsey started to flush with guilt. 'No, but I told her you wanted to speak to her,' she said defensively. 'I even tried to get her to hold on while I came to find you, but she didn't want to.'

'Did you ask if she'd received my messages?'

'Yes, and she has, but she said there was nothing to talk about, and we're not to worry.'

He looked at her gravely. 'See if you can get her on the phone now,' he said.

'But we're about to—'

'Just do it,' he barked.

Kelsey's heart suddenly tightened as the weird feeling that had come over her yesterday welled up again. 'What is it?' she said shakily. 'Dad, you're scaring me. You don't think . . .?'

'It'll be all right,' he told her firmly, 'but we have to find out where she is, and right now you're the only one who can do it.'

'Bingo, sir,' Joy said, coming into Sadler's office. 'You know, you really ought to be a detective.'

Sadler's expression was droll as he looked up from the paper to find a casually dressed DC Joy leaning against his door frame.

'Don't your family mind you coming in on a Sunday?' she asked, stifling a yawn. 'This is the second one in a row. Sorry, sir, late night. Still, at least we got a bit of a lie-in, so mustn't grumble.'

'We're here,' he reminded her, pointing at the paper, 'because of this. Now you were about to tell me why I should be a detective.'

'Jacqueline Hatfield,' she explained. 'Mrs Avery's maiden name, and the one she used to rent a house in Richmond, which belongs to a Mr Peter Gascoigne, currently a resident of Malaga, Spain.'

Sadler's antennae were up. 'Go on,' he prompted.

'I just found an email from DC Ball,' she said, yawning again. 'He's spoken to Mr Gascoigne and apparently the dates fit, so does the description – dark hair, posh, quiet – plus it's a few doors away from where she used to live. Same street, opposite side.'

'Didn't anyone do a house-to-house in that area?'

'They did, but if she was there she obviously didn't answer, and they've only just tracked down Mr Gascoigne.'

'Has DC Ball been to the house since finding out where she is, or at least spoken to her?'

'Yes and no. He went round last night, but there was nobody home, so he's going to try again when he's back on duty tomorrow.'

Sadler's face darkened. 'Get onto Richmond and tell them to send someone now,' he said.

'But sir, it's Sunday and we don't have the authority . . .'

Sadler snatched up the phone as it rang. 'Yes,' he growled. Hearing the voice at the other end, his eyes darted to Joy's. 'Mr Avery. I was just reading—'

Miles cut across him. 'Inspector, I need to know if you've made any progress in finding my wife. She's not answering my daughter's calls, and after this morning's paper . . .'

Sadler was on his feet, but his voice betrayed no alarm as he said, 'As a matter of fact, an email *has* come through telling us where she is. It's an address close to where you used to live in Richmond.'

'Has anyone been over there?'

'Apparently someone went last night, but she wasn't at home. We're about to try again.'

'Please do. And if you have to, break down the door.'

Sadler was already reaching for another phone. 'I'll be in touch as soon as I have some news,' he said, and abruptly ringing off he made the connection straight through to his chief constable.

Having abandoned their plans to lunch at the Nobody Inn, Miles and Vivienne scrambled together some food for Angus and Alice who came over from the cider press to join them in the wait for news. As soon as the meal was ready Miles took a tray for Kelsey and Martha up to Kelsey's room, then, unable to eat anything himself, he disappeared into his study to speak to his lawyer.

'The press are clamouring for comments,' Vivienne was saying as she closed the sitting-room door behind Angus and Alice, 'so Stefan's acting as spokesman.'

'What're they going to do about the Critch?' Alice asked. 'He shouldn't be allowed to get away with the kind of insinuations he's plastered all over that rag of a paper.'

With a sigh Vivienne said, 'I don't think he will. Stefan's already contacted the police, so it's probably only a matter of time before Justine's questioned, possibly even arrested and charged. It depends whether they can make anything stick on the Critch, but they're going to try.'

'What about Al Kohler's brother-in-law?' Angus piped up. 'Isn't he *The News*'s proprietor? Could Miles – or Al – have some sway with him?'

'All I know,' Vivienne replied, 'is that Miles and Al spent a long time talking last night, but whether Al's relationship to Don Dickson was mentioned I've no idea.'

They all sat quietly for a while then, the only sounds coming from the steady patter of rain outside and the hiss and crackle of the fire.

In the end, voicing what was on everyone's mind, Alice said, 'Do you honestly think Jacqueline would . . . You know?'

Vivienne glanced at her, then shook her head bleakly. 'One minute I do, the next I don't,' she replied. 'We know she's made attempts in the past, but the way she's started making an effort with Kelsey . . .' She took a breath. 'I keep thinking of an article I read once about how a person who's arrived at that final decision can become very calm, even kind of happy, as though their stresses and pains have already melted away. It's like the end is in sight, so they're starting to feel free. When we were together she talked about Rufus setting her free.'

'Have you told Miles that?' Alice asked.

Vivienne shook her head. 'Not in so many words. Maybe I should have, but I didn't want to add to how worried he already was. Then, when she and Kelsey started to communicate with one another . . . Well, I thought, at least I told myself, I must have read it all wrong.'

They fell silent again, not wanting to add any more weight to their suspicions as they waited for Miles to come back, or the phone to ring, or something to happen. However, the time ticked monotonously on with no interruption, until eventually Vivienne went upstairs to check on Rufus.

Finding him awake, she hugged him tightly to her and was about to carry him back downstairs when Miles came in, looking more strained than she'd ever seen him.

'No news?' she asked.

He shook his head, and took Rufus from her. 'I'm just going to talk to Kelsey,' he told her, giving Rufus a kiss. 'I'll join you downstairs in a while.'

Another hour passed. After spending some time with Kelsey, Miles returned to his study, while Vivienne sat with Angus and Alice, absently watching Rufus toddling about the room.

'Oh Jacqueline, *ring! Please,*' Vivienne finally urged.

But the phone stayed resolutely silent and the waiting continued.

At three thirty Miles went back upstairs to Kelsey's room and used her mobile to add yet another message to the dozen or so he and Kelsey had already left. After passing the phone back he went to stand at the window.

'She's probably just gone out and forgotten to take her mobile with her,' Martha said, trying, for the umpteenth time, to be helpful.

Kelsey continued to look at her father.

'Martha's probably right,' he said, sensing her eyes on him. He turned round, and seeing the fear in her expression he pulled her into his arms. 'It'll be all right,' he murmured, kissing her hair and wishing to God he could feel more confident.

Martha glanced at him once or twice before, in an embarrassed, tentative voice, she said, 'You know what I keep thinking?'

No one responded.

'Well, it's Sunday, right?' Martha persevered. 'So what if she's gone to church?'

Kelsey became very still, then her head went back to look up at her father. 'She might have,' she said, the tiniest flicker of hope lighting her eyes, 'because she sounds sometimes like she's gone a bit religious. She even said God bless to me yesterday, and she's never done that before.'

Though far from thrilled by the timing of the sentiment, Miles was remembering something else now, and extricating himself gently he said, 'Wait here. I'll be back in a minute.'

As the sitting-room door opened everyone looked up.

'Last week,' Miles said to Vivienne, picking up Rufus, 'when you were talking to Jacqueline, didn't you say she mentioned St Anne's in Kew?'

Vivienne nodded. 'Yes, that's right.' A light of understanding came into her eyes. 'It's Sunday. That's where she'll be. Why didn't I think of it before?'

'We need the number of St Anne's,' Alice said, taking out her BlackBerry.

Both Miles's and Vivienne's expressions showed small signs of relaxing as they allowed themselves to run with the hope, and seeming to sense something of this, Rufus began tugging at his father's cheeks.

Having got the number, Alice switched to speakerphone as a ringing tone sounded at the other end. To everyone's dismay the call was answered by a recording.

'There's probably a service going on,' Miles said. 'But I should let the police know. Perhaps someone can go to the church and check it out.'

He'd barely left the room to fetch Sadler's number from his study when the entryphone at the gates sounded in the kitchen.

Frowning, Vivienne got to her feet. 'Who on earth can that be?' she said, glancing at the window. Though Jacqueline was on everyone's mind, no one voiced the unlikely hope that she was about to stage a surprise appearance. It would be very welcome, but no one really believed it would happen.

Going into the kitchen, Vivienne noticed the time as she unhooked the phone. Almost four o'clock already – though it felt as if they'd been waiting a lifetime. 'Hello?' she said into the receiver.

'It's DI Sadler,' came the reply. 'I'd be grateful if you could let us in.'

Miles was waiting at the front door by the time Sadler stopped his car in the courtyard and got out. As usual Joy was with him, and the look on their faces was enough to tell Miles he'd been right to start preparing himself for the worst.

'Through here,' he said, standing back for the detectives to pass.

Vivienne was at the door of his study, ready to show them in. 'Shall I bring some tea?' she said to Miles.

He shook his head, and taking her hand drew her into the room with him and closed the door.

Sadler came to a stop in the middle of the room and turned round, still looking extremely grave. Joy stood beside him, appearing equally troubled.

'I'm very sorry, Mr Avery,' Sadler said gruffly. 'I'm afraid they weren't able to get to her in time.'

As Miles's grip tightened on her hand, tears of protest flooded Vivienne's eyes.

Miles cleared his throat. 'When . . . When did it happen?' he asked.

'It still has to be confirmed, but they think probably sometime last night.'

Miles swallowed hard and Vivienne moved in closer to him. 'How?' he said, strain roughening his voice.

'It appears to have been an overdose of barbiturates. We'll know more, of course, once the post-mortem's been carried out.'

'Where is she now?'

'I believe she's been taken to the mortuary at Kingston Hospital.'

Miles swallowed again and put a hand to his head. 'Was there . . . ? Did she leave a note?' he asked.

'Nothing's been found yet. The local police are still at the scene.'

Miles nodded. 'Thank you for coming to tell us.' His voice failed for a moment. 'I imagine there a lot of formalities to be gone through,' he said huskily, 'but if you don't mind I need to go and speak to my daughter now.'

As he left the room Vivienne covered her face with her hands and started to shake. 'I'm sorry,' she said, as DC Joy came to comfort her. 'It's just that they've already been through so much.'

Kelsey looked up as Miles knocked and opened the door. The instant she saw his face her own turned white.

'Martha, could you go downstairs for a moment, please?' Miles asked gently.

Martha glanced worriedly at Kelsey, then left the room, closing the door quietly behind her.

Kelsey's eyes were still on Miles. 'No, Dad, no, please,' she begged, as he came towards her.

'Sssh,' he said, taking her in his arms.

'Is she . . . ? I mean . . .'

'Yes, she's gone,' he told her softly.

'No, no, no!' she cried, pressing her fists to her cheeks. 'She can't. Dad, please. Don't let it be true.'

'I'm sorry, my darling.'

She spun away, grabbing her hair in her hands. 'It's my fault,' she choked. 'I had this feeling, yesterday . . .'

'Listen to me,' he said, turning her back, 'it is *not* your fault.'

'But I knew . . . It was like something was telling me, I just didn't want to listen because we . . . We were . . . having a good time. So it's my fault . . .'

'Darling, if anyone's to blame for this, it's whoever took Sam all those years ago, not you. That's what your mother's never been able to accept, and I guess she'd just had enough.'

'But what about *me*?' she sobbed, her face distorted by pain. 'Why don't I matter?'

'You do, more than anything, she was just afraid to show it in case something happened to you.'

'But it didn't, did it? I'm still here and I want her to come back, Dad. Please make her come back.'

'My darling, if I could, I would,' he said, holding her tightly to him as he struggled to contain his own emotions.

'She was always horrible and mean to me, and now she's done this,' she gasped brokenly. 'She shouldn't have done it. Why suddenly be my friend and then go away again? It's like I'm not supposed to have any feelings.'

'I think she was trying to make her peace with you before she went,' Miles told her gently.

'Well, she shouldn't have. It was just mean. She said I could go and stay with her, and get to know Richmond, but she was lying.' Rage was pushing the tears faster down her cheeks. 'I thought I was going to have a real mum at last,' she shouted, stamping her feet. 'I hate her. I'm glad she's gone, because that was a horrible thing to do.'

'She wasn't doing it to hurt you.'

'No, because I don't matter. I never have and I was really stupid to think I did.' She tried to catch her breath, but was overcome by the agony gathering in her heart. 'I think you should kill that editor for what he's done,' she rasped. 'It's because of what he put in the paper. It brought it all back for her . . .'

'The police said she left us last night,' Miles told her, 'so it happened before she saw the paper.'

Kelsey's eyes closed as her face crumpled again. 'So all the time we were enjoying ourselves, she was all on her own . . . Oh Dad, this is horrible. I want it to go away.'

'I know,' he said, pulling her back into his arms.

'Do you know how they found out where she was?'

'Not yet, but she was in Richmond.'

'So she wasn't lying about that?'

He didn't answer, because he didn't need to.

'It's so weird,' she said, after a while. 'I mean I've got this brother who's real, but none of us knows where he is. He's still *there*, though. You know, a part of our family.' Her eyes came up to his, so full of anguish he could hardly bear it. 'I wish I could have grown up with him,' she said, 'and we could have been a normal family. Why did we have to be different, Dad?'

'I don't know,' he sighed, holding her again. 'I wish I did, but I don't.'

It was some time before she spoke again, her voice muffled by his embrace. 'It's been really horrible for her,' she said, 'losing her baby and blaming herself . . . Do you think she might be happier where she is now?'

'I'm sure she is,' he replied, gently stroking her hair.

'She might even be with Sam.'

He swallowed hard. 'Yes, she might,' he agreed.

He felt her starting to shudder as more sobs welled up inside her. 'Do you know if she left a note?' she asked raggedly.

'They haven't found one yet, but they're still at the house.'

She pulled back to look at him again, her eyes burning with more angry pain. 'You know what, if she didn't leave one,' she said, 'then we'll know for certain that we never really meant anything to her at all.'

Chapter Twenty-five

The following morning they all drove up to London, Vivienne and Alice to start dealing with the aftermath of the auction, while Miles took Kelsey to visit the house Jacqueline had rented, before going on to the mortuary alone.

'I felt sure Jacqueline would have left her some kind of note,' Miles said to Vivienne on the phone later, when he and Kelsey were back at home in Kensington, 'but there are no emails or texts, and nothing's turned up in the post either.'

'Did she have a lawyer?' Vivienne asked. 'Might she have left something with him?'

'All he has is her will, which I witnessed myself a year ago. As you might expect she's left everything to Kelsey, though Kelsey's so angry she's threatening to give it all away, the jewellery, the paintings, and whatever money might turn up, since Jacqueline withdrew it all from the bank.'

'Did the police find any cash at the house?'

'Not yet, but she could have opened another bank account, though as far as I know they haven't turned up any statements or chequebooks to say so.' He sighed heavily. 'I guess it'll all come clear in the end, but right now Kelsey's my main concern. And the funeral, of course.'

'Will it happen in Devon?'

'Yes, for Kelsey's sake I think her mother should be cremated and the ashes buried in the family plot at St Pancras in Widecombe.'

'When will it be?'

'The cremation's on Friday at three. The interment some

time next week, we haven't fixed a day yet. Will you come?'

'Of course, if you want me to, but what about Kelsey? I'm sure she won't want me there.'

'At the moment she wants nothing to do with either the cremation or the interment, but that could change by the time Friday comes round, so let's play it by ear for the next few days. How's my boy?'

'Right now he's squashing baked beans into his mouth with his fingers and using his spoon to bang his tray.'

'So that's what I can hear.' He gave a long, weary sigh. 'I'd love to come over and relax in his world for a while, but I can't leave Kelsey.'

'Of course not.'

Changing the subject, he said, 'I spoke to Al Kohler earlier. He tells me that the sums raised on Saturday were even higher than we thought. Which isn't me trying to get out of my five grand, by the way, but it seems I wasn't the only one prepared to make up the shortfall.'

She smiled. 'We're totalling almost four hundred thousand now that Sky and our City gent have kicked in,' she said. 'A very healthy sum to get our good works under way. We're calling it The Sharon and Keith Goss Trust, by the way, and to quote Stella, Sharon was tickled pink when she found out.'

'How is Sharon, really?'

'Tired after all Saturday's excitement, and as nervous as you'd expect about starting more treatment on Wednesday. Having been through it before, she knows what she's in for. However, knowing the children are going to be taken care of by a professional, and that she's going to have transport to and from the hospital is helping a lot.'

'No donor yet?'

'With her rare tissue type it would be nothing short of a miracle if someone else was found now, but let's not give up hope, because you never know. Where's Kelsey at the moment?'

'Upstairs, asleep. Today's been quite an ordeal so I'll leave her for a while and probably send out for something to eat, because the last thing either of us needs is to be stared at and whispered about in a restaurant.'

Since Jacqueline's suicide had made most of the front pages that day, it wasn't hard to imagine how much attention they'd attract if they were to go out. 'Did you see Al's piece in the *Guardian*?' she asked.

'Yes, I did. The Critch won't be too happy about it, that's for sure, but then he's unlikely to be effervescing with joy over anything that's been written about him today.'

'It's amazing – and more than deserved – the way the rest of the press has turned on him.'

'Well, once we knew about Jacqueline it was fairly certain he'd be in for a savaging. He can't be held responsible of course, but the timing was very bad for him.'

'Will he survive it?'

'Possibly, but hopefully not. I take it you know his and Justine's computers were carted off by the police this morning.'

'Yes, I heard. So an arrest could be imminent?'

'Depends what they find. Chances are they've both erased all evidence by now, but we'll see. What matters more at the moment is getting through the rest of this week with as little attention focused our way as possible. Kelsey certainly doesn't need it, and I don't think the rest of us do either.'

Deciding not to tell him about her own bombardment throughout the day, she said, 'It would be a wonderful irony if Critchley's and Justine's disgrace were to replace Jacqueline's tragedy in the media.'

'Actually, I wouldn't rule it out,' he responded, wryly, 'because if my sources are correct then our luck on that front could begin as early as tomorrow or Wednesday.'

'Listen to me,' Critchley growled into his mobile phone, 'the woman topped herself on Saturday night, my paper came out on Sunday morning, so unless the clocks have started going backwards over there in Canary Wharf, don't try pinning the tail on this donkey, OK? There, that's my statement. You have it, now goodbye.'

As he rang off he told his chauffeur to speed it up, even

though the traffic on Aldwych was gridlocked, then checking to see who was calling now, he shut the phone down and tossed it over his shoulder to join that morning's papers on the back shelf.

'Fucking morons can't work out the fucking time,' he muttered furiously to himself. 'Did you read all that crap again today, Paco?' he demanded. 'This is the third morning in a row, and still the idiots don't seem to know which comes first, Saturday night or Sunday morning. They're twisting the facts to make a headline.'

'Which is something you'd know all about,' Justine retorted when he snarled the same words down the phone to her a few minutes later.

'Don't get smart with me. Your ass is on the line here too.'

'I've already resigned,' she reminded him.

'And you think that's going to save you?'

'No, I'll have to pay for what I did, I know that, but I've already explained to the police the kind of pressure I was under to keep my job. Not that pressure's a crime, but it's pretty uncomfortable when it's on, which you're obviously finding out. Can't be very pleasant having half your own profession baying for your blood, but you know what beats me is that you didn't see it coming. How's that for arrogance, I ask myself. Or was it just blind stupidity?'

'You stitched me up with that Barrett woman,' he growled.

'Not true. I told you exactly who she was and what she was about – it was you who decided to slant the story the way you did, and I warned you when I walked out that it was going to bury you. You weren't listening though, were you? You were too high on the prospect of making Avery, how did you put it, "squirm on the end of my line" – bad metaphor, by the way – to realise that using his wife and son to get back at him was as good as putting the noose round your own neck. But I did see it coming, which is why I walked you right into it.'

'Oh, so Justine, the great clairvoyant, knew the woman was going to bump herself off? Yeah, really.'

'*That* was just icing. So whatever else you might think of

me, Critch, remember this, I'm not nearly as dumb as you. Goodbye. I'll see you in court.'

'They'll never get me there,' he roared. 'Unlike some, I haven't committed a crime,' but she'd already gone.

He was still seething fifteen minutes later when he stormed out of the lift and across the newsroom, where heads came up in his wake. They were all still watching, and listening, as he walked into his office to find two security guards waiting.

'What the hell's this?' he demanded, dropping his briefcase and shrugging off his coat.

'Good morning, sir,' one of the guards responded. 'I must inform you that you have ten minutes in which to clear your desk, and then we have instructions to escort you from the building. Should you need it, there's a plastic sack on your chair for your personal belongings.'

Critch's jaw dropped. Then, getting it, he turned to look thunderously out at the newsroom. 'OK, some jerk's having a laugh at my expense. Ha, ha, ha, very funny. Now let's all get to work, shall we?'

'It's not a joke, Mr Critchley,' the guard told him. 'Mr Dickson, the proprietor of this newspaper, issued the instructions himself.'

Critchley's face turned white. 'I know who he is,' he snarled, 'and now I know you're not serious, because there's no way Dickson's going to fire the man responsible for doubling the circulation of this paper. So if you'll take yourself off . . .'

The guard glanced at his watch. 'You're down to eight minutes now, sir,' he told him impassively.

Critch stalked to the door. 'Anita, get Dickson on the line,' he shouted to his secretary.

'Get him yourself,' she shouted back.

Critch's eyes nearly popped out.

'God, that felt good,' Anita grinned at her colleague.

Critch turned back and grabbed up the phone. 'Pauline,' he barked when Dickson's PA answered, 'put him on *now*.'

'I'm sorry, Mr Critchley, Mr Dickson is in a meeting and has asked not to be disturbed.'

'If he's not on this line in the next thirty seconds, I'll come up there and disturb him myself.'

The guard looked at his watch again.

'Hang on, Mr Critchley, Mr Dickson has just come out and he's willing to take your call.'

A moment later the proprietor's gruff Scottish burr came down the line. 'Critch, I'm sorry it has to happen this way, but with the way things are going—'

'Yeah, I'll tell you how they're going,' Critch burst in. 'What about circulation and profit and shareholders? Did they suddenly disappear out the window, or do we want to start this discussion again?'

'They will disappear if as many subscribers and advertisers pull out as have threatened during the past few days. The heat's on, Critch, and it's not going to cool down until you're out of here. Sorry, but that's the way it goes.'

Critch's jaw flapped up and down as he struggled for words. 'I'm going to sue your ass for this.'

'You're welcome to try,' and the line went dead.

As he put the phone down Critch looked at the security guards again, then without uttering another word he began stuffing his personal belongings into the black plastic sack.

With two minutes still to go he started the long walk across a silent newsroom to the lift, a guard either side of him, the bulky sack clutched to his chest. He wanted to shout and rail at them, remind them who was responsible for their Christmas bonuses and lavish expense accounts, but he said nothing. He merely kept his eyes straight ahead, knowing what was waiting for him out on the street, because some treacherous bastard in here would already have called up his mates to tip them off.

And sure enough, as he exited the revolving doors on the ground floor a plethora of flashing lights, TV cameras and microphones was shoved in his face, all wanting to record the Critch's humiliation as he left *The News* and began the next long walk to the nearest Tube.

'You haven't heard the last of this yet, Avery,' he suddenly growled into a camera. 'So don't even think it.'

*

'That man so needs to get over himself,' Kayla remarked, as the screen changed and Vivienne turned back to her computer. 'Do you think Miles has seen it yet?'

'As it's been shown every hour on the hour since ten this morning, I should think he's fed up of seeing it by now,' Vivienne answered. 'Can you email me with a list of the successful bidders, we need to start scheduling the work. Which reminds me, has anyone been in touch from Sky yet, to say whether they're interested in filming the auction results in action?'

'Yeah, and they definitely are, but we need to check with the bidders first, in case any of them want to stay anonymous. List of successful candidates coming up,' she announced, and with a cheery flourish she clicked the mouse to send. 'You will see,' she said, as the email dropped into Vivienne's inbox, 'that we still don't know who bid for Theo. If she, or he, doesn't get in touch soon, we're going to find ourselves short of fifteen grand.'

As Vivienne scanned the list of eleven she said, 'Financially that won't be a huge disaster, but in PR terms it won't do us any good, because someone's bound to accuse us of rigging the bids for TV ratings.'

Kayla shrugged. 'We've got the money, or pledges, now, so what's the difference?'

'It'll damage our credibility for when we do it again, and I don't have to tell you how many enquiries we've already had.'

Kayla grinned. 'Alice was right about this putting us on the map,' she declared, with a triumphant punch in the air. 'We are like so on our way to the big time. Anyway, it's not long since the auction, so our mystery caller could still be in touch. Should we ask Sky to broadcast a request for them to come forward?'

Vivienne's eyebrows rose as she got up from her chair. 'That would be a last resort,' she said, starting to pack her briefcase. 'Alice and Angus are coming over for supper tonight, if you'd like to join us. Pete's going to try and make it too, if he can get away from *Belle Amie*.'

'That'll be great, thanks,' Kayla said. Then, watching Vivienne tuck a sleeping Rufus more warmly into his buggy, 'What's happening with Miles now? Is he still in London?'

'No, he took Kelsey back to Devon this morning,' Vivienne answered, going for her coat. 'Jacqueline's body is being transported to a funeral director's in Bovey Tracey tomorrow. Cremation's on Friday.'

'Have you decided if you're going yet?'

Vivienne shook her head. 'I want to, for Miles, but not if it's going to upset Kelsey.'

'But if she's not going herself . . .'

'She might change her mind. Anyway, time for me to get this little horror home before he wakes up and wants his tea. Come over about seven. It's only shepherd's pie and a supermarket dessert, but Angus is bringing some good wine he tells me.'

To her relief, when Vivienne wheeled the buggy outside, there was no sign of the press, in spite of the number of calls she'd received throughout the day asking for her response to the Critch's abrupt departure and his threatening comment to Miles. Since anything she had to say about the creep was unprintable anyway, she'd followed Miles's lead and referred all press enquiries to Stefan, the lawyer, who'd prepared a statement on Miles's behalf wishing Gareth Critchley every success in a new career.

Easily able to imagine how that must have set the man fuming, if not foaming, Vivienne walked briskly over to the towpath and was just heading towards home when her mobile bleeped with a text. Seeing it was from Stella, she opened it right away.

Might have good news. Can't say more now. Keep fingers crossed. Will ring later or tomorrow. Stella.

Knowing it must be about Sharon, who'd started her treatment today, Vivienne immediately called Stella's number. Finding herself diverted to voicemail, she rang off and tried Sharon herself. No luck there either, as the phone simply rang and rang, meaning she was probably sleeping after the first bout of chemo.

Deciding to try Stella again in an hour, she walked on, and within a few minutes she was wheeling Rufus across the courtyard and in through the kitchen door. Knowing her mortgage arrears were paid off now, and that there might be good news for Sharon, was allowing some brightness to shine through the dark heaviness she felt each time she thought of Jacqueline. The days ahead were going to be far from easy, she was in no doubt about that, but it was Jacqueline's final hours that troubled her the most. It was heartbreaking to think of what she'd been through, and how, in fifteen long years, there had never been any respite. She'd never given up hope of one day finding Sam, until finally, for whatever reasons, she'd come to accept that the dream was as lost as her son. It was tragic beyond bearing, but even so, a small part of Vivienne could almost feel glad for Jacqueline that so much suffering was finally at an end.

After parking the buggy in the dining room, she turned on the lights, poured herself half a glass of wine, then went into the hall to hang up her coat and collect the mail. An electricity bill, a postcard from her mother in Italy, and a small white Jiffy bag that had no identifying logos at all.

Going back to the kitchen, she looked down at the package again, and felt a fluttering in her chest as she registered the Richmond postmark. But it couldn't be from Jacqueline. Today was Wednesday and this . . . had been mailed on Saturday. For some reason it had taken until now to arrive, which wasn't normal, but had clearly happened, so in fact it could be from Jacqueline.

She continued to stare at the handwriting, clear and neat: *Ms Vivienne Kane,* followed by her address and postcode. Since she'd never seen Jacqueline's writing she had no idea if this was it, but an uncanny instinct was telling her it was.

Experiencing a confused sadness and frustration that Jacqueline might have written to her, when Kelsey had never needed to hear from her mother more, she tore open the seal and pulled out a single page with a cheque attached. There was also an envelope addressed to Kelsey.

Putting that aside, she unfolded her own letter and read the address at the top of the page first. This, she realised, was Jacqueline's way of allowing them to find her, not too long after she'd gone, but not before she'd been able to fulfil her intentions.

In a neat, legible hand, she'd written,

Dear Vivienne,

I watched your auction, and because you seemed to be short of £5,000 at the end of it, I am enclosing that sum with this letter. Please accept it as my donation to a very worthy cause.

I am also enclosing a letter for Kelsey. I would like you to give it to her, because it is my hope that it will go some way towards helping her to accept you and move forward into the kind of future she deserves.

Thank you for your kindness when I came to see you. Rufus is a very special little boy. Please take care of him, and always watch over him. A mere moment of risk can, as I've discovered, change a life for ever.

What I am about to do is not meant as a punishment to those I leave behind. I do it for the reasons I am giving Kelsey, as she is the only one I really need to explain myself to.

Thank you, Vivienne, for caring as much as you do. I hope you and Miles will be happy together.

Jacqueline

As she finished reading Vivienne took a shuddering breath and blew it out slowly. Then, looking down at the envelope addressed to Kelsey, she reached for the phone to call Miles.

Chapter Twenty-six

Not wanting to risk Kelsey's letter taking any longer to reach her than it already had, Vivienne set out early the next morning, with Rufus, to deliver it herself.

It was just before midday by the time she pulled up in the courtyard outside Moorlands, with Rufus singing and banging about in the back, and a weak autumn sun struggling to brighten a dull, but dry day.

She found Miles in his study, standing at the window staring down towards the lake. They'd talked long into the night, so she knew, even though he hadn't put it into actual words, how deeply Jacqueline's suicide was affecting him. Their marriage might have been over a long time ago, but he'd never stopped caring for her, nor had he ever ceased to understand or share her pain, since it was his too. What he hadn't realised before, however, was that he'd allowed her to shoulder his hope of finding Sam. She'd kept that flame burning for them both, because he'd truly believed he'd given up on his son a long time ago. Now she'd gone he knew he hadn't, and losing her was a little like losing Sam all over again.

Hearing Vivienne come into the room, some of the intensity left his expression, and his eyes softened as a jubilant Rufus ran towards him, arms waving in the air, baby teeth bared in a grin. Sweeping him up he planted a kiss on his cheek, before pulling Vivienne into a more intimate embrace.

'Are you OK?' she asked, reaching up to cup a hand lovingly around his face. 'You look tired.'

'I'm fine,' he assured her. 'Did Stella get hold of you?'

She smiled and nodded. 'The same donor. Let's just hope that he or she doesn't back out again.'

He started to agree, but his words were garbled by Rufus's sticky fists grabbing his mouth.

'Muh, muh,' Rufus chirped, mimicking a kiss, and pressing his wet lips to his father's he blew a soggy raspberry.

Smiling, Miles hugged him tightly, burying his face in him for a moment, before setting him down to run about the room. 'I had a rather unexpected phone call about an hour ago,' he said, turning back to Vivienne. 'From Don Dickson.'

Her eyes widened with interest.

'Would you believe, he offered me my old job back at *The News*? Double my previous salary.'

She blinked in amazement. 'Are you going to take it?' she asked dubiously.

He shook his head. 'My days on the Sunday tabloids are long over. I've no desire to go back there.'

Not surprised by the answer, she said, 'Have you given any more thought to what you are going to do?'

'It's always in my mind, but for the time being I still have a book to finish, and there's plenty coming in from my non-executive directorships, plus I might accept a couple of the political columns I've been offered.'

'Which means,' she said, cocking her head curiously to one side, 'you'll be working from home?'

'At least for the foreseeable future. It'll give me more time to spend with Kelsey and Rufus, while my wife hits the dizzy heights with her agency.'

As her heart swelled, her eyes showed a subtle mischief. 'I guess that's going to make you a kind of house husband,' she said.

Appearing amused, he said, 'It would if you'd agree to marry me.'

Leaning in for a kiss, she replied, 'I think I could manage that.'

A few moments later he said, 'Does this seem like the wrong time to be asking? Yes, of course it does.'

'You knew I'd accept, and I don't think either of us was planning to announce it just yet.'

'No, of course not.'

Her eyes swept over his face. 'Have you told Kelsey about the letter?' she asked.

'No. Jacqueline clearly wanted you to, so let's do it that way.'

She nodded. 'Where is she?'

Turning back to the window, he gestured for her to look down at the lake. 'She's been sitting there all morning with that goose,' he said. 'I can't get her to come in, so I took a blanket and a warmer coat down for her just now. She says she's fine, she just wants to be left alone with Henrietta.'

Understanding the significance of the attachment, Vivienne smiled sadly. Both Kelsey and the goose had been abandoned by their mothers.

She gave Miles a fleeting kiss on the cheek, then went to take her own coat from the car, plus the letter, and began walking down the lawn. Even if Kelsey was as hostile and rude as before, Vivienne was determined to let it wash over her, while trying as gently as she could to break the news of the letter's arrival. Then she'd beat a sensitive retreat to let Kelsey read it alone.

However, as she drew closer, and began to register how pathetically lonely and unhappy Kelsey looked, sitting on the blanket with Henrietta's fat, feathery body next to her and elegant neck curled over into her lap, she decided at least to try and sit down with them for a while.

She was almost there when Kelsey looked up. The sun was behind her, so Kelsey couldn't make out who she was at first until Vivienne stepped forward. Seeing who it was, Kelsey turned away.

'I have something for you,' Vivienne said gently.

Kelsey kept her head down. 'I don't want it,' she said, her nasal voice betraying how much crying she'd done, but at least there was none of the bitterness Vivienne had been expecting.

Taking heart, Vivienne said, 'Would it be OK if I sat with you for a moment?'

Kelsey neither moved nor spoke.

Hoping the lack of response was a permission of sorts, Vivienne sank down at the edge of the blanket.

Sensing a newcomer, Henrietta lifted her head and eyed Vivienne beadily, before returning to the cosy pillow of Kelsey's lap.

Vivienne took the letter from her pocket and held it out. 'This arrived yesterday, at my house,' she said. 'It's for you, from your mum.'

Kelsey stiffened, and glanced sharply at the letter.

'She obviously intended it to get to you before now,' Vivienne continued, 'but I'm afraid the post let her down.'

Kelsey's eyes remained on the letter, but she made no move to take it.

'Would you like me to leave it here?' Vivienne suggested, putting it on the blanket between them.

Kelsey's nostrils flared as her lips turned pale. 'Do what you want,' she said shortly.

Vivienne left it where it was and gazed out across the lake.

Minutes ticked by.

'Why did she send it to you, and not me?' Kelsey demanded.

Bracing herself, Vivienne said, 'I think she wants to try and help us be friends.'

Kelsey turned away again.

'I'll leave you alone to read it,' Vivienne said and started to get up, but then, hearing Kelsey swallow and seeing two tears form and roll from the bottom of her eyes, she whispered, 'I can stay if you'd prefer.'

Kelsey shrugged dismissively. 'You can do as you like,' she retorted coldly.

Vivienne's heart folded around the pain Kelsey was trying to hide. She didn't want to be alone, but was unable to swallow enough pride to admit it. Sitting down again, Vivienne drew up her knees and hugged them to her chest, giving Kelsey time to decide what to do next.

Time slipped quietly by and Kelsey's gaze stayed on Henrietta, whose silky neck she was stroking with a hand mottled by cold. She didn't even glance at the letter again, but Vivienne knew she was sensing its presence like a ticking bomb between them.

In the end Kelsey said, in a voice that was much tarter

than the words, 'Dad told me the good news about Sharon's donor.'

Surprised by the change of direction, but pleased because it signalled another lowering of barriers, Vivienne said, 'Let's hope it all works out this time. I'm sure it will.'

Kelsey tilted her head to one side, and ran her fingers over Henrietta's golden beak. 'Martha, and my friends at school, think it was really good of you to put on that auction,' she remarked.

Guessing she might be letting the others speak for her, Vivienne said, 'Well, I didn't do it alone. Far from it, in fact.'

'Yeah, but you were the one who got it going.'

Understanding now that this was the excuse she was giving herself to set aside her animosity and open up a little, Vivienne said nothing, only watched her continuing to stroke Henrietta, while sensing her inner struggle and knowing it all had to happen in Kelsey's time.

'The Canadas never came back,' Kelsey said.

Vivienne's heart ached as she looked at Kelsey's face, and seeing a tear drop onto her hand she dispensed with caution and moved to put an arm around her.

To her relief Kelsey didn't shrug her off, but she didn't lean in to her either, merely continuing to stroke the goose. Vivienne wondered if she was remembering how Henrietta's plight had brought them together before. Then quite unexpectedly Kelsey turned her face into Vivienne's shoulder and started to sob.

'Oh, my love, it's all right, it's all right,' Vivienne murmured, holding her close, tears welling in her own eyes. 'I'm here. I won't let you go.'

Kelsey continued to cry, her body shaking and juddering, her voice strangled by too much confusion, until she pulled away again as though angered by her moment of weakness – or, Vivienne realised, afraid that she might be pushed away first.

Not quite sure what to do for the moment, Vivienne folded her arms on her knees again and watched the other geese skimming about the near edge of the lake, as though keeping an eye on the privileged Henrietta, while the ducks paddled and dived imperviously.

Beside her Kelsey's breath was still ragged, and once or twice a latent sob made her jerk and gulp. Then finally she put out a hand and picked up the letter.

As she stared down at her name, written in her mother's hand, Vivienne said, 'Would you like Dad to come and sit with you while you read it?'

For a while Kelsey didn't respond, until she shook her head as another lingering sob made her gasp. 'No,' she said.

Vivienne watched her tear the envelope open. If Kelsey wanted her to go she'd say, so she'd assume, at least for the moment, that she wanted her to stay.

After unfolding the pages, Kelsey looked down at them, and almost immediately flinched:

Darling Kelsey,

I know this won't be an easy letter for you to read, but I hope by the time you finish it you will have at least some understanding of why I believe that what I'm about to do is the best for us all.

Actually, maybe I should deal with a few practical things first, such as the cheque for £15,000 which you've probably already found in the envelope along with my bank details so that Dad can access my account. The cheque is to cover the winning bid for Theo. I thought perhaps it would be nice if he gave some coaching to Sharon's children and their school-friends, do you? And took them for a day out in Bath. That's if she'd like him to, of course. If not, the money is for a good cause, so I'll leave it to you to decide with Theo and Vivienne where it should go.

My will is with my lawyer. Everything that was mine is now yours, including my car. My hope is that Dad will sell it and keep the money to buy something a little more suitable for a seventeen-year-old when the time comes. I've also set things out for you to inherit small amounts from me at various stages of your life, so you'll be reminded from time to time that I haven't really deserted you.

I understand how confused you must be feeling now by the way I've left you, especially when our relationship seemed finally to be gaining some closeness. I'm afraid that has only been possible because I am ready to let go. If I consider staying all the blackness comes over me again, and I know when I'm like that I can never be a good mother to you.

To explain the effect Sam's disappearance had on me would be like trying to explain why it happened. Neither is possible, and yet you've been forced to live with what it did to me ever since you were born. I know we've never discussed it, and I'm sure now that we should have, but every time I tried I found myself thinking of Sam in a way that felt as though I was giving up on him. As soon as that happened I started to panic all over again. I simply couldn't accept that he'd really gone and would never come back, so I didn't want to talk about it for fear of making it real. I just wanted to continue living as though one day he'd be with us again, and when that time came, it would be as though he'd never been taken. I suppose you could say I was like an amputee waiting for a limb that could never be replaced, or a dead heart waiting for its beat to resume.

In the last few weeks, whilst I've been alone, much I wasn't expecting has been revealed to me. First and foremost is the love I have for you that I've been afraid to show, or even feel. After I lost Sam I never again considered myself worthy as a mother. I was afraid to trust myself, and in my grieving mind I believed that if I stopped you from coming close to me it would keep you safe. I have suffered from many tormented and irrational beliefs over the years, mostly caused by the need to punish myself for what I allowed to happen to Sam. I realise now, in a way I never did before, that my obsession with finding him has dominated my life in a way that tore our family apart, even as I used it to keep us together.

With all my heart I regret the pain I have caused you and Dad, the way I have held him to me, while pushing you away. If only I'd realised it should have been the other way round. I needed to let him go, while I poured all my energy into being a good mother to you, but I was so terrified he'd leave me, and so convinced that we needed to stay together for Sam, that I couldn't see beyond it.

I have made too many mistakes, my darling, all of which I can see much more clearly now that my worst fears have come true. Isn't that ironic? I find that instead of destroying me, my fears are finally setting me free. Dad has fallen in love with another woman and they have a son. I never thought I'd be able to say, or write, that with any kind of equanimity, but it turns out that I say it with such a sense of relief that I can only wish it had happened a long time ago.

I don't think I'm a bad person, darling, but I've done some bad things, and bad things have happened to me. You may, for some time, find it hard to forgive me for the way I've treated you, but please keep this letter and let it continually tell you that I am making this choice as much out of love for you as out of a need to escape the daily torment of what might have happened to Sam, or might even be happening now. It's true, other mothers have found a way to live with it, but it seems I can't. As the years go by, my darling, it's only getting worse. All the time I imagine him growing up, becoming a man, maybe even passing me in the street and not knowing who I am. And then there are the darker, much more terrible thoughts of what might have been done to him; thoughts that have all too often driven me out of my mind. I need to put an end to that, for all our sakes. We deserve our freedom, and I believe this is the way to make it happen.

I want you to think only of your future now, and remember that Dad has been there for you every step of the way, and I know he'll continue to be. Vivienne will too, and though you might think it now, I know that deep in your heart you don't hate her at all. Fortunately, I think she's wise enough to realise that, so I'm sure she'll ride the storms with you until you're ready to accept her.

And now here's another thought for you. Maybe she

and Dad would have met and fallen in love anyway, even if Sam had stayed with us. We can't know that for sure, of course, all we know is what life has dealt us, and in your case, you have Rufus. Please believe me, darling, he's a beautiful little boy, full of life and mischief, and I know you two are going to get an enormous amount of joy from one another.

I shall finish by asking you to tell Dad that I'm sorry. He will understand why, but for you I will spell it out: I'm sorry for losing his son, for holding him back from a life that should have been his, and for not treating his daughter as well as I should have. I haven't written to him, because there is no more to be said between us that hasn't been said a thousand times before. I loved him very much once, certainly during the time you were conceived, but our tragedy destroyed our marriage, and now it's time for me to stop letting it destroy everything else.

I go with a lightness in my heart, darling, that tells me I am on the right path. Your future can be bright and sunny, and full of happiness if you let it. It's how I want to think of you as I go to sleep tonight, so please make my dream come true, and always know that I will be somewhere close by, watching over you and feeling so much pride in my girl that the sun will shine from the heavens, even on a cloudy day. Until we meet again, my darling,

Mum

As Kelsey finished reading she dropped the letter in her lap and buried her face in her hands. Immediately Vivienne pulled her into a hug, holding her as she wept, great racking sobs wrenching at her body, despair tormenting her soul. She cried out for her mother, her brother, and her father, while clinging to Vivienne as though only she could keep her from drowning.

Her head went down and down, her hands bunching behind it, and Vivienne grasped her fists, willing her own strength into them as though it might find its way to her heart. She put her head over Kelsey's, covering her hair with her own, and wrapping her so tightly that in the end Kelsey was forced to come up. Then, finally noticing Henrietta watching them with some curious blinks, Kelsey gave a watery smile.

Reaching out, she drew the goose to her, wiping the back of one hand over her cheeks. 'Did you know she's got a new family now?' she said.

For a moment Vivienne thought she was talking about Jacqueline, until realising she meant Henrietta, she looked at the other geese.

'Do you see them watching?' Kelsey said, sounding on the verge of breaking down again. 'Dad bought them when Henri started to pine, and she bonded with them really well, but actually I think she still likes me best, don't you, Henri?'

As though realising she was being spoken to, the goose gave a raucous squawk and brushed her beak over Kelsey's face.

Vivienne smiled as she watched them, then laughed as Henrietta flapped her wings and fluttered her feathers.

Still watching the goose, Kelsey took the letter from her lap and held it out to Vivienne. Then, as though nothing had happened, she said, 'Do you think Rufus would like Henrietta?'

'I'm sure he would,' Vivienne replied hoarsely.

'She's very gentle. She won't hurt him,' Kelsey promised.

'No, I'm sure she won't.'

With her hands still cupped around Henrietta's face, Kelsey said, 'We could go and get him if you like.'

When she felt the time to be right Vivienne rose to her feet, and waited as Kelsey got up too. As they walked back to the house, side by side though not quite touching, Vivienne said, casually, 'Theo's arriving tonight. He's going to see Sharon in the morning, but he thought you might want some company in the afternoon, while everyone's at the funeral. Unless you decide to go.'

Kelsey's head stayed down as she continued to walk.

Vivienne didn't press it any further. She suspected Kelsey had already changed her mind, but it didn't matter if she hadn't. She'd let them know her decision when she was ready. In the meantime, her father was coming to meet them, his expression troubled, but questioning, as his eyes met Vivienne's.

Taking Rufus so he could fold Kelsey into his arms, Vivienne gave him the briefest of smiles to let him know it was all right.

As his father and sister hugged, Rufus watched in silence, seeming intrigued, then worried, as Kelsey started to sob. He looked at his mother, then his father, not sure if this was a game, or if he should cry too. He leaned back against Vivienne, plonking his head on her shoulder, until quite suddenly he gave a scream of excitement and almost sprang from her arms.

Kelsey's head came up; her eyes were red and swollen, her cheeks mottled by tears. Rufus looked so cute and funny that her mouth trembled as she tried to smile. Then she laughed and sobbed as he banged his fists joyously together and screamed exultantly again.

'We're going to take him to the lake to introduce him to Henrietta,' she told her father.

'Look behind you,' Miles whispered.

Kelsey turned round and gave another gulp of laughter as she saw the cause of Rufus's excitement. Henrietta was waddling up the lawn after her.

She looked hesitantly at Vivienne, then watched as Vivienne put Rufus down on the grass.

Swallowing her tears, Kelsey stooped to his height. 'This is Henrietta,' she whispered, as he watched the goose come. 'Be gentle with her, won't you?'

Rufus's mouth was a perfect little O as he turned to look at this new person talking to him. Then all six of his teeth showed in a cheeky grin.

Kelsey laughed and held onto him as Henrietta drew closer – but she didn't hold tightly enough, because he was suddenly running forward to meet the goose, arms open wide as he yelled with delight. Then everyone was laughing as Henrietta, without missing a step, turned tail to hotfoot it back to the safety of the lake.